Keepers of Arden

The Brothers
Volume 4

I0629159

L. K. Evans

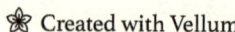 Created with Vellum

DEDICATED

To all the people who continue to buy my books, who so generously took time out of their day to write reviews, and to those who sent me notes of praise and encouragement. You keep me going.

THANK YOU

Thank you to Michael Evans for my cover art.

Thank you to Debbie Coleman and Raini St. John for all your hard work editing this book.

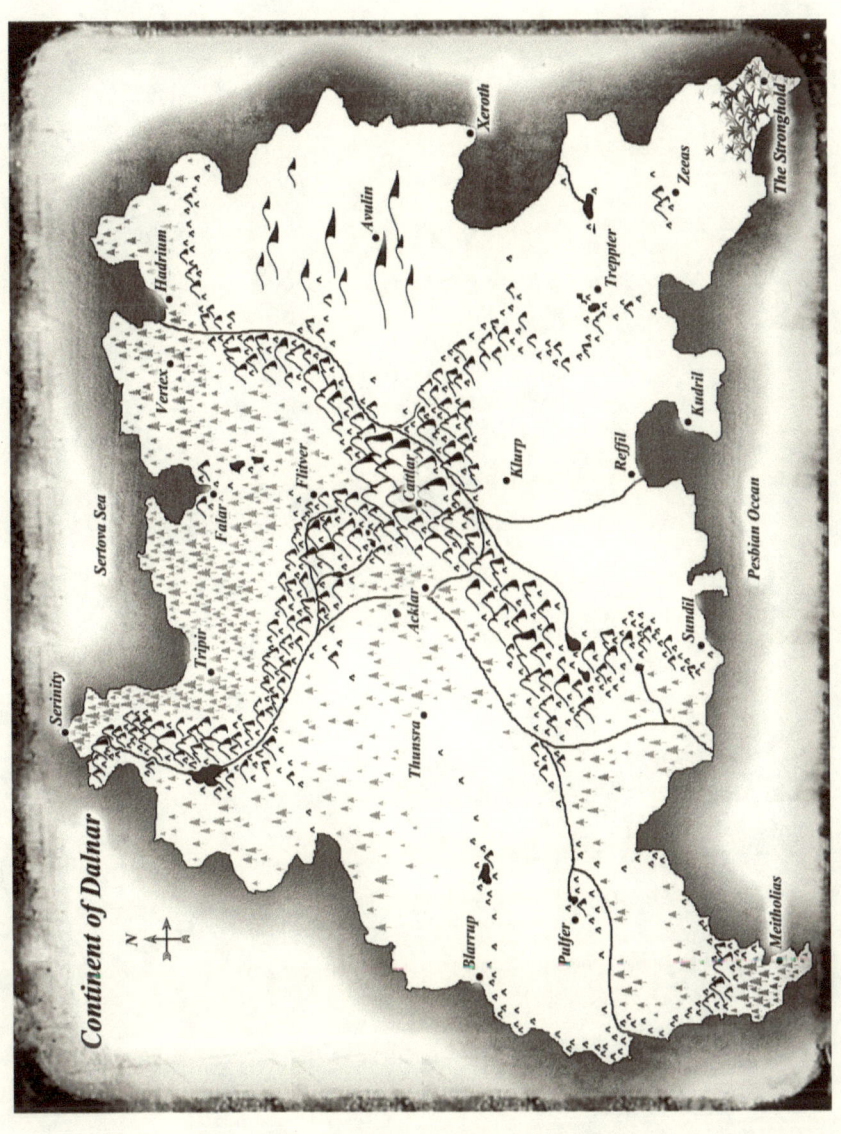

Continent of Dalnar

Continent of Loutsil

SPRING 1022 A.R

Flames flickering in the hearth hypnotized Wilhelm into a listless trance and relaxed his grip on the hilt of his sword. A trickle of sweat inched down his temple, gaining speed until it hit his overgrown beard. The cottage was stuffy—too hot for Wilhelm's taste, but Salvarias would have loved it: curled up by the fire, spell book resting in his hands, whispering numbers to himself. Perhaps counting how many stone blocks had been used to construct the quaint home. Perhaps he would be taking his breathing concoction more often because of the mildewy furnishings and years of dust. Perhaps he would be imagining all the reasons someone would abandon a home.

The loud pop of a burning log snapped Wilhelm alert. Sansis sat quietly, not struggling against the ropes binding him to the chair. The bastard knew nothing could save him now.

"What was first?" Wilhelm asked, voice dry and raw. He'd rarely spoken since his brother's death. "Was it his finger or his ear?"

Sansis turned his gaze to the window, though nothing could be seen through thick woods blocking the moon and stars. Firelight played off the man's wrinkled skin, highlighting the wisps of white hair dotting his scalp.

"Finger," Sansis said.

Wilhelm drew his mother's dagger from his boot, grabbed a rickety footstool, positioned it in front of Sansis, and sat.

"I hardly recognized you," Sansis said. "The beard certainly has changed your appearance, but it's your eyes."

Wilhelm sawed off Sansis's right pinky, just as the bastard had done to his little brother. The man didn't scream—it wouldn't have mattered if he had; the cottage was far removed from any town. Sansis only grunted and hissed through his clenched teeth. Wilhelm tossed the digit into the fire.

"Can't make it grow back?" Wilhelm asked, staring numbly at the stump.

Sansis shook his head. Once his breathing quieted, he slouched against his bindings. "Rest assured, I can sustain my life by whatever means necessary. I will not die this day."

"Today, tomorrow ... doesn't matter to me."

"You think I wanted the boy dead? I loved him as a son. I would have given my life for his."

Wilhelm shrugged. "I believe you. But that doesn't change what I'm going to do to you. I promised Salv I'd hunt you down and kill you. And that's exactly what I intend to do."

He slipped his dagger between Sansis's ear and skull, and sawed, surprised by the ease in which it separated. He tossed it in the fire.

"It was acid you used on my little brother, wasn't it?" Wilhelm asked. He patted his tunic as if looking for some. "I don't have any with me. Honestly, I'm not even sure where to get it. Do you happen to have any lying around?"

Sansis shook his head, puffing air in his cheeks.

"I'll just have to get creative."

Wilhelm picked up a metal rod used to stoke the fire and rested it in the heat of the blue flames.

"Killing me won't bring your brother back," Sansis said. "He's lost to both of us. His soul roams neither Oblivion nor the planes of love Zerana created. There are no higher gods to ferry him from this world." Sansis unclenched his teeth and inhaled a breath. "Tragic, really. Have I told you I have sensed the plane of the dead? When I nearly lost the boy in the barbarian desert, I realized the dead are trapped here. They roam an endless landscape, subjected to relive their death, locked in the agony of their affliction. Every night I imagine the boy suffering such horror, and I weep for him. If you wish to save him, finding my former master and killing him might give Salvarias the peace both of us long for him to receive."

Wilhelm didn't respond.

"I've heard you have hunted any creature not of Nevlar's creation and killed them. How many have you murdered?" Sansis asked.

"I lost track."

"Three years of blood ... such a waste."

Had it been three years? Did it matter? What was time to a man whose body refused to die when his heart had?

Wilhelm pulled the rod from the fire and rested it alongside Sansis's head. Skin smoked and blood sizzled, and the stench reminded him of the shadowfires that had rampaged through Falar all those years ago, the creatures that had bestowed upon Wilhelm the most wondrous gift, one he had squandered away.

Once the flesh had charred and Sansis's screeching stopped, Wilhelm tossed the rod back to the stone hearth and took to his stool. He'd already stripped Sansis naked.

"I remember every cut you made on my brother," Wilhelm said, staring at the blade of his dagger, twisting it to catch the light.

"As do I. He begged for you so many times. I listened to him weep in his cell for eight months before he stopped. For eight months, he thought you would come for him. For eight months, he clung to his hope like a starved child guards his last bite of bread. Then one day he stopped calling for you. I watched the hope die in his eyes. After that, he was resigned to me. He never cried, never begged for you, and never said a word. He simply laid in my arms as I dissected his body, one limb at a time. Did you know that? No, I doubt he would ever tell you. I was fascinated to learn how to mend bone, nerves, and

3

muscles ... so much of the body was a mystery to me before Salvarias. He lived when other subjects died. He taught me, and I loved him for it." Sansis gazed at Wilhelm with sad eyes. "Even now you do not weep upon hearing of his suffering. Has your heart died, Protector?"

"Yes," Wilhelm said simply, and began cutting.

FOR TWO DAYS Wilhelm sliced Sansis to mirror Salvarias's body. For two days Wilhelm left Sansis sitting in his own excrement and blood, denied food and water, denied dignity. Each morning, Sansis's body had healed with no scar left to mark his torment. But the finger and ear never grew back.

On the third morning, Wilhelm sat on his stool in front of Sansis.

"Your blade will dull before I die," Sansis rasped. "Even now, you cannot fulfill your promise. Your brother's death will go unavenged. If you manage to find a way to kill me, what will you do then? Hunt my master? You will never find him. He is beyond your reach. He is guarded by what remains of the Four. Your life has no meaning, Protector. Even if you chose to go home, your son will not recognize you."

Wilhelm hefted the cleaver he'd purchased years ago and tested its weight in his hands. It felt good. Solid.

"This will get you nowhere, Wilhelm."

"I don't care." He propped Sansis's foot on another stool and hacked at the ankle until finally making it through tendon and bone. He threw the foot into the fire. At lunch, he chopped off Sansis's other foot, discarding it in the fire as he had done the other. At dinner, he took both hands, burning them as well. He went to bed shortly after.

The next morning, Sansis still lived. Wilhelm dug out the bones from the fire and sat at the kitchen table with a hammer. He went to work pulverizing the bones into dust. When done, he sprinkled it in the fire before lopping off Sansis's legs and arms. He tossed them in the fire and sat in one of the chairs, watching skin and fat bubble.

Sansis might have been screaming. Wilhelm couldn't hear. He'd slipped into a trance, one where he replayed his brother's last moments of life.

A pop from the fire stirred Wilhelm. The light outside the window had faded. Sansis—nothing more than a stump—sat in his chair, ropes keeping his torso in place. The man had been crying. Wilhelm went to his bedroom and slept.

He woke to a beam of light falling across his face. Lying for several moments, he stared at nothing, thought of nothing.

He made his way into the sitting room to find Sansis still alive. Wilhelm pulled bones from the fire before stoking it to a roaring blaze. Sitting at the table, he ground the bones as he had done the previous day. He finished by lunch and ate a quick bite. After cleaning the kitchen, he returned to his stool in front of Sansis.

"Times up," he whispered.

"During one of my sessions with Salvarias, I gave him a drug," Sansis rasped. "It breaks down the mind and causes hallucinations. At first, it was nothing new. He thought I was his father at one point. He smiled at me. We talked of his childhood. He laughed when he told me of games you concocted for them to play in the guardhouse. He spoke of books you had read him. I was so enraptured by his joy that I gave him another dose. It was a horrible mistake. It loosed too much of his mind. His hallucinations turned violent. He started screaming. He begged for whatever he endured to stop. He said it hurt. I asked him what; I coaxed him to speak. Would you like to know what he said?"

"Shut up."

"You suspicioned it, didn't you? I imagine Tobin did as well. You both knew, but could not bring yourselves to acknowledge it, could you? Not her, not when she was so kind. And who suffered because of it?"

"I said shut up!" Wilhelm belted.

"He said: 'Please, Mother, I will try harder. It hurts, Mother. Please stop.'"

"No! You lie!"

"Go to your brother's tomb, Protector. Feel the back of his head. Feel the scar that runs down his skull. You'll notice she used the same spot each week to drain his blood."

Wilhelm rammed his dagger in Sansis's chest over and over. He was screaming something. Blinded by rage, he saw nothing but red.

When he finally ceased, he was covered in blood, panting from the exertion.

Sansis smiled. "I..." His voice gurgled. "I ... pity ... you."

Wilhelm plunged his dagger into Sansis's chest and carved out the man's heart. He threw it in the fire.

"And that is how you kill me," Sansis choked. "Farewell, Protector. I will see you in Oblivion."

Sansis hitched, his eyes rolled back, and he sagged against the ropes.

Wilhelm wasn't sure how long he stood there, drenched in cooling blood, mind returning to its numb detachment. When he didn't feel anymore, he cleaned his dagger, sheathed it, and drew Tobin's broadsword. He hacked off Sansis's head, tossed it in the fire, and went to sleep.

The next morning, Wilhelm burned the rest of the body and ground up the bones before leaving the cottage in flames. He had no desire to live, but lacked the courage to take his own life.

His mission had been to kill Sansis. It was what he had lived for and what had kept him alive. Now the deed was done, and he had no desire to live, to breathe. With nothing left to drive him, he allowed Lilly to set a course and drew his wineskin.

Eventually he ended up in a dirty part of some city, drunk to a kind stupor. He made out a sign with a cask and promptly dismounted, gave out coin, and muttered to whoever listened to take care of his horse. Inside was busy, people drinking and eating, laughing and singing. He chose a table in a corner and turned over half his purse to the bartender, using the last of his wits to order a room and nonstop flow of strong drink.

A few men tried to talk to him, called him by name, eyes alight with meeting Wilhelm the Unconquerable. The drink robbed him of manners, and he often shoved men away, causing fights. Women came and went, falling in and out of his lap. It all blurred behind his long pulls from his always-full mug.

Eventually, he was in a bed. He didn't remember how he got there. A naked woman was draped over him, moaning in his ear, riding him. He leaned over the bed, threw up, and passed out.

The routine repeated. He didn't know for how long. Sometimes he was alone, sometimes a woman was there. Sometimes he was downstairs, sometimes in his bed. It was a surreal passing of time. He wondered how long it would take to drink himself to the grave. He downed as much as his stomach would contain, hoping it wouldn't be much longer.

He jolted awake to a loud splintering of wood and stomping boots. A swarm of armed men blurred in and out of focus. Glancing around, he vaguely made out a run-down bedroom and a lithe brunette sleeping naked at his side, entirely too thin for his taste. Bottles of wine were scattered across the floor.

"Veedran's wickedness, you look like you spent a year in Oblivion," a voice said.

Wilhelm thought he knew it. It was light, a humorous edge to it. A man squatted down by the bed, avoiding a mess of vomit. He had grass-green eyes, strawberry-blond hair, and a friendly smile.

To the group behind him, the man said, "Pay the whore and settle his debts. Then chain him, toss him in the wagon, and find someone to clean him up." The man glanced at the woman. "You sleep with that when you have a wife at home any man would kill for? She's had propositions, you know. Tons. You do remember your wife, don't you? Varila Laybryth?"

The woman next to him slowly opened her eyes. "What's going on? Who are these people?"

Wilhelm leaned over the bed and threw up on the man's shoes. "I need a drink," he muttered.

"The only thing you'll get out of me is water." The man shook his head. "Salvarias would be devastated to see you this way."

Wilhelm squinted at the man. "Do I know you? Oh ... Okulu. Well, Salv isn't here for me to devastate, so go to Oblivion and leave me alone."

"I don't think so," Okulu said. "Your brother's body has been taken. Time to sober up."

2

SPRING 1022 A.R

Wilhelm rubbed his wrists after the guard removed the shackles. His skin was raw and cut from days of trying to break free and kill whoever stood in his path. The spirits had finally burned out of him. He vaguely remembered weeping, feeling pain he'd long buried. It'd taken a bit, but he'd finally been able to numb everything. Now he jostled about in the back of the wagon with Okulu, placid and uncaring.

"First day you've seemed to be of your right mind," Okulu said and took a swig from his flask.

Wilhelm shrugged. "Where are we going?"

"To see Humar. We're going to fill you in on everything before we set out to find your brother's body." Okulu's gaze steadied on him. "You've been a ghost for nearly three years. I've been tracking you, but I'm always days if not weeks behind. I found a burned down cottage in the woods. There was no body, no bones, but I have a suspicion someone died there."

Wilhelm nodded. "I found Sansis. I cut him apart, burned him, and ground his bones. He's dead."

"Good. Bastard deserved it." Okulu took another swig. "We'll be in Warton tonight. Varila is there, and Lunara as well as their parents.

Your son too. I'll not tell Varila about your lapse with another woman, but if you decide to come back to the land of the living, you should tell her yourself. She deserves to know."

"I'm not married. I told her I wasn't her husband anymore. Now shut up, and leave me alone."

The rest of the ride was silent.

VARILA STARED out the window of her room in Warton, smiling at the unbridled laughter of children. Glancing over her shoulder, she watched the children play a game of chase. The oldest, Prince Dredin, had his mother's rich brown hair and his father's azure eyes. He'd grow up to be a serious man. At three, building blocks and picture books interested the child more than playing outside, and he only engaged when her son and Arias goaded him into it. Princess Belany was a charming child, face round and delicate, bright blue eyes innocent and big. She squealed with delight as Tedris helped her run from Arias.

Okulu's twins were painfully adorable. Their blue-green skin alone was beautiful to look upon, but each had inherited their parent's most alluring qualities. Arias had his father's strawberry-blond hair and his mother's too-bright blue eyes. His features were already masculine, more square than normal children, and his gaze carried entirely too much mischief. More than once the boy had gotten Tedris into trouble, usually breaking something and getting away with it when he flashed his roguish grin. Bri's copper hair was a reflection of her mother's, but her dazzling eyes were Okulu's, and the girl feared nothing. Whirling around on Dredin, she lifted her arms as if to attack and gave a war cry. The prince squealed and fled.

Laughing, Tedris shouted, "Get him, Bri!"

Tedris, though younger than Dredin and Okulu's twins by a season, was the largest of all. He acted five or six, not two and a half. He spoke better than children years older than him, and his mind absorbed knowledge. Of course he was a handsome child. He had his father's square features, bright amber eyes, height, and insatiable appetite. His hair fell somewhere between Varila and Wilhelm's—too light to be brown, too dark to be blond, wavy and wild.

Zehnia joined Varila and locked arms. "They've arrived. Do you want Tedris to stay?"

"I think it best if the children went to the garden. If things go well, I'll call for you."

The queen nodded. "I pray Wilhelm has come to his senses."

Varila mustered up a smile and patted Zehnia's hand. "Thank you."

It took the queen and several servants to round up the rambunctious group. Tedris, normally the first to obey, helped for his part, pausing long enough to pat Lunara's hand. She sat listless in a chair, eyes staring far away. Too often Lunara slipped into one of these trances. Too often silent tears would fall.

The sudden quiet did nothing to help Varila's nerves. Three long years had passed. Three years of missing him. His smell. His laugh. His touch. She doubted time had healed him. More likely, he was further lost to her.

Below in the courtyard, a wagon careened its way through the outer gates and up to the doors, lurching to a stop. Okulu swept from the back, graceful and light-footed as always. Cessia was in his arms before both feet had planted firmly. His laugh reached Varila. Another figure emerged; a massive man seven and a half feet tall, built like a mountain. He'd obviously shaven recently; his jaw was lighter than his cheeks. His hair was longer, cut choppy. Likely he'd done it himself.

Humar walked forward, hand extended, and Varila felt her breath catch in her throat. Wilhelm didn't take Humar's offer of friendship, and instead shot daggers at the king.

Biting back a curse, Varila hopped up from her perch, crossed the room, and knelt in front of Lunara. Dark rings hung around her sister's eyes, cheeks sunken from lack of eating. She'd thinned to unhealthy. "Wilhelm's here."

Her sister blinked and turned a watery gaze to the window. "We should meet him."

Outside the room, her mother and father were waiting.

"You know what to expect?" Edium asked Varila. "He's not in his right mind."

Varila nodded. "Finding Salvarias is what's important."

Once in the receiving hall, she caught sight of Wilhelm marching toward the passageway leading to the catacombs, his voice echoing against the white marbled walls as he spoke to Humar.

"You worthless bastard," Wilhelm growled. "You said this would be the safest place. You said no one would be able to get into his tomb. You know as well as I they want the stone. They'll chop him apart in an attempt to find it. And I just killed the only bastard who could put him back together."

Wilhelm walked past her, not acknowledging or looking at her. The breeze carried his scent: oiled leather and a tinge of sour metal. Her stomach fluttered from the memories. Even when naked above her, he'd smelled of armor.

"We don't know how it was done," Humar said, sprinting to keep up. "No one entered the tombs. I've had guards posted the entire time. I—"

"Save me your horse-crap excuses," Wilhelm snarled. "I trusted you to keep him safe. I trusted you to keep *it* safe."

Mafarias grabbed Wilhelm's arm. "I saw Vuddruk in the city a few days ago. I tried to follow him, but he lost me. I'm sure he's behind this. I ..." The mage glanced at the others and leaned close to Wilhelm. He spoke in secretive tones, but Varila was able to hear. "I've found something out about him. He used to visit Falar. I think he works for the darkness."

Wilhelm's fists clenched. "Let go of me."

Mafarias released his grip. "We find Vuddruk, we find your brother."

"Boy," Edium said, moving between Mafarias and Wilhelm. "Where have you been for the last three years?"

Wilhelm glared at Edium. "I'm no boy, and it's none of your business."

"You can't possibly still blame us," Edium said.

"If you hadn't pushed him, talking of family and a home, he wouldn't have spooked and ran off. Yeah, I still blame you." He curled his lip at Mafarias. "You can go to Oblivion, too."

Wilhelm descended the steps to the catacombs two at a time. Varila was panting by the time she caught up with her husband. He marched through the vast underground cemetery until he found Salvarias's resting place. Humar was quick to motion the two guards aside before Wilhelm plowed past them. Her husband shoved his shoulder against the door, and it ground open. Inside was exactly how it had been three years ago and every week Varila visited. The slab sat on a raised platform wider than Wilhelm and stood as high as Varila's waist.

Wilhelm's gaze swept the room before he roared out in anger. He shoved the lid off Salvarias's tomb, grabbed the pillow and blankets, and threw them across the room. A hole carved out of the bottom of the platform led far underground.

"It had to be Vuddruk," Mafarias said. "He tunneled here like he tunneled his way to the lost city of Quind."

Wilhelm whirled around and leveled Humar before snatching up Salvarias's aspen branch and storming out of the room.

3

SPRING 1022 A.R

I t was late in the night, the time when the moon rose to its luminous glory, bathing the rolling hillside in silver. Winter's last chilly breeze hissed along the grasses, leaving ripples like a snake slithering in the sand. The warm fire at Unupture's back did little to block the wind sweeping over the balcony of the abandoned estate—formerly abandoned.

A month prior, Unupture had arrived in the cold city of Senti, been blindfolded, and deposited in this decrepit home. He was an unshackled prisoner, constantly monitored by the remaining Four and God. No army accompanied them; no guards stood watch, no creatures circled overhead. It was a lonely existence save for the excited air about God. Something was happening. Something Unupture hoped with all his heart involved Salvarias.

He watched dried leaves flutter around a ruined half-wall in the courtyard below. An old gate creaked on rusty hinges. Cold, he tore his gaze from the silent hillside and moved to stand near the fire. The inside of the estate had old furniture that wafted up dust whenever it was used. Shredded burgundy tapestries hung precariously from the walls, and an overused forest-green rug covered the cold stone floor.

A few chairs were positioned here and there, and in the largest sat God, staring at the fire, his fingers steepled. The firelight shadowed his strong jaw and cheekbones, dancing in his dark eyes. Eludar and Devoar, the last of the Four, occupied a corner, heads pressed together in private conversation.

Off in the distance, Unupture heard thundering hooves, and his hands shook in anticipation. He tried to hide it from his master and took to pacing the room.

At long last, the double doors to the room flew open, and a minotaur stepped inside, a limp form cocooned in a gray blanket draped over its shoulders.

Devoar's armor moved like a second skin when it walked to the minotaur. A mirage shimmered off it, and sometimes Unupture heard the souls trapped in that horrid creature screaming. "All went according to plan?" Devoar asked.

"Aye," the creature growled. "The mage dug under the tomb. No one's the wiser."

"On the contrary." Edular's poisonous blood flowed over his form in constant movement, humming like a faraway river. In contrast to Devoar, Eludar gave off a chill. "The King visits the grave every morning and checks the body. Word has already spread."

"I nearly gave up on your plan," God said to Devoar. "Three years is three longer than I wanted to wait."

"Patience is what will win this war," Devoar said. "The tunnel was excavated as quickly as we dared." It turned back to the minotaur. "Any sign of the Protector?"

The minotaur shook its head. "No. The mage hasn't seen him since the boy died."

"He could come out of hiding," Devoar said. "We must be swift before a search party stumbles upon us."

"Unlikely," the minotaur said. "This place is a week's travel from Warton. The watch will tear apart its own city first."

Devoar reverently took the limp body in its arms and laid it out in front of the fire. Unupture fought back tears when Devoar unfolded the blanket and he saw Salvarias's face. Decay had not touched the young man, and he looked as though he were sleeping peacefully. His features were as flawless as Unupture remembered. The firelight flickered orange on his wavy jet-black hair, but his former healthy complexion was now bleak as ash.

God knelt beside the young man and caressed his brow. "He is beautiful, is he not?"

Unupture's gaze flicked between the young mage and God, trying to find physical differences. There were none.

"The Soul has not yet been claimed." God licked his lips. "I feel it waiting."

"Do you sense the stone?" Eludar asked.

"No," God murmured, his black eyes scanning Salvarias. "I feel nothing of it."

"He could have hidden it," Eludar said. "Just as Perek had done."

"Then our master would surely have sensed it by now," Devoar said. "The boy has done something. Something truly powerful."

God's jaw rippled. "What now, you worthless creatures? I have waited three years for nothing!"

"I feared this would be the case," Devoar said, unflustered by God's threatening tone. "And I have planned accordingly. It is once again time to call upon your birthright. It is time Balance be restored."

God's cold eyes brightened. "Of course!" He raised his head and said, "Show yourself, servant."

A woman stepped forth from the shadows. She was neither tall nor short, nor beautiful or ugly. One would not even look twice at her in passing. "Yes?"

"I am owed, Balance" God said. "I wish for the boy to be brought back."

"As you command," Balance said. Speaking to a dark corner of the room, she purred, "Come out and face the consequences of your actions. You defied Father when you used your power in defiance of His rules."

It took Unupture a few breaths to realize the darkness moved, catching light, writhing as if alive. Then a shadowfire stepped forward. In the form of a human, Unupture could not discern if the being was shadow or fire. The two forces had birthed a trick of the eye. The center of the creature looked like a shadow, dull and empty, but the edges licked the air like black flames, alive and dangerous. Each step hissed against the stone floor, leaving charred footprints.

"You cannot ask this of me," it snarled at Balance. "Make them leave the boy, and then I will bring him back."

"You are in no position to make requests," Balance said coldly. "You helped him when he was dying. You gifted him respite, fought for him, and showed him the voice in his mind was not to be trusted. You did so with *your* power. How can you think this is not your fault?"

"You are asking me to give him over to that monster. I cannot."

"You do not have a choice," Balance said. "Father is growing weary of this game. Do as I say or else He will take the boy's soul for Himself. And you know what that means."

God smirked at the shadowfire. "Let us battle once more. Or do you have so little faith in your chosen?"

"Damn you," the shadowfire hissed. "Damn you both." It slunk over to Salvarias, empty eye sockets sweeping over the room. Its eyeless gaze rested on Unupture. "You must help him. He will go mad on his own and be nothing for either your master or myself. Block everything from his mind. Let it come to him slowly."

Throat too tight to speak, Unupture nodded as his fingernail grew double the length of his finger. He gently pushed it into the base of Salvarias's skull. Unupture had done this several times before, and each time he was struck by the sheer presence of Salvarias, of his intelligence and the constant motion of his mind. Now there was nothing. Where life once flowed in his veins, there was a sense of waiting, as if blood had merely been suspended in time.

"Oh," Balance said, holding up a hand, a cruel smile curling her lips. "I almost forgot. Father has forbidden you to speak to the boy again. You cannot walk by his side anymore."

"Ha!" God shook his head, chuckling. "I'm afraid this will be over rather quickly, dearest *therro*." God grinned at the shadowfire. "About time, is it not?"

"Curse you," the shadowfire snarled. "My son will find a way to free her, and he will free me. Then you will feel my wrath!"

The shadowfire thrust its flaming hand inside Salvarias's chest. "It is not time to rest, my son. You must awake."

The shadowfire morphed into a ball and submersed itself inside Salvarias's heart. A slow drum beat in Unupture's mind, and he had a sensation of movement, of life. Slowly, faint beat by faint beat, the drum beat louder, steady. Salvarias shuddered in a breath.

"Faster!" God demanded.

The shadowfire poured the last of its power into the young man. Salvarias's lifebeat thumped quickly and color flushed his face. Unupture actually felt the force of Salvarias's soul plunge into his body, coursing life through once dead veins. The mage inhaled sharply, and his eyes fluttered open.

When the shadowfire slithered out of Salvarias's chest, it was no bigger than a worm. It lurched along the ground, reaching for the shadows. Salvarias hitched and his eyes rolled back. Unupture could not even attempt to sort through the hurricane of confusion and thoughts raging in Salvarias's mind.

God curled his lip at the shadowfire. "Now you are blind, *therro*. Do not fret. You will know when I have obtained victory. I will not give up until the boy is mine. His soul will succumb to me, and once I use him to cleanse this forsaken world, I will come for you. This time, I will not spare your life, my dearest *therro*, my brother."

The shadowfire stretched out longingly but lacked the strength to crawl to safety. With a shudder, the fire flickered out, and the shadow faded in the moonlight.

God placed his finger on Salvarias's forehead. Red fog poured from God's hand, encasing them both, caressing Unupture's skin. He recoiled and wanted nothing more than to withdraw his nail, to flee from God's power. It embedded a feeling of dirt, of a stain on his skin, of something not meant to be touched or witnessed. Salvarias curled up, and a building scream burst from his throat.

"You see the darkness within you," God hissed. "Reach for it. Accept it. You have no choice."

Power boomed to life inside Salvarias. Magic.

"You think you can beat me?" God growled. "You are nothing. Magic is the weakest of all the powers. You cannot win this fight."

God's power tore at the magic's connection to Salvarias. The two forces fought viciously, ripping into each other like two wolves, leaving a taste of blood in Unupture's mouth. Power fighting power: the most awful battles to ever be waged, one done within the mind and soul. To be witness to it left an aching wound on Unupture's own soul.

It took little on God's part to sever Salvarias's mind from the magic, leaving it flowing like a volatile river inside Salvarias; now separate, now dangerously out of control.

Sapphire light exploded from Salvarias, filling the estate, and when it spoke, it seemed to surround Unupture. "He is under my protection!"

"You are no match for me," God sneered.

"Do you think me a fool?" the magic demanded. "Do you think I do not know what has happened to my wizard? I know, owner of darkness! I knew what he was the instant you brought him back. He doesn't belong to you! He is mine!"

Another light flickered over Salvarias, this one a warm green and within that one, black flames rose out of Salvarias, subtle enough Unupture initially doubted his eyes.

Salvarias's magic addressed another force within the young man. "We must save him, and to do so you must make me stronger."

The green and blue light flashed brightly, blinding Unupture for a breath before blinking out. The black flames extinguished, and then brilliant sapphire light shot at God, hurling him from the mage. He smacked into a wall and toppled into a heap on the ground.

The red fog seeped inside Salvarias, and God screamed, "No!"

Salvarias convulsed and blood jetted from his mouth. God's powers, what it did to Salvarias's mind, was too much for the young man to bear. He slipped toward insanity, his thoughts a whirlwind of pain and grief. Unupture frantically tried to help the mage cling to reality, but Salvarias was drowning.

"You have left him unguarded," God wheezed. "You honestly think merging with Vuddruk and Mafarias's power will save him? You are as big of fool as he. He is mortal, trapped in this form, subjected to its hinderances, just as I. The human mind was not made to harbor such powers."

The sapphire light flashed, then with a rush of air it plummeted back inside the mage.

Salvarias's cry choked off in the river of blood. Unupture gently turned the young man on his side. Unupture reached out his powers and sensed the magic trying to protect Salvarias's mind, to shield it from the new influx of power. The magic turned its fury toward Unupture, but before dealing a lethal blow, it paused. It seemed to recognize him.

I will withdraw, the magic said, its words echoing in Unupture's mind. *You must be present to help him when he calls me forth. Without our link, I will unintentionally kill him. There is no way to repair it. It is up to you to help him release me. Beg his forgiveness for me. I was ignorant.*

It receded deep inside Salvarias, to some quiet corner in an attempt to hide from his mind. Ignoring it, Unupture used his power to haul Salvarias back from the abyss of insanity.

"He will be mad now," God said, his voice heavy with defeat. "I have lost."

"No," Unupture murmured, his concentration wavering. "I can save him. He is not too far gone."

"Impossible. That amount of power will make him insane."

Devoar sucked in a breath. "Do you sense it, master? He has become one of the Gods of Magic."

God snorted. "You're as mad as he. The boy could not accomplish such a feat unless he's a ..." God's eyes widened.

"I told you the boy was evolving. All we've done to grow his power, all he's been through ... Perhaps once he was mortal, his godhood locked away, but at some point, we unlocked it, cracked its shell. That is why Balance used a shadowfire. She lacked the power to bring the boy back." Devoar pressed a hand to the wall as if to steady himself. "We've unleashed a higher god. Do you not feel it? The power? Surely, it is a mistake. Surely He did not mean to make him so powerful."

God's eyes lit with fury. "Father has tricked me!" Raising his gaze skyward, he shouted, "You give him a son but deny me? Am I not what you have made me? Have I not earned your love, Father?"

Unupture's heart ached at the pain flowing from his master's voice. Turning from him, Unupture directed his entire mind to helping Salvarias.

UNUPTURE PASSED Salvarias another cup of tea. The mage looked near death, pale and shaky, a sheen of sweat glistening on his face. It had taken a week to reach this point, to get Salvarias to eat and the blood dripping from his nose to stop. Unupture was exhausted from using his powers nonstop to help Salvarias control the new power he had stolen from God. More than once, Unupture worried he would lose the young man. What a dark world it would be if such a thing were to happen.

With the fourth cup of tea, Salvarias raised his head. For the first time, his eyes were clear, alert. "Thank you. Without your help, I fear I would not be alive."

Unupture smiled, realizing he missed hearing the young man's melodic voice. "It was my pleasure."

Salvarias surveyed the room. Unupture hoped it was calming. He had taken great care to keep the fire going, warm and inviting. Two chairs were positioned near it, each dusted at length to help with the man's breathing condition. He'd laid out a few books and added more rugs than needed. Thick blankets covered the bed Salvarias sat on, stuffed with feathers instead of hay. Unupture had even taken a painting from another room and hung it above the fire; a beautiful scene of a meadow and a couple picnicking together.

Salvarias inhaled a slow deep breath. "I have been taken."

It wasn't a question, but Unupture answered. "We are in Loutsil, though exactly where I fear I do not know. Eludar and Devoar are here. God as well."

Salvarias tensed, but nodded. "I died?"

"What do you remember?"

"Pain and then ... my brother came for me, but my wounds were fatal. I ..." His face twisted in a grimace, his breathing increasing. "Death. I was surrounded by the dead."

"Indeed, you died. It has been three years."

Salvarias sat straight, his eyes widening. "Three ..."

"There is nothing to be done for it now. Save your strength." Unupture went to a crate he had by the fire and riffled through his personals until he found the two palm-sized eggs. Cradling them close, he went back to Salvarias and deposited them in his lap. "I have created something for you. And I promise, no animals or people were harmed in their making."

Salvarias set aside his cup, his eyes brightening. It filled Unupture with more joy than he liked to admit. Sitting on the edge of the bed, Unupture said, "Our talks inspired me to explore my powers. I had been trained to use them cruelly, and I never thought to try otherwise. But you inspired me, and I learned I can create with no pain to the creatures involved."

Salvarias hesitantly reached out and ran his fingers along the hard shell. As Unupture had planned, the egg cracked upon Salvarias's touch.

A furry lion's head poked through the shell. With a fair amount of struggle, the creature's body burst free and it crawled mightily out, spreading its wings and swishing its lion's tail. Its clawed feet dug into the blanket with each hop as it made its way into Salvarias's open hands. He gently touched the second egg and it cracked immediately. This one emerged with much more force, its tiny brown eyes finding Salvarias. It leapt into his lap, curled up, and started purring. A wide smile slid across Salvarias's face, and a soft, joyful laugh escaped his lips. "How truly remarkable."

~

LUNARA RODE in the back of the group, despondent and uncaring of what passed by them. She wasn't sure why she had decided to accompany her parents, sister, Okulu, and Wilhelm. Even if they managed to find Salvarias's body, it would not change the fact the man she loved was dead.

Three years and the loss was no less terrible. She ached with emptiness, a shell of a person. Even so, she doubted her pain came close to Wilhelm's. He'd locked away his entire self. All she sensed in him was an unquenchable anger.

While Humar and Mafarias tore apart the city in search for Vuddruk and Salvarias's body, Okulu had gone exploring for clues. It had taken him three days to find the tracks of a minotaur who had ventured from the main road after a mile. It was at least something.

Wilhelm had left upon hearing of the news, not bothering to gather supplies or ask anyone else if they wanted to come. It'd taken her family and Okulu the entire afternoon to catch up to him, and now he set the pace. He rested little and ignored everyone. He hadn't even looked at Varila. Indeed, her sister was wise in keeping Tedris clear of the man. Wilhelm was dead, and Tedris was fatherless.

They stopped late in the night and set up camp in a cluster of trees just off the main road. Lunara went through the motions of gathering her bedroll, blankets, and helping her mother with the pots. Her mind must have wandered because the next thing she knew, she was holding a bowl of stew. Wilhelm sat alone at the edge of the campfire's light.

"Should we try to get him to talk?" her father asked, reclining against a fallen pine as he stared at Wilhelm's back.

"No, dear," her mother said. "He'll talk when he's ready."

"It's been three damn years," her father growled. "He has a family, responsibilities. He can't go on like this."

Talura sighed. "Actually, I think he has every intention of going on like this." She held Varila's hand tightly and smiled.

Warmth washed over Lunara, like Salvarias's breath on her lips when they'd almost kissed. The world brightened, and an emotion Lunara had long forgotten fluttered in her heart: joy.

Wilhelm's bowl fell from his hands, and he sprang to his feet. Lunara had risen without realizing. Wilhelm whirled around and met her gaze.

"He smiled," she breathed.

4

SPRING 1022 A.R

Salvarias's smile broadened when the creature gnawed on his finger. Its tail wrapped around Salvarias's wrist as it perched on his hand.

"They are beautiful," Salvarias said.

Unupture smiled and ran his finger along one of the creature's wings. "The griffins of old were superbly intelligent and had a human-type mind. And a god created them, something I am far from being. These are the closest I could make."

"Remarkable," Salvarias murmured. He reached out his mind to the creatures. Just like Unupture's other creations, Salvarias could not speak to them. Regardless, it did nothing to discourage his affections, and he cradled them close and stroked them soothingly. "I cannot thank you enough for such a gift."

Unupture smiled shyly. "You're the first friend I've ever had." Unupture frowned and looked away. "Which makes what I'm about to tell you all the more difficult. I fear your joy will soon end. I have put them off, but Eludar and Devoar will come for you. They will take what they want, and they will use me to do so. They will discover your fears and what you have done with the stone."

"My brother will come for me." He did not disclose he had lost his connection to both Wilhelm and Lunara. The thought of losing something so valuable was heartbreaking, but what stole his breath was the probability they were dead. The more he dwelled on it, the more it became the only explanation.

The door flew open, and Devoar stepped inside. Its glowing red eyes focused on Salvarias, and a cruel smile twisted its lips. Heat drifted up from its lava-crusted body as it bowed deeply. Salvarias heard the souls trapped inside Devoar screaming.

"I'm pleased to see you awake, Salvarias Laybryth."

Unupture shoved the creatures under the blanket.

"I think it is time you met your Master," Devoar said.

The fight Salvarias always clung to loosened his throat, and he said, "I have no master."

"On the contrary." Devoar strode up to the bed and offered its hand. Its gaze drifted to the blanket moving. "What is this?" It tossed back the blanket. The little creatures looked up with wide, innocent eyes.

"Unupture, you continue to disappoint me." Devoar snatched up the creatures before Salvarias could. It threw them into the fire.

The shrieks tore through Salvarias, and he struggled to rise from the bed, fighting his tingling legs and stiff muscles. By the time he lurched his way to the fire, the creatures were shriveled husks.

"When will you learn, boy? We're going to kill everything you love. Now come along. We can't keep your master waiting."

Unupture started to rise but Devoar clucked its tongue. "Not you, Unupture. You stay here."

Fighting back tears, Salvarias hauled himself up and headed for the door. After a few short steps, his bad leg crumpled beneath him, and he latched on to a chair to stay upright.

"There, there," Devoar said, coming to his side. "It's been three years since you walked, young man. That kind of damage cannot be repaired, even by one as powerful as my master. A little stiffness is to be expected. Let me help you."

Salvarias flinched from the creature. "Do not touch me." He developed a picture of his staff in his mind and called it to him. It appeared at his side, and he snatched hold before it fell. Steadying his voice, burying his grief, he motioned to the door and said, "Lead the way."

LUNARA'S HEART hammered in her ears as she stared at the spot where Salvarias's aspen branch had once rested. Wilhelm had staggered back until he tripped over his own feet and had toppled to the ground. No one man should be subjected to the amount of pain consuming his soft cry.

"How—What—Can ..." Her father glanced at them.

"Don't just sit there!" Okulu snapped. "Pack!"

Her mother started putting out the fire. Wilhelm's eyes were brimmed with tears. It was the first sign of something besides anger. Yet, as Varila walked toward him the life behind his amber eyes melted away. His tears dried instantly, and his heart cringed back behind its wall.

He got to his feet, and a scowl cascaded over his features. He shoved aside Varila's outstretched hand and marched to Lilly. Not bothering to help the others, he saddled his horse, mounted, and rode out of camp, ignoring her father's call.

Varila watched Wilhelm for a short moment before helping their mother pack. Lunara went to help, though she barely knew what her physical body was doing. She was too focused on trying to find a link to Salvarias. It'd been so long, and fear she might be wrong hindered her efforts to connect with him. She wouldn't be able to handle the pain if her fears were realized. He couldn't be alive. Three years ... Three ...

"Lunara!" Her father was shaking her. "Do you sense him? Is he alive?"

Fear burgeoned in her, dreadful fear. Was it hers or could it be his?

SALVARIAS HOBBLED down the hallway with all the confidence he could muster. Terror gnawing on his body made walking difficult and breathing a near impossibility. He did not want to see what awaited him.

They passed abandoned rooms along an eerily quiet hall. He had expected screams, to pass rooms of torture, to see creatures from the Long Wars roaming the estate. Instead, he felt incredibly alone, removed from the world, from help.

Devoar opened a door and motioned him to enter. Salvarias clung to his courage and stepped inside. A hooded figure sat in a chair by the fire. The flames made his red robes look alive with a fire of their own. Salvarias recognized the man from Falar. The man who made him swim in an ocean of blood, who wore death like a favorite cloak.

Devoar closed the door, leaving Salvarias alone with the being.

The man's thin hand reached out and motioned to a chair in front of him. "Sit."

There was something hauntingly familiar about the voice. Swallowing his terror, begging himself to be strong, he crossed the room. He thought of Wilhelm. His brother would not be frightened. His brother would draw his sword and lop off the man's head without pause. With all his being, Salvarias wished he were that strong. But fear had raised Salvarias, owned him, and he was a slave to its will. Reluctantly, he sat.

"You are difficult to find, my pet." The figure tossed back its hood. Salvarias's vision swam with dizziness as he gazed upon his mirror image. The man's face was Salvarias's, his build was Salvarias's, and his hands were Salvarias's. It was only when he looked into the eyes did he see a difference. This man's irises did not move. They were dead of life, lumps of hate.

Unbidden, Salvarias breathed the word, "Father."

The man's eyebrow arched. "Father?" He reached up and touched his cheek before bursting into laughter. "Father!" He leaned back, wiping his eyes. "Yes, I am your father, my pet."

Tears welled in Salvarias's eyes as everything clicked into place. "You are God. The shadowfires are of your design."

"I am, and they are." God smiled. "Now tell me, son of mine, where is the stone?"

Hot tears trickled over Salvarias's cheeks. "I will never give it to you. My brother will come for me, and he will kill you."

"You carry much confidence," God purred. "But you've yet to discover just how powerful I am. Your brother will not defeat me."

Fight. It was all Salvarias could cling to. Fight. Gritting his teeth in determination, he ignited his magic. Hot lava flowed in his veins, and he swore some creature was eating him from the inside out. Pressure compressed his skull, and he screamed in a pointless attempt to relieve it.

We are no longer connected, his magic said. *This being severed our link. It's time to let me go, my wizard. Release your hold on me so I can die.*

Never!

Then we both die. This is the only way! Release me!

Salvarias had not realized he had fallen from the chair. He was writhing on the floor, sweating, spitting up bile and blood as the magic tore into him.

Please, his magic said. *I beg you, let me die! You cannot endure this!*

Salvarias refused. His magic was a friend, a dear friend, and he would not let it die without a fight. Clamping his jaw to keep in another scream, he desperately searched for the core of his power.

"Call it forth," Salvarias ordered.

He sensed the hesitation in his magic before it reached deep inside and ignited the power. He felt the anger of blackfire and clung to it, coaxing it to him. Unsure what to do with it, he did the only thing he knew how: he enchanted. This time, the recipient was his magic, and Salvarias's order was for the blackfire to mend their connection. He did not know if it was the correct path, but desperation was his only option.

The blackfire surged up within and exploded with understanding. Salvarias's world went black. He floated in an ocean of tangible darkness pressing in on him from all sides. It took him a moment to realize he was drowning in his lake. Beneath the surface, horrible memories hunted him. His heinous acts stalked him, striking like a whip across his heart. He heard himself sobbing. He did not want to be here anymore, but he was lost, alone.

It seemed he sank for an eternity in that horrible place before he saw a speck of light. It glowed with the brilliance of a sapphire and was surging toward him. Then he felt it. His magic. But it was not his old magic; it was so much more powerful. The light cocooned him in safety and carried him up from the darkness.

I am here, his magic whispered, its words calming Salvarias's terror. *I owe you my life. Truly, you are a remarkable wizard.*

Salvarias saw light and blurred objects. He blinked several times, and the haze cleared. He was lying on the floor in front of a fire. God still sat in his chair, eyebrow arched.

Salvarias swallowed the taste of bile and blood and slowly shoved himself to sit. He leaned back against his chair, utterly exhausted, but thrilled at the power coursing through him. His magic was alive, its anger burning Salvarias's own blood.

He met God's gaze. "You thought to strip me of my magic?"

God shrugged, his gaze anything but indifferent. "Apparently, I failed." Disappointment did not frame the words; triumph did.

"What have you done?" Salvarias said, running the sleeve of his robe across his mouth. His arm shook badly.

It is my fault, my wizard, the magic said. *I have done something to us. I have made us like your grandfather and Vuddruk. I beg your forgiveness. I have added yet another strain to your mind, my wizard.*

"Where is the stone?" God asked.

"I will never give it to you."

"My powers surpass yours, my pet. Check for yourself. Eventually, you will give me what I seek. It is inevitable."

Salvarias reached out his mind to God's power. It far exceeded Mafarias and Vuddruk's. It was beyond Salvarias's comprehension. It was also a familiar foe. It was the same as his evil.

No, my wizard, look deeper, his magic urged. *I will show you how.*

Salvarias had no desire to reach further inside God, but he trusted his magic. With the slightest hesitation, he allowed his magic to lead him. As Salvarias hunted deeper, he found a kinship to the power within God, a power God was a master over while Salvarias was merely an apprentice. Yet, what God had mastered seemed ... hollow, missing something valuable, something terribly important.

To lessen more of God's potential was another power, one so familiar it brought tears to Salvarias's eyes. Zerana. Her powers were eating at God's, weakening that mighty force and draining him just as his powers drained hers. What he sensed was not her grace left in patches over Arden. It was *she,* and the instant Salvarias discovered it, pain burst over his body. Her power fought the son as it did the father.

We must look deeper, his magic urged.

Through blinding pain, Salvarias followed his magic beneath the layer of God's power. It was then he touched God's soul. It was more beautiful and horrific than anything Salvarias had ever seen. He felt the humbling presence of being inside a true god, not some lesser god like Crutar. This was a higher god. Tainting the beauty of God's soul was a disease. It ate at him, infecting God's beauty with decay.

Even as Salvarias processed this, he realized its essence was something he had come across before. He rummaged around his memories and found it: Humar's crown, the curse of the Lilkous bloodline, *Veedran's* curse. Sucking in a huge breath, he bolted clear of God's soul and mind. When he met God's eyes, they were alight with anger.

"How dare you!" God roared, springing up from his chair.

"Veedran," Salvarias breathed. He had not realized he was scrambling backward. His gaze was locked on Veedran, on the Dark God, the god that brought pain and suffering to Arden. The god that was his father.

The door flung open, and the Four rushed inside. Devoar glanced at Salvarias and then at Veedran.

"How could you let the boy know?" Devoar shouted.

"I didn't," Veedran snapped. "His magic discovered it!"

Unupture rushed into the room. "What has happened?"

Betrayal stabbed Salvarias's heart when he looked at Unupture. "How could you not tell me?"

Unupture looked genuinely surprised. "Tell you what?"

"That you serve Veedran!"

Unupture's eyes widened as his gaze darted to God. "Veedran?"

Scanning the room, Salvarias saw a window. Without thinking, he rushed for it. He would rather throw himself from the estate than spend another moment with the dark god, with the evil living inside him, with his father.

Before he reached it, pain flared on the side of his head and darkness claimed him.

UNUPTURE COULDN'T TEAR his stare from Veedran standing over Salvarias's limp body, hands balled into fists, cursing in languages never uttered on Arden.

"Did you kill him?" Veedran demanded.

"No," Devoar said, shoving the mage over with its foot.

Blood trickled from a cut on Salvarias's temple.

"Now what?" Veedran asked, sinking into a chair.

"We go on as planned," Devoar said. "We use the one who can exploit his fears and show us a way to break him."

All eyes turned to Unupture.

Veedran snorted. "He's betrayed me. No doubt he will not push the boy. He will be gentle. He will tell us he is trying, yet he will do nothing."

"The choice will not be his," Eludar said. It walked slowly up to Unupture, a cruel smile on its lips. "There are few creatures you have not made yourself, servant. Can you think of any that could control you?"

Unupture knew klusher blood flowed in his veins. He'd obtained their ability to mind read, but a full-blooded klusher could control a man. "But none survived the Long Wars," he said aloud.

"Do you think we were fools?" Devoar said. "Veedran created us to think of every complication. We hid away pairs of the species you and Veedran created. They've been breeding for near a thousand years."

Unupture took a step back toward the door. "How did you hide yourself?" he asked Veedran.

The god curled his lip. "That is not your concern."

Unupture took another step. He was in the doorway. "We would have served you if we'd known."

Veedran's glare faltered, and his gaze flickered to Unupture. There was a lack of confidence in his eyes Unupture had never seen before. "You would have laughed if I told you who I was. You wouldn't have believed me. I am weak compared to what I once was. My power does not feel the same. He stole it!" Veedran stared at his hands. "Now I am trapped in this hideous form. A broken god."

Perhaps he was right. Unupture remembered Veedran as a cloud of red hate, no form, and no weakness save the goddess herself. His power had been astounding, his hate unrelenting. What sat before him now was more man than god. Unupture wondered what had happened to Veedran and his powers.

Answers were not as precious as freedom. He would escape, hunt down Wilhelm, and return with the entire Loutsil army on his heels. They would save Salvarias, and perhaps the mage would look upon him with fondness.

Unupture whirled around and was greeted by a klusher. It smiled wickedly before it jammed its claws into Unupture's skull.

5

SPRING 1022 A.R

Salvarias did not know how long he had been battling Unupture's power. The man mercilessly pummeled Salvarias's walls, and soon they would crumble. He clung to the promise he had made to his brother: to never give in, to fight until Wilhelm came for him. And his brother would come. Wilhelm never broke a promise.

The last thing Salvarias remembered was being shackled to a wall. Unupture had been chained at his side and next was a creature Salvarias guessed to be a klusher. Its orange skin and luminous green eyes were characteristic of klushers, yet Salvarias had read they had all been killed. He did not know what to believe anymore. After all, Veedran and Zerana were alive, Nevlar missing or dead.

A sharp jolt of pain pulled his attention back to Unupture. Salvarias saw nothing in front of him. He had been blinded by the concentration needed to battle Unupture's powers. He did not know if he was hungry or if his nose dripped blood. He only knew of the war inside his mind.

Unupture flung a surge of power, and Salvarias braced himself, but it was too late. His walls toppled, and every dark memory tucked below his lake of indifference exploded to the surface.

. . .

SALVARIAS TREMBLED WITH FEAR, watching his mother pace. He was curled in the corner of the room in the home by the docks. Ever since Jyfil started asking questions, his mother had brought him here so his cries would not be heard. The home was similar enough to his own that Salvarias sometimes forgot he was not above the baker during his mother's more violent beatings. The only difference he clung to was the rancid odor of fish. His home smelled of fresh breads and sweetcakes, not fish guts.

A figure sat in a chair, shadowed except for slate-blue robes pooling in the small ray of light streaming through the broken window. Salvarias mouthed the words, "help me," but the figure did not move. Each session, the person would watch. Each session, his mother's frustration had intensified, frantic in her endeavor to rid Salvarias of his evil. There was a gleam in her eyes that had been growing brighter.

Ashra stopped pacing and stared at Salvarias. "This is your last chance."

"I am trying," Salvarias wept softly. "I promise, Mother. I am trying."

Ashra's eyes hardened, and she grabbed his arm. He cried out when her fingers dug into his flesh bruised by the frying pan she had hit him with earlier.

"I swear to you!" Ashra said, dragging him from the room. "I will make it leave you!"

She tossed him inside the washroom. His bones smacked the hard stones, and he whimpered. There was a chair centered in the room with short belts nailed to the arms and leg posts. A washbasin sat on the floor behind it.

"I finally know how to get rid of it," Ashra said.

Salvarias looked up eagerly. "You can make it go away?"

"Yes."

"Help me!" he pleaded, crawling to her. He clawed at the bottom of her robes. "Help me make it leave!"

His mother sank to her knees in front of him. She gently touched his cheek. The gleam lessened, and her eyes brightened. "I will help you," she whispered. She brushed aside a clump of his bloody hair, wiped tears from his cheeks, and smiled.

"I love you!" Salvarias wept and flew into her arms. "I love you, Mother!"

She cradled him tightly while kissing his forehead.

"Please," he whispered. "Please love me."

"I ... I—" Ashra shoved him. "No! You will not tempt me, monstrosity! I will not be tempted by your evil!"

She slapped him hard across the cheek, knocking him to the floor. He hugged himself, rocking back and forth, and wept from his stinging cheek and her denial.

"I will drive it from you!" she said shrilly.

His mother yanked him to his feet and shoved him into the chair. He cried out when she yanked the straps tight around his wrists and then his ankles, the leather biting into his skin.

"I will drain it from you," Ashra said. "I will force it from your body. From our home!"

She grabbed his hair and jerked his head back. A strap went across his forehead, holding is head in place. He stared wide-eyed at the dark gray ceiling.

"Please, Mother, I am scared."

"I don't care," she whispered in his ear. "I will save you. I have to. It's what a mother is supposed to do. I'll drive the evil out of you, and then we can be a family. I can have the family I've always wanted."

Salvarias caught the glint of a blade in his mother's hand.

"Please!" Salvarias begged, squirming to free himself. "Please, I am trying! I promise, Mother!"

"No, monstrosity, you are not or else it would be gone. The evil owns you, controls you. Now, hold still."

It took a moment to feel cold steel slip into his scalp on the top of his head. His eyes widened as the metal sliced down the back of his head.

"It hurts," Salvarias breathed. "Please, Mother, it hurts."

"This is for your own good," she said.

Salvarias cried out. "It hurts! Please stop! Please!"

"Shut up!"

Salvarias did not know how long he sat listening to the unsteady dripping of his blood into the bowl on the floor and the low keening of his own voice, nor how much time passed before the sparrow came to visit him as it did every week. It squeezed through a crack in the window and peered at him with its glossy eye. Salvarias softened his sobs so he could hear the bird's cheery song.

When darkness pressed in his vision, he felt drained of life, barely able to stay focused on the bird, on his lifeline, on hope. He saw his mother's needle glisten in the candlelight. He caught sight of the figure robed in slate-blue cross the room.

"Please," Salvarias mumbled. "Please help me."

The figure paused at the door as if on the verge of helping, but instead it slipped out of the room.

His mother hummed while she threaded his scalp together, tugging his skin closed. Light dimmed, and the room blurred through his tears. He sensed the bird's sadness and tried to smile reassuringly at it, but he did not have the energy.

"Remember," his mother whispered in his ear. "Tell your brother, and you'll never see him again."

Then all was dark.

He woke while choking on something warm running down his throat. It tasted of iron. He sputtered up the liquid.

"Stop it," she snapped. "It'll make you better. My blood is pure. It'll help with yours."

Salvarias did not want to drink his mother's blood. He coughed it back up. She slapped him, and then pinched his cheeks between her fingers. "You will drink it. Do as I say!"

Sobbing, he swallowed.

"Good," she murmured, pouring the rest down his throat. "You'll be taken tonight. Then you'll know who you really are. Maybe that will give you the strength to fight."

Salvarias squeezed his eyes shut and gagged down more blood.

· · ·

SALVARIAS JOLTED awake when hands grab him. He was in his bed in his room, and a pale blue hue tinted his surroundings. He latched on to the edge of his mattress but hands pried away his fingers.

He was about to scream for help from his slumbering brother, but his mother hissed, "Stop fighting."

A hood went over Salvarias's head, and he was picked up. As they moved through the home, Salvarias counted. They were in the sitting room, out the front door, down the steps, and then he knew where they were going: his second home of horrors near the docks.

He heard loud laughter from a tavern, smelled gamey roasts and boiled vegetables, then the overwhelming stench of the docks. Rusty hinges creaked and boots thudded on a stone floor.

He was forced into a chair, ropes went around his wrists, and then the hood was ripped off. The room was pitch black, heavy with the scent of cloves and the stench of fish.

"It is time you understand your evil," Ashra said.

Salvarias trembled. A candle lit on a small table six feet in front of him. Two men were tied to chairs facing Salvarias. A warm finger rested on his forehead and pain stabbed at his mind, but it lasted only a breath.

"Your evil is strong, monstrosity," Ashra said.

"No," Salvarias wept. "Please stop."

A hazy blue blanket draped over Salvarias's mind, and he hovered on the cusp of sleep. Then pain lanced across his head, and he was suddenly alert, and ... angry.

"See what you are capable of, child of the dark," Ashra hissed.

Another candle ignited to life and revealed a woman chained to the floor, her eyes wild with fear.

Salvarias turned his cold gaze to the man on his right. "Kill her." His voice no longer sounded like his own. It was cold, calculating, and heartless ... feminine even.

The man trembled and shook his head.

"Do it or I will kill you," Salvarias whispered.

The man's bonds fell away, and a shard of ice floated at his throat.

"Her life or yours," Salvarias said. A dagger was lying on the table. "It is right there. End your torment."

The man shakily picked up the knife and stumbled beside the woman.

Salvarias then understood it was the man's wife, and his smile grew. "Choose, weakling. Your wife or your life?"

The man gently touched the woman's cheek, and she begged him to kill her. He drew the dagger on himself, ramming it right into his heart, and Salvarias chuckled. He turned his attention to the next man.

"Kill her," Salvarias whispered.

The man's bindings disappeared, and he ran to the other man, snatched the knife, and stabbed the woman repeatedly, despite her cries for mercy.

"Let me go," the man sobbed, dropping the weapon. He was covered in the woman's blood. "I did what you wanted."

Salvarias was no longer tied and accepted a dagger handed to him. "I never told you I would release you. I never told you I would not kill you."

Grinning, he raised the dagger and plunged the blade into the man's neck. The blue haze lifted, and he blinked at the heavy dagger teetering in his tiny hand, slick with hot blood. He dropped the weapon and screamed.

6

SPRING 1022 A.R

Wilhelm crouched behind a pile of dark brown rock, examining the derelict estate in the moon's brilliant light. He wished it were overcast. Though it would have made his job a little harder, it would have provided extra cover. The moon seemed brighter than the sun.

Overgrown hedges, broken trees, and tall grasses had devoured the garden. The surrounding wall had crumbled to nothing more than rubble, and a rusted gate swung in the faint breeze, adding a foreboding creak seeming louder than a charging army. Most of the windows on the first and second floor were broken. Only dull light shone through two leaded glass windows on the third floor. By the spacing, he guessed they were at least five or six rooms apart. Off to the side of the entrance, a carriage was hitched and ready, as well as three other saddled horses.

Wilhelm made one last cursory glance at the door leading to the estate before he darted from cover, crouched over. He leapt a bench overgrown with creeping vines and stopped behind a tree. He smelled the stench of decay and piss and heard a faint buzzing. His gaze fell to a decomposing body of an octril. In the moonbeams, he saw several additional corpses. Not all were octrils, but he didn't recognize the creatures.

Something snapped behind him, and his head whipped around. It was Edium. Wilhelm curled his lip. Why couldn't they let him do this alone? He didn't want anyone near him.

He caught sight of a blonde braid in the moonlight and looked away quickly. Emotions brought pain, and Wilhelm had endured enough of that to last him a lifetime. With as shriveled as he was inside, he wasn't sure he had enough presence of mind to care if his brother was alive.

Gaze sweeping over the estate, he cursed. The fact they'd yet to see a guard worried him. "God" wasn't an idiot. He would know Wilhelm would come, wouldn't he? Yet Wilhelm had made record time. Maybe "god" thought he had days left.

Taking in a chilly breath, Wilhelm crept from the tree and sprinted across the garden. He plastered himself to the wall just to the left of the door. It was wooden; ironwork held together thick oak planks. It was ajar.

Edium slunk to the other side and raised a hand. Slowly, he peered inside.

"No one," he breathed.

A horse nickered softly.

Edium nudged the door just wide enough to fit through. Wilhelm opened it a bit more and squeezed inside. He smelled strawberry oiled leather and felt warmth at his side. He ignored it. Slowly, he drew his broadsword. Light fell across packs piled up near the door. Wilhelm saw Salvarias's aspen branch.

Lunara tiptoed over and picked it up. She cradled it to her chest. Tears glistened on her cheeks as she stared at the grand entrance. Two staircases flanked the side, spiraling up continuously to the third floor. Turned over furniture littered the area, and shredded tapestries fluttered in the occasional breeze.

"Varila," Edium whispered. "Clear the bottom floor with Okulu, and keep an eye on this entrance."

A breeze caressed Wilhelm and bathed him once again in straw-berries. He winced. His chest hurt.

"Come on," Edium breathed.

Wilhelm sidled along the wall and up the staircase, testing his footing each time to ensure absolute silence. Edium followed his steps, Lunara her father's, and Talura her daughter's.

Wilhelm paused on the second-floor landing. He should clear this level and ensure no one snuck up on him, but his feet wanted to keep going. Lunara didn't seem interested in the second floor either. Her eyes were focused on the next set of stairs, and she licked her lips. He kept going, despite Edium's hissed objections.

They ended at a landing flanked by two long corridors. Based on what Wilhelm had observed from the outside, he took the hallway on his left.

He passed three closed doors before he stopped by one that had a stream of light glowing from underneath. Pressing his ear against the cool wood, he listened.

"Is everything packed?" a voice asked.

"Yes, we can leave at any time."

"And Unupture? He survived as well?"

"Yes, much to Devoar's surprise. We'll bring him along. He might still be of use to us. He's the only one who can touch the boy's mind directly."

Wilhelm shuffled by, not caring or needing to hear anything else. His gaze locked on the fourth door down and the light leaking into the hall. This door was cracked open.

Heart beating too fast and mouth absurdly dry, Wilhelm closed the distance. He almost didn't look in. He was afraid of what he would find ... or of what he wouldn't find.

Inhaling a shaking breath, Wilhelm peered inside. He made out two figures shackled to a wall next to each other, a fireplace, three chairs, two side tables, and a frayed rug. No one else was present.

Wilhelm slipped inside far enough to make room for the three people at his back. When his gaze landed on the figures, pain lanced through his heart and locked him in place.

One figure's head was bowed. Silky black hair fell to cover his face. His robes were soiled and reeked of piss and vomit. A stream of saliva ran from his lips.

"No," Wilhelm croaked.

The pain was too intense. He couldn't endure this again. Blinking aside wetness in his eyes, he shoved away the surge of emotion. Securing the Guardian's body, dead or alive, was all that mattered. That was his purpose. Even so, it took concentration to move his legs. Slowly, he sank in front of the figure and lifted the man's chin.

It was Salvarias. His brother twitched and choked out a line of brown bile with ribbons of red mixed in it.

The last time Wilhelm had seen his brother, Salvarias's face had been ashen, dead, eyes closed and expression peaceful. What Wilhelm gazed at now was a man whose mind had been lost. Salvarias's swirling black eyes stared at nothing. His pallid face sported a sheen of sweat. Drool still fell from his mouth, which was opened slightly. As Wilhelm raised his brother's face higher to catch the light from the fireplace, Salvarias hitched and hot bile ran over Wilhelm's hand.

"Wilhelm," a voice rasped.

It took every ounce of willpower to turn his gaze from Salvarias to the man shackled next to him. Unupture's orange skin glistened in the light, and its gooey covering made Wilhelm want to retch. Unupture's large eyes were focused and clear, if not exhausted. There were six punctures in his skull seeping blood.

"They've drugged him," Unupture said, his voice rough like sandpaper. "It'll take days to wear off. He's barely maintaining control over his evil. He can't have anyone touch him." His gaze flickered over to Lunara. "Especially her. When the drug wears off, he'll go through withdraws. It'll be like a fever. You must get him far from here." He turned to Lunara. "Whatever you do, child, do not touch him until he wakes and is of his own mind."

"I've... I've lost our connection," Lunara said, voice breaking.

"Death is the unknown," Unupture said. He closed his eyes and rested his head against the wall. "He knew you would come for him. He never doubted. The key is on the wall."

"Gods," Edium breathed from behind. "What did you do to him?"

Unupture opened his eyes and regarded Edium, then Talura. He smiled slightly, but it fell quickly. Tears filled his eyes as he spoke to Talura. "I tortured his mind until he couldn't fight me anymore. Then I wrenched out his worst memories and exploited them. He ... he needs your help. Gods, you have to help him."

Talura sank by Wilhelm's side and slipped a key into the shackle holding Salvarias's right arm. Once loosed, Salvarias fell limply forward. Only the left shackle kept him up. Bile ran from his mouth.

"Stop," Unupture hissed. "I'm hurting him."

Wilhelm noticed the rope tied around Salvarias's neck. Tracing it, he found it bound Unupture's hand in place. The man's fingernail was embedded in the back of Salvarias's neck.

"Untie it," Unupture commanded.

Talura did as he asked. Wilhelm hadn't found the courage to move. The rope fell away and Unupture slowly withdrew his nail. Salvarias hitched and vomited on Wilhelm's hand.

Talura undid the last shackle, and Salvarias fell forward into Wilhelm's arms.

"Go," Unupture said. "Take him from here. Tell him I beg for his forgiveness. I beg ..." Unupture's voice choked off.

"We can take you with us," Talura said.

"No," Unupture said. "I promised I would feed Salvarias information. It's the least I can do. He's lost every battle with the Hunters. Be prepared."

A strong hand squeezed Wilhelm's shoulder. "Come on, boy," Edium said. "We need to get out of here."

Wilhelm rose on shaking legs, cradling his brother in his arms. When he turned around, he saw Lunara using the aspen branch to lean on, one hand covering her mouth. Tears stained her cheeks.

Something snapped inside of Wilhelm. Feeling numb of thought and emotion, he shoved by Lunara and left the room.

Glancing up and down the hallway, Wilhelm started the way he had come. He stopped when light flooded the corridor four doors up. Whirling around, he silently sprinted around the next corner. It was three rooms long and led into another hallway. He took off at a run, hearing soft footfalls behind him. He didn't care who else made it out. All that mattered was the Guardian not coming to anymore harm.

The next corner led down another hallway, and moonbeams shot through the windows, lighting his way to the third-floor landing.

"NO!"

The roar sent Wilhelm barreling carelessly forward. He reached the stairs and took them two at a time. There were shouts echoing through the estate.

He flew by the second-floor landing. Sparing a glance over his shoulder, he saw the Bellerums sprinting behind. No one pursued them, but the shouts were getting louder.

He made it down to the first floor and saw the front doors gaping open. Okulu stood beside Varila. Upon seeing Salvarias, both looked at each other, cursed, and darted outside.

"The carriage!" Okulu called.

Varila flung open the carriage door as Okulu hopped in the driver's seat. Wilhelm leapt inside, and the door slammed shut behind him. A protesting nicker followed a crack of the whip, and then the carriage lurched forward at a reckless speed.

Wilhelm sank into the seat and looked down at the Guardian. Salvarias's eyes were still unfocused and blood now ran from his nose. He'd vomited all over the front of Wilhelm, and he didn't care one bit.

VARILA SLID OFF HER HORSE, beyond happy to be off the mare's back. She stretched her legs as she watched Wilhelm climb out of the carriage, holding tightly to his brother. Salvarias shivered, yet his body was drenched in sweat. During their flight, he had screamed or muttered incoherently almost constantly. He never was of his right mind.

Even with his brother alive, Wilhelm had yet to leave his emotionless state. His cold eyes tracked anything nearing Salvarias, and he had the look of a predator before it killed—tense, too alert, too eager. Everyone stayed his or her distance.

The doors to the castle flung open with a boom, and Humar and Zehnia barreled out until their gazes fell to Salvarias. The king looked to have run into a wall. He stopped dead, eyes growing wide.

"By the gods," Humar breathed. "He's alive."

"Barely," Edium said. "We need to get him to Serenity, as far from this place as possible."

"Yes, yes," Humar said, though Varila doubted he heard Edium. He seemed frozen in disbelief.

Mafarias swept down the few stairs and approached Wilhelm. "What happened?"

"We found him in an abandoned estate," Talura said. "We were told he had been drugged."

"Yes," Mafarias murmured. "He is extremely ill. Let us—"

"We're taking him home," her father growled. "Far from this place. Do you have a portal up in Serinity?"

Mafarias nodded.

"We leave now," Edium said.

"I'll get Tedris," Zehnia said.

If the name meant anything to Wilhelm, he didn't show it. His gaze still swept the courtyard, his stance ready to pounce.

Varila shook her head and walked up to the queen, leaning in close to whisper, "I'd prefer he stay with you. Wilhelm's not ready, and I need to be there for my sister right now. Give me a week, and I'll come back for him."

Zehnia clasped Varila's hands tightly. "The boy can stay as long as you need. It's really no trouble."

"Let's gather our things," Talura said. "Then we'll go, dear."

Edium nodded slightly. "Hurry. I want off this continent and home where I can keep guard on the boy."

"I'll pack for you," Lunara murmured.

Varila smiled at her sister. Lunara was still in a sort of shock. She rarely looked at the mage.

Varila followed the queen through the estate and outside to her private garden. Prince Dredin was fiddling with a wooden block, and Princess Belany was chasing a frog along a cobblestone path. Tedris sat under a shady tree with a picture book. She saw his mouth moving and smiled. With help from Lunara, he could read simple words, and he was apparently sounding them out.

He looked up, and his crooked grin spread. Book forgotten, he rushed into her waiting arms.

"I've missed you, Mama!" he said, the words tumbling over one another.

She laughed and squeezed him tightly. "I've thought about you every time I breathed."

Tedris laughed. "Don't be ridiculous! No one can think about anyone *that* much. Did you find Uncle Salvarias?"

Varila buried her face in his wavy hair. "Yes. I'm sorry, son, but I have to be gone a bit longer. Another week or so."

Tedris's arms tightened around her shoulders. "It's all right. Don't cry. There's nothing to apologize for, Mama. You have important things to do. I understand. Can ... can I see Uncle Salvarias before you go?"

"No, sweetie," she said. "We'll talk about it when I get back."

She'd taken him to visit Salvarias's grave weekly. She'd used the time to tell Tedris stories of his father and uncle. Now she wondered if it had been wise. How could she explain a man coming back from the dead? How would a child process that kind of information?

"What about Father? Can I meet him yet?"

"No, sweetie." She blinked aside building tears. "Your father is still very sick."

SPRING 1022 A.R

W ilhelm's gaze flicked between the door and the window. They'd been in Serinity for two days, and already Salvarias had battled away the fever and bouts of vomiting, and his nose only dribbled blood a few times a day. Lunara had mixed Salvarias's breathing concoction and tea each morning, and Wilhelm managed to get the Guardian to choke it down along with vegetable broth. Given the circumstances, Salvarias had recovered at a rapid pace.

Now, Wilhelm sat on the bed beside the slumbering Guardian, looking for signs of danger. He didn't care Edium had doubled the patrols and posted twenty guards at the door. No one could keep Salvarias safe. Something would eventually come for him.

Wilhelm had yet to allow himself to sleep. Exhaustion tugged on his eyes but he refused it. He'd stay awake for eternity. He wasn't sure if it was delirium talking or his need to fulfill his purpose: to keep the Guardian safe. That was all that mattered.

The sun had just painted the evening sky a brilliant purple when Salvarias jerked violently. His eyes slowly opened, and his gaze lurched over the room. Tears brimmed when he looked up at Wilhelm.

"Brother?" Salvarias reached out a hand.

Wilhelm blinked, then turned his gaze back to the window, then the door, then the window, then the door. Safety was all that mattered.

"Brother," Salvarias wept, his sobs crescendoing. "I am scared."

Vaguely he was aware of Salvarias clawing at him for comfort. He sank himself further in his trance. Nothing else mattered but the Guardian's safety. He blinked and looked at the door, then the window.

SALVARIAS SHOOK HIS BROTHER, desperate for someone to help, to tell him where he was, to tell him he was alive, to tell him this was not a dream. Nothing was as it should be. *He* was not as he should be.

Wilhelm's gaze merely switched between the door and window.

"Brother!" Salvarias cried, shaking the man's shoulder. "Help me!"

He was plummeting toward panic. The last thing he remembered was being chained to a wall with Unupture. The man had ripped away every last stone Salvarias had built up to shield himself from painful memories, and now his horrid past was exposed, out for all his mind and heart to witness. And he could not bear it.

Salvarias dug his fingers under Wilhelm's breastplate and shook. "Brother! Help me!"

The door flew open and people rushed inside. Salvarias scrambled backward until the walls stopped him. His heart faltered, and he clutched his chest, wincing. He was so terribly afraid, so alone.

"Son," a man said.

Salvarias looked up at Wilhelm. His gaze swept from the group to the window and repeated.

"Son," the man said again.

"W-where am I?" Salvarias stammered.

"Salvarias..."

He looked at a smiling woman with ice-blue eyes and raven hair. She was familiar, a face of light in the horror of a nightmare.

"My name's Lunara. Do you remember me?"

"No," he choked.

"You're safe," she said. "You're in Serinity. Do you remember my father?"

Salvarias looked at the man she pointed to and shook his head. He grabbed his brother's arm. "Help me, please."

Wilhelm did nothing.

"My mother?" Lunara said.

A woman stood behind Lunara, piercing blue eyes, hair done in a braid laced with white flowers.

"It's all right if you don't," the woman said. "It might take you a bit to remember. Do you need your tea?"

Salvarias should recognize them. He knew he should. "Where am I? What has happened?" His words started tumbling out. "What is wrong with my brother? Why do I not remember you?" The more questions that surfaced, the more petrified he became.

"We're home," Lunara said. "We rescued you. Do you remember where you were? The abandoned estate? We—"

A cry left Salvarias as he remembered sitting across from the dark god, from his father. "Veedran ..." he choked, pressing himself further into the corner.

"Veedran?" the man said. "What about him?"

Salvarias shoved Wilhelm. "Help me!"

"Veedran's..." Lunara shook her head. "Veedran's not here. I swear you're safe. Salvarias, look at me."

He met her gaze. She was calm, her voice steady.

"We're all right," Lunara said. "I swear it on your life."

She would not lie to him. Not his light. He looked around again and then back to her. He nodded.

Smiling sweetly, she said, "Sleep. You're safe here."

He shifted and slumped against his brother's side. Salvarias was not sure how much time passed before sadness and loneliness hauled him into nightmares.

∾

S<small>ALVARIAS WOKE WITH A START</small>. His frantic gaze darted to his brother sitting next to him. Wilhelm was as motionless as an old mountain. Salvarias fought another bout of panic and studied his surroundings. The room was familiar. The bed was soft and comfortable, the blankets clean and smelling of jasmine. The crackling fire was inviting, and the furniture mutely elegant. The cold stonewalls were dark gray, and a massive window let in moonbeams through half closed drapes. Home, a place lived in love. It was the Bellerum's estate, and he suddenly remembered everything.

He buried his face in his hands and wept. Nothing felt right in his world. No longer did he live on a placid lake of indifference. His emotions were a maelstrom, and his mind a tornado. He was a spawn of the dark god. His magic was unfamiliar. There was no wolf to lecture him on his mistakes. There was no soft fur under hand and no strong presence to give him strength. There was no light touch on his mind, no caress of her thoughts on his, no subtle sense of her emotions fleeting across his own. He was alone.

He did not allow himself much time in self-pity. It was a weak emotion, one benefiting no one. He would rise from this bed and fight. It was all he could do, all he could focus on. If he sat still for too long, he would be forced to think, forced to remember.

He tossed aside the blankets, crawled out of bed, and saw a steaming kettle of tea sitting on a small table. He hobbled over to it and drank three cups to ease his pounding head. Not only was he suffering from the usual effects of his evil and the Hunters, but also, he was enduring the ribbons of pain left by Unupture. It lanced across his mind and made him fight down waves of nausea. Besides those, there was a new strain, an unfamiliar pressure in his skull, and a tightness to his skin as if his blood was seeking escape.

It is my fault, his magic said. *I was losing you. I panicked and asked the blackfire to make me stronger. It did, my wizard, but at a great cost to your mind.*

"What has happened?"

I fear it has given us godhood. It has turned us into a God of Magic.

"How ... I do not understand how it could accomplish such a thing."

It is more powerful than you can imagine. I think it is time to explore it, listen to it, and embrace it as part of yourself.

Absolutely not. He still heard the screams of those in Oblivion, felt the unnatural joy coursing through him as he savored the suffering of the damned. Tears burned his eyes. *I will use it as needed, but I will never embrace it as a part of me. I do not trust it. Look at what it has done to us. I can barely handle our new power. I am not meant to be a god, yet it did so anyway.*

It protected you. It saved your life. The power is growing, and soon you will have no choice. Let us use it, acquaint ourselves with it, and learn of its intentions. With time, you may see what I see.

He mulled over the idea. With his foe being the dark god himself, Salvarias grudgingly realized he needed all the power he could find. *I will do as you say. I will continue enchanting.*

And I propose we try to create, my wizard. It will show us the power's true self, what it desires.

Are you certain it is safe? I cannot bear to create something murderous again.

I am certain, but we will start small, contain our experiments, and control our environment. I will not fail you. Trust me, my wizard.

Always, my dear friend. Salvarias breathed in the warmth and comfort seeping into his bones.

A soft knock sounded on the door. With a hand on the hilt of his sword, Wilhelm crossed the room and eased open the door. "What do you want?" he growled.

"I'd like to talk to Salvarias," Varila said.

Salvarias raised the hood of his robes.

Wilhelm's jaw clenched, and he hesitated before stepping aside. After she entered, he closed the door and resumed his seat on the bed, eyes drifting between the door and window.

Salvarias motioned to a chair next to him. "It is good to see you, sis."

Varila's voice was forcibly light when she spoke. "Good to see you, too. You look good."

Salvarias lowered his voice. "How are you, truly?"

She looked down at her hands. "Fine. Lunara's been anxious to see you. She's—"

"Do not change the subject."

"You have a nephew," she said.

Salvarias rocked back in his chair. "A ... a nephew? How? When?"

Varila cast him a small smile. "The 'how' we'll have to talk about later. The 'when' was shortly after you died. I named him Tedris."

Understanding overshadowed his happiness. "He has yet to meet his father."

Varila glanced at Wilhelm and spoke soft enough he would not hear. "That's not my husband. I won't have Tedris meet him like this."

"It could help my brother."

Varila shook her head. "He's not the same man, Salvarias. He's traveled for three years killing, screwing, and drinking."

"You must forgive him. It is my fault. I—"

"I have forgiven him," she said simply. "But it's not your fault. I knew when I married him if anything happened to you, I would lose him. What time I did have was wonderful, and I don't regret it. I got a remarkable son."

Salvarias blinked aside his tears and stared at flickering flames. "I am sorry. Tell me about him ... about Tedris."

"He's just like Wilhelm. Crooked grin, same eyes. His hair's a little lighter, wavy like mine. Lunara's been teaching him to read."

"Remarkable." A drop of warm blood landed on Salvarias's hand. He quickly retrieved his cloth and pressed it to his nose.

Varila arched an eyebrow. "Something tells me what's happening inside you is masked by how well you look."

"Just remnants of Unupture's power," Salvarias said. He closed his eyes for a moment to allow the sharp pain to subside before opening them. "I believe whatever powers lurk within a Protector enhances his ability to learn. The child must be impressive."

Varila grunted. "This coming from a man who was reading at six months."

He shrugged off the comment. "Tedris was a good choice."

"I was hoping Wilhelm would think so. I'm bringing him home tomorrow. There's no point in delaying. If you can't get him out of this ..."—she looked over her shoulder at Wilhelm—"shock, then I don't hold hope. And I'm not going to be separated from my son another day. I'll just have to think of something to tell him." She turned back to Salvarias. "And explain how his uncle came back from the grave."

Salvarias nodded. "A difficult conversation. However, as I said, I assume his mind is more capable of understanding than the average child. I would be honored to meet him, if you approve."

"Of course."

Salvarias closed his eyes when his mother glided across the room. It was not real. It was not real. When he opened them, she was gone.

He drank another cup of tea and snatched up his aspen branch. "Let us meet with your family. There is much to discuss."

When he approached the door, Wilhelm bolted over and stood in front of it.

"No," Wilhelm grumbled. "It's not safe."

"Brother ..." Salvarias searched Wilhelm's features for any sign of life, but the amber eyes were dead. Gods, three years. What had happened to his brother? What had Salvarias done to him? Of course he knew. He had left his brother's protection, gotten himself captured and cut up, then had died in his brother's arms. Salvarias had killed them both that night. Swallowing his guilt, he said, "I must see the Bellerum family."

Wilhelm growled and flung open the door. Twenty guards snapped to attention. "Take me to Edium," Wilhelm snarled.

The men bumped into each other as they not only recoiled from Wilhelm's menacing tone and expression, but tried to go in the general direction of the stairs.

They were led through the estate and eventually into a windowless study. It was a beautiful room. Candles warmed the otherwise dark, gray space, and the hues of green fabric and lighter woods compensated for the lack of light. The fireplace was larger than the one in his room, and though a roaring fire heated the space, a faint draft came from the left side of the room, which would undoubtedly hide another hidden chamber. By the drafts Salvarias had felt throughout the estate, Lord Bellerum had made each commonly used room escapable.

Lord Bellerum sat behind a massive desk, papers strewn across it. He looked up when they entered, and an instant smile spread across his face as he sprang up from his chair. "Salvarias! By all the gods, I've missed you."

Salvarias bowed. "Lord Bellerum."

"For the love of Zerana, call me Edium, Son."

The word cut like a knife across his stomach, more so now than ever before. Turning to Lady Talura, he bowed. She was sitting in a chair by the fire and looked to have been sewing, but she stuffed a wad of fabric behind her chair before he could tell for certain. "My Lady."

"We've missed you," she said.

Salvarias shifted to face Lunara. Varila slumped down on the couch next to her sister and both grinned at him. Lunara's eyes were lit with pure joy, and he could tell it took all her willpower to stay in her seat. He was not pleased by her success. She looked thin to him, eyes slightly sunken, cheekbones more pronounced. He bowed. "My lady."

Her smile beamed brighter than the sun. He bathed in its warmth for a short moment before facing Lord Bellerum. "I would like a word, if you both have time."

Lady Talura motioned to a chair. "Of course, dear."

Salvarias bowed before he took his seat. Wilhelm remained by the door, scowling at everything.

Salvarias inhaled a nice long breath to steady his voice for what he was about to confess. "I have met God."

Lord Bellerum's eyebrows shot up. "When?"

"In the estate."

Lord Bellerum slammed a fist on the desk and sank into his chair. "Dammit! I knew I should have searched it."

Salvarias turned to address Lady Talura. "My lady, may I see your right hand?"

She hesitated a breath before she raised it, palm up. In the center was a white mark, as perfect and round as the moon.

Lord Bellerum shifted in his seat, his gaze darting between his wife and daughter. "It's just a birthmark, passed down from mother to daughter."

Salvarias glanced at the squirming man. "You are not that naive, my lord."

Lord Bellerum truly looked pained, and his voice was a rasp of dread. "What is it?"

"A mark from the goddess Zerana," Salvarias said.

Lord Bellerum paused in his distress. "Zerana?"

"I spent much time reading and searching for the cause, and I discovered it in Windlous. A very old book. I learned the goddess marked her clerics. She linked them directly to her." Salvarias turned back to Lady Talura. "You and Lady Lunara are the last of Zerana's clerics and have a direct link to the goddess. I have touched my mark to Lady Lunara's before. It is what caused the streak in her hair. When I did so, I could hear someone calling to me, but I did not touch our hands long enough to learn. I think with my power and yours, we can uncover some truths. However, I must warn you it could be our death. I do not understand what happened to Lady Lunara. I—"

"I'll do it," Lady Talura said. "If it can get us answers, let's try it."

"Absolutely not!" Lord Bellerum said, jumping up from his chair.

"If it is Zerana, I have no fear of her," Lady Talura said. "It's either me or Lunara, dear."

Lord Bellerum's gaze darted to his daughter. "It's neither!"

"My lord, if—"

"Edium."

Salvarias continued, "If we uncover Zerana's location, we might be able to rescue—"

"Now hold on!" Lord Bellerum said. "You're talking like she's alive."

"I am. I—"

"It's her," Lunara said. "In my dreams."

"My lady?" Salvarias asked.

"I have dreams where I walk through a desolate land. I come to a pit, and there's someone at the bottom who asks for my help. The voice was never identifiable in the beginning, but after you touched my hand, it was clearly a woman who spoke to me. She was the one who told me I could destroy the orb when Serinity was attacked."

"I've had the same dream," Lady Talura said.

"The decision is yours," Salvarias murmured, meeting Lady Talura's gaze. "I have told you the risks." Though he doubted them highly. It was the only reason he considered this path. He believed Zerana would not allow her cleric to come to harm by means of her own grace. The goddess would die first.

"But ..." Lord Bellerum looked on the verge of tears. "We can't try this without knowing ... without understanding!"

"We have no choice, dear," Lady Talura said. "This is our chance to get the upper hand once again."

Salvarias turned a quizzical eye to Varila.

"It's the army," Varila provided. "It took over Windlous before word even reached us or Humar. The entire continent is his."

"Don't burden the boy," Lord Bellerum said. "There's time to discuss it later."

"We must do all we can, dear," Lady Talura said to her husband.

Lord Bellerum plopped down in his chair. "Gods ..." He closed his eyes and ran a hand over his face. "Gods help me."

"I'll take that as a yes," Lady Talura said. She sat straight. "What do I need to do, Son?"

Salvarias knelt down in front of her. "For now, nothing. Just open yourself to me."

Lady Talura nodded and smiled. "Whenever you're ready, sweetness."

Salvarias glanced at Lunara. "You understand her powers will harm me, but I will stop before they kill me. Do not interrupt."

Lunara nodded gravely.

After a deep breath, Salvarias touched his mark to Lady Talura's. As he suspected, he was initially debilitated by the images bombarding his mind. They were pleasant ones of the Bellerum family, full of love and warmth, and he was amazed to see so many of Wilhelm and himself. More startling was the amount of times she had stayed by his side when he slept. He swore he could actually feel love from the image.

Gritting his teeth, he shoved it aside and ignited his magic. It called forth a small portion of the blackfire, and Salvarias used it to search for Lady Talura's power. He found it relatively quickly and followed the ribbon of it into the depths of her soul.

His path dumped him in an arid landscape where the ground was nothing but dried cracked mud with wisps of brown grasses clinging to a miserable existence. He walked forward, shielding his eyes with his hand as he gazed up at the sun-drenched sky. There were no clouds, and the air was oppressively hot.

He did not walk far before he found the pit. Calming his nerves, he sat beside it and looked down into the chilling darkness. There was something unnatural about the shadows, something that made his skin crawl.

A woman appeared in the single ray of sunlight. Her hair was whiter than snow, and her ice-blue eyes were hauntingly familiar. When she gazed up at him, instant tears welled.

"Hello," she breathed. "I have waited a long time for you." She recoiled to the side and stared frightfully at the shadows. "We do not have much time. You have to find me."

"You are Zerana?"

"Yes."

"Where are you? How can I free you?" He reached down and glided a hand over the top of the darkness. It responded initially with affection, but quickly switched to confusion, and finally to malice and hate, so much hate and ugliness. He yanked his hand back. It was a trap for anyone besides Veedran. Or possibly a child of light. Only two powers were allowed in. "Is it Veedran?" Salvarias's voice was hoarse, reluctant in asking. He had held on to a wild hope he had been wrong. That the dark god had not spawned him.

"Yes. He begs for my love, but I cannot give it to him. I cannot lie, even to free myself." She looked once again to the shadows. "We have no more time. I do not know where I am. Ne—"

Some slithering shadow shot from the darkness and knocked the goddess from the light. She screamed.

What felt like a troll's club rammed into Salvarias's head. How he was conscious, he did not know. Nothing was before him but brilliant white light. It was peaceful, but only for a breath. As if it were a thousand wretics, it burst alive and ravaged his body, tearing through skin and tendons, ripping him apart from the inside out. He screamed, but nothing came from his throat.

Then it stopped. He was gasping and indeed screaming, but familiar arms were hauling him somewhere. He collapsed, and those same arms let him fall to the ground. He reached blindly, choking out the word "brother," but no one came to help him.

"Salvarias! Son!" It was Lady Talura's frantic voice.

Hot wetness covered him, and he knew any wound healed by Veedran or Sansis had reopened. He blinked several times, and finally the study blurred into focused. Everyone was knelt around him save the one person he longed for. Wilhelm had moved to the door once more, bloodied arms folded over his chest, eyes glaring at Salvarias.

"He is my father," Salvarias whispered hoarsely. Tears welled unbidden. "Veedran is my father."

Wilhelm's gaze never softened, and he never crossed the room to hide Salvarias in safety. And that was all Salvarias sought. He turned to see Lunara smile, her eyes red with tears.

"Veedran?" Lord Bellerum breathed. "It can't be."

"It doesn't matter," Lunara said, her gaze never leaving Salvarias's. "It doesn't matter who it is, we'll fight him and defeat him."

"He is my father," Salvarias wept. "Veedran!"

"It doesn't matter," Lunara whispered.

And he knew her words carried two meanings. She still loved him. She still loved the son of the dark god. Salvarias buried his face in his hands. He had lost three years of his life. When finally he was alive once again, his brother was not there. He was alone, without the touch of the woman he loved, without the safety and love of his brother. His magic had turned him into a god. His blackfire harbored some kinship to Veedran's power, which led him to one terrifying conclusion, one he had not disclosed to anyone. So utterly petrified of it, he refused to even voice the thought to himself.

He was so terribly alone and afraid. He curled up on the beautiful brown rug he was staining with his blood and allowed the waiting darkness to haul him into new nightmares.

8

Lunara sat in one of the oversized chairs in the library. It was the middle of the night, but she couldn't sleep. The room was dark and cold, and she pulled her shawl closer about her shoulders. Her nightdress wasn't nearly warm enough, but something about the frigid air made her insides feel less cold. The fact she still couldn't sense Salvarias had stolen all the warmth from the world.

The door creaked, and she looked over to see a tall figure enter the room. She didn't need to be connected to know it was Salvarias. He did not pause; he did not ask to join her. He had sought her out.

He closed the door, limped across the room, and sank to his knees in front of her. His head was bowed, face hidden in shadow, but she saw his shoulders shake.

Raising a trembling hand, she pushed down the hood of his robes. Moonlight glistened on the tears streaking his face. He met her gaze, and her heart broke. He'd been beaten. It was clear in his eyes. He was a man who'd learned horrible things and had no comfort. A man lost, even to himself, devoid of hope and fight.

"Help me," he whispered. "Make me disappear."

She was petrified to touch him, petrified to know their connection had been severed permanently. What if she couldn't help him?

"Hide me," he pleaded. "Take me from this place. I beg you."

Tentatively she reached out a hand and brushed aside his hair. The spark flared and blazed into a roaring fire as their connection burst to life. A soft sob left Salvarias, and he slowly lowered his head to her lap. Not fighting her own tears, she ran her fingers through his hair. She fought away his pain and suffering with light and warmth. She bludgeoned his defeat and helplessness with hope. She overpowered his loneliness with her love.

His sobs deepened as he clung her.

SALVARIAS WOKE to fingers tugging through his hair. He was stretched out on a couch, his head resting in her lap. Reluctantly he left the peaceful meadow he had been wandering in and forced his eyes open.

Her smile greeted him. What would it be like to wake to that every morning? Sunrises would seem so dull.

"Morning," she whispered.

The estate was quiet. The sky outside the windows was black, but the few stars betrayed the early morning hour.

"Morning," he said, inhaling a deep breath. Finally he had slept and felt as if his mind were functioning once again. His misery was a distant memory. If he did not focus, he could even forget his mother's beatings, his brother's withdrawal, and the knowledge he was the son of Veedran.

"How did you escape your brother?" she asked.

Salvarias ran a hand over his eyes. "A sleeping spell. He needed it as much as I."

A soft finger traced his brow and eased a furrow he had not realized had formed. "So serious," she murmured.

Salvarias caught her hand and rested it on his chest, covering it with his own. "Thank you."

"I'm happy I could help. I was so worried we had ..."

Was he caressing her fingers? He snatched his hand away. "Forgive me. How is your mother?"

"Fine." Lunara held out her white lock of hair. "She has one matching my own, but nothing else. Speaking of, Mother and Father will be looking for me soon."

"It was improper of me to detain you from your room. We are not traveling any more, and we should not be alone together. Forgive me." Reaching up, he ran a finger down her cheek. "Have you been ill?"

"In a way, yes. I'm feeling better, though."

"I am pleased to hear."

Inhaling a calming breath as he sat up, he braced himself and released her hand. He suspicioned it would happen, and apparently not wanting to disappoint, his mind burst to reality. A groan escaped. Warm blood trickled from his nose, and he quickly caught it with his hand while fumbling for his cloth. He found it and tilted his head back, grimacing at the crusty fabric he had forgotten to clean. It took time to adjust to the rush: the images of death, his mind suddenly processing multiple thoughts at once. He took to counting the stones of the ceiling until it evened out.

"Worse?" she asked.

Salvarias nodded and slumped on the couch. "Much." He cleaned the blood from his upper lip and accepted a cup of water from Lunara.

The door flew open, and Lord Bellerum and Lady Talura rushed in, Varila right behind, sword in her hand.

"Damn you two!" Varila spat. "You scared us half to death."

"Death was far from you," Salvarias said.

Varila rolled her eyes. "Just because you've been a visitor doesn't mean you know everything about it."

Salvarias's pounding head flogged down any smile he might have come up with. "Of course, sis."

"Tea, dear?" Lady Talura asked. Without waiting for a reply, she left the room.

"So dark ..." Lord Bellerum said, glancing between Salvarias and

Lunara.

Salvarias's cheeks burn with embarrassment. "My apologies, my lord." He ignited his magic and lit a few candles.

Lord Bellerum raised an eyebrow. "Nice spell."

There were dark shadows in the far corners, and Salvarias resisted the urge to light the walls on fire; what he had sensed in Zerana's pit continued to haunt him.

"So," Lord Bellerum said, forcing a too casual note in his voice. "Veedran you say? You're certain?"

"Yes."

"I would have thought Veedran could overpower us at any moment he chose."

"He is weak. Something is missing from him." Salvarias shook his head and regretted it when his brain thumped his skull. "I sensed something was wrong, but I do not understand. I am still working to figure it all out. I—"

Wilhelm burst into the room, eyes aflame. "Damn you!" he snarled. "Don't you dare leave me again!"

Salvarias flinched from the fury in his brother's voice and nodded mutely.

"He's safe here," Lord Bellerum said.

"Go to Oblivion!" Wilhelm barked. His brother took several deep breaths and leaned against the wall by the door. His gaze calmed and flicked from window to window.

Lady Talura returned with a steaming kettle. "One of the servants is fetching your herb pouch, dear."

"Thank you—"

Mafarias strode into the room. "What in Nevlar's fury is going on? Who's here?"

"What are you talking about?" Lord Bellerum asked.

"A ..." Mafarias glanced around, and his eyes narrowed at Salvarias. "Another mage. I ..."

Salvarias regarded the man for a moment before he spoke. "Did you mean another god, Grandfather?"

"Whoa! Grandfather?" Lord Bellerum said, bolting up from his seat.

Mafarias straightened himself. "I don't know what you're talking about, boy."

"Which part?"

"What's going on?" Lord Bellerum demanded.

"Nothing," Mafarias said. "The boy's not in his right mind."

Salvarias ignited his magic and stripped it of the illusion diminishing his power. Gasps filled the room, and he glanced at Lunara's wide eyes and her skin covered in gooseflesh.

"What ..." Mafarias staggered back a step. "What have you done, boy?"

"I have shown you mine, now show me yours."

"You're a fool! What have you done?"

"What was necessary!" Salvarias shouted, his anger surging forward stronger than he could control. "Who are you? When—" Then it hit him. "You! You were the one who brought magic to Arden!"

Mafarias's eyes widened. "Hush, boy. You don't—"

"I know plenty, Grandfather," Salvarias growled. "You lied to me! To my brother!"

Mafarias glanced around the room, looking like a trapped cat: unpredictable, capable of violence. Salvarias kept his magic ready.

"Yes," Mafarias said reluctantly. "I came here during the Long Wars. I didn't care about the higher gods and their petty fighting. I ... I ..."

"Had a penchant of bedding women," Salvarias provided.

"You could say that. I didn't know Nevlar and Zerana had made their creations so weak they couldn't handle a little power. By the time I saw what it did it was too late. My magic infected any woman I bedded, and it passed down randomly to any children they bore."

"Ashra was your daughter?" Lord Bellerum said.

"The first one I had since the Long Wars," Mafarias said. Sadness weighed on his voice. "When mages became feared, I never passed along my magic to another until Jepine. She was remarkable. I loved her. I really did. She knew my habits so she told Ashra I was an uncle." He waved a hand as if what he was about to say was unimportant. "Magic appears randomly. I've helped as much as I dared, giving simple spells to mages."

"Wait, doesn't that make Ashra a ..." Lady Talura pressed a hand over her heart.

"A demigod? Yes," Mafarias said. "I fear her mind was fragile with the amount of power she had. It explains why Wilhelm was such a sharp boy."

Mafarias sank into a chair in a dark corner. Shadows enveloped him except for a stream of light falling on his slate-blue robes pooling on the floor. Fear blossomed.

"What is it, boy?" Lord Bellerum said.

Salvarias's gaze darted from Mafarias to Wilhelm. He could not tell his brother and beg for help. If he did, he would have to confess what their mother had done. Yet, Salvarias could not stand to be in the room. He was petrified.

His mother stepped from the shadows, a dagger in her hand. Salvarias stumbled backward, tripped on something, and scrabbled over it. He fell to the ground and crawled to the nearest corner. He looked over his shoulder as he fled. She followed him, dagger clenched in her fist.

He was weeping by the time he found the corner. He felt the breeze of her approach.

"Hold still," she hissed.

Salvarias shut his eyes tight when the blade slid into his scalp. "Please stop, Mother!" he cried. "It hurts! It hurts!"

WILHELM FELT like he got kicked in the gut. Air rushed from his lungs, and bright lights flashed across his vision.

Talura snatched up a blanket and rushed to Salvarias huddled in a corner. After covering him, she hummed a soft song, her widened eyes coming to rest on Wilhelm. She'd known. Varila's eyes were guarded as well when their gazes met. She'd known. Lunara had pressed a hand over her mouth, eyes full of shock. Edium looked equally stunned, but what shook Wilhelm was Mafarias's fearful gaze. He'd known all along.

"I'm here, Son," Talura whispered. "You're safe."

Salvarias looked up at her, hand clamped to the back of his head, tears streaking his face, eyes clouded with a desperation Wilhelm didn't understand.

"What happened?" Talura whispered to Salvarias.

"He watched," Salvarias sobbed. "He watched her do it."

Whatever might've been left of Wilhelm's world crumbled to ruin. "That's it!" he roared. "We're leaving!"

Salvarias flinched and turned his confused gaze to Wilhelm, then Talura.

"I'm so sorry, dear," Talura said. "You said it was her."

Salvarias's eyes widened.

"All this time!" Wilhelm shouted. "All this damn time, you've lied to me!"

"Please, forgive me." Salvarias got shakily to his feet and walked toward Wilhelm. "Forgive me, Brother. I never wanted you to know. I-I had to lie. She—"

Wilhelm backhanded Salvarias. He staggered, catching himself with a chair.

Wilhelm switched his voice, imbuing it with the slight influx that made it a command. "Pack now!"

Salvarias's shocked expression mingled with subservient obedience. He walked toward the door, pausing once to run the back of his hand across his mouth. It came away with a streak of blood.

"You bastard!" Varila shouted. "What in Oblivion is wrong with you?"

Wilhelm ignored her and marched after his brother. He knew a line of people followed. He heard shouting, but didn't bother to listen to exact words. The only command reaching through his fog was Edium ordering the guards to imprison Mafarias, and if the mage escaped Edium would take his anger out on the man who let it happen. It should have comforted Wilhelm—to know another cared for his brother—yet all that consumed him was rage. His life was full of lies, but worse, they came from his brother, the one Wilhelm should have been able to trust above all others.

His life was lies and failures.

Once in the room, Wilhelm looked around. He didn't have anything he needed but fresh clothes. He threw them at Salvarias. "Put those in there."

Salvarias obeyed.

"Son," Edium said. "You can't take the boy from here. You can't protect him. I can. I have an army. You—"

"You want me to stay here?" Wilhelm asked exasperated. "Here where there's people that can hurt him? You think I trust you?" He looked at Talura. "Or you? No, you can all go to Oblivion! No one else will hurt him." His mind raced with his next actions. "I'll take him away, keep him secret."

"He's not an object!" Edium roared. "He's a man, your brother!"

"He's not my brother!" Wilhelm exploded. "The brother I thought I had wouldn't have lied to me! That man is a Guardian. I'm a Protector. I have a purpose. I have to fulfill it. That's all that matters!"

He turned to see Salvarias staring at him, eyes pouring tears, a full pack falling from his hand.

"Are you done?" Wilhelm growled.

Salvarias mutely nodded.

"Pick it up. Let's go."

Wilhelm shoved through the crowd of guards outside their room.

"I could stop you," Edium said.

"And you'll have twenty dead guards in your hallway."

"Don't go," Varila said to Salvarias. "Tell him no. Stay."

"He can't," Lunara said, her voice thick. "Wilhelm has broken his promise."

Sharp pain stabbed Wilhelm's chest. He had to leave, to get out of here and complete his purpose. He grabbed Salvarias's arm and yanked him through the estate and toward the stables. He'd keep his Guardian secret, tucked away in the wilderness where no one would ever find them.

9

SPRING 1022 A.R

Salvarias followed Wilhelm through the thick forest. Spring flowers covered the mountainside, gifting him another counting source besides the trees, pinecones, and rocks he came across.

They had nearly run Mithal and Lilly to the ground for the past week, and now they walked. The peaceful setting was in blatant contrast to the horror Salvarias experienced. He was a prisoner to Wilhelm's beckon and call. The commanding tone held a power over him, the need to not upset his brother, to do as Wilhelm ordered. Salvarias tried several times to disagree, but on the second command, his will crumbled.

For the past two days, his sole company was the horses and his magic. His reunion with Mithal had been the only pleasant aspect of his trip.

He had used the time to work with his magic on a possible spell to help his brother come from whatever shock held him captive. The one they had so far would be devastating for his brother, and Salvarias was not yet desperate enough to try it.

However, with every step his anger grew. He missed the Bellerum home, the feasts, and library, but to a greater extent, he missed Lunara. Over the past few days, he had thought about her eyes when she had said it did not matter that he was Veedran's son. Through everything, she loved him. Yet, could he love her? Could he allow another person besides Wilhelm inside his heart? And if he did, would she eventually deny him as his mother and Tobin had done? He could not bear the pain if she were to do so. Yet he could not bear the pain of not loving her, of pushing her away when all he wanted was to hold her and to tell her what dwelled in his heart.

The dense trees parted way to a small clearing wreathed by redwoods. "We should rest the horses," Salvarias said.

Wilhelm nodded, went to Lilly's pack, gathered some food, and ate.

Salvarias got a hunk of bread and ate slowly, noticing the food tasted of nothing.

"I want to go back," he said for the seventh time.

"I don't care."

"Your son needs you, Varila needs you."

"They're better off without me, just as I was without my father. They'd have died if we'd stayed together."

"No, this is not the same. I—"

"Shut up."

Salvarias snapped his mouth closed. Anger began to boil.

"Let's go." Wilhelm shoved the rest of the ham in his mouth.

"They need more rest."

"We go."

Lilly was on the verge of falling over. Carrying Wilhelm's weight up the side of a mountain pushed her limits.

"She cannot go on, Brother."

"She will."

Salvarias put himself in front of Lilly and blocked his brother's way. "She cannot. You will kill her."

"I'll buy another one. Mount up."

"No. She is my friend."

"I said, mount!" Wilhelm commanded.

"No."

"Now!"

Salvarias's resolve wavered. He was about to take a step away when Lilly pleaded him again. Jaw clenched, he said, "No."

Wilhelm grabbed Salvarias's arms, fingers digging in his flesh. He winced.

"Do as I say!" Wilhelm roared.

"No."

Wilhelm backhanded Salvarias. The force sent him to the ground and blood ran from his split lip.

"Do as I say!" Wilhelm snapped.

"No!" Salvarias yelled back. "I want to go home!"

"We have no home!"

"We do, and you know it!"

Wilhelm pounced on him. The first blow to the side of his head darkened Salvarias's vision. His head pounded with the next strike, and his breath whooshed out when a fist landed in his gut.

"Stop!"

Salvarias caught a blurred glimpse of Lord Bellerum as the man leapt on Wilhelm's back. Varila pulled on Wilhelm as well as the rest of the family. It gave Salvarias a chance to choke in a breath of air.

Wilhelm shoved Varila and Lady Talura down, grappled Lord Bellerum off his back, and tossed the man across the clearing. Lord Bellerum smacked into a tree and crumpled to the ground.

"Wilhelm!" Lunara cried.

Wilhelm backhanded her. She fell to the ground, holding her cheek. Salvarias saw nothing after but a massive fist. Wilhelm's incoherent roars droned in and out with the Bellerum's shouts.

Wilhelm paused to knock someone else out of the way. Salvarias tried to rise, disoriented by his head swimming in a pool of honey. A foot kicked his ribs, and he cried out when a bone snapped.

"You bastard!" Wilhelm roared. "All my life has been a lie! You'll do as I say now! Get up!"

No amount of command in Wilhelm's voice could have made Salvarias's body move. He grunted when what felt like a tree rammed into his head.

He rolled to his side and coughed up bile and blood. "Forgive me,

Brother," he rasped, and managed to cast his spell before the encroaching blackness claimed victory.

~

WILHELM JOLTED back as if struck with a battering ram. Whatever the force, it knocked him to the ground, and his mind drowned in Salvarias's spell.

He lived through three years of Varila's pain, of her loneliness. For three years he listened to his son begging to meet his father and felt his son's pang of abandonment. For three years he experienced the grief of two parents weeping for their son who'd disappeared right after their other son had died.

As if that wasn't enough, Salvarias's suffering bludgeoned his heart. For weeks his baby brother had relived beating upon beating from their mother, had learned he was the son of Veedran, and had gone through it alone. His brother's desperation for Wilhelm's comfort, to be safe and loved, tore out Wilhelm's heart.

Wilhelm's mind snapped under the assailment of his family's emotions, and all those walls shielding him from pain caved in around him. His own suffering bled back to him; pain as fresh as it was three years ago. Hugging himself, he cried out, sure his heart would break under the barrage.

He blinked aside the haze of pain and saw Salvarias curled up on the ground. Blood covered his face. One eye was swollen shut, his lip cut in three different places, his cheeks bruised and bloody.

"What have I done?" Wilhelm choked. He scrabbled over to his brother and scooped him up. "Salv! I'm so sorry!" He shook his brother. "Forgive me! Salv!"

Hands hauled him away, and Lunara and Talura knelt by Salvarias. Using water and a cloth to clean the blood, they tended to his injuries.

Wilhelm doubled over on his knees, resting his forehead on the damp grasses. "I ... I can't do this. I can't! I'm not strong enough." He hugged himself. "I can't." His failures surged forward: the times

Salvarias had been hurt, the silent tears his brother shed at night when he was a small boy, his screams from the nightmares, the bruises, her glares toward her own son. How had he not seen it before? How could he be so blind? How could he bear the weight of everything he'd done wrong?

Arms wrapped around him, and he smelled strawberries. The pain he'd caused her rushed forward, beating him with shame. He tried to pull back. He didn't deserve her comfort. He didn't deserve *her*.

"No," she whispered in his ear. "You're not alone, Wilhelm. I ... love you, and I'll never leave you. No matter how hard you try to push me away."

An agonizing cry left his lips. "I can't do it anymore! I can't take it!"

"Yes, you can. And you will. *We* will."

WILHELM SAT by his brother's side, staring at his bruised face. They were halfway down the mountain; another three days or so and they'd be home. Home. Wilhelm hugged himself, curling around his pain. He had stayed clear of the Bellerums, only replying with short comments when they tried to talk to him, but he made sure his voice was kind. They didn't deserve his anger. Especially after learning they had followed them. Edium knew he couldn't change Wilhelm's mind, but the man said he wanted to be there for the brothers when they would need him. Such dedication to two men who were not even his own children.

Gently he pulled the blanket tighter about his brother. Salvarias rarely woke, and when he did it was barely long enough to drink a small bowl of broth. Wilhelm had yet to have an opportunity to beg for his brother's forgiveness.

Lunara knelt on the other side of Salvarias and applied a fresh salve to his bruises. The one on her cheek had already faded. Luckily, he'd had some semblance of control not to hit her hard enough to break anything. Even so, he wondered if Salvarias would forgive him for striking her.

"He'll be fine," she told him for the hundredth time. "The rib is healing remarkably fast."

"I'm sorry," Wilhelm whispered hoarsely.

She met his gaze, and the amount of empathy in her eyes gave him a comfort. They shared a love for Salvarias, and she was all too familiar with the hole it left when Salvarias had died. She placed a hand over his. "Of course I forgive you."

"Will he?"

She smiled. "Do you really have to ask?"

She squeezed his hand and left to rejoin her family by the fire. Not much time passed before Salvarias jerked awake, a soft cry leaving his throat as he grabbed the back of his head.

"It's all right," Wilhelm said soothingly. "I'm right here."

Salvarias's gaze darted over to him. Not a drop of fear toward Wilhelm was in his eyes. He did not cringe or act at all tentative. Instead, much to Wilhelm's surprise, his brother flew into Wilhelm's arms, fingers digging into his shoulders, his brother's hold painfully tight.

Confused, grateful, guilty, and utterly relieved, Wilhelm gathered his brother gently to him. The Bellerums were kind enough to leave the campsite and wander the forest. The instant they were out of sight, Salvarias's sobs burst free.

"Veedran is my father," his brother wept. "Veedran!" His breath came in halting chokes, too little of it, and he curled up tight, either ignoring or oblivious to his pain, and held on to Wilhelm's arm as he shrank in upon himself.

Of all Wilhelm thought his brother would do when he woke, this had not once crossed his mind. Gently rocking Salvarias, Wilhelm said, "I know, Salv. I know. It's going to be all right. I promise. I'm here, and I won't let anything happen to you. But you have to breathe, Salv. Just like me."

Salvarias pressed an ear to Wilhelm's chest. It didn't take long before his brother calmed, breathing steady, and his tremble reducing. "Forgive me," Salvarias said. "The spell was cruel, but I did not know what else to do. Please forgive me."

Wilhelm's own tears streamed hot down his face. "You didn't do anything wrong, Salv. It was my fault. It's all my fault." He passed over the puzzle box.

Salvarias's tension drained out of him the instant his fingers began to manipulate the pieces, and he sagged in Wilhelm's arms. "You have done nothing wrong either. I lied to you. She lied to you. You must not hold guilt, my dear brother. I beg of you. You must not."

As always, it seemed Wilhelm could do no wrong in Salvarias's eyes. It should have shamed Wilhelm, but instead he drank from that bottomless well of love until he felt strong enough to face the world.

10

SPRING 1022 A.R

Wilhelm dabbed his clammy hands on his trews, cursing the spring sun despite it being a cool day. Lazy clouds sauntered across the sky, sweeping in with the gentle breeze. In the forest outside the bustling city of Serinity, the soft calls of birds and the wind whispering through the pines seemed unusually loud.

"You shouldn't be nervous," Varila said. "He's going to love you."

Wilhelm chose not to respond and still couldn't bring himself to look at his wife. They'd only been back for a day now. Salvarias had rarely woken. It seemed as if his brother hadn't slept in years and was on a mission to make up lost sleep.

Though the effects of Salvarias's spell were fading daily, guilt would never leave him, nor could he return to his shell and hide. For now, he could summon the strength to rise out of bed in the morning and look upon those he'd hurt, except Varila. He'd yet to speak to her except a few short replies here and there, yet to smell her, touch her, or taste her. Shame kept his gaze from hers and his head lowered whenever she was near.

The portal shimmered brighter, and Zehnia stepped through carrying a boy on her hip. The child had Wilhelm's eyes and looked almost exactly as he had at that age save an inch or two in height and a few pounds. His dirty-blond hair was wavy like Varila's, but he had the same crooked grin as Wilhelm. It spread instantly when his son looked at him.

Squirming in Zehnia's arms and holding out his hands to Wilhelm, Tedris exclaimed, "Papa!"

The word brought tears to Wilhelm's eyes. Blinking them back, he took his son in his arms, holding him tightly. His son clutched his neck, squeezing. Wilhelm wasn't sure he'd ever be able to let go.

"Are you better?" Tedris asked. "Are you going to stay with us?"

Wilhelm couldn't loosen his throat to speak, so he merely nodded.

Tedris clapped his hands. "Mama told me about your swords, Papa. May I see them?"

Wilhelm squeezed his son before lowering him to the ground and drawing his great sword. Tedris's eyes grew big and bright as he ran a finger along the hilt.

"Will you teach me to use it?"

"Someday, Son" Wilhelm said.

Tedris grinned at him. "Mama said you're almost as good as her."

Wilhelm laughed. "Almost."

"Thank you," Varila was saying to Zehnia. "I'm surprised Humar didn't come."

"He wanted to, but our scouts just returned from Windlous. The news wasn't good."

Varila nodded. "I'm sure once things settle down here, we'll be in touch. Take care of yourself."

Zehnia hugged her, tilted her head in farewell, and went back through the portal. Cessia emerged a breath later, two children running behind her. Their skin was an alluring shade of blue-green, a pastel form of turquoise. The little girl's mess of copper curls framed her bright green eyes brimming with entirely too much boldness. The boy's hair was as strawberry blond as his father's, and his blue eyes glittered with mischief. They both grinned at him and then sprinted to Varila, showering her in hugs and kisses.

"Okulu is at the estate," Varila said past a chuckle. "He said he's proofing the rooms for Bri and Arias's arrival."

Cessia laughed. "As he should. I'm sure Talura has started hiding the breakables. Come on, kids, let's go find your father." Snatching up a hand from each child, she led the way to Serinity.

Varila knelt down in front of Tedris and brushed back his hair. "We need to talk to you about Uncle Salvarias."

"Is he missing again?"

"No," Wilhelm said. "But your uncle is special. He's not like everyone else."

"He's alive," Varila blurted. "A powerful creature brought him back from the dead."

Tedris grinned. "An uncle and a father in one day!" He leapt in Wilhelm's arms. "Can I meet him?"

Wilhelm shifted his son to his shoulders and rose to his feet. "As soon as he wakes up."

Tedris wrapped his arms around Wilhelm's neck and rested his chin on Wilhelm's head. "Is there anything you want to know about me, Papa?"

"Everything."

Tedris inhaled deeply, and the stories began to pour out of him.

WILHELM BROODED ALONE in his room, gazing at the steady flame of a single candle. He'd put Tedris to bed hours ago, yet couldn't bring himself to join Varila. She'd asked him to, and her eyes had shot daggers at him when he'd refused. He couldn't. He didn't deserve her, but he had taken advantage of Salvarias sleeping for the past two days and had gotten to know his son. A son he could not have been prouder of, one who saw no flaws in him, and who beamed at him from the stories his mother had told. A son he didn't deserve.

Running a hand across his face, he leaned back and stared at the dark ceiling. Though exhausted, sleep was nightmares—reenactments of what he imagined his mother had done to Salv. He was tired of such visual pain. It was easier to think on it, to allow light to fall on all he'd been blind to in his youth. He hated his mother, despised her. If she stood before him now, he'd run her through with a sword. Tobin too. The man should have seen it.

Despite knowing so, Wilhelm blamed himself above all others. A lifetime of torment, and yet Salvarias emerged from it with a kind and forgiving heart. Wilhelm would have never been as strong. He would've hated anything, anyone. But for the first time, Wilhelm truly understood his brother. It did little to ease his pain. Wilhelm's mistakes were always a monster in the room, chasing and taunting him.

Just thinking of Salvarias made Wilhelm edgy. His imagination concocted all sorts of images of Veedran, robed in blood-red, sneaking into Salvarias's room and snatching him away. Or perhaps Mafarias had escaped the prison Edium had shackled him in. The more Wilhelm dwelled on the possibilities, the more he couldn't stay in his own room.

For the third night in a row, Wilhelm went to the next room, passing the twenty guards posted. He eased opened his brother's door, wincing at a creak it made. After Wilhelm shut the door, he fumbled around blindly in the dark, eventually making it to a chair.

He wasn't sure how much time passed before Salvarias sucked in a sharp breath. The sheets rustled frantically, and his brother choked out the word, *"Lumous."* A white sparrow blossomed to life, floating above Salvarias's bed. His brother's eyes were wild as he surveyed the room. When his gaze fell on Wilhelm, tension seemed to drain from Salvarias. It was the first night Salvarias had woken. All the other times, Wilhelm had stayed unnoticed, slipping out before his brother woke.

"Are you not well?" Salvarias asked, sitting up.

"I'm fine," Wilhelm answered. "Go back to sleep." His brother looked remarkably better. The swelling of his entire face had gone, leaving a few angry bruises and a small cut on his lip. Salvarias raised the hood of his robes. Wilhelm knew his brother did so to spare him pain.

"I feel quite rested," Salvarias said. He crossed the room and sat in the chair beside Wilhelm. "I must apologize to the Bellerum family. I fear I have been rude, shutting myself in here for days."

"You needed the rest," Wilhelm said. He got up, started a fire, gathered a few blankets, and draped them over his shivering brother. His anger burned at the servants for allowing the fire to go out. Spring was fresh upon Dalnar, and the nights were cold. Growling at the room, he picked up Salvarias—chair and all—and moved him in front of the fire. After moving his own chair next to his brother, he sat down again, staring into the flames growing with life.

"Thank you," Salvarias murmured, huddling in the blankets.

Moments of silence passed before Wilhelm said, "What do we do now?"

Salvarias gave a short, sardonic laugh. "Do not ask me, my dear brother. My decisions have gotten us nowhere. Matter of fact, I have done well to put us in danger time and time again. No, my decision days are at an end. I would only suggest we talk with Mafarias and learn what he knows."

"He betrayed us. He deserves to die."

"Perhaps."

The response startled Wilhelm. He brother was usually so forgiving. "You mean it?"

Salvarias shrugged. "He nearly got you killed, captured, and taken to Zeeas where they would have tortured you. Yes, I feel he deserves whatever you and Lord Bellerum decide."

Wilhelm grunted. "Always about everyone else besides yourself."

His brother shifted in his seat.

"You're not angry at him?" Wilhelm pressed.

Salvarias whispered something, and the candles in the room flared to life. There wasn't a dark corner left. "Perhaps. But ... my fear is stronger than my anger. It is foolish. He cannot hurt me anymore, yet ..." Salvarias shuddered and then waved a hand as if dismissing his feelings. "He is a god. We could use him."

Wilhelm sat in thought for a long time. Salvarias had made the decisions since his rescue from Zeeas. Certainly he paid mind to

Wilhelm's suggestions, but everyone knew who ultimately made the choices. Now Salvarias had placed the responsibility in Wilhelm's lap. For the first time, he could keep his brother safe. But if he chose to cower and run, Salvarias would rebel. His brother was trusting him to do not only what was right for the brothers, but what was right for Arden. Now he understood the weight that had hung on Salvarias's shoulders all these years.

Inhaling a deep breath, Wilhelm said, "We take our place in the Knighthood. We use them to defeat Veedran. We'll do what no one else has done before. We'll kill him and everything that follows him. We'll take back Arden. Screw any gods who stand in our way."

In the shadows of his hood, Salvarias's white teeth shone in a fierce smile. "Well said, Brother."

"But this ..." Wilhelm motioned to the two of them. "This has to change, Salv. The lies, hiding stuff, running away. It has to stop."

Salvarias's smiled faded. Returning his gaze to the fire, he sat silent for several moments before he said, "Ask me what you will. I will not lie."

A simple offer that stated Salvarias's agreement. An offer allowing Wilhelm to maintain his ignorance or hear the truth of what happened in their youth, to hear voice given to all his failures. He didn't want to know, but by some sick need he asked, "It was when Tobin took me to practice, wasn't it? It was never bullies."

"Yes."

Air fled from the room. He hadn't prepared himself for this. "Did Tobin know?"

"I do not believe he did. I would like to think he would have done something if he had."

Of course Tobin knew. Just as Wilhelm had known. Both had decided it was easier to ignore the signs and keep Ashra on her pedestal. "You're sure it was Mafarias in the room and not Vuddruk?"

"No ... Yes." Salvarias shrugged. "I find myself trusting Vuddruk more than our own grandfather. Sansis told me Mafarias was a traitor, but I cannot believe such a creature." Salvarias winced and recoiled from his left side, rubbing a hand on his arm.

"What is it?" Wilhelm asked alarmed.

"It is noth—" Salvarias clamped his mouth closed, inhaled a deep breath, and relaxed. "I see her. Sometimes she stands next to me; sometimes she hits me. It ... it feels so real."

"You just saw her?"

"Yes." Salvarias raised a shaking hand and pointed to a corner. "Sansis is there. Soon he will come to me, cut me, and it will feel as real as the day he did it." Salvarias's smile was closer to a sneer. "I am going insane, Brother. Slowly, certainly, but nevertheless, one day I will be a blubbering idiot. What is real and what is not is a growing mystery. I cannot remember where I am when I wake up. When Veedran resurrected me, he was trying to take over my mind. My magic helped, but at a great price."

When his brother didn't speak, Wilhelm shifted his chair closer, facing Salvarias, ignoring the heat of the fire burning into him. "I'm here, Salv. I'm real. You're safe."

"I am a God of Magic," Salvarias blurted, voice hoarse and barely whispered. "Just as is Mafarias and Vuddruk. I have tried to deny it, tried to convince myself it could not be true."

Wilhelm grinned, and it felt *good* to have something to smile about. Salvarias gave him a questioning look. "I always knew you were special," Wilhelm said. "I always said you were the most powerful mage alive. I was right. And now we have a God of Magic on our side to fight Veedran, train new mages, and to make things better for them."

"Mortals are not meant to control this kind of power," Salvarias said. "It will drive me mad."

Wilhelm shrugged it off. "You're the strongest man I've ever met, Salv. It'll try, it might play these tricks on you, but you'll beat it in the end."

Salvarias glanced at the corner, cringing ever so slightly.

"As for Sansis," Wilhelm said, drawing the puzzle box from his pocket. He grew it to its normal size and passed it to his brother. "He's dead."

Salvarias jerked and met Wilhelm's gaze with wide eyes. "Truly?"

Wilhelm's smile stretched across his face at the hope in his brother's eyes. This he could give his brother. He could eliminate one of Salvarias's nightmares. "Dead. I burned him, cut out his heart, and pulverized his bones. There's no coming back, Salv. He's gone. For good."

Salvarias's light laugh filled the room, a laugh overflowing with such relief it was painful to know how much horror his brother had lived in.

Contagious as always, Wilhelm found himself chuckling. Noticing a pot in the corner of the room, he shoved up from his chair and crossed the room to it. Intricate flowers dominated the dark leafy plant, petals bursting in layers of white. "Where did you get this?" Wilhelm asked.

Salvarias glanced at it and a slight smile spread, the clicking of the box never pausing. "I made it."

Wilhelm didn't hide the shock on his face when he turned to his brother. "You mean created it?"

Salvarias nodded. "I've given it healing properties. It has already aided in my breathing and eased the pain in my heart."

"But ... last time ... I mean—"

"I used a different power, Brother. The same I use for enchanting. I made it yesterday, and it continues to evolve: adding petals, increasing the potency of its healing properties. While I will never use the power I did in Xeroth, I feel this power could be quite useful. I plan to make companions for Lunara. An animal to guard and keep her company. I had hoped ..." Salvarias shifted in his seat. "That is, with your permission, I had hoped to give them to her as a wedding gift."

Shock froze Wilhelm.

"I have denied it for far too long," Salvarias continued. "Against all I'm sure her better judgement is telling her, she loves me. Even with the knowledge of who fathered me. Do you approve?"

Wilhelm swallowed hard a few times before he could get this voice back. "Of course, Salv. She's perfect for you."

Pure, unbridled joy filled Salvarias's eyes, and with it, Wilhelm's world brightened. He was sure the sun would shine brighter, the sky would be bluer, and the air would never be heavy again.

SALVARIAS STOOD in front of Lord and Lady Bellerum's door. He had tried to knock four times but had failed. The twenty guards constantly following him had stayed slightly back, giving him room to battle his fears.

Lord Bellerum would deny him Lunara's hand, surely. How could a father approve of his daughter marrying a man spawned by the dark god? How could anyone think something as evil as Salvarias was worth an ounce of love? Lady Bellerum would laugh at him. She would grab his hair and drag him to some dark room, beat him and cut his head open. Mothers, after all, saw into the soul. That was how Ashra had known. Taking a step back, he reached for the scar along the back of his head. What in Oblivion was he thinking?

"Oh, look at you, alive and awake."

Salvarias glanced at Okulu sauntering toward him. "And look at you, soberly drunk as always."

Okulu threw his head back in a laugh. "You'd be impressed. I've cut back on my drinking quite a bit."

Salvarias tilted his head to Okulu's left hand. "Married life has agreed with you?"

The merc raised his hand, looking at the wedding ring with false alarm. "Oh my. Did some woman wrangle me into marriage? Must have been pretty drunk for that to happen." Okulu leaned on the wall and observed the Bellerum's door. "Nasty thing, isn't it? All that wood. Decorative iron. I've heard Oblivion itself resides beyond it."

Salvarias rolled his eyes and reclined beside Okulu. "I fear you are right."

Okulu chuckled. "What has you standing out here?"

Salvarias shifted uncomfortably.

"Ah," Okulu said. "You looking to finally marry Lunara? Ask for her hand from her parents?"

"Am I a fool?" Salvarias looked at Okulu in all seriousness. "Would you let your own daughter marry a man like me?"

Okulu shrugged. "Wouldn't be my decision. I plan to raise a smart girl, one that can take care of herself and isn't afraid to take a risk. When Bri chooses a man, I will trust it is the right one. And if I'm any judge of people, I think Edium and Talura feel the same about Lunara." The mischievous twinkle in Okulu's eyes snuffed out, leaving them darker, and his voice lacked any slur. "You deserve her, certainly. But Lunara ... Well, Lunara deserves you more than anything. She's waited for you, even after death. She's rejected suitor upon suitor. Respectable men. Good men. She's in love with you, and she is one woman who deserves to finally be happy." He pointed at the door. "Don't go in there for yourself. Go in for her. Give her what you've denied her for years."

Salvarias inhaled a deep breath of courage and stood straight, fixing his robes, and set his expression against what they might say. Taking one last look at Okulu for support, Salvarias knocked on the door.

Okulu winked, then took off down the hall, leaving Salvarias alone with his fears. The door swung open, and Bellara greeted him. Despite not having seen the servant for years, she had not change. Her silvery hair shone bright in the candlelight, and her eyes were alert and thoughtful. She smiled broadly and curtsied. "Master Salvarias, it is good to see you."

Salvarias breathed shallow in an attempt to avoid the overwhelming scent of cloves coming from the woman. "Madam, it is good to see you as well."

"I trust your room is in order."

"It is. I was hoping to see Lord and Lady Bellerum."

"Send him in," Lady Talura called.

Bellara stood aside. After he was in the room, she curtsied again and left, closing the door behind her.

Inhaling a deep breath, Salvarias faced the room. It was cozy, warmed by a fire and fluttering candles, cooled by a window opened to the early spring air. The furniture was mutely elegant; soothing hues of pale blue fabric stretched over rich brown wood. A balcony near the size of his room overlooked the city, its lights winking at him in the late evening hours. The scent of jasmine permeated the air, and the vines themselves were crawling up the balcony railing.

Lady Talura smiled sweetly and motioned him to join them. "Why hello, dear. You look rested."

"Good to see you, Son," Lord Bellerum said. He patted a chair beside him. "Have a seat."

"Thank you, my lord, but—"

"Edium, Salvarias. For the love of the gods, call me Edium."

"I will not be staying for long," Salvarias finished. He swallowed, wishing for nothing more than a glass of water. His mouth was dry, his hands clammy, and he felt faint. Barreling on, he said, "I have come to ask you a question."

"Certainly, dear," Lady Talura said, passing him a glass of water. She always seemed to know what he needed.

He drank it quickly. Why had he not planned on what to say, how to ask? He was unprepared. This was stupid of him.

Passing the glass back, he was about to beg his leave, run to his room, shut the door and huddle in his bed, hold his fears close to himself as he had always done, let them own him in seclusion and safety. His goodbye was on his lips when he remembered what Okulu had said. Salvarias was not here for himself. He was here for Lunara. It made him feel conceited, as if his hand alone would bring her happiness, but he pushed away the feeling and blurted, "I want to marry her." Blinking aside a shiver of shock at spouting the words so carelessly, he quickly tried to smooth over his announcement, doing everything in his power to ignore the Bellerums' widening eyes. Calming his voice, he said, "I have loved your daughter for years. Though I do not deserve her, I will spend my life trying to be worthy of her love and make her happy. With Durak's inheritance, I have plenty of money to support her and offer a life as comfortable as the one she has led."

Lord Bellerum barked out a laugh and Lady Talura clapped her hands, a girlish gesture that almost had Salvarias smiling if not for the denial he was certain he had heard Lord Bellerum speak. Bowing, Salvarias said, "I understand. I will do my best to avoid her and respect your wishes. Good evening."

"Salvarias," Lady Talura said, her smile still wide. How cruel of her to show such joy in rejecting him. He always knew she would betray him, hurt him. "Son," she said gently. "Listen closely. Yes. We could not be happier for you and Lunara. Yes, we want you two to marry as soon as you're ready."

He realized he had never prepared himself for approval. He had them denying him before he even asked. Now, with their permission, with their approval, with their joy, he had no excuse.

He had somehow clung to a false future, one where he was denied the woman he loved. One where he could offer himself up to her, but one where she could never marry him because of her parent's disapproval. One where she would be safe. But here the Bellerums had snatched away that hope, and he was left exposed to a new future. He would be a husband. Lunara would be his wife, and the forces of darkness would hunt her as a means to find him. They would carve her up to get him to surrender to his evil.

He was a natural born idiot.

"Zerana," Lady Talura said, as if the word should squelch all his fears. His confusion must have shown, because she continued. "Zerana owns Lunara. I feel the goddess close to her, connected beyond what I understand, and now I am as well, ever since you touched my mark. Zerana will not let us be harmed. She kept Lunara alive after your death. She watches over us both. Do you understand?"

He did. A part of him knew it to be true. For his entire life fear had owned him, its claws sunk in so deep that seeing hopeful truths was beyond him. He managed to nod.

"Good," she said. "You're part of this family, Salvarias. You are our son. And ..." She took Lord Bellerum's hand, both smiling at him with so much love it made Salvarias sick, made him recoil from it. "We love you," she finished.

Every moment of Salvarias's life was so vivid, a product of his perfect memory, and every memory of horror as real as the day he lived it. Tobin's betrayal cut him as deep as it had the day he proclaimed it, the day Salvarias's once-father's words burned a hole in his heart that would never be healed. 'You are no son of mine.' Betrayal. Denial.

Lunara he trusted. Lunara would never cause him pain. He knew —*felt* it in her. But these two—parents, people who saw into souls— no, he did not trust them. Not one bit. Steeling himself, he raised his head and said, "I am not your son. I will live where Lunara wants to live. I will eat dinners with whomever she chooses. But you are not my parents." Blinking aside building tears from Tobin's words, he said, "I do not want your love nor will I ever give mine to you. Is that acceptable or would you prefer to rescind your approval?" His voice was harsh in his own ears, thrown out as a challenge.

Lord Bellerum's smile faded, but Lady Talura's grew. "We are not saying you must love us, my dear," she said. "Nor are we saying you have a choice in how we view you. In our hearts, you are our son. In our hearts, we love you. And there is nothing you can do about it." She smiled sweetly. "Now go speak with Lunara in the gardens. When she agrees, come see us, and we'll begin planning the wedding."

Salvarias bowed stiffly, grinding his teeth to keep any rebuttal down, and left the room. He fanned the flames of his anger, directing them toward hate, and the fire burned along the scar down his skull. He would not be weak and beaten again. He would not be cut, and he would not be hurt ever again.

SPRING 1022 A.R

L unara weaved through the cluster of aspens in her family's garden. The sun had set some time ago, and normally she would have fled to the safety of her home to avoid shadows and the frightening noises only heard at night, but she did not want to see anyone. She was tired of assuring her parents and sister that she was fine. She was tired of smiling fake smiles. She wanted to be alone with her sorrow, with his sorrow. It weighed on her; sat on her chest like a brick. The small moments of happiness Salvarias had found since his rescue had usually been snatched away so quickly, she wasn't sure they had even happened. She wanted to tell him of her love, to comfort him, but he had been fast asleep for days, and she had reluctantly given him time to rest. He certainly needed it after Wilhelm had beaten him bloody and after being resurrected by the dark god—by Salvarias's father. She shuddered off the thought.

His confession never sat right with her. Veedran alive was a truth she believed, but him fathering Salvarias seemed ... wrong; an assumption by Salvarias, a need to explain the darkness within him. But she pondered if there wasn't another answer.

Something squawked from above, bringing her mind back to the present. Nighttime always frightened her. Shadows swayed all around, and the moon glinted behind aspen leaves rustling in the night breeze. She'd walked far into the garden all alone. Fear squeezed a rush of blood through her, and she whirled around toward her estate, ready to flee to safety. A scream burst free when a figure towered behind her. It only took a blink to recognize Salvarias.

"My lady," he said. "I am sorry I startled you."

Resting a hand over her heart, she forced out a light laugh. "I'm fine."

Frowning, Salvarias surveyed the garden. "It is safe here. The gardens are well protected."

Smoothing her dress, she inhaled a deep breath. "It's silly of me, but the dark has always scared me ever since I was a girl. But now you're here, and I've nothing to fear."

"*Lumous.*" Salvarias's gaze dropped to hers, his eyes swirling with their usual hues of dark gray, brought to life by the light of his sparrow. He stood rigid, and she now noticed his fear tightening her own throat. His eyes gave him away though, showing a longing—a love—she'd seen once before.

Smiling she took a step toward him, reached out, and shifted back his hood, allowing the full light to illuminate his handsome face. "Why have you come?"

His fear mingled with another emotion she couldn't quite grasp. Swallowing hard, he took a step back and ran his hand along the trunk of an aspen. "It was the first time I knew." He walked to the other side of the tree, putting it between them. "In our dreams, I never walked through forests or gardens. I walked among the dead, the same field you once saved me from. It was always the same wheat grasses, same putrid sky, bodies, the same rivers of blood. But you ..." He glanced at her, uncertainty in his eyes. "You brought something beautiful with you."

"A butterfly," Lunara said, smiling at the memory.

"A sunset."

"A rose bush."

"But it was the aspens when first I knew I loved you."

For three years she had waited for him to say those words, and when he had, he'd followed it by saying they would never be together. Three years later and here he was again. She braced herself for his excuses, the reasons he would give her of why they could not be together. Already her heart was breaking and tears were threatening to surface. She blinked several times and raised her head high. She would wait for him for another six, sixteen, sixty years. However long it took before he was ready.

Salvarias looked back at the trees. "We should not be together. The further you are from me, the safer you will be. Yet ..."

Lunara nearly choked on her breath.

"Yet I can no longer deny my heart," he whispered. "Gods forgive me, but I cannot."

"Salvarias ..."

He raised a hand to stop her. Taking in a huge breath, he faced her, his expression twisted into a plea. "Deny us. Cast me aside. I beg of you, do not love me. I am born of darkness. You *must* see it. You must open your eyes."

"My eyes have been open since our first meeting. It is you who has been blind."

His expression fell into utter anguish. "I beg of you—*I beg you*—seek happiness with another."

"There is no other." She walked around the tree and stood in front of him. He cringed from her, his eyes seeking escape, his fear so strong it pulsed her own vision. Rising on her toes, she cupped his face in her hands, turned his gaze to hers, and said, "You have owned my heart for years, Salvarias. It belongs to no other." She ran a finger along his brow and smiled. "Always so serious."

His kiss was quick, his lips trembling. It was not how she imagined it, but then again, it seemed he surprised them both by his attempt. When he pulled away, he searched her face for something, perhaps rejection, perhaps disapproval. There was some sick hope in his eyes, as if he wished her to slap him, to spit on him. His emotions were a hurricane of uncertainty, fear, and sadness, but also a new kind of hope free of its usual darkness and call for others to hate him. This hope wanted acceptance and love.

"I will never leave you," she whispered. "I will never stop loving you. And I will *never* hurt you."

Closing his eyes, he bowed his head as tears trailed down his cheeks. Resignation and fear battled elation for his attention. It all roiled within her, muddying her own happiness. Tentatively, she reached out to his mind. He tensed immediately, the wall surrounding his thoughts snapping taut to guard whatever lurked behind it.

Opening his eyes, he regarded her for several moments until he whispered, "It is not a pretty sight, my lady."

"Do you think I will see something I haven't before? Do you not believe me when I say nothing will change how I feel about you? Trust me," she urged. "You have to trust me, Salvarias."

Despite his body remaining tense, the wall around his mind sagged, folding in upon itself brick by brick. She wasn't sure when it had happened, but the world had faded from view. She stood in a dimly lit space, the same as when he had called upon Zerana's powers in Windlous except for one difference. Now within the cavernous space of churning gray fog, pulses of deep blue peeked out. Power vibrated the air itself, sending gooseflesh over her arms and legs, snaking a shiver up her spine.

He stood by her side, regarding her with calm eyes. The caves that had been shrouded in darkness were now awake, the shadows boiling with pain and anger. Unable to stop herself, she headed toward one, and with each step the cries of a child grew louder. The shadows took shapes: a boy huddled in the corner of a room and a woman stood over him, holding a knife. Light pierced the dark, and the woman took form. She was striking. Auburn hair shone bright in the dim light, her jaw slightly square, highlighting strong cheekbones. Full lips were pulled back in a sneer that marred her otherwise kind eyes. The woman grabbed the child's hair, and when it looked up, Lunara clamped a hand over her mouth to stop her cry. He would have been such a beautiful child if not for his thin frame, sunken eyes, and deathly pale skin. His hair was short, cut choppy and a little wild from its natural wave. Large black eyes were raining tears as he grabbed his mother's hand, trying to alleviate his weight, kicking his legs along to keep up. He begged for her forgiveness, pleading for her not to hurt him, not to cut him.

Lunara whirled around and ran a few steps from the memory until she found herself in the center of calmness where Salvarias stood staring at the cave.

"As I said," he murmured. "This is not a pleasant place."

Looking around, she could see it. So many of those dark caves, so much pain and anger, despair and loneliness. But there were spots of light, joyful memories sprinkled here and there, and within those was more love and happiness than she had ever known.

"There's something I want to show you," Lunara said, taking his hand.

Unsure if it would be the same, she nevertheless thought of what Zerana had shown her all those years ago, of how Salvarias's soul was entwined with Lunara's. It took a bit of concentration, but in a blink, they stood in a space half occupied by Salvarias's gray fog and the other half consumed in white. Where the halves met, two vines existed. At the base, each was planted in its respective half, the black vine climbing from the gray, the white blooming from white. After a short while, the two weaved into one, a beautiful braid of light and dark.

"What is this place?" Salvarias said.

"Zerana showed it to me." She pointed toward the light. "That is my soul. This is yours. And this"—she motioned to the vines—"is our connection. This is what I did when first we met." She studied far up and saw the vines had separated for a span before coming loosely together. "I assume that was your death. Somehow, it broke our connection." She blinked aside tears. "I hope it never happens again."

"Then let us ensure it does not." Salvarias whispered under his breath, held out his hand, and a burst of brilliant blue light blinded her. Covering her eyes, she looked away. Cold brushed over her followed by heat that made her sweat instantly. Shuddering off the feeling, she peered out between her fingers. The light was still there, bearable to witness as it surged over each of the vines.

"What is it?" she asked.

"My magic," Salvarias said absently, his attention focused on the blue light. "I have asked it to help us." His attention shifted back to his magic, their low murmured conversation echoing in the space.

Lunara waited, but soon became bored. Looking around, she headed off on her own. She stayed clear of those dark caves but chose to visit a few of his happy memories. Wilhelm owned the majority of those bright moments: the times they played games, joked, and wrestled. They contrasted the ones with his mother, and she wondered how they could come from the same child.

Deeper and deeper she ventured until ending up on a precipice where everything ended. No fog rolled over it; no light illuminated whatever lurked below. Biting her lip, she contemplated stepping over. After all, this was only his mind. No real harm could come to her. If she found herself frightened, she merely needed to think of a different place, and she would be there. This was more like a dream. And nothing could hurt her in her dreams. Smiling to herself, she jumped over the edge.

In a blink, she was in a space with what appeared to be a marble the size of the castle in Warton. Churning within was the same gray fog that lived in Salvarias's mind. She was certain it was alive. She had the distinct impression it was some sort of seed, something planted within Salvarias, but not yet grown.

As she walked around it, it seemed as if it followed her; eyes that were not there, life that she could not touch. She stopped in front of a crack along the sphere's surface. The tiniest of holes could be seen, and from it leaked a thin tendril of blackfire. It snaked around her ankles, making her skin warm.

"It is not safe here," a voice said from behind.

Yelping in surprise, Lunara whirled around. A ball of sapphire light floated in front of her. His magic.

"I-I'm sorry," she stammered.

"My wizard is too frightened of this place to visit, but I believe one day he will embrace his true self, break open what is rightfully his."

She looked over her shoulder at the sphere. "This is his true self?"

"Yes," the magic said. "But something else dwells in the shadows of this space. Something that has infected him that he cannot cast out." Sadness seeped from the light. "I am scared."

Lunara gazed around, and then she too felt it: wrongness in the air, a malice that watched her.

"I cannot save him," the magic said. "He was doomed at birth."

"Do you have such little faith in him?" She took a step back from the magic. Its statement appalled her, but more so, she was frightened of whatever else lived here. "Do you not want more for him?"

"I want him to live a life of peace and joy. But what I want will never come to fruition. He will die young. He will die saving Arden. I am telling you so you can prepare yourself as I am."

"I have faith in him. He will defeat Veedran."

"I have no doubt of that either. But he will do so at a great cost. You were right when you once said he was something beyond a mere man, and it will kill him. I am doomed with him because I will willingly die to protect him, but even now I am not powerful enough."

"I can help."

"No, I fear not." It shifted to the blackfire. "It has shown me a future I cannot avoid. I only ask you give him love and peace for his remaining days. Drown him in it, for it will carry him through hardships he would otherwise not survive. Now go to him. I am almost done helping him, and he will be missing you. Do not mention our conversation, I beg you. Let him live his last days in hope and love."

Backing away, shaking her head, Lunara thought of the vines. When she blinked, she was in the space once more, gazing up at her and Salvarias's souls. He was still studying them as if she had never left.

Swallowing a wave of tears, she set her jaw and pushed aside the magic's words. She would save the man she loved. After all, she had the goddess of light on her side. How could she lose?

Nodding to himself, Salvarias said, *"Rulose."*

A loud clap vibrated in Lunara's head, a shiver of pleasure coursed its way up her spine, and she felt a strong pull on her heart, leading her right to Salvarias.

"Nothing will break our connection again," Salvarias said. "It can be weakened, but never will our souls separate. Not even in death."

Lunara smiled up at Salvarias. "Thank you."

He bowed, but his gaze was focused on the white space, seeming to try to see what lie beyond.

"You are welcome anytime," she said, motioning him toward the light. "I will always be open to you."

He glanced at her, then back toward the light.

"You are a curious man," Lunara encouraged. "It is one of the things I love about you. My heart is yours, and my mind and thoughts forever open to you. Please, I must insist."

Frowning, he walked toward the light. She took a few quick steps and caught up to him, taking his hand in her own as she did. When they passed into the light, it momentarily blinded her then faded, leaving her and Salvarias in a space similar to his own. Here, most of her caves were filled with joy and love, only a handful were dark with pain.

Salvarias grimaced at her side and leaned a bit of weight on her as he wrapped an arm around her shoulders. She had not noticed in his mind he was a whole man. He did not limp, and all his fingers had been present. Now he barely put any weight on his bum leg, and he flexed the two remaining fingers on his right hand.

"I'm sorry," she said quickly, standing taller to take on more of his weight. She willed him whole, demanded it, spoke it, but nothing changed.

"It is fine, my lady," he said, gaze sweeping over the cavern.

"I don't understand," she said apologetically.

"This is how you have known me. I was once whole, and it is how I wish to be, so that is what my mind shows me."

He stepped to the closest memory and reached out to it. The instant his fingers touched it, Lunara gasped in blinding pleasure. It weakened her knees, lungs laboring for breath, and her heart pounded in her chest. It was such an intimate sensation. Never before had she considered her soul—her essence—as tangible, but now he had found it, touched it, and it shook her to her core.

"Are you all right, my lady?"

Lunara opened her eyes she had not realized had closed. They were in the gardens again, facing each other, close. The scent of lavender mixed with jasmine and the freshness of spring.

"Fine," she said, resting a shaking hand over her heart. "It was such an odd sensation." She still ached with need, a throbbing she had never felt before.

Salvarias's face reddened as if she had voiced her thoughts, and she might as well have. Despite not being as seeded in her mind as a moment ago, they had opened a mutual path to one another, and he could sense her emotions as she did his.

Nevertheless, their shared shyness did not stop him from sliding an arm around her waist and pulling her close. She gazed into his eyes, so dark, so alive, and so full of desire. Heat warmed her body, building up in her cheeks. Tilting her head back, she invited him with parted lips, pleading him with her eyes. He leaned forward; enough that his breath washed over her mouth and the scent of herbs stole away the lavender. Closing his eyes, his lips brushed against hers, soft, almost teasing, causing her stomach to flutter, her heart to stammer, and her knees to nearly give out. A soft thud of his staff falling from his hand was followed by the warmth of his fingers caressing the back of her neck, holding her there as his kiss deepened.

The world fell away for them, disappeared, hid so they could be alone, so they could finally have what they had wanted for so long. To be together.

When at long last he pulled away, his lips only left hers far enough for him to whisper, "Marry me?"

"Tomorrow," she breathed, and kissed him again.

TALURA KNOCKED SOFTLY on Salvarias's door. It was early, too early for the servants to be up, but she couldn't sleep. Light flickering underneath her son's door said he had the same issue. Tucking the wrapped bundle tighter under her arm and juggling the tray of steaming water, she rapped on the door again. It opened before she finished.

Salvarias bowed and took the tray. "Good morning, my lady."

"So it is," she said. "Might I come in?"

Salvarias stepped aside. "Of course."

The room smelled of lavender and soil. On the table, he had sprigs of dried herbs spread out along with his mortar and pestle. "Running low on anything, sweetness? I can get you whatever you need."

"Thank you, my lady. I intend on going to the herb shop today to purchase a few."

"Nonsense. You're getting married this evening. Today should be spent with your brother. Write me a list, and I'll have the herbs fetched for you."

He opened his mouth as if to argue, closed it, sat at the table, dipped his quill in ink, and wrote on a clean sheet of parchment.

"No argument?" she teased.

"I find you are a stubborn woman. Mountains bend more than you," he said dryly.

"Oh come now, dear. I'm not that bad." She settled herself in front of the fire, smoothing her dress. "I'm happy for you. And for Lunara."

His quill paused before flowing along the paper. "Thank you, my lady."

When done, he sprinkled sand on the ink, dusted it off, and sat beside her at the fire, handing over the parchment. She skimmed it, admiring his smooth and elegant penmanship. "I have something for you." She picked up the bundle wrapped in white cloth and held it out for him.

Salvarias shifted back in his seat, looking at her offering as if it would grow teeth and tear him to shreds.

"Open it."

"I ... I cannot accept any gifts, my lady. I thank you—"

Using her motherly tone, she said, "Open it, Son. Refusing would be to insult your new mother-in-law. Not wise."

He swallowed hard and took the package in shaking hands. She looked away from his two-fingered hand. She wished she had been there when Wilhelm had cut up Sansis.

The fabric fell away revealing the new slate-blue mage robes she'd been sewing him for months before his death. She had never known why she'd finished them after his passing. It seemed right, and now she was delighted she had. All his burgundy robes were old, far too large, faded and torn, tattered at the bottom. Only his thick black cloak had survived time due to the small fortune Wilhelm had spent on it years ago.

Talura had chosen coarse fabric for the outside, material that would stand up better to wear and tear, and lined the inside with softer cotton. Also in the bundle were summer robes, made of lighter material. Biting her lip, she watched him closely, but he just stared at them.

Eventually the silence was too much, and she said, "I know you usually wear burgundy, but you would look so handsome in blue. And see here." She pulled out one of the robes and showed him the secret pockets she'd sown into the sleeves and a few at the hem. "You can hide spell components here." She dug around the bundle until she found his cloak. She'd had Bellara sneak it out of his room after he had fallen asleep last night so she could make the adjustments. "I made a few in your cloak too. See, here's one for your smaller spell book."

Still he sat there staring at them.

Blinking aside her tears, she waved a hand and tossed the robe and cloak into the bundle. "Silly, I know. You probably have your clothes worn in, and they fit you the way you like. These will surely be uncomfortable. I'm sorry about the cloak. I can take the pockets out without any damage to—"

"No," Salvarias blurted, gathering up the clothes. "Please, I ... I ..." When he looked up at her, she was surprised to see tears standing in his eyes. "I love them."

"Oh." Joy blossomed into a smile. "Very good then, sweetness. Let's see one on you."

Salvarias gingerly set the bundle on the footstool as if it were breakable porcelain. Picking up one of the winter robes, he went behind a partition to change.

"Are you nervous about the wedding?" she asked.

A pause and then, "Slightly. I was hoping it would be small."

"Of course, dear. No one but your closest friends and family. I will have to invite Brice though. Lunara grew up with him, and he is a dear friend of hers."

"Thank you, my lady."

He stepped into view, and Talura could not stop her smile. Hopping up, she circled him, studying the fit for any flaws. There were none. She'd been right when she'd assumed there was more behind the fabric his slouch could not hide. No brother of Wilhelm's could be a thin man. This new robe fit across his shoulders, displaying their impressive width, and fell against a muscled chest. Regardless of her underestimate, the robes hung perfectly around him, highlighting his build without sticking to him.

Pushing down his hood, her smile grew at seeing how the lighter fabric brought attention to his eyes and the richness of his hair. "You are quite a handsome man. You should wear these to the wedding."

Salvarias blushed and went to raise his hood, but stopped when Talura clucked her tongue.

"Remember," she said. "When it's just the two of us, keep the hood down." Motioning him to follow, she guided him to a mirror. "What do you think?"

Salvarias avoided looking at himself, nodding while shying away. "They are wonderful."

"Come now," she scolded. Grabbing the edge of his sleeve, she pulled him in front of the mirror again, sure not to touch him. "Look."

"I prefer not," he said.

"Do as I say, Son."

Reluctantly, he raised his head.

"What do you see?" she asked.

"A monster. A demon."

"That's what she saw. That's what she told you. Look again."

His grinding teeth set hers on edge, but he did as she asked.

"I see a kind man," she said gently. "A handsome man. I see what is truly there, not what someone tells me to see. Now, what do *you* see?"

Ever so slightly, he raised his head, looking himself over. His brow furrowed as he stood straighter. "I ..." He inhaled a deep breath. "I see a selfish man who is going to marry a woman he does not deserve. I see evil behind black eyes." His gaze shifted to hers, lacking any anger but full of truth. "*I* see I am a monster." Looking back at himself, a slight smile played on his lips. "But now I am a well-dressed monster."

Despite herself, Talura burst out laughing, and Salvarias's smile spread into a wide grin.

12

SPRING 1022 A.R

Lunara's father plopped down in a chair. "It's absurd to plan a wedding in a single morning."

"Honestly, dear," her mother said between teeth clenched around the pins she was using to hem Lunara's wedding dress. "The two have waited long enough. Salvarias would be uncomfortable with a big wedding. There's really nothing to plan."

"But ... but we need to invite our friends."

"*Our* friends, dear, not Salvarias or Lunara's. Only Okulu, Cessia, Kisra, Wilhelm, Brice, and Varila will be present. And of course, the two of us. That's it. Final."

Edium frowned at Lunara. "You're sure this is what *you* want? I know Salvarias is a private person, but you can have whatever wedding you desire."

"I promise," Lunara said. "This is perfect."

Edium mumbled some more before rising from his chair. "I'll see how the garden is coming along."

"Lots of flowers," Talura said. "Every color we have."

Lunara's father muttered all the way from the room.

"He just wants it to be perfect for you," her mother said.

"I know."

After the pins were in, Lunara stripped from the dress, threw on a robe, and joined her sister on the balcony. It overlooked Tedris's favorite grassy lawn. He was there now with Wilhelm and Salvarias.

"He loves Wilhelm already," Varila said. "He snuck out of his room last night and into Wilhelm's."

Tedris flung himself into Salvarias's lap, laughing as he clasped his arms around his uncle's neck. Salvarias's soft voice didn't reach their balcony, but whatever he said sent Tedris in a fit of fake shrieks of fear. Bolting up, Salvarias swept Tedris up in his arms and tossed him high in the air. Wilhelm leapt up, caught him, and tossed him higher. Tedris's infectious laugh soon had Varila and Lunara giggling along as the brother's lobbed the child between them.

"He's going to be an amazing father," Talura said from behind.

Lunara nodded. "He will give them all the love and happiness he was denied."

"How is it Salvarias can touch the child?" Talura asked.

"The first time had the usual effects," Varila answered. "But Tedris wouldn't let go of Salvarias. He said he could make it better. It lasted a while, and Salvarias was near passing out, but then whatever he endured stopped, and he seemed fine. Tedris said he shared everything with his uncle. Salvarias looked perplexed, but didn't offer any explanation beyond what Tedris provided." Varila cast Lunara a mischievous smile. "By the way, I did have a talk with your soon-to-be-husband. I imagine Wilhelm never bothered to ... how should I put this? Educate his brother on the finer points of taking care of a woman's needs."

Lunara's face burned hot. "You didn't!"

"Oh, I did."

Talura laughed and strolled back into the room. "Come along, my dears. We have a lot of work to do."

The rest of the day was filled with sewing, laughter, and nerves. The sun set low in the sky sooner than it had ever done before; Lunara was sure of it. Her hair had never been so unruly as her mother and sister argued over its arrangement, finally settling on pinning it back at the sides, making her face feel too big for her head.

When she said so, Varila—with a wicked smile—had said the pin was so Salvarias had a place to start tonight.

Once all the fussing ended, she looked herself over in the mirror and blanched. Oh gods, had her cheeks always been so pale? She pinched them. Now they were too red.

"It's time, dear," her mother said.

"Are you having second thoughts?" Varila asked. "You seem out of sorts."

"Of course not. Let's go." Gathering up her dress, she left the room and followed her mother through the estate.

Lunara didn't doubt her feelings for Salvarias, but she was nervous for her wedding night. Varila and her mother had been all too keen to share what to expect, but it did nothing to alleviate her anxiety. More than anything she feared after so many years of denying himself, when now Salvarias finally had what he had sought, she would not live up to his expectations.

All too soon they stood at the door leading to the gardens. Her father was waiting with a smile and misty eyes.

Varila squeezed her hand and then disappeared into the garden.

"You'll be fine," Talura whispered, and then she too left.

"You look pale," Edium said, frowning. "Nervous?"

"He loves me, I know. But ... but what if I'm not what he expected? What if I'm not strong enough? He needs me to be." Tears built, and she cursed her weakness. "So much darkness stalks him. He needs a strong woman, not this!" She angrily brushed away her tears.

"Have you lied to him? Have you shown him a person you are not? Faked who you are?"

"No, of course not."

"Then you've nothing to fear, do you?" He smiled. "You are exactly what he needs. If I did not think you were perfect for him, I would have denied him when he asked for your hand. If he was unworthy of your love, I would have cast him out of my city." He hooked his finger around her chin and lifted her head. "You are my daughter, Lunara. I don't have weak children. And I would never allow you to be unhappy."

Flinging her arms around his neck, she held him tight. "I love you, Father."

He kissed her forehead. "I love you, too. Now let's get you married."

Outside, the sky was painted plum, orange, and brilliant yellow. Flowers were everywhere, a myriad of colors and smells, petals folding under her feet as she walked with her father.

Seated in the garden were Talura and Cessia, Tedris curled up in his grandmother's lap. He smiled crookedly at her, his amber eyes just like his father's. She winked at him. Behind them, Kisra was sidled up to Brice, who was already lost to the woman's charms. Suppressing a giggle, Lunara looked to the raised platform her father had hastily erected. Varila stood waiting in a robin-egg blue dress, sword hanging at her side. She grinned, and Lunara grinned back. Wilhelm towered over everyone, dressed in his full armor polished like new. A sword hilt over his shoulder, another at his hip, and one from a dagger sticking out of the top of his boot glittered in the fading sun. A slow smile spread across his face, and he stood taller, tears sparkling in his eyes. She hadn't seen him look this happy since his own wedding over three years ago. Okulu stood ready to conduct the ceremony. He was dashing as always, dressed in deep purple that played off his olive skin and brightened his grass-green eyes. His son Arias and daughter Bri were clinging to his legs, grinning up at her.

She'd avoided looking at Salvarias because she knew she would be lost to him once she did. After inhaling a deep breath, she kissed her father's cheek, stepped onto the platform, and raised her gaze to Salvarias.

The first thing she noticed were his eyes. His hood was down, and the churning of his irises caught the colors of the sunset. A slight smile was on his lips, his wavy hair falling effortlessly around his shoulders, shimmering in the last rays of sunlight. When she tore her gaze from his, she admired his new robes, no doubt sewn by her mother. The body she'd always felt was now on display, and he stood upright, abandoning his former slouch.

Salvarias's own gaze roved over her, and she smoothed out the white fabric stitched tightly around her upper body, the neckline lower than she would normally wear. The skirt hung to the ground, artfully sewn to be full without the ridiculous layers of the latest fashion. She hoped he liked it, and by his growing smile, he did.

Taking her hand, they faced Okulu.

"Gods," Okulu said dryly. "I never thought this day would come."

The merc rambled on for several long, long moments before he finally asked for the rings. Lunara had insisted she be the one to design them and had found a jeweler who took his task seriously and had worked all night and most of today to finish them. She passed them to Okulu. Arching an eyebrow at them, he shrugged and continued on for more long, long moments before passing her Salvarias's ring. With shaking hands, she slid it on. She had mirrored the entwining of their souls; two metals, each a different hue, braided around one another in the same pattern. He studied it for a breath before meeting her gaze.

It is perfect, he said in her mind.

She beamed a smile at him.

After he slid on her identical ring, Okulu spread his arms and proclaimed, "Nothing came to kill us! No lightning struck from the sky! No beasts stalked our shadows! Love! Love has scared them all away!" He winked at Salvarias. "And the fact they don't know where you're at yet." Clearing his throat, his serious gaze shifted between Lunara and Salvarias. "Come Oblivion or Zerana's grace itself, you two will forever be bound to one another. For the love of all the gods, be happy. There's no other couple who deserves it more than you two." Turning to Salvarias, he said, "Now kiss her before I do it for you."

Lunara blushed from the eyes watching them, but Salvarias seemed not to care. His kiss was lingering, tasting of herbs. When he finally broke away, he whispered, "Never have I been happier."

Grinning up at him, she said, "Nor I."

"Let's drink!" Okulu roared.

Clapping turned Lunara's attention to the group, and she found herself whisked up in a bear hug, Wilhelm's chuckle vibrating out his chest and into hers. "I have a sister," he said. "A little sister!"

She hugged his neck, laughing as he swayed her back and forth, her feet not coming close to the ground.

He kissed her cheek and whispered in her ear, "Thank you for seeing him for who he truly is. Thank you for loving him for it."

She squeezed Wilhelm tighter. "I promise to make him happy."

"I know." He lowered her to the ground and immediately swept Salvarias up in a hug. Whatever Wilhelm whispered to his brother caused Salvarias to laugh lightly.

Everyone had gathered around them by then, wishing them well and ushering them along to the dining hall. Lunara glanced behind, hoping to see Wilhelm and Varila in each other's arms, but Wilhelm had joined Brice, Tedris riding on his father's shoulders. Varila walked with Kisra, though her sister's gaze was on Wilhelm. He seemed not to notice.

The dinner Lunara's mother had prepared was ridiculously large, but Wilhelm made short work of any leftover meat. Lunara couldn't bring herself to eat much. Her stomach was a knot of nerves, and by Salvarias's small plate, he fared no better. A part of her wanted the meal to last forever, and another part could not wait to be alone with her new husband.

In the end, the meal flew by, and one by one their friends left until it was just the two of them. Unfortunately, Wilhelm went his own way, leaving Varila to walk to their room alone yet again.

Salvarias frowned after his brother.

"He must forgive himself soon," Lunara murmured.

"I doubt he has any intention of doing so," Salvarias said. "I have tried to talk to him about it, but he will not listen." Sighing, he shook his head and looked back at her. "We have been hasty."

"What do you mean?"

"We have not discussed where we will live or where we will stay tonight."

"Oh." Lunara had assumed they would live here. She'd never considered he would want a home of their own.

"Of course," he said with a smile. She gave him a quizzical look, but it only made him laugh. "You do not shield your thoughts in the least, my lady."

"Oh," she said again, blushing. She'd not realized his light presence had never left from the day before. "I'm sorry. We—"

He raised a hand. "Please. This is a wonderful home, and I would never ask you to leave it." He shifted in his chair, his smile fading. "Nor have I been privileged to see your room."

Heat rushed up Lunara's cheeks. "To tell the truth, my parents had rooms made for my sister and I should we ever marry. They had assumed we would always live here, so our residence is spacious and private. I'm sorry I never thought to mention it before."

Salvarias stood from his chair and offered his hand. "As I said, my lady, we were hasty in our plans. We had no time for such discussions. Please, lead the way."

The twenty guards her father had posted on them followed at a respectful distance, but it was awkward hearing the thudding footsteps behind them, all knowing what would be conducted behind closed doors.

At the end of a T-shaped hall, Lunara motioned to the right corridor ending in a double, thick iron door. "That's Varila and Wilhelm's rooms. The left is ours."

After they entered their room, Lunara shut the iron door and bolted it. It was as she remembered. The sitting room was off the entrance, comfortable furniture strewn about. On a desk in the corner rested Salvarias's herb pouch and a teakettle hung on a bar over the fireplace.

An expansive balcony overlooking the ocean and gardens would be behind the closed drapes. Salvarias stepped farther inside and opened another door. Beyond was a spacious four-post bed. Heavy curtains were pulled back, revealing cushy pillows and feather-stuffed blankets. Another set of curtains along the wall would open out to another balcony. Each room had its own fireplace.

Salvarias ventured into the bedroom and opened the last door. Their private washroom was the size of a small bedroom. Centered and steaming with hot water was a tub. On the far side was another door.

"That's for the servants," Lunara explained. "There's a bell outside we can ring when we need the room cleaned or fresh water for bathing."

Salvarias nodded, still looking around.

"Do you like it?" she asked.

"It is lovely."

They stood in awkward silence before she found the courage to motion to the bath. "Would you join me?"

He nodded. She sat at the vanity and found another tie for the rest of her hair. Once she got it up, she stood and turned her back to him. Trying to keep her voice from trembling, she asked, "Would you help with the dress?"

Warmth reached her, a tickle along her neck from his breath, and she heard his deep inhale. "You smell wonderful," he murmured.

The corset loosened and his soft hands slid over her shoulders, taking the dress with them until it fell in a pool at her feet. His touch lingered for a moment before he stepped back. Fabric rustled as he took off his robes, and she used his distraction to tiptoe to the tub and sink into its warm waters.

They sat across from each other and talked of nothing important until the water turned cold. As conversation lulled, Salvarias's intense gaze rested on her for a long moment before he rose from the tub. Her heart hurt every time she saw his maimed body, all the angry gnarls of old burns and raised scars. His side was still bruised from Wilhelm's beating. But even his mutilations did not hide his physique; arms strapped with tight muscle, the chisel of his chest and stomach, the broadness of his shoulders.

Snatching up the nearest towel, he wrapped it around his waist, picked up another towel, and held it open for her. Hoping her face wasn't as red as it felt, she rose from the tub and walked into the towel as he folded it around her. She dried in silence and traded the towel for a robe.

Salvarias walked up to her, kissed her hair, and said, "I need a cup of tea."

She watched him leave, never realizing how attractive a man's back could be, or how a towel wrapped around a waist could be so tantalizing. Sighing in contentment, she padded into the bedroom, wincing at the cold floor, stirred up the fire, and then peeled back the curtains to the balcony. Lights from the city twinkled at her, and moonbeams danced off the hypnotic waves halfheartedly crashing into the rocks far below.

She glanced over to see Salvarias leaning in the doorway of the bedroom, still only wearing a towel, a smile on his lips.

"You shouldn't stare," she scolded, hiding her smile by turning to the window.

"Then you should not be so beautiful."

Gods, this could be a dream. Never had she imagined this day would come, that they would marry. Perhaps it was a dream. Perhaps she would wake in a cold, dark room, alone and grief ridden.

Arms slid around her waist, his warm body pressing against her back. "It is not," Salvarias whispered in her ear.

A soft kiss lingered on her neck, shuddering a ripple of pleasure down her, making her knees weak. His arms kept her steady, his hot breath moving farther down. His hand slid along her arm, taking her hand and moving it from the curtains. Staying behind her, he guided her to the bed, his lips gliding along her neck.

He stopped by the bed and turned her to face him. No words were spoken as he removed the pin holding her hair. Frozen in terror and aching want, she stood shaking as his fingers untied her robe. It slid off and his towel fell to the floor.

"I love you," he whispered.

"I love you, too."

Leaning forward, he kissed her as his arms slid around her, and the weight of his body took them to the bed.

There were two things about Salvarias she had taken for granted until now. First was the smoothness of his hands. They glided along her

skin, sending tingles and shivers over her body. Next was the purposeful-
ness in which he made every movement. His lips drifted from place to
place, his hands caressing without hesitation, all with the intent of
discovery. Each stroke and kiss taught him what made her moan, what
made her body rise and fall in sheer pleasure. She was victim to her
desires, to the revelations of what a simple touch could do to her. When
she tried to explore him, he gently took her hand in his until she
succumbed to selfish pleasure once more. All he allowed was for her to
thread her fingers through his hair, holding him longer to where she
wanted, or to clench his arms as waves of blinding need washed over her.

By the time his body settled between her legs, she was slave to her
own hunger, her breath laboring as she kissed him. He took her
gently, sinking into her slowly, building up a soft cry in her throat
that made her pull her mouth from his so it could escape. He moved
slow and rhythmic, his soft exhales of pleasure mingling with her
increasing moans of ecstasy.

A groan of agony left her throat when he stopped. His slick forehead rested against hers, his eyes shut, his breathing harsh.

"What is it?" she whispered.

"Nothing." He kissed her softly, and his body shifted away.

She quickly wrapped her legs around him, holding him to her.
"Tell me."

"We need to stop," he said, his eyes closing tighter.

"I don't understand."

He looked at her as if she must know, as if whatever was in his
head was written across the wall. "We ..." His brow furrowed, his eyes
lighting as if he just thought of something. "Surely you realized we
cannot have children."

"Whatever are you talking about?"

"I am a Guardian. You are a cleric. I doubt the two forces would
even allow us to conceive, and if they did, do you really want to curse
a child to such a fate? Not to mention it will surely be infected by my
evil."

She hadn't thought of it, but he was wrong. "We will kill Veedran and free Zerana. There will be no reason our child would be cursed. There will be no danger to them. And you are not evil."

"But—"

"Enough," she breathed, lifting up so their lips almost touched. "I would not willingly conceive a child I knew to be doomed. And I hope, with all my heart, our child will be exactly like you. For once, trust me. Trust I am right."

"So much hope," he said. "Lunara."

It was the first time he had addressed her informally, and it sent a shiver along her skin. His voice had power itself, and with a word he conveyed the depth of his love.

His lips upon hers, they sank back to the bed.

SLEEP DID NOT COME to Lunara as she lay encased in Salvarias's arms, listening to his deep breathing. Partly because she still bathed in the pleasure radiating through her body, the other part because she was thirsty and ridiculously hot.

Finally giving up, she untangled herself and crawled out of bed. The room spun, and she had to grab hold of the bed to keep from falling. It passed quickly enough and, shrugging it off, she made her way to the sitting room by the dying fire's light while draping on a robe.

She drank two glasses of water, wiping a building sweat from her forehead. Gods, it was so warm, stifling. Gasping and groping through the thick drapes, she found the balcony doors, flung one open, and stumbled into the cold night. It washed over her in blessed relief. Sucking in huge lungfuls of air, she rested a hand on her belly. Her skin was hot to the touch. Turning her back to the city, she untied her robe and looked down. A dark stain was under her skin, moving, churning slowly, shrinking in size.

A scream lodged in her throat when sharp pain went straight through her belly. She fell to her knees, cradling her stomach. Another wave of heat washed over her, spinning the balcony wildly. Her stomach heaved, but she swallowed it down.

She wanted to scream, wanted Salvarias, but her throat and teeth were clenched. Darkness bled into her vision, followed by pulses of blinding white light. She collapsed completely, her body jerking in spasms of pain.

What have you done? Zerana said in her mind.

Then Lunara felt the spark of life inside her.

Your son will suffer, Zerana said. *Certainly there will be joy and love, but he will endure pain. I can unmake him, if you so choose.*

"No," Lunara gasped, wrapping her arms protectively around her belly and curling up. She couldn't explain it, but she had already connected to her son, a love that bloomed the instant she sensed his life.

You know as well as I Salvarias holds a dark power. And you hold the light within you. Your child will be born to both, and they will war inside him. I say again, I can stop his pain before it begins.

"You will not," Lunara snarled between clenched teeth.

You should tell your husband. He will understand the two of you should not have conceived, that such extremes of light and dark should not be housed in one man or god. And you ... Do you not feel it? The unnatural pain of his seed taking? The burn of it? Salvarias is ignorant of his powers, child, and he has created ... something. It is forbidden for gods to create gods. To create beings containing so much power. I cannot even begin to imagine what your child will be like, what powers he will wield, and what horrors he will endure. I beg you, let me end the child's life now, while he is too weak to fight me.

No! You will not!

Sadness bled into Zerana's voice when she said, *So be it, child.*

When the dizziness faded, Lunara stared up at the blanket of stars. She wiped tears she hadn't known she had shed and hauled herself up. The pain was gone, leaving behind a warmth in her womb and the instant bond between a mother and child.

"I won't let anything happen to you," she whispered, rubbing her belly. She locked the conversation in a corner of her mind, hidden from Salvarias until she decided what to do. Tightening her robe with shaking hands, she stepped back inside and closed the doors.

Salvarias staggered in from the bedroom, rubbing his eyes as he surveyed the room. "Are you all right? I thought I felt ... something."

"I'm fine. Just thirsty."

"Mmm," he murmured, seeming half asleep. He crossed the room, poured himself a cup of tea, downed it, and turned sleepily back to her. "Did you want to stay up?"

Frowning, she peeled back the curtains and stared at the lazy ocean. She should tell him, of course. But he had so many worries, so many burdens. Knowing he had a child could change his decisions, and he needed to be clear minded for what he would face in the coming months.

Soft hands moved aside her hair, and his lips lingered on her neck. His solid form pressed against her back calmed her fears. There was nothing in life they could not overcome together.

"You're tired," she said, trying to ignore the weakness in her knees as he moved his hands around her waist. "We should sleep."

"Mmm," he whispered, and untied her robe.

Tilting her head back, she closed her eyes and succumbed to him. She would tell him ... eventually.

SALVARIAS WOKE in the late morning hours, his new wife encased in his arms, his heart too full for words.

The drapes around the bed were pulled closed, hiding them away from the day outside. Inhaling a contented breath, he whispered, *"Lumous."* His dim sparrow lit enough for him to see her face. She slept soundly, a slight smile on her lips, her body warm against his. How could life ever be more beautiful than this moment?

Lightly he kissed her cheek then unraveled his body from hers. It took him a moment to bludgeon down the rush of his thoughts, but once in control, he slipped from the bed, blinking at the harsh stream of light sneaking between a gap in the window coverings.

After his ablutions, he headed into the main sitting room. Bellara was hanging a fresh kettle of water above the lazy fire she had started.

Salvarias bowed. "Madam."

Bellara curtsied. "Lady Bellerum said you'd be needing this. I hope I didn't wake you."

"Not at all. Thank you." He stood far from her, avoiding the heavy sent of cloves always clinging to her and the harsh memories it brought about.

"If you need anything else, ring the bell."

Salvarias bowed. "Thank you."

Once she left, he made his tea and drank two cups quickly to ease his building headache. Moseying around the room, he stopped when he came upon the plant he had created. Lady Bellerum must have moved it from his old room. Igniting his magic, he ran his fingers along the stems of the flowers and the petals. No thorns sprouted, no poison bled into his fingers.

The plant's healing properties are increasing in potency, his magic said. *Its evolution is in no way sinister, nor its intent. It is as docile as a daisy.*

How can something so wonderful come from blackfire?

The power has greater depths than you see, my wizard. Perhaps if you accepted it as part of you, you will see its wonderful potential.

Salvarias stepped out onto the balcony and watched the lazy waves kissing the cliffside. *I cannot ever imagine a time when I would embrace that power, my friend. I still hear Durak's screams, his pleas.*

You cannot hide from yourself forever.

I have accepted my godhood, Salvarias said defensively. *I have embraced being a God of Magic.*

His magic's voice was gentle when it said, *You know as well as I you are more than a mere God of Magic. You know as well as I what created you gave you unequaled power. I will not harp on it every time we talk. I am not here to force or coerce you into anything you do not want. I only beg you to think on it. That you explore the blackfire with your heart open to it.*

Salvarias switched topics. *I want to create something for her, something she would adore, and something that would protect her.*

What did you have in mind?

I have explored her mind and found she had a love of griffins when she was younger. In one of her favorite memories, her father gave her a stuffed griffin doll. She decorated her room with them and read every story containing one. I have pondered the subject and fear a traditional griffin would not do. They were independent creatures, as intelligent as man, and would never stay with her once they were grown. I would like to make a version of a griffin with the heart and soul of an animal, something neither good nor evil. Something that loyalty can be earned. Like a dog, perhaps.

That sounds extremely complicated, my wizard.

I am determined to gift her something wonderful to show her the depth of my love.

Then let us try. You are making two, I assume?

Salvarias drew two stones from a hidden pocket in his robes. *Yes, a male and female. I want them to have companionship.*

Let us begin.

Salvarias sat on the ground, leaning his back against the balcony railing, and set the two stones in front of him. Creating was different than enchanting. Opening a link to energy was relatively easy in his mind. Creating the flower had taken much more imagination; all those details, all those characteristics he sought. He had no inkling what to expect this time. His last creation was simple by comparison. To create something with a heart—with a *soul*—was entirely intimidating.

Nevertheless, he was determined to give his wife something magnificent, something she could cherish for all her years.

Closing his eyes, he constructed an image in his head. Unlike griffins of old, he made these completely black, save the female he marked with a white diamond on her neck. The head and neck were of an eagle, feathered and soft. The front and back legs were those of a lion. The body was a lion's with a silky coat for his wife's comfort. The wings would be spectacular, long, and powerful. Eventually his creation could carry up to two humans with little effort. The more details he added, the more his smile grew. They were stunning creatures.

After every detail was in place, he imbued them with an eagle's intelligence and hunting prowess, a lion's bravery, but most of all, he gifted it a dog's bottomless well of love and loyalty, of compassion and joy.

When all was as precise as he could make it, his magic voiced its approval and called forth blackfire. It burned hot in his blood, seeking his attention, but he denied it. It was simply a tool for his use, one he would toss aside if it ever dissatisfied him. As the blackfire wrapped around his image and soaked up his wishes, the heat in his body grew wondrously comforting. He bathed in that warmth, sinking into the euphoric pleasure and contentment pulsing through his veins. Life budded up from his very soul; filling him with such joy it brought tears to his eyes. Blackfire reached into that tiny portion belonging solely to Salvarias, to that portion of himself he saw as good, and fed it into the stones, planting his seed of life. As it flowed out of him, he exhaled heavily, feeling it leached from his soul, from his very blood, from some deep part of himself he hid from.

When it all finally drained out of him, he slumped, gasping for air, wincing at his brain thumping his skull, at the soreness of every muscle, and at the uselessness of his limbs. He merely sat sprawled out, sweating and shaking. Sleep beckoned to him, but his growing excitement denied it. Sitting before him, blinking their large black eyes, the griffins spread their wings and ... purred. Laughing lightly, he reached out his mind to them. Theirs were awash with curiosity and excitement, with wonder and instant joy. As with all creation except Unupture's, these were born with names. The girl was Sira and the boy Saval.

They called him father as they hopped into his lap, both the size of a house cat, fighting for his attention, squawking loudly. It took time to calm and quiet them, but when he did, he scooped them up in his arms and made his way back to his bed.

Lunara still slept as he crawled over to her and deposited the griffins next to her. He introduced her as their mother.

Sira nuzzled up to Lunara's belly and purred contently. Saval kept to Salvarias, using his talons to crawl up his chest until it perched on his shoulder.

Lunara inhaled deeply, and her sleepy smile brightened Salvarias's world.

"Morning," she murmured.

"My lady, I cannot begin to tell you how happy you have made me. For all my days, I hope to make you as happy as I am in this moment."

Her smile grew, and her eyes slowly opened. "I cannot imagine being happier." She frowned and looked down. Her squeal of delight was instant as she fully woke. Reaching out, she stroked Sira's head. Lunara's joy made Salvarias lightheaded. His wife looked up at Saval and squealed again.

"They're beautiful!" she exclaimed.

Saval flapped his wings and leapt. He was too young to fly, but he managed his way down and immediately snuggled up to Lunara.

"I love them!" She laughed in delight and flew into Salvarias's arms. "Thank you!"

He buried his face in her hair, inhaling her scent and smiling. "You are welcome, my lady."

His smile faded when he sensed a corner of her mind shielded from him. It had not been there yesterday. Her walls were not nearly built as well as his, and no doubt he could knock it down with the tiniest of efforts, but he withdrew. Her mind was her own, and if she chose to hide certain thoughts, he would respect her privacy. Nevertheless, it wounded him.

13

Wilhelm shifted in his seat, cursing the carpenter that made such small chairs. The Knight Council had reluctantly gathered at the urgent behest of Edium, insisting they meet at the Knighthood's headquarters in Sundil. One of Mafarias's old portals was all that got Wilhelm and Salvarias to Sundil in time for Wilhelm's appointment. All that rushing seemed to be for no reason. He had sat outside a meeting room for near an hour, his girth spilling over the flimsy chair struggling to support his weight. Salvarias sat calmly; his hood pulled low, his whispered numbers and the clicking of the puzzle box the only things soothing Wilhelm's nerves.

Edium had no inkling what trials awaited Wilhelm. His father-in-law had mentioned in over the thousand years since the Firth brothers' disappearance, several had tried to lay claim to Firth birthright. Those men where never heard from again.

Wilhelm had politely declined Edium's offer to come along. Selfishly, Wilhelm wanted time alone with his brother, to embark on something together, free from the pressure of a group. To have an adventure, just the two of them. And though it had only been two days since his brother had married, he already saw a change in Salvarias. His brother was content. Wilhelm believed whole-heartedly that his brother would have been happy if not for the army occupying Windlous, becoming a God of Magic, and finding out he was the son of Veedran. Those truths weighed on Salvarias, dampening any joy he'd been blessed to find since his resurrection. Even so, contentment was more than Wilhelm could have hoped for at this point in their lives.

Shifting again in his seat, it protested loudly, and he feared he heard a crack. "This is ridiculous," Wilhelm growled. "I don't have all day."

"You must see it from the Council's point of view, Brother. They were commanded out of their beds by Lord Bellerum to yet again endure a poor soul claiming to be a Firth. For them, you are just another man trying to gain ownership over the knights. They do not know you are a true heir."

Wilhelm grunted. "Doesn't mean they couldn't offer us a nicer chair while we wait."

The double doors to the meeting room swung open, and a young knight motioned them in. His smirk vanished when Wilhelm rose to his full height and cast the cocky ass a scowl. He caught the puzzle box when Salvarias tossed it, shrunk it discreetly in his hands to the size of a blueberry, and dropped it in his shirt pocket

"They will see you now, gentleman," the man said. "However, the mage must wait outside."

Wilhelm strode up to the man and looked down at him. "You want to stop me from bringing him with me?"

The man shook his head.

"Step aside," Wilhelm growled.

The man dodged inside the room and out of the way.

The room was rectangular with a table stretching nearly its entire length. A fireplace warmed the stones, making the room too hot for Wilhelm's taste. Seated facing him were thirteen men, the majority old and tired looking. At the center, a sturdy old man rose, his brow heavy and his eyes small. Wrinkles and age spots covered his face and hands, but when he spoke, his voice was strong and commanding. "I'm Councilman Creed. State your name, boy."

"Wilhelm Laybryth."

"And what makes you think you're the descendent of a Firth?"

"My father told me I am."

Creed rolled his eyes, and a few others chuckled. "Just because daddy said so, doesn't mean you are."

Wilhelm held up his mark. He wasn't sure if Wilhelm Firth had one, but it didn't hurt to try. By the man's blank stare, it meant nothing. Biting back his annoyance, Wilhelm said, "Is there some test I need to complete? Some old man that would recognize a Firth?"

Creed's eyes narrowed. "You're certainly big enough to hold such ideas of grandeur. You a farmer's son?"

"No."

"What did your father do, boy?"

"It doesn't matter."

"You need a mage to protect you?"

"This is my brother."

"Ah, another laying claims to the Knighthood."

"No, he's not." Wilhelm's patience was at an end. Sitting in a damn chair for an hour, making his nerves build past control, only to walk in here and have them mock him. He was about to throw out a nasty remark when Salvarias's light hand rested on Wilhelm's arm.

"Patience, Brother. This is new to you, but redundant for them. They must ask these questions. They must be sure you are sincere."

Inhaling a calm breath, Wilhelm unclenched his fists. Ever since he'd beaten his brother, his temper threatened to unleash itself. Fighting was a stress reliever for Wilhelm, and he'd yet to have a reason to draw his swords, to unburden his pent-up rage and self-hatred.

Creed sat in his chair and leaned back casually. "I tell you now, boy, turn and leave. If you choose not to, I promise you will not walk out of here alive."

"I'm not leaving."

"So be it. Follow me."

Creed led him through a door in the back and down a long hallway, a guard of ten marching along behind them. With no windows, the only light came from the man's weakly lit torch. Eventually the hallway ended at a wide spiraling staircase, which the man took.

At the bottom was another hall, dark and guarded by four knights. When Wilhelm passed them, he heard a grunt and a thud from behind. Whirling around, his brother was on the ground, a knight standing over him holding a club.

"What in Nevlar's fury!" Wilhelm roared, reaching for his broadsword.

Cold metal pressed into his neck, and the knight in front leveled a sword at his chest. The man behind him snarled, "I warn you, boy, draw that sword and you'll find this knife in your jugular. We just knocked your brother unconscious. Nothing more."

Wilhelm released the hilt and raised his hands in surrender.

"Thirty-three men have laid claim to the Knighthood since I've been on the council, which has been forty years. All of them died, boy. All of them. I give you one last chance to walk back up those stairs and leave. If you fail the test, you will die. If you fail, I will kill your brother. What will it be, boy?"

"I am a Firth," Wilhelm growled. "I'll take your damn test. And you," he pointed at the man that had struck his brother. "When I'm done, I'll introduce you to my fist. No one hurts my brother."

The dagger left his throat. "The choice is yours. Let's go."

"I'm not leaving my brother."

"I swear on my honor and name, no harm will come to him unless you fail. If he is not laying claim, he cannot proceed. I swear he will be guarded here."

Wilhelm reluctantly nodded and followed Creed. If his brother woke and was threatened, no doubt Salvarias could protect himself. Wilhelm killing knights was no way to start his rule.

The hall ended at a double door, barred with a thick wooden beam that took three knights to lift. When the doors swung open, a cold breeze rushed from beyond. A single sputtering torch lit an empty room.

"Inside is a portal," the man said. "Go through it and, if you are a Firth, claim your birthright."

Mafarias's betrayal was always fresh in Wilhelm's mind, and he found himself untrusting of portals. "Why a portal? Who made it?"

Creed's eyes narrowed. "For a man with a mage for a brother, you seem untrusting of magic."

"I have a mage uncle who's betrayed me time and again. I'll not be a fool."

Creed chuckled and clapped Wilhelm on the back. "This was built over a thousand years ago by a servant to Travard, a friend of Nevlar himself. Unless your uncle is a thousand years old, this cannot be his work."

"I didn't know Travard had a mage in his company."

"Oh yes, a powerful one sent by Nevlar to watch after the Firth brothers. The god trusted his two sons to no other. The mage was rumored to stay with the Knighthood for some years after the Retribution, but soon the people learned mages were as much to blame as Veedran. They drove the old man out."

"Ignorance," Wilhelm muttered. "Mages fought beside Zerana."

"Fear is the worst sort of power, boy. It can convince a populace that bunnies evolved into flesh eating monsters."

"And what do you believe?"

Creed shrugged. "I believe everything and nothing. What I can tell you is the mage was trusted by Nevlar, and if Vuddruk were alive today, I would welcome him into the Knighthood once again."

Wilhelm raised an eyebrow. "Vuddruk built this?"

"You know the name?"

Wilhelm snatched up the torch and entered the room. The shimmering air was barely visible. As he walked through the portal, he said over his shoulder, "I know the god himself."

He wasn't sure what to expect on the other side, but a door wasn't it. It was barred just as the last. The stench of decay was heavy in the stone room, and the sputtering light of his torch was the only illumination. A grumble echoed in the room. Initially he thought it was his stomach, and while he was hungry, he doubted his stomach ever protested loud enough to vibrate the floor beneath his feet.

After depositing the torch in a holder, he spread his legs, shimmied his shoulder under the beam, and heaved. Sweat burst on his brow, and he felt the veins on his neck stand as he lifted. The wood groaned in protest, and once free of its iron holders, he dropped it left of the door. It thudded loudly.

Wincing, Wilhelm waited, but no noise came from beyond. Drawing his broadsword, he pressed his shoulder against the door and shoved.

It groaned and creaked and squeaked and wailed. Gritting his teeth, he boldly stepped into the room, crouching in his fighting stance. Bones were piled up along the walls, all human. One corpse was fresh, bloated and rotting. The room was long, and his torch did nothing to shine light into the opposite end. But he heard breathing.

"I'm Wilhelm Laybryth," he shouted. "And I've come to claim my place as Lord Knight."

A rumbling laugh echoed. It took a breath to realize it was in his head, not the room.

Yet another poor soul, the creature muttered, mirth draining from its deep voice. It sounded old, and when it spoke next, sadness weighed heavily on its words. *Oh Wilhelm, oh Travard, when will you free me from this prison? Why have you left me alone?*

"Who goes there?" Wilhelm called.

The voice sighed. *Well, I may yet have room for another meal. And this is a large one. Meaty indeed.*

"I'll not be eaten this day, beast. Give me what I came for, and I will be merciful and let you live."

A roar vibrated the room, sending dust drifting from the ceiling. The ground quaked with pounding footfalls. Barreling from the darkness came a grizzly bear larger than any Wilhelm had ever laid eyes on. He could have ridden the beast. Its canines were bigger than Wilhelm's hand, and its eyes too intelligent to be a normal bear.

Dodging barely in time, he fell hard to the creature's right. Scrambling to his feet, he held his sword ready.

The bear rounded on him, stance ready to pounce. *How is it you have heard my thoughts?*

"I don't know," Wilhelm responded.

The bear's eyes narrowed. *You look like my Wilhelm, but you are not he.*

"I'm a descendent of Wilhelm Firth."

The bear relaxed, cocking its head to look Wilhelm up and down. *I am inclined to believe you, boy. Only Wilhelm and Travard could speak to me. You are one of their sons?*

"I'm sorry to be the one to tell you, but you've been down here a thousand years. Wilhelm and Travard Firth are dead."

Curse that mage. He caged me here, said it was for my own safety while he went off to find my brothers. He never returned.

"Vuddruk lives. He's helped my brother and me on several occasions."

Of course he has. He is loyal to our bloodline. Loyal to Nevlar. The bear sniffed the air. *I sense my father's power in you. You are a son of Nevlar?*

"I'm ... I'm a son to Tedris Firth."

I see. You were born of a man and a woman?

"Yes."

Nevlar himself created my Wilhelm and Travard. They were good men. Worthy men. It leaned close, sniffing deeply. *Tell me, boy. Are you good? Are you worthy of my loyalty as they were?*

Wilhelm sheathed his sword and stood straight. "I try to be a good man. I intend to help Arden and kill Veedran. I intend to rule the Knighthood and carry it into a peaceful era."

Give me your blood, boy.

"Um." Wilhelm lightly rested his hand on his sword hilt. "I need my blood to survive."

The bear rolled its eyes. *Not a clever one, are you? Cut yourself. I only need a drop.*

Wilhelm drew his mother's dagger, nicked his hand, and held it aloft. The bear leaned forward and licked Wilhelm's hand. A tingle spread across his palm, and he wiped it on his trews.

You have suffered much in your short lifetime. Your pain saddens me. Such responsibilities. Such a weight. It gently pressed its forehead to

Wilhelm's chest. *You are worthy of me, boy, of my loyalty and the strength I can give you.*

A cooling ripple went through Wilhelm's body, easing the sweat pouring from his forehead, ridding himself of a feverish feeling in his bones he never noticed before. All his pain felt bearable, easily carried.

Your road both ahead and behind is paved by sorrow. For all your days, Sadness will shadow you. But I will help you. If need be, I will even carry you through it.

Wilhelm blinked back his tears. "My brother?"

I will not know until I meet him.

"You'll not tell him anything about his future until you've discussed it with me. His burdens are tenfold of mine. I'd not trouble him more than is needed."

You are as protective as Wilhelm was of Travard, though his brother didn't need it. Travard was stronger than Wilhelm ever gave him credit. I am curious if I will find the same when I gaze upon your brother.

"My brother is the strongest man to have ever walked Arden."

I will be the judge, boy. Take me from this place.

"No killing anyone."

The bear chuckled. *I only killed those claiming to be a Firth. Coming in here with swords and bows, trying to kill me. They were warned, and their arrogance led them to my belly.*

It took effort on the bear's part to fit through the door as it complained of how fattening people were to eat. When it dumped on the other side of the portal, it inhaled deeply.

I was growing weary of the stench of death. Here I smell life.

On the other side of the door, the men's eyes widened as Wilhelm stepped into the room, the bear looming behind him.

Creed sucked in a breath. "Gods, could it be?" He swallowed and blinked a few times before turning to his men. "Attention!" The knights snapped straight and banged a fist to their chest.

Salvarias stood among them, his gaze fixed on the bear, his eyes growing wide.

You are a mage? How unexpected.

Salvarias bowed. *It is an honor to meet you, Vegos.*

You know me?

"Uh, how can I hear this?" Wilhelm asked.

Because your brother is a powerful being, boy. And educated. Very educated. Give me your blood, mage.

"Just a nick," Wilhelm said.

Salvarias drew his dagger, cut his hand, and offered it to the bear.

Vegos licked it and closed his eyes. A breath passed before the bear said, *Your brother cannot hear me, boy, but I see what you mean. You are stalked by Sadness; he is stalked by Terror. Terror in His most brutal form. Your brother's weight could not be carried by a man. Any mortal enduring what he has endured would have died from a broken soul years ago. What stands before us is a god. A god who has yet to learn of himself and is too terrified to think he could be such a wonderful creation.*

The bear's golden gaze seemed to reassess Wilhelm. *My dearest boy, you have single handedly saved a god. A god! You stand on the knife's edge with him, constantly saving him from falling into a bottomless pit of despair. You hide him from Terror's seeking gaze when he needs it most. He has claimed you, and when a god lays claim on a soul, there is no end to what the pair can achieve.* The bear blinked a few times. *Now I see why your heart is so full of love and why you have come from Sadness's grip time and again. To be owned by a god ... how wonderful it must feel.*

"I don't understand," Wilhelm muttered.

You two are entwined for eternity; your soul will forever be his, and his forever yours—despite the efforts of the girl. No force in all the worlds will ever sever his hold on you. No force will ever steal him from you forever. Take heart in this, boy, because Salvarias's future is bleak indeed. Death will claim his mortal body when he is young, but do not let that break you. Remember, in time, he will return to you. Always will he return to you.

Vegos nuzzled them both, and once again Wilhelm's heart lightened. Salvarias even inhaled deeply.

Thank you, Salvarias said. *I am honored to be accepted by you.*

You have Nevlar's power flowing through you, Salvarias, just as your brother does.

His brother stiffened. "How? I do not understand."

Vegos rumbled a soft chuckle that shook Wilhelm's chest. *All in due time, boy. All in due time.*

Wilhelm clapped his brother on the back and then turned to the room. "Did I pass?"

Creed smiled slightly before clearing his throat and snapping to attention. "Yes, my Lord Knight. I am at your service."

"This is my brother, and he has also been accepted by Vegos. He is a Lord Knight as much as me. We will guide the Knighthood together."

"A mage?" Creed said tersely. "Is that wise?"

"Yes," Wilhelm said. "It's time Arden learns to accept magic."

The man's jaw rippled, but he bowed his head. "As you command. We will set up a room for you both, and tomorrow we will perform the ceremony."

"After that, it's right down to business. We plan to take back Windlous and kill Veedran before summer's end." Wilhelm winked at his little brother when the cacophony of alarmed questions rang in the room. He took advantage of the confusion and found the man who'd hit his brother. The knight looked at him with grim acceptance. Winking at him, Wilhelm leveled the man. The arguing stopped, and Wilhelm turned to them. "No one touches my brother. The next man who's stupid enough to do so will find my sword in his throat."

WILHELM SAT in his chair watching his brother toss restlessly in his sleep. Soft, urgent words tumbled from Salvarias's lips, all some form of pleading, begging whatever he endured to stop. So much pain in his tone, so much loneliness.

It is never easy to watch a loved one suffer, Vegos said.

Wilhelm pulled his gaze from his brother and regarded the bear. Creed had given them the only room big enough to fit the three of them, and Vegos took up nearly half the space. The bear swallowed the remnants of the salmon, pin bones and all, before setting a serious gaze on Wilhelm.

"Three fish in one hour," Wilhelm noted. "Hungry?"

I've only fed on human for Nevlar knows how long. And every day I was locked in that damn room I thought of salmon. I applaud your planning, by the way. For one so young, your mind is sharp. Much as your ancestors.

Shrugging, Wilhelm said, "I don't have a lot of faith in it. Luck has not been kind to us."

Luck ... that is something you make for yourself. Besides, I think you boys have been plenty lucky. You've escaped situations few would.

"Always at a great cost." Wilhelm didn't have to think hard to recall the times his brother had pushed his magic to save them, the times blood leaked from his mouth and he nearly died.

Vegos nodded and cast a sympathetic gaze. *As I said, it is not easy to watch loved ones suffer. It is why, I assume, you never tried to save your brother when he perished.*

Wilhelm stiffened, his heart stuttering, wincing at the tearing pain in his soul. "I can't heal my brother. His wounds were fatal. There was nothing I could have done."

True, your powers cannot help his physical body. Yet, you did not try. You did not pray as you used to when he was hurt. Remember, I have access to your memories, Wilhelm. You did nothing but weep over his body. Tell me why.

"You have all these insights. You tell me."

Shame covers whatever your reasoning might have been.

"I'm a crap excuse for a brother," Wilhelm growled.

Many things you are, but never that. Beneath guilt lies a virtuous reason.

Wilhelm blinked back his building tears. That horrible night was so clear in his mind: his brother's fading smile; the rare peace Wilhelm saw in his brother's eyes; the odd joy that hung in the air. Salvarias had been happy in his last breaths, happy and at peace. The only things Wilhelm could have hoped for. He remembered the prayer that had been on his lips, remembered his hand twitching to grab his brother's mark. He remembered the unbearable pain when he chose to remain quiet, when he clamped his hand into a fist. He remembered too well the hole carved out of his heart when he let his treasure die.

I see, Vegos said, voice heavy and sad. *You gave him what he had begged you for for years. Peace. He was tired of fighting and being hunted. For years he had pleaded you to let him go, and finally you listened. You let him slip into the beyond, knowing you would leave behind your wife and all you loved. Knowing you would die with him.*

"I wonder sometimes if he hates me for what I did," Wilhelm said thickly. "I wonder if he knows I let him die."

I say again, you could not have saved him. But yes, he does know of your sacrifice. I have seen his memories of that night, and I feel his sorrow and gratitude. He weeps not for himself and his death, but for what he knew you gave up for him. Your true heart will never be hidden from Salvarias. He sees into you deeper than you see into yourself. Take comfort in this, boy. Release your guilt and shame, because it weighs on your brother as heavily as it does on your heart.

Wilhelm stared at his hands, remembering them covered in his brother's blood, remembering how cold his brother's skin had felt.

"Vegos is right, Brother."

Wilhelm looked over to see Salvarias sitting up in bed.

"If only you forgave yourself as easily as you forgive me," Salvarias said. "If I could, I would shoulder your pain, Brother. All you have suffered has been because I was selfish."

"It's not your fault, Salv. We've done the best we could. We did what we thought was right. It's all we could ever do. Just try."

"Perhaps you should be telling this to yourself," Salvarias said, a small smile forming. "My guilt will only leave with yours."

Wilhelm shrugged and turned his gaze back to his hands. "I'll work on it, Salv."

Warmth spread through Wilhelm's chest, and the world around him brightened. For all his life, he had never realized he had felt this every time his brother focused on him, every time Salvarias conveyed his love by mere thought and uttered the word 'brother'. Life never seemed so hopeless when that warmth filled his heart.

Inhaling a deep breath and closing his eyes, he swam in that bottomless lake. It cleansed him of his sorrow over that fateful night, ridding the boulder of shame from his heart as easily as brushing away a pebble. When he opened his eyes, he felt stronger, renewed. The world did not seem so dim.

Vegos growled out a chuckle. *He worships you, Wilhelm.*

Wilhelm had no idea what he had done to deserve such devotion, but he didn't let his mind dwell on it. The brothers were back, together, and they'd kill anything that needed killing. He grinned at his brother, and when his brother grinned back, Wilhelm knew, eventually, everything would be all right.

14

SPRING 1022 A.R

Wilhelm looked over the docks, leaning his weight comfortably against Vegos as he watched Humar's ship navigate Falar's port. Salvarias stood by his side, his brother's whispered numbers spilling out in a soothing cadence as always. Edium paced behind Wilhelm, muttering about the smell. Indeed, summer had made an early showing, and the stench of warm fish was potent. Vegos had taken his fill of a pile of spoiled fish that had been tossed aside.

People walking by cast wide glances at Vegos, but none fled or screamed out or caused panic. Vegos had assured Wilhelm that by desire alone the bear could ease the fears of people, making him easily accepted. Vegos had proven himself right time and again.

Okulu swaggered up and took his spot beside Salvarias.

"Report," Wilhelm said.

Okulu gave him a sour look. "Nothing's changed since yesterday, Lord Knight."

Wilhelm grimaced. He didn't care for the title of Lord Knight Wilhelm, but the Council had insisted out of tradition and respect. None of his friends called him that aside from Okulu who seemed to take pleasure in irritating Wilhelm.

"Okulu is coming along nicely," Salvarias provided. Wilhelm caught the scolding look his brother shot at Okulu. "Though I must say he has not taken to his new title well."

"I'm only doing this to keep an eye on you," Okulu muttered to Salvarias.

"Regardless," Salvarias continued smoothly, "our training is far ahead of schedule. However, we have an incredibly long way to go before I would even contemplate working together in a battle. Learning the movements of fifty men is a challenge."

Wilhelm nodded approvingly. "And how are the men accepting the mages?"

Okulu grinned. "After seeing what Salvarias here can do, they are more than willing to die to protect him because it's obvious he's going to be saving their asses when it comes time to battle. Cessia and Kisra have earned their respect as well."

As they should, Vegos said. *Your brother's power is stunning.*

Wilhelm exhaled another piece of his worry. The Vipers were an elite fifty-man squad of the highest skilled knights led by Okulu—who'd reacquired his Knighthood title to stay close to Wilhelm's brother. Salvarias and Kisra—each knighted into service—were integrated into the group, making it a lethal force. To be honest with himself, Wilhelm did so to ensure his brother's safety on the battle-field. If Salvarias guessed as much, he never said.

"My training effort is also going well," Salvarias supplied.

Ten other mages had joined the Knighthood. Wilhelm had watched them for days and swelled with pride at how far they had come under Salvarias's tutelage. Matter of fact, the entire Knighthood had fallen in line with his vision faster than he anticipated.

Graciously, Edium had gifted Lord Gunder's estate to the Knight-hood as their headquarters. It kept the brothers close to the Bellerum family, and Salvarias under Edium's watchful eye. Not to mention it gave Wilhelm a chance to be close to his son.

Investing funds from the inheritance Durak had left him, Wilhelm had bought properties in the major cities and staffed it full of knights, there to aid the local guards and keep the cities safe. The fee he had charged each city was paid easily with a slight tax to the public. They were all too eager to pay after the creatures of Veedran's army had tormented them for so many years.

"Dame Mira is on her way to Sundil," Salvarias continued. "Our own portal should be active within a week, and then she will close the one Mafarias made."

Over the past month, Salvarias had sent Dame Mira—a mage he trusted—to each city to open up a portal so Wilhelm could visit any time he needed. It would help keep the Knighthood functioning to his standards, at least in Dalnar.

"And Sir Blain and Sir Rhyn?" Wilhelm asked.

"Preparing to return with Humar," Salvarias said. "Once in Loutsil, Sir Rhyn will begin to purchase properties, and Sir Blain will set up the portals."

"And Sir Rhyn is respectful of mages?" Wilhelm asked Okulu.

"We've gone over this," Okulu complained. "And nothing has changed since the last time I told you. Yes, Rhyn will protect Blain with his life and vice-versa."

"And Cessia's efforts?"

Okulu shook his head. "Going poorly. I don't see the Knighthood managing to persuade Watythms to set up a navy branch. Possibly she might secure a few ships, but not enough for any kind of force. More likely they'd just be ferrying our troops."

Wilhelm nodded. He'd not expected her to succeed, but it was worth a try.

"She's offered to teach a few savvy Erthlas how to properly construct ships," Okulu offered. "Perhaps under her guidance, we could build up our own fleet. She could train them to sail as well."

"A wise plan," Salvarias said.

Varila sauntered up. "Damn it's hot."

Wilhelm grunted an agreement. He still hadn't looked at her, despite Salvarias and Vegos's encouragement.

Okulu bowed. "Dame Varila."

She grinned at him. She did not seem to tire of her knighthood being referred to whenever she was addressed.

"Report, please," Wilhelm said, keeping his gaze on Humar's ship as it sidled up the dock.

"Training is going well," she said. "Inventory is starting to poor in from our smithies in Cattlar. I expect to have at least enough to outfit everyone. By end of year, you'll have the best armory in the history of Arden. I've also managed to employ three prized Cavrul smiths. I'll send one to each continent, and they'll have their choice of employees. Soon, under their instruction, I'll have a trained smith at every station."

Wilhelm nodded his approval. He'd appointed Varila Master of Arms, where she managed not only outfitting the knights with the best weapons available, but also trained them on how to use them. Secretly he enjoyed watching men sneer at her and belittle her behind her back, only to have her beat them down in a fight. If a man couldn't handle a woman in the Knighthood, Wilhelm didn't want them. Varila was perfect for the role, and from what Salvarias had told him, she relished it. Not only was she an excellent trainer, but her ability to maintain a wide range of exceptional weaponry and handle the cash flow of outfitting their numbers made her invaluable. To top it off, she was an inspiration for women and already weakening archaic traditions. Soon there would be an uprising as women fought for equality, and the Knighthood would support them every step of the way.

A ramp lowered from the king's ship, and Humar walked down before it'd been secured. Wilhelm never remembered his friend looking so haggard, but then again, he didn't remember much over the last three years. Humar's normally bright azure eyes were dull with fatigue. Gray streaked through his mousy hair and trimmed beard. He'd given up his knighthood shortly after Salvarias's death so he could focus on his duties as king and therefore had given up his armor. The man's new tunic and trews fit him loosely. The king had lost weight. He walked heavier, as if the weight of the world rested on his shoulders. Whatever burdens he felt did not touch his smile when he looked at Salvarias. It was warm as the sun, and his eyes sparkled with a joy Wilhelm hadn't seen in them for some time.

"Salvarias," Humar said. "By the gods, it's good to see you alive, boy."

Salvarias bowed and gifted Humar a small smile. "My king."

"And married?" Humar laughed. "I can't tell you how much that pleases me."

"I find myself ... remarkably happy," Salvarias said.

Humar looked Wilhelm up and down. "Lord Knight." He tilted his head in respect. "I feel the Knighthood is finally in good hands. I've learned of some of the changes you've made, and I must say I highly approve."

Wilhelm offered his hand, and Humar shook it with a growing smile. "Thanks, Humar. I learned from the best."

The king laughed again and pulled Wilhelm into an embrace. "You bring me happiness, Wilhelm, in a time when I sorely need it."

After a clap on the back, Humar made his greetings to the others, taking extra time to marvel over Vegos's size. Zehnia and what Wilhelm assumed were Humar's children joined them. The little ones were introduced as Prince Dredin and Princess Belany. The children rushed into Varila's arms, calling her aunt, and telling her how much they had missed her. Wilhelm clenched his jaw and stepped clear of the reunion. Three years had been lived without him; three years he had abandoned all he loved.

When Zehnia moved to Salvarias's side, it came back to Wilhelm that his brother had murdered the queen's father. He tensed, hand drifting to the hilt of his sword.

"I am happy you are well," she said, though her voice was a tinge cold.

Salvarias bowed. "My queen."

"You've yet to ask my forgiveness for killing my father."

"With respect, I do not seek it. If given the chance, I would do the same. My wife was tortured by his order."

Zehnia studied him a moment before nodding. "I see. Despite my understanding of why you did it, I can never forgive you. That does not mean we cannot respect one another and work together to help my husband and Arden."

"I am pleased to hear so, my queen."

She guided him a little ways from the group, and Wilhelm kept himself close enough to hear.

"My husband does not sleep," she said. "Nightmares own his dreams. Defending and securing Loutsil consumes his days. Thwarting assassination attempts and poisonings from the nobles has taken a toll on his body. I fear for his life."

Salvarias nodded. "I noticed immediately. I will blend some herbs to aid his sleep, and there are a few potions that will save him from nearly any poison. Those I will give to you."

Relief eased hard lines around her mouth, and she smiled. "You have my thanks. To see him alive again would make me very happy."

Once the reunion died down, Wilhelm led the way back to the sprawling estate he had purchased for the Knighthood. The lower floor had been converted to meeting rooms on one side, and the other was consumed by a kitchen and mess hall. The upper floors had been renovated into barracks.

Any knight they passed banged a fist to their chest in salute, and then bowed to Humar. Their first loyalty would always be to the Knighthood, and Wilhelm had been quick to separate it from the king and any allegiance to a specific continent. He wanted them independent of rule and to have their own honor and missions guide their decisions. Needless to say, their ranks had been thinned, but he had every intention of rebuilding it with the most honorable of men and women. Okulu had told him he'd aimed too high, but Salvarias had merely tilted his head, a sign louder than words. His brother's opinion was the only one that mattered, which was why he'd given the title of Lord Knight to Salvarias as well. There would never be a time when Salvarias did not stand by his side as an equal.

Wilhelm chose the largest meeting room with a map of each continent taking up one wall, and on the opposite hung the command tree Wilhelm was developing. A window let in the afternoon sun, heating the room so sweat burst on his brow when he stepped inside, despite Brice having opened the window to let in a meager breeze.

"Damn hot," Varila muttered again, lifting her braid from her neck. "Cursed city."

Wilhelm tore his gaze from a trickle of sweat hitching its way down her neck.

"Idolar!" Humar exclaimed, and clasped hands with the knight. "Good to see you."

"You as well," Idolar said.

Wilhelm stood at the table, which took up the entire room, leaving only enough space for chairs, and grunted his approval at the map lying in its center. He'd hired a talented cartographer to make a model of Arden, including raised mountains, blue paint for rivers and lakes, and even mini cities.

The land looks so different now, Vegos said, voice heavy with sadness. *Nevlar's fury was great indeed.*

"Impressive," Humar said. "This will definitely help." Snatching up a few red blocks of wood, he started positioning them across Windlous.

"How accurate are your reports?" Wilhelm asked.

"I've had my spies there for two years," Humar responded. "It's accurate. Our only problem is every three months or so Veedran's army will add troops to one city, strengthening it while weakening another. It's made it impossible to invade. Even when we begin to muster our forces, there's suddenly a fleet of enemy ships sailing for Loutsil or Dalnar's boarders. Of course we hold and reinforce our ports, but nothing's come of these sightings yet."

"Distractions," Wilhelm muttered.

"Possibly, but Veedran's keeping his movements unpredictable enough we can't chance it."

Wilhelm nodded. "Half your army should stay in Loutsil as Edium's should stay in Dalnar. I'll take the Vipers and fifty other knights here," he said, motioning to a beach near a day's ride from Bellend. "It'll be the safest place. I'll send the remaining two hundred and fifty knights and the other half of your army around to here." He pointed at Bren. "The main force will hold their attention while the rest of us sweep across Windlous and recapture it one town at a time. We'll herd Veedran to Bren and take him between our forces."

"A sound plan if you had more men. By the time you push his army into one mass, his numbers will be in the thousands."

"Mages can even the playing field," Salvarias said.

Humar shook his head. "No, we've reports he has creatures in his service that have magic themselves. It's how they captured Windlous so effortlessly."

"Any word from Neithelas?" Wilhelm asked.

"No, not for weeks," Humar said.

"There were eggs in the swamp fortress," Salvarias offered. "I did feel magic within, but it was weak. With a few spells, we can eliminate them."

"When you take Bren," Wilhelm continued, "you'll be tasked with building up a bank around the city." He clapped Salvarias's shoulder. "My little brother here plans on creating a storm big enough to flood out the entire area. It'll wash away half of Veedran's army."

Humar raised an eyebrow. "You can conjure a storm?"

"Yes, however I cannot maintain it nor control it once I do. It will be up to you to protect Bren from flooding."

"I'll have enough men if all goes well," Humar said, more to himself. "When we free the citizens they can help."

"The mages I will send with you will have specific spells to assist," Salvarias said. "I have also been concocting a protection spell that uses a component. I am close to mastering it, which will be used to strengthen the wall around the city, which will ensure it does not flood."

Humar leaned back. "I applaud your planning, Wilhelm. I never knew mages could sway the outcome of a battle so unequally sided. Even so, with a mere one hundred men, taking the larger cities will be near impossible."

Wilhelm grinned. "You haven't seen the Vipers in action. We'll take them, rest assured."

"And after we take Windlous, what then?"

"We find Veedran," Wilhelm said. "And we cut out his heart and set it aflame."

"You do realize he has an entire army we've yet to discover. His numbers were near twenty thousand, and I can account for barely half of that force."

"We hope to take prisoners," Brice said. "Perhaps one will tell us where the army is and where Veedran is hiding."

"Zerana's Armies of Light failed to defeat him," Humar said in an apologetic tone. "I have faith we can save Windlous, but Veedran ... If the goddess of light could not kill him, what makes you think we can?"

"He is weak," Salvarias said. "I felt it when I met him. I doubt his power is half of what it once was. I think that is why he is after the stone. It can grant him the power he lost."

Your brother lacks confidence, Wilhelm, Vegos said. *Without it, your fight will be difficult. With it, he could annihilate the armies housed in the cities with a simple thought. I will think on a way to build his confidence. I fear at this point, he is held too tightly by Terror. Convincing him of what he is will take time and patience.*

"Let's focus on one thing at a time," Idolar said. "We take Windlous, gain information, and then set about a new action."

"How long do you need?" Wilhelm asked Humar.

"I can be ready in two months, if I hurry."

Wilhelm stood straight. "Then I suggest you hurry."

"Yes, of course," Humar said. "But we have some business to take care of before I leave." His eyes hardened. "Now where are you holding your grandfather?"

HUMAR FOLLOWED the brothers down the narrow winding staircase and let his mind drift. All those years ago after Durak's death, Humar had been so angry and confused. He thought he hated Salvarias, but upon seeing the boy alive, joy was all that filled his heart, and he followed it instead of his brain. Apparently with his acceptance of

Salvarias, Wilhelm had decided Humar worthy of trust and friendship again, and that had only given Humar more peace and comfort.

At the bottom of the stairs facing a narrow hallway of cells, Salvarias paused, his shaking hand reaching to the back of his head, the shadows hiding whatever expression might have revealed his thoughts.

"It's all right, Salv," Wilhelm said soothingly. "I'm here."

Salvarias seemed to shrink in upon himself, and when they started walking, the boy was so close to Wilhelm he stepped on the back of his brother's heels. It reminded Humar of the boys' youth when Salvarias had been a scared child, never venturing far from his brother. The imaginings of what must be playing through Salvarias's mind tightened Humar's chest. Knowledge was power and so often pain. For years Humar had trusted Mafarias, and come to find out, the bastard had stood by while his daughter had beaten a child.

Quick steps behind them made Humar glance over his shoulder. It was Edium. Humar had no illusions the man wanted anything other than Mafarias's head on a stake. Surprising himself, Humar did not object to Edium's presence. The two fell in line, and in one glance Humar realized he shared Edium's thoughts. The lord smiled wickedly. If there was one soul in all of Arden that scared Humar, it was Edium. Any crossing the man's family found horrendous ends. Humar had learned the fate of Varila's parents and the man who'd raped her when she was sixteen. He shivered.

A guard quickly unlocked the cell Wilhelm approached, and when the door swung open, the boy never paused. He ducked inside, hand on the hilt of this sword. Salvarias did pause, but soon stepped inside, standing half behind his brother. Wilhelm loomed tall, eyes dark and dangerous. By contrast, Salvarias seemed to shrink, folding in upon himself, head lowered to stare at the floor—the submissive child he had once been.

When Humar and Edium were inside, the guard locked them in the cell. Overall, it was surprisingly clean. The mage had a mattress covered in fresh linens, a cleaned chamber pot, and the walls themselves looked to have been recently scrubbed.

Wilhelm scowled at the room. "I'll have to see to the conditions of your cell. I never planned for you to be so comfortable."

Mafarias looked tired and sad. He sat on his bed, back against the wall, feet resting on the edge, his arms hanging on his knees. Dark circles ringed his eyes, and he had a look of defeat Humar had never seen on the man before.

"At least I have one grandson that treats me like family," Mafarias said.

Wilhelm glanced at Salvarias who somehow managed to make himself seem smaller.

"My brother has always been the kind one," Wilhelm said. "It was his idea we talk to you. Ever since Salv was taken to Zeeas, we've suspected a traitor. Was it you?"

"Yes," Mafarias said.

Wilhelm rocked back a bit, an expression of hurt fleeting over his features before they set to stone. "Talk."

"And what would you like me to say?" Mafarias said mildly. "I've been working for Veedran since before you were born. He took Ashra's mother and used my love for her to make me do things. Terrible things. And I'd do them all again for her."

"Our grandmother is alive?"

Mafarias shrugged. "She was the last time I talked to Veedran. You have to understand, I didn't know it was the dark god himself."

Edium snorted. "And if you had?"

Mafarias looked about ready to say the right thing, but instead he slumped. "Of course you're right. For Jepine I would do anything."

"What were your instructions?" Humar asked.

"To watch over the boy. Veedran wasn't ready to overthrow Arden yet. When it was clear Wilhelm had his power, Veedran's focus shifted from Salvarias. He wanted me to watch the boy, do what I could to tempt him toward darkness. The goal was to grow Salvarias's power enough so he could annihilate Arden, which is why Dethal was sent."

"You left us," Wilhelm said hoarsely. "They were murdered and you left us."

"No. No, you don't understand. I told the men there was buried money in the woods. I knew if they saw a mage, they would kill her and therefore end Salvarias's torment. I didn't think they would hurt children or Tobin. You must believe me. When I found out what they had done, I secretly ended Humar's contract in Sundil. I knew he would return to Tobin, and I knew the two of you would cross paths and that he would care for you."

"So you knew all along Tobin was my brother?" Humar asked. "Your surprise after Salvarias was taken was a show?"

"Yes. I had to be careful to keep you all in the dark."

"And the slave mines?" Humar asked.

"I couldn't help. Veedran had me creating portals all over Arden so the army could travel faster. When the boy was found, I'd hoped they would send me back to you, but they sent Dethal instead."

Humar shook his head. "When I sent for you after the boy was taken, you took your time."

"I had to. Veedran could never know I was helping you. I tried to find a way to rescue Salvarias myself, but Veedran kept me occupied."

"You were never looking for him," Wilhelm said.

"No. I knew where your brother was, and I sent you far from him for your own safety. But then you found me in the mountains. I was creating portals at the time. I was told to send you to the farm. Sansis had men going there to capture you. I had no choice."

"You told them where we were after we rescued Salv," Wilhelm said. "That's how they found us so quickly at Varila's estate."

Mafarias nodded. "Following that, they didn't want me around you. They feared you would discover my betrayal, and they would lose me as your trusted uncle. I did my best, boys. I truly tried to help while keeping Veedran's trust. If he suspects me, he'll hurt your grandmother."

"What are Veedran's plans?" Edium asked.

"I don't know. Ever since Salvarias's death, I am given few orders, and none of them have shown me their plan."

"It was you who stole Salvarias from his tomb, not Vuddruk," Humar realized aloud.

"Yes. It took me three years to burrow under the city and up into his tomb. Devoar was adamant we not draw attention to our plan. He wanted the stone." Mafarias looked at Salvarias. "But you've done something to it, haven't you boy?"

Salvarias remained quiet.

Mafarias nodded. "You've no reason to trust me. I know." He leaned forward, his eyes shimmering with a swell of tears. "You have to understand, boy. Your mother's mind was fragile from her power. She saw within you Veedran's touch. She didn't understand and it made her ... mad with fear. When she started ..." He glanced at Wilhelm then back to Salvarias. "When she started, I stayed in the room to make sure she didn't kill you. When the storms came, Veedran knew what was happening, and I couldn't stop it or else he would suspect me. You understand, don't you, boy? You can forgive me, can't you?"

Salvarias did not speak, but his breathing turned harsh and irregular. He leaned closer to Wilhelm.

"You can rot in Oblivion for all I care," Wilhelm growled. "You'll never see the light of day again."

Salvarias rested a shaking hand on Wilhelm's arm and said, "We could use his help. He is a God of Magic. His spells are as powerful as mine."

"You want me to free him?" Wilhelm said exasperated.

"Keep him in chains if you must, but we need all the help we can find to defeat Veedran's armies."

"He'll betray us again," Wilhelm said. "We can't trust him."

"No, I won't," Mafarias said. "You understand my predicament now. Keep me in chains, let a creature escape and pass word to Veedran. The dark god will know I am a prisoner and being forced to help you. He'll have no reason to harm your grandmother. When finally we find him, we can kill him and free Jepine. Don't you see? I can help you. Together we can beat him."

Wilhelm's jaw tightened. His gaze turned to Edium. The lord shook his head. Wilhelm looked to Humar.

Instincts told Humar to leave Mafarias behind, yet his mind whirled with all the mage could do for them. He'd seen Mafarias's spells and how powerful of a god he was. To defeat Veedran, they needed every advantage. Slowly, he nodded.

Wilhelm closed his eyes, took in a slow breath, and then turned to his brother. He bent slightly and whispered, "I'll kill him, Salv. We don't need him. Whatever you want me to do, I'll do it."

Salvarias's fists clenched, his knuckles whitening. He stood that way for a long moment before he whispered in a trembling voice, "We need his help, Brother."

Uncertainty warred across Wilhelm's expression before finally melting into defeat. He stood tall and faced Mafarias. "All right. You'll help us take back Windlous. You'll be shackled at all times. I'll leave instruction with the guards that if you try anything, they're to kill you."

Mafarias nodded. "Of course. I would expect nothing less."

Wilhelm ground his teeth, wrapped an arm around Salvarias's shoulders, and led his brother from the room. The mage couldn't get out quick enough.

Edium spat to the side. "You're a worthless piece of horse crap."

Mafarias smirked. "The boys trust me, Edium. Wilhelm sided with me, not you."

Edium's dagger whipped out so fast Humar didn't even realize it until the lord had planted it into Mafarias's chest.

"I won't kill you right now," Edium growled. "But if you lay a finger on my sons, I swear to all the gods that Salvarias's pleas won't save you. I'll chop off your head, shove it in my chamber pot, and piss on your face every day." He yanked the dagger from Mafarias and stormed out.

Mafarias sagged against the wall, pressing a hand over the wound. It didn't bleed enough, and Humar understood Mafarias's godhood was no different than Crutar, and therefore the means to kill him would be the same.

"You hate me," Mafarias said through clenched teeth. "I love her though. And all the hate in all the worlds would never make me regret what I've done for her."

Humar regarded his once friend. "No. You're not worth my energy. I care nothing for you. Nothing at all."

Mafarias blinked at him, pain filling his eyes. And that was how you hurt a god.

～

NEITHELAS SAT in his throne room, the trees singing to him in an effort to ease the agony in his heart. Three years had done nothing to dim the pain of her second rejection. He had been certain that with Salvarias's death, Lunara would love him. He was a king, after all. He was handsome and good. Yet still she denied him.

Now, the creature before him brought news of Salvarias's rebirth. Once again darkness threatened Arden, and once again he would watch Lunara fall prey to the man's evil.

"We can end him once and for all," the creature said.

It was one of the Four, Neithelas was sure of it. Devoar, he guessed based on the molten armor and distant screams coming from the depths of the creature.

Neithelas pondered at the creature's ease in which it had gained entry to his home. The trees were frightened of it, but had never sent warning. Neithelas should have had the sense to be scared, but he wasn't. Deep emotion was no longer his. Not for a man with a broken heart.

"You cannot be entertaining this beast's proposal," his wife hissed.

He glanced over at her. He'd searched high and low for a Winsire woman who resembled Lunara. What he found only left him wanting his love more. His wife's raven hair was not as soft, her lips not as full, eyes not as alive, and her skin not as milky. What was the same was the lack of love in her gaze. Her family had urged her to accept the king's hand, to be a queen. He doubted, if given the chance, Jenthia would do so again.

Turning back to Devoar, Neithelas said, "You can end this darkness? Bring Arden into the light once more?"

"I can," it said. "A brief period of hardship will befall this world, but I will keep it from your home. The Winsires will remain protected. Soon the shadow will lift from Arden, and this world will thrive in peace."

"In exchange?"

The creature shrugged. "Simple. Keep the Winsires protected here. Do not respond to Humar's calling."

"I've already sent word that I would aid him."

"And I've intercepted it. If you deny me, I will gladly relay the message to King Lilkous and ravage your home. Accept, and I will burn the message and leave you in peace."

"You think Winsires would side with such a beast?" Jenthia snarled. "You come into our home, spouting your lies, and you think we're fool enough to believe it!"

"You are a fool not to," Devoar snapped. "Your husband sees truths, Queen. He has his eyes open to the world."

"You want nothing else from us?" Neithelas asked.

"One thing, though I would speak to you privately, King Neithelas."

Neithelas rubbed his cheek, contemplating his options. "Leave me, wife."

A hand rested on his. "Certainly you cannot think this best," Jenthia whispered.

"I said leave," he growled.

His wife rose, curtsied to him, and glided from the room.

Devoar tilted its head. "Rumors are you burned all of the thryn trees. Is that true?"

Neithelas frowned. "What would you do with the oil?"

"I would kill him."

Neithelas regarded the creature. "On one condition."

"Yes?"

"Include the Bellerums. I want them as protected as my people. No harm can come to any within the family, including Wilhelm."

Devoar bowed. "Consider it done, King."

"Then we have an accord."

"I feel it my duty to tell you he married her. Even now I feel her soul darkening with his evil."

Neithelas never thought his heart could break anymore, but it did.

Devoar cooed in sympathy. "Rest in knowing it will be you who saves her."

After Devoar received what it needed, the creature left as quietly as it had come. Neithelas took to his room and drank himself full. When his mind buzzed with numb detachment, he gathered up a fresh bottle of wine and staggered to his son's room. Paithone slept soundly, his black hair that of his mother's. Behind closed eyes was the sole trait taken after Neithelas. Violet eyes. Nothing else about his son reminded him of himself.

Even so, Neithelas smiled. He'd saved his people this night. He'd saved a son he resented for not being born from the womb of the woman he loved. But most of all, he had saved *her*. She might never discover it was he, but he knew, and that was all that mattered.

When his bottle was empty, he stumbled from his son's room and into one down the hall. He did not knock before stepping inside. Jenthia was brushing her hair, a thin white nightdress hugging her curves.

Neithelas had only visited her bed once so he could have an heir. Now he visited her out of despair, out of hate, and out of carnal want.

She rose from her chair and silently slipped free of her clothes. Untying his trews, he lurched over to her, spun her around, and bent her over the table so he would not have to look upon her. Ignoring her soft sobs, he took her with urgent lust, staring at her black hair and imagining it was Lunara bent before him, urging him on, moaning her approval.

When he climaxed, he called out her name.

15

Wilhelm leaned on the ship's railing beside his brother, both studying the beach coming into view.

Salvarias waved an annoyed hand at it. "Have our lives been so dangerous that such a tranquil scene makes me believe there is a trap awaiting us on that sunny beach? I do not trust peace."

Wilhelm wrapped an arm around his brother's neck and ruffled his hair. "Come on, Salv. Wouldn't it be a little fun to finally see some action? All this paperwork and planning has been boring." A strong elbow landed in his ribs, making him wince. "Ouch," he muttered.

Salvarias grinned up at him. "You have become soft, my dear brother."

Wilhelm rubbed the spot. "No, I've never felt stronger. I think married life has agreed with you far too much."

Salvarias sighed, turning his gaze to the white beach. "Even the month before we left, I hardly saw her. And now I must endure two more without her. I admit, I am disappointed Lord Bellerum tricked her into staying behind."

Edium had told her she would be coming on a second ship with Tedris and Talura. Wilhelm was glad he wasn't there to witness her anger when no second ship arrived.

Salvarias slumped further against the railing and ran a hand across his eyes. It shook more than Wilhelm would've liked. Then again, the month of preparation had taken a toll on his brother. Salvarias practiced with the Vipers from sunup to sundown. Then at night he stayed up creating new spells and performing them repeatedly until he felt they were safe enough to pass on to other mages. Wilhelm had hoped a month at sea would have given his brother a break, but without Lunara, nightmares stole any rest his brother might have gotten. Not to mention his continuous study of his spell book. He was up to four cups of tea a day and three breathing concoctions.

Running a hand over his own face, Wilhelm doubted he looked any better. He'd spent so much time preparing for their departure that he'd just taken to sleeping at Headquarters. It saved him from Varila's offer to join her every night, which was worth all his hours of work. It gave him excuses to be far from her, though he made sure to spend a few hours with Tedris each day. Now at sea, it'd been harder to avoid his wife, but he'd made excuses that Salvarias needed him when he woke from nightmares—a lie all too close to the truth. His brother rarely remembered where he was when he woke, and often Wilhelm had to convince Salvarias that their mother was not in the room.

Not for the first time, Wilhelm wished the ship could've accommodated Vegos. Strength seeped into Wilhelm's heart whenever the bear was near, and now without it, he felt the old familiar weight pushing him into the ground. But they had required a small ship, one stealthy enough to slip past any patrols Veedran might have set. The one they'd obtained barely fit the crew and supplies were short, and much to Wilhelm's dislike, rationed. He hadn't been this hungry since his youth when his mother could only afford stew.

"I fear I have become paranoid," Salvarias murmured.

"What do you mean?"

"I am certain I saw something move in the woods."

Wilhelm squinted at the forest.

"It was as tall as the trees themselves," Salvarias said. "My eyes must be playing tricks on me."

They very well could have been. Salvarias's hallucinations were frequent enough, but they were always of their mother, Sansis, or Veedran. Wilhelm had never known his brother to imagine living creatures.

Varila joined them, resting her back against the railing. "You got everything you need for the portal spell?"

Salvarias patted a pouch of dirt tied to the rope around his waist. "I do, sis. As soon as we land, I will create it."

Wilhelm frowned at a dark shadow amongst the trees. "Perhaps we should check things out first, just to be sure we're not delivering our men into a trap."

Varila turned to face the beach. "You think something's out there?"

"Salv saw a shadow move." Wilhelm pointed to a dark spot in the trees. "See that?"

She nodded. "Doesn't fit right. There should be some sunlight through the canopy."

Wilhelm grunted his agreement.

When the ship was as close as it could safely get, Wilhelm, Salvarias, Varila, Okulu, and Brice loaded themselves into the rowboat.

Speaking to Cessia, Wilhelm said, "Once we've cleared the shore, we'll send a signal, and you can ferry over our supplies."

She kissed Okulu long enough to make everyone uncomfortable, and then her men pulled on a bunch of ropes. The rowboat lowered gently to the lazy ocean, and they all began to paddle.

The beach gave way to swaying tall grasses after a mere twenty feet, and densely packed trees soon ate those up. The natural inlet kept the bay waters serene, making Cessia's ship look like it floated on a dead lake instead of the ocean. The paddles effortlessly cut the clear waters, and the waves barely aided them as the rowboat slid onto the sand. Wilhelm hopped out first and pulled the boat farther up. After helping his brother out, he offered his hand to Varila without fully thinking it through. Her hand was warm in his, their callouses scratching against one another, her long nails reminding him how wonderful they felt when they used to sink into his back. The sight and memory froze him, so when she leapt out of the boat, she bumped against him. The scent of strawberries mingled with the saltiness of the sea and the crispness of the forest behind him. He wanted to kiss her. Gods, how he wanted to taste her, ravage her right there on the beach, but memories of the faceless women that had ridden him after he killed Sansis flashed in his mind. Dropping her hand, he turned to face the forest. Guilt clogged his throat, and it took a couple tries before he could swallow and breathe easily.

"Looks safe enough to me," Brice said.

"Let's check it out," Wilhelm said.

The five of them walked up to the grasses. Every shadow drew Wilhelm's attention, but no creature burst forth from the trees. The farther they walked, the more his brother shifted, the faster his gaze swept the area. Something was here.

"I wish we would've brought Vegos," Okulu muttered. "He could have checked it out for us."

"Don't be such a chicken," Varila scolded.

"I'm cautious," Okulu snapped. "You and Wilhelm seem fond of dashing off into danger. The rest of us prefer to stay in one piece."

Brice grinned. "That's not the spirit a knight should have."

"I don't want to be a godsforsaken knight," Okulu growled.

"Too bad," Wilhelm said. "You are. Now grow a pair and shut up."

"You hear that?" Okulu hissed, stopping and cocking his head to listen.

Everyone else stood still, and Wilhelm held his breath so he could better hear. Nothing at first, and then a far-off rumble, like thunder only continuous, building but never reaching a climax.

Salvarias took a few steps from the group and knelt down, pressing a hand to the grasses. Wilhelm's lifebeat pounded, pushing blood through him at an exhilarating rate. He missed the rush, the danger.

Beneath him, the ground began to vibrate, subtle at first, but quickening with each breath.

"I'd say something's coming," Varila said, drawing her sword.

Wilhelm drew his two, waved one to get his brother's attention, and said, "Get behind us."

No sooner had Salvarias stood than a row of trees burst up from the ground, flinging clods of soil and stones. Trees crashed into one another, spewing splinters and felling nearby weakly rooted trees. The crack and snapping muffled the building roar as dust and leaves clouded the air.

Shielding his eyes, Wilhelm squinted at the path of destruction. That's when he saw it. Some creature was tunneling its way below ground, like an unseen gopher.

"Salv!"

The mound shot past on Salvarias's right, but the speed in which the creature moved through dirt and the massive size of it tossed his brother to the ground.

Brice's startled cry whipped Wilhelm's head around. The man was dangling six feet off the ground. A vine was wrapped around his ankle and another was rushing from the woods toward the helpless knight.

Not one creature. There were two.

Wilhelm took two massive steps and leapt into the air. He barely got high enough to slap the incoming vine aside with the flat of his blade. The great sword rang out from the impact, vibrating down Wilhelm's arm. He landed awkwardly on a fallen log, and it sent him toppling to the ground.

Sparing a glance behind, the once tranquil bay was a riot of waves and screams and splitting wood from Cessia's ship. Salvarias was already hobbling toward the waters, Okulu sprinting ahead. Leaving the ocean creature to his brother, Wilhelm turned to face what lived in the woods. Gods, he wished he hadn't.

The thing towered up into the trees. It was the size of a troll, only instead of flesh the thing was made of tree roots wrapping around one another, writhing in some nightmare of twisting vines dripping tar. The bulbous top had no eyes, no mouth, but Wilhelm swore it glared at him. The trunk-like base crawled along the ground on thousands upon thousands of roots that tossed aside whatever got in its way. Smoke hissed and sizzled from any living thing the tar touched, and now that Wilhelm saw, he noticed Brice curled up on the ground, clutching his ankle, the smell of burning flesh trumping the scent of summer.

"Try not to lose any of your valuable parts, love," Varila said.

He couldn't stop his grin, and when she winked at him, his heart stuttered. Gods, she was stunning.

"Shall we?" she asked, eyes alight with adventure and daring.

Wilhelm bowed to her. "After you."

IF SALVARIAS HAD to describe the beast, he would have said a snake twice as long as a troll. It had scales like one, ranging in pattern from striped to diamond to solid and then back again. The colors were a mishmash of browns, yellows, and oranges, all dull and putrid looking. No light shined on the creature's scales, and wherever it went in the water it left behind a floating black oil-like substance.

The ship was a ruin of chunks heaving in the violent ocean. Surviving sailors had made their way to larger rafts, shouting and drawing swords that would do no good.

Cessia was an accomplished mage—extremely accomplished— but her spells lacked brute force, raw power that would allow them to deal a deathblow to a creature this size. He saw a few shards flying here and there, lightning striking out from the chaos, but still the creature constricted around heaps of wood, shattering them and raining down chunks on whoever was around.

The head finally rose out of the sea. The sight of it stumbled Okulu to a halt. It was like a cobra, flattened and half as large as the boat. It swayed above where Cessia stood, the fire of her hair catching the sun, her stance straight and unafraid.

"Salvarias!" Okulu cried.

Salvarias had already generated an ice sword the size of Wilhelm and sent it sailing. The creature reared back for a strike, and Cessia sent off one last spell of light in order to disorient it. The spell did not work, but it did not need to. Salvarias's sword sank deep into the creature's neck. It hissed and spat, thrashing in the waters, capsizing Cessia's raft.

Okulu had stripped from his armor, and he dove into the ocean.

The snake righted itself and spun toward the beach. Fangs dripped yellow poison, and its hideous red eyes locked onto Salvarias. He was certain the wound was fatal, but apparently, the creature had plenty of time to wage more destruction before it succumbed to death.

You are tired, his magic said. *We have not rested enough.*

Forgive me, my friend, but we must push ourselves.

Salvarias was chanting his next spell when the creature did the completely unexpected. It launched itself across the bay. Water glistened off it, cascading down in a waterfall dazzled by the sun. Its eyes gleamed as it opened its mouth. The body was longer than Salvarias had suspected, and the creature had no problems crossing the distance.

Cursing himself, Salvarias collapsed into a ball and shouted out his protection spell right as the mouth closed in around him. The creature chomped down, but the spell held. It hissed, spitting up poison to encase Salvarias's bubble, blinding him to what was happening.

Ending the protection spell would drench him with poison, but doing nothing was not an option. Cursing again, he grabbed his dagger, though his mind stayed blank. He saw no way to free himself without dying in an instant.

Then the creature dropped. Salvarias frantically moved his spell to keep up with the beast's descent. The poison disappeared and blue surrounded him. The creature had dove underwater. It whipped its head back and forth like a dog shaking a toy. Regardless of how easily Salvarias maintained the bubble spell, he could not keep up with the movement. Water drenched his sides as the spell failed.

Taking a deep breath, Salvarias ended the spell on the seventh shake. Water closed in around him, freezing despite the sun being high in the sky. Clenching his jaw, Salvarias rammed his dagger upward. It felt like he hit stone at first, but his momentum carried the blade through the hard outer shell and into a soft center. It was only a dagger though; a pinprick to a creature this size.

Ripping the blade free, Salvarias pushed off with his feet and swam for the dot of sunlight sparkling overhead. Glancing down, the creature spat again, but the pressure of the water kept the poison from reaching Salvarias.

One quick ripple from the creature's body and it was close enough to nip at Salvarias's feet. He was almost to the surface, just a few kicks.

Scales flashed in front of him, a whirl of colors and spinning water, bubbles tingling up his legs. It took a breath for him to figure out what was happening, but it was a breath too late. The creature coiled around him and dove deeper into the waters. Darkness pressed on the edges of Salvarias's vision as the creature squeezed, pushing precious air from his lungs.

Straining against the beast's hold, Salvarias freed his left hand enough to draw out his rune, and then using the last of his air, he chanted out a spell. His fire sword appeared, and he gagged out *"Rulose."*

The sword shot through the water with enough force to send shock waves along Salvarias's skin. The blade plunged between the creature's eyes, flying with such force it shot straight through. Brain matter and blood exploded out the back, and its eyes glazed over.

Shoving with every ounce of strength, Salvarias managed to free himself and began swimming. Only a speck of light reached through his dimming vision. Pins stabbed his lungs, and his body seized up from cold. He swore he kicked with all his might, but the light never got closer.

His eyes grew heavy, and he felt himself sinking; sinking down, down into darkness. Something hard rapped against his arm, and it woke him enough to see Okulu's sword hilt in front of him. The merc had a cloth wrapped around the blade he clung to.

Movement was agony, but Salvarias lifted his heavy arm and grabbed hold. Water passed by him, the sun growing bright and big. Gods he wanted to sleep. Nothing else mattered. Blessed sleep.

He broke the surface and sweet air rushed into his lungs. Hands grabbed hold of his soaked robes, and he found himself curled up on a chunk of wood, spots flashing across his vision from uncontrolled bouts of a racking cough. One image and his staff appeared in front of him. He hugged it close, feeling the rays of warmth seep through his clothes.

A loud crash forced his eyes open. The sight bolted him upright, and he choked out, "Brother!"

VARILA SUMMERSAULTED UNDER A SHOOTING VINE, somehow avoiding skewering herself on her sword. A drop of tar landed on her arm. She hissed at the burning sensation and rubbed her arm against the ground before springing back into a sprint.

The creature had kept its body hidden amongst the forest, only sending vines to try to snag them up. Squinting through the dust and leaves, she saw Wilhelm had outdistanced her, his strides one for her two. He sailed over fallen logs, weaving and bobbing to avoid the vines unfurling toward him. She missed watching him fight: his agility, his strength, and his courage. He never hesitated in battle.

One vine shot past Wilhelm, hanging too long before it retracted. Her husband swiped down with his great sword, cleaving wood as if it were water. Tar shot from the wound, spraying about as the appendage flopped to the ground. Smoke sizzled off his skin. He never paused or cried out.

A thinner vine swept toward her, aiming lower than the others. Spewing out a curse, she timed her jump as best she could. On her drop, she brought down her sword, angling awkward in an attempt to reach it. Her sword connected with a thud and a ring. A smile was almost to her lips before she realized her sword was stuck. As the vine whipped away, she held on for dear life, unwilling to drop her only weapon, and it yanked her off her feet and sped her through the forest.

Why did everything look so easy when Wilhelm did it?

Cursing him, she contorted her body right to avoid a tree. Another one was barreling toward her. Shouting in annoyance, she let go of her sword and tumbled along the ground, grunting and cursing as sticks and rocks poked her. When finally the world stopped spinning, Wilhelm was standing over her, crooked grin stretched, holding out the hilt of her sword for her.

"Lose something?" he asked.

"Go to Oblivion, you giant ogre," she muttered and snatched up her sword.

Wilhelm grabbed her free arm and began to pull her up. Behind him, another vine was heading straight for his back.

"Look out!" she shouted.

Too late. The vine smashed into him, catapulting him face first into a tree. He crumpled, but it'd take more to beat her husband than a mere tree. Shaking his head, droplets of blood rained down, and when he turned around, she saw his nose had been smashed and the skin on his left cheek had been ripped away, chunks of bark stuck in his flesh. It only made him mad. His eyes darkened, he spat out a glob of blood, and readjusted his grip on his swords as he marched forward.

Gaining her own footing, she took his right flank, looking back in hopes of seeing Salvarias, Okulu, or Brice. No one.

"How do want to do this?" she asked.

Wilhelm looked at her as if she'd asked the stupidest question. "Kill it."

Laughing, she sidestepped a vine. "Suggestions on how to go about that?"

He winked at her. "Swing away."

Both grinning like giddy children, they darted forward. She knew she was a good fighter. It wasn't conceited for her to think so because it was a plain truth. But Wilhelm was a master. While she grunted and groaned with each swing, he swirled his blades in a hypnotizing rhythm. The loud whistle they generated could be heard over the cracking of wood as he chopped his way through the vines, taking them closer and closer to the main body. She kept the roots off their right, trusting him to fend off the left. Regardless of her skills, his sword repeatedly flipped out to take off one she had missed.

As they chopped and shuffled onward, the vines retracted along with them, pummeling them continuously, but they were still drawing closer to the bulk of the creature. What they would do when they got there was a mystery.

Sweat poured down her face, and her sword arm trembled with each strike. Fatigue would take over soon. No one—except her husband, of course—could swing a sword that long without tiring. Gritting her teeth, she did her best to keep up with Wilhelm. Each step was agony, and for every one of her swings, Wilhelm was forced to catch the two she missed while maintaining his own side.

Cursing, she pushed herself harder. She wouldn't let him down. Couldn't.

Breath came to her in sharp gasps, her strikes weakening, and her hand numbed. Nevertheless, she fought on. She fell into an exhausted trance, her mind ordering her body to move.

A curse from Wilhelm turned her attention. Sweat rained down his face, his swords spun haltingly, and his steps faltered with hers.

"Retreat," he growled between clenched teeth.

She could have kissed him. They both backed off together, but the vines merely followed, not easing up in the least.

"I ..." She couldn't breathe to talk.

Wilhelm stepped forward, shielding her, and it gave her enough of a break to gasp in air and readjust her grip. Then Wilhelm was gone. Just ... gone. There one moment, not the next.

Plunging forward, she didn't try to hack off the roots. She merely pushed them aside so she could see. Through one gap, she saw him cocooned in vines, arms pinned at his sides, face red as they tried to squeeze the life out of him. Fear clenched her throat, and she bolted forward.

How she managed to raise her sword, she'd never know, but she brought it down with a shout and every ounce of strength she had left.

The blade bit through wood holding her husband, jarring her teeth on an especially thick vine. It was enough. Wilhelm flexed his arms and tumbled free. He kept tripping forward until his hand grabbed hers.

She ran as fast as she could. His footsteps pounded behind her, urging her faster, but she merely tripped and staggered, air lancing her lungs. The ground shook as the creature charged after them in an ear-shattering crash.

An enormous weight landed on her back and drove her to the ground. A rush of air stirred up the dirt, stinging her eyes as she watched a vine cleaving by.

Wilhelm's arm around her waist lifted her and pushed her forward. "Run!" he roared from behind.

Her feet fought one another, but her mind sorted them out eventually. They were near the edge of the trees. She'd not known they'd made it that far into the forest. A raft was bobbing its way ashore, and she made out Okulu and Cessia dragging it from the waters. Salvarias was curled up on it. She wasn't sure he was alive.

Glancing behind, Wilhelm was on her heels and limping. Badly. Blood covered his left leg, and a stick stuck out of his upper thigh.

She wanted to scream for help, but air wasn't her friend. Then Salvarias sat bolt upright, his eyes large. He said something but his voice didn't reach her. It didn't need to. Stumbling to a stop, she spun around.

A vine was wrapped around Wilhelm's torso, lifting him off the ground. The creature's bulk was once again in view, and it pulled Wilhelm to its chest, the vine coiling tighter, and Wilhelm shouted out in pain, his face red, veins sticking up from his neck.

A small voice in her head told her not to panic. Salvarias could heal Wilhelm. But all the blood gushing out of his mouth told the voice to go to Oblivion. It was impossible to hear his bones breaking above the creature's ruckus, but she swore she did. His chest caved in, and his body hung limply.

As if that wasn't harrowing enough, the creature dove to the ground and began to burrow, taking her husband with it. Salvarias couldn't heal his brother if they never found Wilhelm's body.

"No!" Salvarias skidded by on his knees, leaning far back to make himself fit between the ground and the stomach of the creature, and disappeared under it.

Shock passed, and she sprung a step before arms grabbed her.

"Let me go!" she cried.

"You'll only get yourself killed," Brice snapped.

"Salvarias will get him," Okulu said on her other side, but his voice was uncertain.

Fire exploded in front of them, bathing them in suffocating heat, and throwing them backward. The world went black.

16

SUMMER 1022 A.R

Light blurred in Varila's vision. She blinked slowly, feeling as if someone shook her brain loose. Every part of her body throbbed and every muscle tensed in pain. Ash fell around her, hazing the sky, and waves of heat beat against her. A loud deep drum thumped in her ear, married with a constant ringing.

Okulu was crawling past her, shouting but she couldn't hear him over the ringing in her ears. His hair was singed, clothes blackened, and smoke rose off his back.

Okulu shouted again, and she heard his muffled cry for Salvarias. She raised her head, squinting at smoke burning her eyes. Where the creature had once been was nothing but a massive mound of flaming branches, an inky black smoke curling skyward, cutting through the flakes of ash.

Stars dancing in her vision and pins stabbing her skin, Varila managed to roll up to her hands and knees. Sound began to bleed through the ringing in her ears. Wood crackled and popped, and Okulu kept calling for Salvarias.

The entire mound of smoldering branches left the ground as if resting on a clear stone floor. It took a few blinks to wet the dryness in her eyes so she could see underneath it. The mound had made it two feet off the ground before it stopped. Peeking out from a crater was a slate-blue sleeve and a two fingered hand.

"Salvarias!" Okulu called.

Crawling on his stomach, Okulu wriggled his way under the suspended mound and to the crater, Varila not far behind.

Salvarias lay beside the crushed form of Wilhelm. A hacking cough choked Salvarias, and blood streamed out his mouth, nose, and ears. No color reached his face, and sweat rolled down his forehead, leaving clean streaks along his soot-covered skin. A branch had pierced his shoulder, pinning him to the ground.

Wilhelm's torso was flattened, bones protruding through skin, organs pooling around him.

"Easy," Okulu said softly. "We'll get him out."

Okulu and her snaked their way to Wilhelm. Grimacing, the merc dumped Wilhelm's insides into the man's lap, then wiggled himself underneath Wilhelm's left side and began to shimmy his way backward, grunting and groaning under her husband's weight.

Salvarias wrapped a hand around the stick protruding out his shoulder. He took a few quick, short breaths and yanked it free. A cry escaped him, and he rolled to his side, clutching at the wound.

"Let me help you," Varila said.

He shook his head. He must barely have had the Hunters and evil under control.

"Help me," Okulu panted.

Squirming her way over, she took Wilhelm's other side and heaved. His body moved in a way no body should. Limbs flopped around like they were boneless and were slippery with blood.

She was certain eternity had passed but when she crawled into the sun, it couldn't have been long. Twisting on to her stomach, she looked back. Salvarias was clawing his way out, leaving a trail of blood down the front of him, his body shaking so badly she feared it'd rattle apart.

"Come on," she encouraged. "You have to make it out to heal him."

Salvarias shuddered and seizures took hold. He flapped around, grunting and contorting.

Okulu cursed and lunged underneath the mound.

"You can't touch him," Varila snapped.

It wasn't the Hunters she feared. Salvarias could very well lose his mind to the evil.

Okulu ripped off his shirt, wrapped it around Salvarias's arm, and pulled. Brice scrambled under and did the same on Salvarias's other side. The instant they made it out, Okulu said, "We're clear. End it!"

Nothing happened.

"End it!" Okulu barked.

Salvarias jerked, rolled on his side, coughed up a pool of blood, and muttered something. The burning mound toppled to the ground, forcing Okulu and Brice to stumble backward as sparks and branches tumbled around them.

"Gods be cursed," Okulu breathed and cast her a wicked grin. "These brothers will be the death of us."

VARILA SMOOTHED Wilhelm's hair from his forehead and applied a cool cloth. Sweat poured off him despite his shivering. Blood flecked his lips with each gasping cough. His fleshless cheek had crusted over. Angry contusions splotched his entire torso. It'd taken four sessions with Salvarias to get her husband this far along in healing. Her little brother was hardly recovered enough to do any of it, but he'd insisted, and Varila shamefully agreed.

Raising her tired gaze, she examined Salvarias. The wound in his shoulder had been stitched up, the burns along his left arm treated with a balm, and the other bruises and scratches were all healing nicely. Physically, he was fine. Mentally was an entirely different story. They'd been forced to strap him down to stop him from fleeing every time he woke. He only recognized Wilhelm, and seeing his brother in such a condition sent him into a fit of panic. It took less and less time to calm him when he woke, but it hurt to see him so frightened.

Varila adjusted the covers on the brothers, kissed Wilhelm's cheek, and stepped outside. Luckily, Cessia had managed to find what she needed to open the portal shortly after their skirmish yesterday. Okulu had been quick to rush in the healers and squires so a tent could be erected immediately. Over the long night and most of the day, Okulu had effectively orchestrated the rest of the troops. Tents circled Wilhelm's, and a few of the Vipers had taken up guarding it. She still marveled over how quickly Salvarias had earned their devotion. Life had been so hectic as of late she never had an opportunity to discover the reasons.

The young knight at the entrance banged his chest in salute. "Respectfully, Dame Varila, may I inquire after Lord Knight Salvarias?"

"A man loyal to a mage is a rare thing," she said, fishing for hints.

She hadn't even cast out the line when he willingly explained. "Lord Salvarias overheard me talking with a few men about my daughter's failing health and how our healer had told us she wouldn't make it another season. Salvarias came over and promised he could make her well. And he held true to his word. A handful of other Vipers also had sick family members. He cured them all, refusing payment of any sort, and never asked for a thing in return. Not our acceptance or protection." The man's cheeks dimpled with a smile. "But he had it. I told him we would follow him to Oblivion, and he merely said he wasn't worthy of such devotion, but he hoped we would do everything in our power to save Arden. Not for him, but for our families and his brother. I'd be hard pressed to find a humbler man. Especially after witnessing the power he wields."

"Have you seen his eyes?"

The knight brushed back a mass of blond curls from his forehead and shrugged. "No, but I've heard rumors. I don't think it'd change my mind in the least."

Varila nodded, but chose not to argue. That was normally the issue. Salvarias was quite likable these days, but it was his eyes that scared the sanity out of most. As he always said: "The world fears what it does not understand."

"I don't remember your name," she said.

"Qwyn, Dame Varila."

"Ah, Okulu's right-hand man. He speaks highly of you."

Qwyn's watery blue eyes widened. "I didn't know. He's constantly saying we're going to get Salvarias killed and end Arden with our lack of focus and skill."

Varila laughed. "Sounds like him. Okulu is rather protective of Salvarias."

Sir Paull bustled up to her, his white healer robes catching the last rays of the setting sun. He was older than her father, hair completely gray, his build tall, lean, and healthy looking with hands steadier than a mountain.

She'd initially disapproved of Wilhelm's decision to knight healers. After all, the five he had found couldn't lift a sword. Despite them being the best healers across all the continents, this was the Knighthood, not a service of healers. He'd changed her mind with one explanation.

"We'd all be dead if it weren't for healers," Wilhelm had said. "They save lives. We take them. Which one of us is more worthy of an honorable title? Of respect?"

That'd shut everyone up.

"Dame Varila," Sir Paull said. "Do the Lord Knights require my attention?"

"No, they're still resting."

"Very well. Zerana's grace bless you." He saluted and continued on his way.

"I think we're set," Okulu said from behind. "After Vegos and the last of the squires come through with the rest of the supplies, Kisra will close up the portal. Cessia is on her way to Bren."

"And we're sure the portal's location is secret? No one could have snuck through that wasn't supposed to?"

"Paranoid?"

She glared at him. "How many creatures and gods are after Salvarias? Of course I'm bloody paranoid. Wilhelm was clear the portal would only be known to the hundred men, their squires, and two healers."

"And so it was." Okulu frowned at her. "Have you slept?"

"An hour here and there." She looked him up and down and doubted she looked worse than him. "Have you?"

He winked. "An hour here and there." He pointed at a tent to the right. "That's yours." Then the left. "That's Salvarias's when he wakes."

Varila nodded. "I'm hoping in another two days we can be on our way. We're already behind schedule."

"Pesky evil is so inconsiderate," he drawled.

Scowling at him, she went back inside the tent. Wilhelm was awake, gasping, fists clenching the bedding. Blood stained his gritted teeth.

"Paull!" Varila shouted. They'd been able to keep Wilhelm drugged so the man didn't wake in excruciating pain. Rushing to his side, she placed a hand on his forehead. He was burning up. "It's all right," she said. "Salvarias is resting. When he wakes, he'll heal you some more."

Tears rained from Wilhelm's eyes, his gasps flecking up blood. Paull strode inside, a vial already in his hands. Leaning over her husband, he frowned and started feeling along Wilhelm's ribs.

"Dammit," Paull muttered. "That rib punctured his lung. He's drowning in his own blood."

Closing her eyes, she repeated to herself that Salvarias would save him. Wilhelm wouldn't die forever. He wouldn't leave her again.

The commotion stirred Salvarias awake. Whether he recognized where he was or not seemed to drown in his short cry as he grabbed Wilhelm's hand. Her husband groaned, latching on to Salvarias hard enough to turn his brother's skin white. A few breaths passed before Salvarias fell back to the bed, his eyes distancing, and a drop of blood trailed down his cheek from his nose. A snap sounded in Wilhelm's chest, his skin moved, and he leaned over and gagged up blood.

"By the gods," Paull breathed. "I'll never get used to that."

Wilhelm sucked in massive lungfuls of air, and his eyes shut tight. Gripping Salvarias's hand tighter, skin bloomed along Wilhelm's missing cheek, flaking away the scab until nothing but smooth flesh remained. The bruises on his chest faded in a blink, leaving behind unmarred skin.

Salvarias curled up, choked out a cry, and gurgled on a rush of blood spewing from his mouth.

Cursing herself, she pulled on Wilhelm. The man didn't budge. His full strength was back. "Help us!" Varila yelled.

Her husband grew right in front of her. Muscles bulged against his skin, and his exhale was one of euphoria. "Wilhelm, you have to stop!" she shouted.

If he heard, he gave no sign. He only tightened his grip. Then men were there, ten of them pulling on Salvarias and Wilhelm's arms. They pried apart their hands, and Salvarias collapsed in a heap of limpness, sweat pouring off him and blood trickling from his nose.

Wilhelm sat straight, his wide eyes scanning the room. "Where in Oblivion am I?"

"The camp," Varila said, motioning the other men out.

He flexed his hand and glanced down at Salvarias. "You let me go too long."

"Your strength is back," she said defensively. "It's hard to stop you when you're better."

Wilhelm hopped out of bed like he'd never been injured. It was disorienting for her to see him go from death to complete health in a day. His alert eyes scanned the tent while he pulled on a tunic.

"Report," he said.

"You son of a bitch," she said. "You died and now you want to carry on as if nothing happened?" She couldn't shake the sight of him from yesterday: disemboweled, body broken, blank eyes staring at nothing.

Wilhelm glanced at her, a frown tugging down the corners of his mouth. "Salv was here. I wasn't going to die. Permanently."

Perhaps she'd held in her feelings for too long, or perhaps she was angrier than she thought. Perhaps he was just an ass. Whatever the reason, it boiled her blood and made her want to run him through with her sword. After all, the bastard didn't care if he lived or died, or what it would do to her.

"You and I need to settle some things," she said in a low voice.

"I don't have time right now. Maybe—"

She slapped him. And it felt damn good. "You're coming with me."

His eyes grew wide, but she saw he wouldn't argue again.

Stepping outside, she tried to keep her voice steady, to keep her hate and anger from it. Turning to Qwyn, she said, "Keep guard on Salvarias. No one goes in. He should sleep for the rest of the night. If he has a nightmare, leave him be. If he wakes up, come find me."

"Where will you be if needed?" he asked.

"In the woods," she muttered and stormed off. Purposefully passing by the armory wagon, she snatched up two practice swords sheathed in wood to stop lethal blows. She had to admit it was an artful design on her part.

Wilhelm said nothing as he followed her; he merely tilted his head and saluted other knights as he went. She ventured far into the forest, far enough she was certain no one would hear her yell or his shouts as she beat him to Oblivion. When secluded enough, she whirled around and slapped him again.

"You bastard!" she snarled. "For three years I had to be alone. I raised a son alone. I gave excuses to any asking where you'd run off to. Now ..." She jabbed a finger at his chest. "Now you've returned and what did I get? A thank you? A kiss? You won't even look at me! After all I've done! For months—MONTHS—I've put up with your crap. I've waited for you to come to me. I've invited you to my bed every night I could find you. Nothing. Nothing from you!" She slapped him again and then again, but it didn't ease the anger flaring to life the longer he stood silent, the longer he wouldn't look at her. Grabbing a wooden sword, she chucked it at him. "Pick it up!"

"Varila, this isn't going to do—"

"Go to Oblivion," she snarled and charged.

It might have been a wooden sword, but the weight of the inlaid metal still hurt. Hers smacked against his raised arm, and he grunted, stumbling back while snatching up his own wood sword. She swung again and again, no form to her advance, just brute overhead strikes. Cursing him the entire time, she finally gained enough of her own mind to spit out, "Is it because I'm not a whore in some tavern? Do I not have enough diseases for you?" She hit home on his ribs. He wasn't wearing armor, and no doubt they'd bruise. When he grunted and stepped out of her range, she snarled, "What's wrong? Your brother can heal you. Death is nothing to you. It's only the people that love you that have to watch you bleed and suffer. But that doesn't matter does it? Cause you don't give a damn how I feel. That's been obvious!"

Wilhelm's face darkened. "You think I don't know how much I betrayed you? Hurt you?"

His expression twisted into rage as great as hers, but she never feared him. He wouldn't do any real damage to her, but facing that anger made her realize why creatures fled before him, and she couldn't help taking a step back.

Unshed tears glistened in his eyes, but his jaw set and he advanced. Finally!

Sword flipping right, she parried his lazy jab, but it was merely a distraction. The flat of his hand landed on her stomach. Her armor took some of the impact, and gods knew he only used a portion of his strength, but it knocked her back on her bum.

"Every day I wake up, and I don't think I could hate myself more," Wilhelm growled. "What else do you want from me?"

"Ugh!" she shouted in frustration. "I want my husband back! I want us to be a family! I want you to forgive yourself just as I've done!" Jumping up, she charged him. He parried her effortlessly, and it only drove her more insane. *Anger,* her father had always said, *will make you lose every time.* And she wanted nothing more than to kick his ass to Oblivion.

Backing off, she steadied her breathing and glared at the man she loved. He was thinking. She saw it clearly in his distant eyes, his brow creased, lips turned down in a frown.

"What?" she snapped.

"You honestly still love me?" Wilhelm asked. "I slept with other women. I left you alone and pregnant. I abandoned our family. Honestly, how can you?"

Hurt lanced across her heart. Of all the people in all the worlds, she thought he would be the one to understand her. It left her feeling lonelier than the day he walked out on her.

Tears blurring her vision, she struck out. She'd been a fool. She'd committed her heart to him, and it was plain he'd not done the same. If he had, he wouldn't wonder how she could still love him.

There she was again: vulnerable, exposed, hurting.

"You son of a bitch," she spat. Their swords were a blur, his massive frame a mirage of betrayal, but she didn't care if she lost anymore. She wanted to hit him, to hurt him as much as he'd hurt her.

The next time she lunged, he leaned back from the sword, grabbed her wrist, and twisted. Crying out, she dropped the weapon. A leg hit the back of hers and then she was falling. The bastard caught her on the way down and eased her fall. She went to slap him but he snatched her hands and held them at her side. She wrestled against him, tears streaming down her face.

"You think I don't care?" he snapped. "Don't you understand me at all? I've betrayed you. Hurt you. How could I ever look you in the eye after doing that? How could I ever forgive myself? I don't deserve your love or forgiveness. I don't deserve to be your husband and the father of our son. You gave yourself to me, and I threw it away. I hurt the one person I love as much as my brother. How can I ever make it right? If you'd done what I'd done, would you look me in the eye?"

Yes, she would. Certainly she would feel guilt, feel undeserving of him, but Varila had built her life around moving forward. Crap happened. Kick it off your shoe and move on. That was her motto. But she never put herself in Wilhelm's mind. He was a worrier, a thinker, and over-analyzer. Sometimes she forgot how similar the brothers were, how much they placed on their own shoulders, how high a standard they held themselves to. In his mind, he had done the unforgivable. Honorable men were eaten alive when they betrayed a loved one. And she had let that disease feed on her husband instead of talking to him, instead of helping him. She'd wanted him to be the one to make the first move, but of course his shame would never have allowed it.

How could she have been so blind to him, so oblivious to what he needed from her? How could she have let him live so long in such pain?

Tears filled her eyes, but she blinked them aside. "I get it," she said softly. "I do. And I love you all the more for how much what you did is hurting you. For how honorable a man you are. But it's time to forgive yourself, to think about what *I* need, what *I* want. Not *your* guilt or *your* shame. None of that is coming from me. And as for deserving me, I'll decide for myself," she said sternly. "Don't you dare tell me what I can and cannot have. You're my damn husband. Now act like it, you bastard." She kissed him quickly. It wasn't romantic or passionate. She did it fast enough he couldn't pull away or stop her. She did it so he knew how she felt.

He blinked in surprise, then that passiveness in his eyes began to fade. His gaze dropped to her lips, and the first embers of desire ignited in his amber eyes. Still he paused.

"The mighty Wilhelm Laybryth," she purred. "Paralyzed by a woman." Tilting her head up, raising her lips to his, sliding a leg up his side, she breathed out her challenge. "Come now, Lord Knight, take from me what you will, if you can." She grinned wickedly.

His kiss was as hot and passionate as she remembered. Bucking her hips left and upward, she knocked him off balance and rolled on top of him. Rough hands snuck under her armored skirt and grabbed her thighs, squeezing. Unbridled want roared through her, and she tasted sweet blood from his lips as she bit down. A rumble of approval vibrated from his throat, and it drove her mad. Fumbling at the neck of his tunic, she found the weak spot and ripped it off. Pulling her lips from his, she bit along his chest while working to untie his trews. The instant he was free, he grabbed her hair and yanked back as he sat up, bringing her lips to his.

Want owned her, building and building, throbbing to near

uncomfortable, making her beg for him. He never bothered taking off her armor. As soon as he shifted aside her undergarments, she slid on to his length. Her body arched as he drove inside her, and she anchored her nails in his back, riding him, reveling in his groans, how tightly he clasped her thighs, how sweat followed the curves of his chest and stomach. He sent her over the edge quickly and followed her a breath later.

Spent, they both collapsed back to the ground, panting and sweating. The moon glistened overhead, peeking through reaching tree limbs. Somewhere off in the distance, a wolf howled.

"Stay with me tonight?" Wilhelm asked.

Rolling over, she propped her head on her hand and ran a finger down his chest. "Only if you get me dinner. I'm famished."

He brushed a lock of hair from her face. "I love you."

Warmth penetrated the cold cocooning her heart. Grinning, she said, "I know," and kissed him.

A SUMMER BREEZE kissed over Lunara's balcony, lifting her hair and making her dream of spring. Normally Serinity took longer than most to surrender to summer, but this year, the city had not even fought. One day it was cool, the next warm.

Exhausted as she was from helping Salvarias heal his brother, sleep was an elusive friend. She wanted to be by her husband's side, comforting him, helping him, but like always, she was perceived as a sheltered girl who offered nothing to the fight. She hoped her husband wasn't party to the trick her father had played. She feared to think Salvarias viewed her as baggage. Certainly she could not fight herself, but she could aid her husband, stand by his side, calm his mind, and gift him peaceful nights.

Of course she had tucked away her disappointments into a dark corner of her mind. Salvarias needed her support and love. With what he faced, his heart could not be troubled with guilt or concern for her happiness. And though she knew he sensed her hidden corner, he remained respectful as usual and never tried to uncover her secrets. A part of her wished he would.

Just thinking of the warmth of life within made her smile. Massaging her belly, she said, "Soon I'll tell your father. I want him to be focused right now." She hummed her son a cheery song.

Sira and Saval rubbed against her legs before climbing up the balcony railing. Their purr rumbled deep in their chests as they pruned their wings, perching as steadily as birds. Already they'd grown to the size of a wolf and had managed to fly short distances.

They had rarely left her side over the past two months since their creation. When they did, it had been to find Salvarias when he would stay late at his office at the Knighthood estate, practicing his spells until all hours. The last month they had taken a liking to Tedris, and played often with Vegos and the boy. However, they were never gone long. Always they returned to her, purring and weaving around her in affection. Before Salvarias had left, the two griffins had slept at the foot of the bed, but once he had gone, Sira had taken to sleeping with her head pressed against Lunara's belly, purring and nuzzling. Saval moped around, smelling anything Salvarias had touched, and issuing soft, forlorn cries. The griffin took her comforts, but his sad eyes broke Lunara's heart.

Reaching out, she stroked each of their necks, gliding her fingers along their soft feathers. With all the planning for invading Wind-lous, Salvarias had barely slept, had barely talked with her, and had only bedded her a few times since their wedding night. She often mused it was why he had bestowed the griffins upon her, to help fill the gaping hole of his absence. After all, they had been created by him and, intentional or not, they carried with them a sense of his presence. It was as if a part of him was always with her, and she loved the creatures for it.

A soft knock on her door was followed by Tedris saying, "Aunt Lunara? May I come in?"

Frowning up at the gray sky just lighting with the morning sun, she called, "Of course." Tedris was never up before sunrise.

The boy walked in wearing his rumpled nightshirt, his hair a mess of waves sticking this way and that. He yawned as he stepped into the room, and behind him, Vegos loomed.

"He said you need to go," Tedris said. The child looked over his shoulder at the bear, rolled his eyes, and said, "I know! But you woke me at a godsforsaken hour!" Turning back to her, he said, "There's not a lot of time. He wants you to hurry."

"Go where?"

Tedris yawned. Vegos gave the child a gentle shove.

"All right, all right!" Tedris snapped. Lunara marveled over how quickly the child had taken to the bear. Vegos intimidated her to no end, but here Tedris was, talking back to the creature, unafraid. Then again, he had played with the bear nearly nonstop for the entire month. The two had become inseparable. Vegos had even taken to sleeping in Tedris's room.

Tedris jammed a thumb over his shoulder. "Vegos said that Uncle Salvarias needs you, even if he doesn't know it yet. He said he's going to sneak you through the portal. He said he can hide you in the army until you think it's best to show yourself."

Lunara was already running to pack. "What do I need?"

"Just undergarments. He's going to get you some healer robes and squire outfits. Put up your hair and grab Uncle's ratty cloak." Tedris looked over his shoulder. "You're sure I can't come? I can help Papa." Frowning, Tedris nodded. He turned back to her. "He'll lead you. He said I need to be back to bed before Grandma and Grandpa come. He said you should write them a note so they don't worry."

Lunara finished throwing her undergarments in her pack, swept Tedris up in a hug, kissed his cheek, and said, "Thank you, sweetie."

The boy grumbled some reply and rubbed his eyes. "I don't understand why they didn't knight you as a healer and take you with them."

"Me neither. Now off to bed. Don't forget to practice reading."

"I will." He gave Vegos's leg a hug. "Take care of my papa and uncle, please."

The bear gently nuzzled the boy then gave him a shove out the door.

After pinning up her hair, writing a short letter to her parents, and saying a lengthy goodbye to Sira and Saval, she followed Vegos down the hall, through the estate, and to the back wall where the secret entrance to the Knighthood hid behind thick vines. She fumbled until finding the brick that opened the door. Slipping through the narrow entrance, she looked back at the bear. "I assume you want me to wait here?"

Vegos nodded and trotted away.

The sun seemed to be racing the bear. Too much light would make it harder for her to sneak in. Her stomach rumbled a protest at missing breakfast. Her son had gifted her a healthy appetite. Cherries and milk. She couldn't get enough cherries and milk. Of course there would be none in the army's rations. Patting her belly, she whispered, "Sorry, Son, but we'll have to go a while without your favorites."

Vegos came sauntering over from the shadows and dropped a tent and a pile of clothes at her feet. He sorted through them with his nose before separating out a pair of brown trews and a green tunic.

"Turn around," she murmured.

The bear rolled his eyes and used his body as a privacy screen. She changed quickly, donned her cloak, and raised the hood. After throwing the rest of the items in her pack, they set off.

Vegos proved artful in avoiding wandering knights and the young set about on a variety of tasks. Outside the armory, he nudged her back into the shadows of a tall hedge and continued on his own. Waiting was agony as she watched the sun chasing the last stars. When finally Vegos returned, he carried a sack in his mouth of something clanking loudly with each of his lumbering strides.

When they arrived at the entrance to the loading yard, hiding was no longer an option. Standing tall but keeping her head down, she walked beside the bear as it confidently strode to the knight on watch.

The man stood at attention and banged his fist on his chest. "Vegos, Okulu has been looking for you." The man's gaze flicked to her. "Is this your squire?"

The bear nodded, giving off a low growl that made the knight immediately step aside.

"You can't miss the portal," the man said. "They're still ferrying through supplies."

Vegos grunted as he passed, and Lunara did her best to walk as gangly as possible, trying to mirror the other youths fumbling about.

"Vegos!" Okulu called, waving his hand. "Over here."

The bear switched directions, keeping her on the opposite side of Okulu.

"Been a nasty business," Okulu said when they were close. "Wilhelm died, but Salvarias brought him back already. We have probably another day until the mage is ready to travel. It took quite a bit out of him."

Vegos nodded.

"Want me to have someone take your armor?" Okulu offered.

Vegos shook his head and lumbered onward.

The portal was larger than any Lunara had ever seen, near two houses wide. Wagons went in three rows deep, and by the line, they would be another hour or so. Vegos wormed his way in between two wagons, growling at both sides, making the horses go wide-eyed.

When they passed through, darkness claimed the rising sun, and sputtering torches lined a path leading to where the wagons were camped.

Vegos headed north toward the tiny campfires sprinkled about.

"Thank you," Lunara whispered.

Vegos regarded her for a moment with his large brown eyes before nodding. He stopped at a cluster of neatly rowed small tents barely fitting a single person's needs. She then understood the bear's intent. She would hide among the squires and healers.

A booming laugh whirled her around. Wilhelm was ambling along, his arm draped around Varila, her sister's smile clearly stating what had just occurred along with Wilhelm's ripped tunic. Joy surged up in Lunara, and she fought the urge to run to her sister and share in Varila's happiness.

Vegos didn't. The bear gave a short playful growl and barreled toward Wilhelm. His attention was too focused on Varila for him to notice anything else. His laugh cut off when the bear rammed into him, tackling him to the ground.

"Vegos!" Wilhelm's laugh erupted again. "I've missed you!"

Though joy filled his voice, she couldn't help noticing a heavy relief, as if he'd just received news of Veedran leaving Arden. When he finally stood, he closed his eyes and inhaled deeply. "I can't tell you how much I've missed that."

The three wandered off toward the center of camp, leaving Lunara alone and, thankfully, unnoticed. Looking around, she didn't doubt her ability to blend in with the other youths. The Knighthood was new, and few were familiar with each other. The squires were all watching one another in a manner of observation, learning each other's character.

Smiling to herself, she began setting up her tent. Soon her husband would tell her how much he needed her, would beg her to come to him, and here she would be. Then he would apologize for leaving her behind, and maybe, just maybe, her sister and parents would see her as more than just a girl and would finally admit she had something to offer in this fight.

17

SUMMER 1022 A.R

"Four hundred octrils," Idolar said. "Ten minotaurs, and about fifty creatures we've yet to identify."

Salvarias narrowed his eyes at the city nestled against the ocean. Bellend was as dark and gray as he remembered. The last rays of sun shot purple and orange beams across the sky, piercing the baleful clouds scudding in from the north. They would have rain come nightfall. Both a hindrance and a welcome cover.

From their perch on the hill, hidden along the forest's edge, they could see the layout of Bellend. And the destruction. Half the buildings had been razed to the ground, the fires long ago squelched, but the charred and broken stone spoke mutely of the horror visited upon them. No light shone through windows of the few standing homes, and the streets themselves lacked life.

Salvarias shifted in his saddle and glanced at his brother. "Those odds are not in our favor. Perhaps we should use our Grandfather?" Mafarias had been chained—using shackles Salvarias had enchanted to keep the man from utilizing magic—and was held in camp, guarded by no less than five knights. "We could use the guards as well as his magic," Salvarias added.

"No, we don't need him yet," Wilhelm said.

I agree, Vegos said. *He is unreliable. I sense deceit in him. You are not yet desperate enough to trust him. Not yet.*

Salvarias was not so sure. He was tired. Without Lunara, his nights were never restful. Without her smile, his life was not as bright. For the past month, he hardly had a chance to talk to her. Time was different across continents, and his free moments rare. Now, with a battle and the lives of men reliant upon his magic, he cursed himself for staying silent when Lord Bellerum had tricked her into remaining behind. No doubt she was furious with him, though in their few conversations she showed no signs. More so was his shame for inserting himself as a decision maker in her life. Her choices should have been her own.

"There," Brice said, pointing to the three largest standing estates tucked up against one another. "According to Humar's scouts, that's where they're keeping prisoners. Rumors are, only a few thousand lived through the invasion."

"There were about ten thousand citizens living in there," Okulu said and took a swig from his flask.

"I read Humar's reports," Varila added. "Windlous has no armies, and their cities were never well protected. A gift from Lakvra, no doubt. Bellend didn't stand a chance."

"They have one now," Wilhelm muttered. "Brice, gather your choice of five men that will go with us. Make sure they're stealthy. We head out as soon as it's dark. Idolar, prepare the rest. After I give the signal to Salv, your men will come in behind the Vipers." He shifted in his saddle so he could look Okulu full in the face. "Are the Vipers ready? If they're not and my brother gets one scratch on him, I'll take your head off."

"They are ready," Salvarias said. "I will be fine, Brother."

Wilhelm's gaze stayed locked on Okulu.

The merc took another swig and grinned. "Remember, it's my hide too. Kisra will be with them, and Cessia will have my other head if I screw this up. They're ready."

Wilhelm grunted and turned back to face the city. "Get them suited and lined up," he said to Okulu.

"I'm ever at your service, Lord Knight," Okulu said, bowing in his saddle. He winked at Salvarias and then followed Brice and Idolar back to camp.

"Okulu's good," Varila said. "His men are the best. Your plan is solid. Trust it."

Wilhelm rubbed his cheek, his gaze roving over the city. "I know. That doesn't mean I have to like it."

Salvarias glanced at Varila and tilted his head toward camp. Taking his hint, she leaned over in her saddle, yanked Wilhelm closer, and kissed his cheek.

"I'll have everything ready," she said.

"Thanks," Wilhelm said.

Once she was gone, Mithal sidled up to Lilly. Over the two days ride to Bellend, Salvarias had seen Wilhelm's eyes brighten, and his jovial mood increased each time he stepped out of his tent in the mornings, Varila on his arm and both full of smiles. Wilhelm's laugh often boomed through camp, and the morale of the knights had improved. Yet ever since their evening meal, Wilhelm had become quiet, his eyes distant, his thoughts whirling. Salvarias had felt the hurricane of it in his own mind.

Wilhelm was made to command armies. He was strategic, his plans calculating and thorough, and his preparations remarkable. Wilhelm knew he was good, no matter how humble he appeared. But today men would die—Wilhelm's men—and it would be by his order; a weight heavier than any one man deserved.

Salvarias understood his brother better than any other person, so he knew no words could help. Instead, he sat beside Wilhelm in silence. Ever since Salvarias first opened his eyes to the cruel world, his big brother was a hero to him. A courageous, self-sacrificing man worthy of all the happiness and rewards life could offer. These thoughts consumed Salvarias until he felt his brother's eyes upon him.

"Thanks, Salv."

Vegos gave Salvarias an approving nod. *You two feed upon one another. Use one another's strengths to battle your weaknesses. Truly, I have never known two people more entwined in each other's souls. Trust in that, if nothing else.*

"Tobin always said our relationship wasn't healthy," Wilhelm said.

Bah! If you were normal children, I would agree. But what you face must not be done so alone. Your relationship has saved Arden, my dear boys. Together ...

Salvarias grinned. "Together, we can do anything."

You two carry the fate of the world too willingly. You are but two. You will do what you can, and what will be will be. I'll not have either of you succumb to the pressures. But I cannot deny what Salvarias has said.

Salvarias inhaled a deep breath along with his brother as his heart lightened. The battle did not seem so doomed. The world was not so dark.

Nevlar gifted me this power, and I intend to use it to my full ability. I am here for you both, and as I did with your ancestors, I will help carry your burden. As long as you fight, I will fight by your side. Today will not be our end.

Wilhelm's crooked grin infected Salvarias with joy. "Let's give Veedran something to worry about, little brother."

"DAMN ALL THE GODS," Wilhelm muttered as the first raindrops drummed on his armor.

"Let's not damn Zerana yet," Brice said. "She might save us one day."

Wilhelm grunted disagreement. As far as he was concerned, the gods could go to Oblivion. Not one had helped them. Not one had stopped the torment nipping at his brother's heels.

The moon had disappeared some time ago, and though the darkness helped hide them from the octrils patrolling the wall, it also blanketed the ground in black. Wilhelm had slipped and slid over the rocky terrain, but he'd managed to keep his brother from experiencing the same blunders. Salvarias's bad leg barely had much of a function anymore after Sansis had broken it and Salvarias's foot.

Tightening his grip on his brother's shoulders, Wilhelm navigated a dry creek bed and breathed a sigh of relief at the wall looming on the other side.

"Take your time on the way back," Wilhelm whispered to Salvarias. "You're no good to us if you break your leg again."

"I will be fine," Salvarias said in between his whispered numbers.

I will aid him, Vegos said.

At the wall, Salvarias ran his hand over a few stones, muttered to himself or perhaps his magic, and then nodded, apparently finding what he needed. He glanced Wilhelm up and down, looked back to the stones, and frowned.

"What?" Wilhelm asked.

"I might have to remove three," his brother said.

Wilhelm took a quick measure and shook his head. "I'll fit through two."

"As you wish." Salvarias whispered words of magic and traced a rune in the air.

How his brother managed to remove a stone from a wall without a single sound, Wilhelm would never know, but his chest swelled with pride when one of the knights behind him gave a soft whistle of admiration. The second stone shimmied free as silently as the first.

The opening was tight, and as Wilhelm squeezed his way through, he had to wiggle and grunt and groan as he inhaled here and exhaled there. He birthed on the other side bruised and drenched in as much sweat as rain.

After seeing the street empty, he peered back at Salvarias and grinned. "Be careful, little brother. Remember, no exerting yourself. I'll be too far away to help, and we're on a campaign here. Steady will win it."

"Yes, Brother." Salvarias hesitated, and his uncertainty mingled with Wilhelm's, the surge of it making him light headed.

"I'll be fine," Wilhelm assured him.

Neither wanted to separate, and Wilhelm's doubts about his plan were starting to fester again.

"For the love of Nevlar," Varila muttered. "You'll both be fine. Now get out of here, little brother."

Salvarias flashed her a smile. "Of course, sis."

With that, his shadowed form turned and headed back, Okulu and Qwyn flanking him.

Vegos said, *You can change your play.*

"I can't risk it."

Salvarias had trained with the Vipers for a month, and his brother knew of their movements. He had been adamant that adding Vegos would only hinder his spells. Reluctantly, Wilhelm had agreed and assigned the bear to support Idolar. Vegos was not thrilled.

"Salv has his guard. They'll keep him safe."

Vegos grunted and then went out of sight.

By the time the other five knights, Brice, and Varila had wormed through, the clouds had unleashed their fury. The downpour was straight and sharp, but thankfully no wind. His brother would already be freezing, even with the warmer summer air.

Despite having just separated, Salvarias's focus honed in on Wilhelm instantly. The whirlwind of his brother's chaotic mind gave him a headache, so he forced his own thoughts to his surroundings, easing the intensity of his connection with his brother as Wilhelm snuck further into Bellend.

The city had always been dirty and gray, but now death had laid claim on it, and whatever light might have lived in the city had long been devoured by darkness. They passed toppled homes, blackened by soot, carpeted with broken furniture, kitchens in disarray, beds overturned, and children's toys burned of their innocence.

The glimpses he caught of charred bodies turned Wilhelm's blood cold. Gooey blackened corpses lay prone, hands and feet trussed up behind them. Too often he saw entire families huddled together in death, and by the few surviving boarded windows, Wilhelm did not have to guess what happened. Any home that had survived the fires looked forlorn, their emptiness reflected in the deserted streets.

At one intersection, Wilhelm raised a hand for a halt and pressed against a home, the others following suit. He'd been certain he'd heard something—a plopping of feet in a puddle perhaps.

"Sick bastards," Varila muttered beside him.

Tracking her gaze, he saw a husk of a child, rotted and maggot infested. It clutched on to a stuffed toy bear, one similar to a toy Tedris favored. The sight tore through his heart, and an overwhelming urge to see his son nearly made him give up the entire campaign. Perhaps it would have been wiser to whisk his family away.

Vegos's voice rang clear in his mind. *Focus, boy. Do not let the horrors eat away at your fight. And fight you must. Do not be afraid, be angry. Imagine that child is yours. Imagine the creatures imprisoning this town killed him. What will you do, boy?*

"Kill them," Wilhelm growled, clenching the hilt of his broadsword.

Then do it.

Hissing out a curse, he peered around the corner. Up three houses, four octrils were ambling along, thankfully going the opposite direction. Their feet planted loudly, splashing the water and explaining what Wilhelm had heard. Once they went out of sight, he continued onward.

The trek surely took forever. By the time they reached the three estates holding the prisoners, Wilhelm feared the sun would rise, but one glance at the dark sky gave him hope it hadn't taken as long as he'd thought.

Three sets of ten guards patrolled each estate. Of the thirty Wilhelm observed, half were octrils. The other half were some sort of reptilian creature in humanoid form. Their faces were pointed like snakes, their bodies scaled in a dull tan, and their swishing tails were clearly lizard-like. They stood a head taller than the octrils, and their arms and legs were thickly muscled. They carried halberds and looked to know how to use them.

Adding voice to his thoughts, Varila said, "Those creatures actually look trained."

"Scared?" Wilhelm grinned at her. "You can go with Brice if you're not up for humiliation."

Varila rolled her eyes. "Trying to get rid of me so I won't show you up in front of your men?"

"I still think I should be the one going with you, Lord Knight," Brice said.

If there were another knight Wilhelm would want at his side other than his wife and brother, it would have been Brice. The two had sparred together daily, and because they were close in age and had similar interests, they had become fast friends. But Varila could beat Brice, and with the amount of creatures Wilhelm would be facing, he needed the best.

"Your job is to free the prisoners and get as many able-body men and women to help us," Wilhelm reminded him. "That's what's important."

Brice nodded without much agreement behind it.

Wilhelm winked at his wife and jerked his head south. She cast him a quick grin before creeping off into the shadows and disappearing. With the rest of his group in tow, Wilhelm traversed two more streets until they were huddled in an alley closest to the first estate.

"Stay hidden until they're all cleared," Wilhelm instructed Brice.

Without waiting for a reply, Wilhelm darted off. Clinging to the shadows, he went a few streets before he stopped at one centered with the middle estate. Inhaling a long, soothing breath, Wilhelm stepped from the shadows and walked with slow purpose up the middle of the street.

It didn't take long before shouts of alarm erupted from one of the groups circling the prison. Wilhelm stopped at the end of the street and waited.

Creatures flooded around the sides of the other two estates, and soon thirty crouched before him, weapons drawn. Another ten or so barreled out of the prisons. Wilhelm slowly drew his swords, savoring the hiss they made. He was no stranger to how intimidating his height could be, so he used it to his advantage and stood straight, glaring down at the creatures before him.

"Come now," he roared. "Is this all you have?"

An additional five stepped out of the prisons.

"Pathetic," Wilhelm spat. Spreading his arms wide, he shouted, "Who would claim the life of Wilhelm the Unconquerable? Who dares challenge me?"

They started forward, swords and halberds lowering for a charge. Wilhelm turned on his heel and fled. The pounding behind him confirmed the troop had taken up pursuit. Clearing his mind of all his planning and worries, of the rain pelting his face, and of the slippery ground hurrying by underfoot, he thought only of his brother. A rush of relief relaxed his own shoulders and the whirling of Salvarias's fast paced mind made him dizzy. Quickly he said, "Now!" both in mind and aloud, then let his senses return. Far off he heard the steady drum of the Knighthood thumping and thumping in time with a march. Cries rose from the walls and a loud horn bellowed out over the city. As he had hoped, the group at his back continued their chase.

Wilhelm gritted his teeth and sprinted ahead, lengthening the distance between his hunters and himself. Barreling around one corner, he ended up at the narrow, dead-end alley. Varila stood there with her sword drawn and a smile dancing on her lush lips.

"About damn time," she said. "I get half. Don't go crazy and leave me nothing to fight."

"It's not my fault you're slow," he countered, giving her wink.

"Selfish bastard," she muttered, then whirled around and kissed him deeply.

He almost dropped his swords, swept her in his arms, threw her against the wall, and took her right then and there. He might've if she hadn't pulled away when she did.

Unable to stop his grin, he plunged into the swarm of creatures rounding the corner. Blood rushed in his veins as limbs and organs flew from his swords' sweeping strikes. Joy built with each swing, with each casual parry, and with every body crumpling at his feet. Laughter erupted from him, and for the first time since his brother's death, Wilhelm felt alive.

18

SUMMER 1022 A.R

Salvarias squinted through the rain at the formable gate of Bellend and rested a calming hand on Mithal's neck. Behind him and in cover of the woods, squires beat on massive drums, the sound vibrating his chest, and the feet of fifty Vipers kept time as they marched toward the city. Wilhelm had chosen the drums for pure intimidation, and Salvarias had to admit his brother's idea had merit. The cries of alarm and fear rising from the city were highly satisfying.

"Now?" Kisra asked for the sixth time.

"Not yet," Salvarias murmured, and nudged Mithal forward. The Vipers were still a ways from the gate, and as Wilhelm had said, timing was everything.

The rain came down in earnest, thunder clapped, and lightning fingered across the roiling clouds. The sour odor of wet metal tainted the air, and Salvarias swore he already smelled the blood that would be shed this night. In war, no one ever won. After they killed these creatures, they would move on to the next city and kill those. And so on and so on until they finally killed Veedran. Salvarias would have liked to think it ended there, but humans were human. They would find another enemy, something else to kill, some reason to fight. It was the way of the world, the continuity of the wheel.

The Vipers were within arrow range, but the city appeared not to have any archers, so he waited.

Kisra shifted in her saddle, muttering about how slow knights marched. Salvarias knew she was anxious to try her new spell, and he was excited to witness it. Unlike Cessia's precise magic, Kisra's talent was a bull. Her spells blasted where Cessia's cut. For sieges, Kisra's magic was ideal.

"They're almost in range of the tar," Kisra pointed out.

Salvarias nodded, trying to keep his heart steady and breathing regular. He had asked Kisra to perform her spell thirty-three times before he felt comfortable with her timing: how long it took her to chant her spell, how quick her fingers danced out the rune, and how fast she sent her projectile. Surely her nerves would hasten her actions, which made Salvarias's job a hundred times more difficult. His spell could not be cast until the last possible moment. If he missed the timing, the octrils would not bother to dump the tar or worse, the first three to four rows of Vipers would be shredded.

Straightening in his saddle to obtain optimal view, he said, "On my count, Dame Kisra."

Her aqua eyes lit, and she licked her lips, sitting straight and raising her hand in preparation.

"Three ... Two ..." He saw the cauldrons of tar start to turn. "One!"

Kisra hissed out her spell, snapped her rune out, and released the energy. The instant she did, Salvarias cast his own spell, cursing himself for underestimating Kisra's eagerness. His magic surged with extra effort, catapulting his spell to make up the time.

Kisra's spell was wind, simple and effective. It shot overhead, flattening grasses and howling above the thunder. The knights, having expected it, braced themselves by pausing in their march and taking a knee. As the wind sailed over them, they shook like weak trees in a hurricane. At the same time, Salvarias's protection wall slammed down in front of them, shaking the ground with his hasty casting that

189

had amplified its potency. The wall fanned up and backward, creating an invisible canopy over the Vipers. And none too soon.

Kisra's spell hit the gate with devastating effect. Wood exploded, and the deafening boom trembled the ground. Thousands of wood shards hurled toward the Vipers with deadly force, but upon meeting with Salvarias's protection wall, the shrapnel bounced back and flew into the city. The first two waves of octrils fell.

The impact of not only his spell, but Kisra's as well, had tipped the tar backward, and it cascaded down upon the creatures hoarding the entrance. The screams were harrowing.

The Vipers would have felt nothing in Salvarias's protection, so shock did not stop them. They let out a war cry and charged. The protection wall, however, charged first. It drove back the hundreds of octrils blocking entrance to the city and allowed the Vipers free range of motion.

The drums behind switched to double time, and Idolar's roared order of charge was felt more than heard as fifty mounted knights burst from the trees and descended upon the city at frightening speeds.

After the first wave of creatures fruitlessly attempted to attack the Vipers, Salvarias dropped the spell and charged into the city with Idolar on his heels.

Once through the decimated gate, Salvarias veered left while Kisra went right. As remembered, an opened staircase led to the top of the wall. Swinging off Mithal, Salvarias clambered up the stairs, gritting his teeth at the pain in his knee.

One octril atop the wall cried out and rushed to meet Salvarias. It barely got within striking distance before Salvarias lashed out with his staff and struck the beast on its side. It went toppling to the ground below.

Sparing a glimpse behind, he saw Kisra at the top of the wall opposite the gate from him, her guard of five Vipers parting way through a group of octrils. He cursed himself for forgetting to wait for his own guard. Glancing down, he saw Sir Qwyn struggling against the tide of battle. Salvarias could either wait or continue up. From here, his vantage point was good enough, and the throbbing in his knee demanded a break.

Leaning on his staff, Salvarias chanted his spell. All those hours upon hours of watching the Vipers fight and he still felt unprepared. Regardless, now was not the time for doubt. Idolar had arrived, and despite reinforcements, the knights were grossly out numbered.

Inhaling a soothing breath, Salvarias took a few precious moments to observe the flow of battle. A single, finger-long ice shard floated at his side, waiting. Wilhelm had taught him to slow down the battle, to look at the fight as a planned dance with figures gliding in a purposeful pattern.

It took too long for his tastes, but eventually he saw it, and for the first time he was thankful for his ability to focus on more than one thing. The boiling mass of bodies consumed his vision, his mind, until it was clear what would happen next. The first ice shard he sent into the brain of an octril raising a sword against Sir Qwyn, missing the knight's skull by a few inches as the man dodged left, just as Salvarias had anticipated. No sooner had the shard left his rune than two more materialized.

Unexpected, his magic observed.

Indeed, Salvarias had only been able to generate one shard at a time when using this simple spell, one he could keep up for some time. The shards were smaller than his regular spell, but for these cases, he did not need the power or girth of larger shards.

Let us test our limits, shall we? his magic asked.

Salvarias could not help but smile. Without any drain on his energy, five shards appeared. Picking his five targets, he sent them off while ten more appeared in his rune.

Brilliant! his magic exclaimed. *Our godhood has brought us at least one positive in a pool of negatives.*

Indeed, my friend, Salvarias confirmed.

"Salvarias!"

Sir Qwyn's cry jolted Salvarias at the same time pain splintered through his chest. He collided with the wall, air whooshing from his lungs, his head rapping smartly against stone. Everything spun in a blur of gray before he blinked his vision clear.

Too late.

A massive hand clamped on to the collar of his robes and lifted him off his knees, which he had not realized he had fallen to. He was raised eye level with a minotaur. Rain streaked down its muzzle and slicked its horns. The smell of wet cow was nearly overpowering.

"We've been looking for you," it growled.

Salvarias gasped in a breath, prying at the beast's hands. "You can tell your Master he is not the hunter any more. We are coming for him, and we will kill him."

"What makes you think you can beat a god?"

Salvarias had no chance to reply. The minotaur smashed him into the wall. Pain radiated along his spine and the back of his skull. The world went deaf and white and reappeared a blink later. The creature slammed him again, as if he weighed nothing, like he was a doll. Pain consumed him in a wave of nausea.

Salvarias felt the strike coming. Partly because of instinct, the other because he heard his brother's roar of anger from across the battle, echoed by Vegos. Salvarias's spell was still active, but his brain merely swam in agony, unable to focus the shards.

The sickening wet sound of a sword piercing flesh was followed by the sweet smell of blood and the crunch of bone. Whatever held him up let go, and Salvarias crumpled to the ground, clutching at his sporadic heart and gasping in lungfuls of air, eyes shut tight against the pain.

"Lord Knight," Sir Qwyn said. "Are you all right?"

Salvarias nodded and forced open his eyes. He was on his side, rain pelting his face, and his hood had fallen back.

Sir Qwyn sucked in a breath and staggered backward. No matter how many times it happened, it hurt Salvarias as if it were the first. He averted his demonic eyes and raised his hood.

"Thank you, Sir Qwyn," he rasped.

Using the wall and his staff, Salvarias managed to get to his feet, ignoring Sir Qwyn's gaping stare.

"Sir Qwyn, you must focus," Salvarias said.

The knight just stared.

"You blubbering idiot," Okulu snarled.

The merc was descending the staircase. He grabbed Sir Qwyn's cuirass and shoved him. "Get down there. You and I will have words later."

Qwyn fumbled his way down, glancing back every few stairs.

"Worthless bastard," Okulu muttered. "I've got you. Get to work."

"Thank you, my friend."

"Don't. You and I are having words as well. I can't believe you took off without your guard."

"I fear I am nervous and was not thinking. I apologize."

Okulu grunted, motioning three men to Salvarias's other side.

Salvarias searched the city for his brother. Wilhelm had roughly fifty freed prisoners at his side and had flanked the enemy, squashing them between the two weak forces. One quick scan showed him a strip of octrils that had not managed their way into the fight, perhaps sixty of them.

Chanting and drawing his rune, Salvarias generated an ice sword at least as tall as Wilhelm.

"What in Oblivion do you plan to do with that thing?" Okulu asked.

The merc did not have a chance to wait for Salvarias's explanation. He engaged two octrils heading down the stairs.

"Rulose," Salvarias whispered.

His sword flipped parallel to the ground and dove into the mass of unengaged octrils. The force was more than what Salvarias had intended, and the strength of his spell seemed to sap out of his muscles.

Shrill cries rose as the octrils saw their end speeding toward them. They had nowhere to run. They were packed together between the two sides, shackled in place by their own troops. The sword passed at chest level and cut them in half. The spectacle turned the heads of three lines of the enemy. The knights closest to the blood-spewing half-bodies utilized the distraction brilliantly. Mercilessly they cut down any creature gaping at their fallen comrades. As beneficial as it was, it did not level the playing field.

"That's something," Okulu said. "You need to teach Kisra that spell."

Inhaling a breath, Salvarias drifted off into a trance, allowing his mind to take in the battle as a whole. Shards from his original, still active spell flew from his rune. He paid no heed to the numbers he spawned, only that they hit their target. Vaguely he was aware of Kisra's lagging efforts, of her leaning against Brice as he held her up. Regardless, she kept going. They both had to because the tides had not turned in their favor. Yet.

Smiling to himself, Salvarias drew his dagger, ran it down his left hand, and held it up. "Brother."

From across the battle, Wilhelm's gaze turned to Salvarias. His brother staggered back at seeing Salvarias's blood, and the rush of power surging alive in Wilhelm sent a shiver up Salvarias's spine.

His brother's laugh boomed over the deafening clang of steel on steel, the drums beating off in the distance, the cries of the dying, and over the bellow of thunder tearing at the sky.

The tides turned, and the enemy fled.

LUNARA PULLED the hood of her meager cloak tighter about her face as the knights covered in blood and reeking of death plodded back into camp. The other squires were too busy cheering to notice her sinking into the background.

For the past two days, she had snuck around, changing disguises from squire to healer's apprentice to chef's assistant to latrine digger. Her entire body was sore, her fingernails dark with dirt, and she never felt clean anymore. Nevertheless, she would do it all again just to be close to Salvarias, to be there when he finally realized he needed her.

Standing behind a tall young man, she peered around him. There. In front of the group, Wilhelm strode forward, victory lighting his face with joy, Vegos lumbering alongside him. Her breath exhaled in sharp relief when she saw her husband under Wilhelm's arm. Salvarias's feet weren't moving right, but Wilhelm held him up as he often did. Salvarias's face was death white except for an old trail of blood smeared under his nose.

Kisra slept in Brice's arms, and a set of squires fussed around the pair, offering water and to carry the unconscious woman. Brice merely held on to her tighter, shaking his head at the offers.

Taking one last long look at her husband, Lunara turned from the crowd and crept among the tents. At Wilhelm's, she crouched and waited.

It didn't take long for light to flare to life. A group of perhaps ten crammed inside, silhouetted shadows to Lunara, but she recognized Wilhelm's build and her sister's curvy figure.

"Report," Wilhelm said.

"One dead," Sir Paull said. "One more will be dead by morning. Three will need weeks to recover. The rest should be ready by the next city."

"All things considered, that's better than we could've hoped," Idolar said.

"No, it's completely unacceptable," Wilhelm muttered. There was a pause before he said, "We need a different approach."

"I agree," Salvarias said, voice heavy and slow. "And I will suggest again what I did before."

"No," Wilhelm growled.

"I think he's right," Okulu said. "Honestly, it's safer for him and Kisra. You saw that minotaur nearly killed him. Kisra was almost taken too. I had to add five knights to each of them. The creatures see them as the threat when they're out in the open."

"Then we hide them," Wilhelm snapped.

"We cannot be hidden and have a view of the battle," Salvarias mumbled.

Wilhelm growled deep in his throat. "Varila?"

A long pause, then Lunara's sister said, "I think Salvarias is right. We need to trim down the Vipers. Make them a small force, stealthiest of the bunch. Sneak them into the cities and have them free the prisoners while we distract. Then they can find defendable positions and help from there. When they're on the front lines, it's impossible to protect them."

"I'll think about it," Wilhelm said.

"We ..." Salvarias inhaled a deep breath. "We must make better time between cities."

"Absolutely not," Wilhelm said shortly. "I'll not have you doing that spell. It takes too much out of you."

"I'm starting to think it wasn't a good idea to leave Lunara behind," Okulu said. "She could help." Another pause. "We could create a portal and bring her here."

Wilhelm laughed, but it lacked any humor. "I'm sure Edium would let his untrained daughter traipse across Windlous when it's infected with the enemy. They'll be looking for a way to get to Salv, and using his wife is surely at the top of their list."

"I agree," Varila said. "Lunara and Salvarias are safer apart."

"Salvarias?" Okulu said.

Another pause, and Lunara held her breath.

"I think the decision should be hers," Salvarias said eventually. "She is her own woman, and it is not my place to say what she does or does not do."

Lunara's breath exploded out in relief.

"My father will never agree," Varila said.

"Let's table the issue for later," Wilhelm concluded. "We need some rest. The day after tomorrow we move out."

Peering around the corner of the tent, she saw Salvarias emerge with Okulu. Another man was waiting, younger than Varila, with a mass of blonde curls crusted with gore. He stood at attention.

"You sent for me, Knight Commander Okulu," he said.

"Qwyn," Okulu drawled. "The man who let down our Lord Knight, who almost got him killed. Tell me, what do you think would've happened tonight if Salvarias had not been present?"

"We would have lost, Sir."

"Okulu," Salvarias chided.

The merc held up a hand. "Don't defend him, Salvarias. There's more at stake than just your life. You saved countless in that battle. Lower your hood."

"I do not—"

"Please," Okulu said, his tone dead, eyes dark. To Qwyn, Okulu said, "And if you look away, so help me I'll flog your ass to Oblivion."

Her husband seemed too exhausted to argue. He tossed back his hood and met Qwyn's stare. She never understood why people cringed from Salvarias, but Qwyn was no exception. He looked about ready to break, but Okulu grabbed a chunk of the man's curls and held his head in place.

"Salvarias is my friend," Okulu growled. "You will look him in the eye until you see what I see."

Qwyn squirmed, whimpered, his eyes wide and filled with horror. Pain lanced across her heart, the pain of a man who wanted acceptance so badly that each time he was denied it, it was like being stabbed over and over.

"Please," Salvarias said softly to Okulu. "There is no—"

Qwyn stopped his struggles, his eyes growing wider, awe struck instead of petrified. Falling to his knees, he bowed his head and choked, "Please forgive me, my lord. I beg you."

Salvarias looked as shocked as she felt. He blinked, glanced at Okulu, then sank to his knees in front of Qwyn.

"There is nothing to forgive," Salvarias said.

"I betrayed you," Qwyn said in a voice near tears.

Salvarias's expression fell into helplessness. He reached out, but curled his fingers back. "I swear on my brother's life I hold no grudge against you. Please rise and feel no guilt or failure. I gladly place my life in your hands."

Qwyn nodded and rose to his feet, Salvarias following.

Okulu beamed a smile as if nothing had happened. "Very good, then." Turning to Salvarias, he said, "By the gods, go get some sleep. You look about ready to fall over."

Salvarias, eyes still wide, pulled up his hood, bowed to the men, and stumbled away.

"What did you feel?" Okulu asked once Salvarias was out of earshot.

"Awe," Qwyn responded. "Love. Power. I ... I want his approval more than anything. I would follow him to Oblivion." Raising his gaze to Okulu, he said, "What is he?"

The merc frowned. "My guess? A god. A very, very powerful god that doesn't know what he is yet. You understand me?"

Qwyn nodded fervently. "Forgive me, Knight Commander. I swear I will give my life for his."

"Find nine men you trust to do the same and to keep what I've told you secret. We'll repeat this exercise with them in the morning."

Lunara snuck around another tent until she caught sight of Salvarias. He hobbled into his own tent.

Keeping her face down, she walked by. Unintentionally she caught a glimpse of him through a gap in the tent flap. He'd taken off his robes and stood with his back to her. It was covered in red blotches, already darkening with bruises, and he inhaled a sharp breath when he twisted to the water basin. By the color, his entire back would be black and blue tomorrow.

Striding past, she switched direction and headed toward her tent. No doubt her husband would not seek a remedy for his pain when others were worse off, nor could he apply his own mixture. She, however, had continued studying herblore for the three years Salvarias had been dead. She knew exactly what he needed.

Her tent was big enough for a bedroll and her pack, and was so squat she could barely sit up in it. Awkwardly, she struggled out of her loose trews and tunic and into her baggier healer robe. Donning her thin cloak, she pulled the hood low and headed to the healer's tent.

When she arrived, it was quiet. Sir Paull drifted from knight to knight, ensuring they were comfortable, that bandages were clean and balms applied. She'd met Sir Paull years ago, and had artfully avoided him until now. Bowing her head, she tried to keep behind him and headed toward the herbs.

"What is it, child?" he asked, never turning her direction but clearly addressing her.

Trying her best to change the tone of her voice, she said deeply, "Lord Knight Salvarias has bruises forming on his back."

"Bad?"

"Yes."

"I see." He frowned at her. "Do you know what to mix?"

"Yes," she said.

He studied her for some time before smiling. "Then do so and take them to him."

"I think it best if another healer delivers them."

"Nonsense, child. He obviously feels comfortable with you if he showed you." He shooed her. "Hurry along now. We can't keep him in pain."

Fool! Lunara cursed herself.

Mixing the herbs and oils gave her a chance to calm and think this through. All she had to do was find another healer and pass along her mixture to him, tell him to deliver and apply it, and her problem would be solved. Happy with her solution, she hummed her mother's favorite song as she ground up witch hazel and chamomile.

It took some time to smooth the witch hazel before she added the oils. Satisfied, she gathered her things and walked as quietly as she could to the tent exit. Outside, Sir Paull was whispering with Sir Qwyn.

"Ah," the healer said, breaking his conversation and turning to Lunara. "My apprentice. Do escort her to our Lord Knight, would you, Sir Qwyn?"

The knight bowed to her. "It would be my honor."

"There's really no need," Lunara said.

"Nonsense, child," Sir Paull said. "Hurry along."

Begging her brain for a plan, it betrayed her and fled. Muttering one of Salvarias's favorite curses, she followed Sir Qwyn to Salvarias's tent.

"Wait here," he instructed.

He wasn't in her husband's tent but for a breath before he came back out and held the flap open for her.

"He's asleep," he said. "Will that be a problem?"

Lunara peered inside. Salvarias was on a cot, lying face down, his arms dangling off the sides, a blanket pulled up to his waist, his bare back reddening. She'd never seen him sleep in such a way. Normally he was on his side, curled up to a near fetal position and dressed. He must have been in more pain than she had assumed.

"It's fine," Lunara said.

"Take your time."

Qwyn dropped the tent flap behind her. She stood motionless, battling the fear of being discovered against the need to ease her husband's pain.

He twitched, and the motion sent spasms up his back.

That decided it. Tiptoeing to the cot, she knelt beside it and dumped half the herb mixture into her hands. After rubbing them together to warm up the oil and her fingers, she gently worked the oil into his scarred back. The effect was immediate, whether because of her touch or the ointment she didn't know, but tension drained from him, the furrow in his brow eased, his breathing lightened, and he seemed to sink further into the cot.

Once his skin absorbed the first dose, she poured the remaining in her hands, warmed it, and massaged it into his back.

"I would recognize that touch in the darkest of rooms," he murmured.

Lunara froze, fear stammering her heart, her breath catching in her throat. They'd send her back. Ship her away from her husband.

Slowly he rolled to his side, and his dark eyes regarded her for several moments. "Am I dreaming?" he asked.

She hesitated a blink. "Yes."

Wincing, he reached out a tentative hand and pushed back her hood. A smile lit up his eyes. "I have missed you."

Then his lips were on hers. His hands owned her wholly the instant they pulled her into his lap. She wasn't sure how long it had been before she noticed the cold air on her naked skin, or how long his lips and hands had explored her, but when he took her, he did so slowly, with those purposeful motions that drove her insane with desire and hauled her over the brink quicker than ever.

Afterward, he wrapped her in his arms, buried his face in her hair, and fell asleep. Sure he wouldn't wake, she kissed him softly, slid free, and dressed. By the time she left the tent, the furrow in his brow had deepened and his head tossed restlessly.

Qwyn had fallen asleep outside, and she snuck by. Smiling at the pleasure still radiating through her, she strolled to her tent, her disguise intact, her husband cared for, and the world brighter than it had been.

19

SUMMER 1022 A.R

Salvarias woke with a start and nearly cried out when throbbing pain vibrated down his spine. He looked around, begging his mind to remember where he was. Sunlight filtering through canvas warmed the tent. A steaming kettle of tea waited on a nearby table. Outside, silhouetted shadows moved about, and he heard the droning of conversations and smelled cooked bacon.

It came back in a rush, and remembering the battle made him groan in pain. Burying his face in his pillow, he hid from the afternoon sun blaring through his tent. The scent of a spring meadow filled his nostrils, and he inhaled it deeply, feeling a pang of longing.

Forcing his body up, he careened his way to the table and plopped down in a chair. He drank three cups of tea to hammer away the building headache. As it receded, he remembered the dream he had had last night: the warmth of Lunara under him, the sound of her moans in his ear, and the taste of her on his tongue.

He bolted upright and gave a sharp exhale at the spasm tightening his back. It had not been a dream. He could still taste her and smell the scent of her lingering on his skin.

Dropping his cup, he grabbed his robes, pulled them overhead, and marched outside, not bothering with shoes or a belt.

Okulu lounged on a stump. "What's got you all riled up?" he drawled.

Salvarias ignored him and walked to the healers' tent. Inside, none of the white robed people were of the right build. Turning around he nearly ran into Okulu.

"What's wrong?"

Salvarias shot by and surveyed the camp. "She is here."

"Who?"

Salvarias strode to the horse pins. Nothing. He asked Mithal if he had seen her, but the horse had not. Of course she would stay clear of the stallion. Mithal would have told Salvarias.

The squires. Marching to his right, he found the open area where the young squires sat around campfires. Wilhelm had taken in any child that came to them looking for food and a place to sleep, but only the older ones had been permitted to accompany them on their campaign. The youths were mostly slender, grappling with the lankiness of teenage years. Lunara was slim, long limbed, and only her gracefulness would make her stand out.

Then he saw her. She sat alone, hood pulled low, polishing blood and gore from a cuirass. He could not see her face, but he knew those motions, how they felt upon his skin. Then she looked up. Her eyes widened, and she stood, dumping the cuirass to the ground. Fear melted from her stare, and her eyes hardened, her fingers curling into tight fists.

"Oh my," Okulu said from behind. "Varila is going to throw a fit."

Salvarias crossed the area, ignoring the eyes following him. He stopped in front of her, the group quieting.

"You can't make me go back," she said, lifting her head, tossing her hair. Gods she was stunning. "I'll run away," she threatened. "I'll find a ship to bring me back. I'll escape whatever dungeon my father throws me in. I'll do it. I swear it!" Tears brimmed in her eyes, and she blinked them away. It seemed to make her more furious. "I'm staying, Salvarias Laybryth! And there's not a damn thing you can do about it!" Her voice cracked and tears broke free. "You can't make me go back! I can help you!"

So many emotions warred for dominance, but one stood out from the rest: shame. "Forgive me." He sank to his knees in front of her. "Forgive me for making you stay behind. Forgive me for not listening to what you wanted."

Uncertainty fleeted across her face. She had expected him to be angry, to send her away. It shamed him more.

Then she launched herself into his arms. He gathered her tightly to him. "I beg you," he whispered. "Forgive me."

"Of course I do," she said past a laugh and tears. "I love you."

"This is all fine and good," Okulu said. "But you two are in for some arguments. Varila is going to kill something when she sees you."

SALVARIAS CONCLUDED that Okulu's insights were more honed than the merc ever let on. Salvarias had expected Varila to be upset, but the instant the woman laid eyes on her sister, he feared Varila's anger would erupt the tent into flames.

"What have you done?" Varila snapped at Lunara. "Father's probably dying of heart failure right now."

"I left him a note," Lunara mumbled, her head downcast.

Varila threw up her hands. "A note? A damn note? You think that's going to help him? Or mother?"

"I want to be here," Lunara said.

"So you can screw your husband?" Varila snapped. "So you can be captured and tortured again? What could you possibly contribute to this cause?"

Anger tinted Salvarias's vision, but he knew Lunara could handle herself, and interfering with arguing sisters would be as smart as standing in the middle of a tornado.

Lunara's head shot up, and her eyes narrowed at Varila. "If anyone would take the time to look upon me as the woman I am and not some child, you would know I'm versed in herblore. If *anyone* in my family took the time to see me as something other than a sheltered girl, you would have knighted me in with the healers. But all you or father ever do is treat me like a child. I am married, Varila. I have a husband. I have a mother, a father, and a stubborn sister who I want to help. I love Arden, and I want to raise my children in Serenity. If we don't kill Veedran, that hope is lost." Lunara turned her glare to Wilhelm. "Why wasn't I asked to be knighted? Why was I cast aside while you made all your plans, found positions for your friends?"

Wilhelm glanced at Varila and then Lunara. "Because I knew your family would kill me if I did. They love you, and they want you safe. Salv and I love you and want you safe. We did it because—"

"Do you not love your own brother? You had no problems knighting him. Or how about your wife?"

"That's ..." Wilhelm's voice trailed off. He glanced at Salvarias, but he merely shrugged. They had treated Lunara poorly. There were no excuses. Wilhelm cringed from Varila as he said, "You're absolutely right. It wasn't my place to tell you no and exclude you."

"You can't be serious?" Varila said exasperated. She turned fire-eyes to Salvarias. "They'll take her. They'll cut off the rest of her fingers."

"Her decisions are her own," Salvarias said, though his own heart ached with the same fear.

Okulu clucked his tongue. "If you two ladies want to go outside and wrestle for it, I think the ground is still nice and muddy. It'd be all soft and accommodating."

Varila growled at him. "I suppose you support this."

Okulu raised his hands in surrender. "No, absolutely not. I'd side with you and that lovely sword any day." He cast Lunara a not-so-secret wink.

"You've all gone mad!" Varila bellowed. "She can't fight. She can't defend herself! We're at war! WAR!"

"Sir Paull can't use a sword," Lunara countered.

And there it was. All eyes fell to Varila. No argument could be made against Lunara's point.

Varila looked stricken. Tears welled in her eyes and a feeble, cracking voice came from her lips. "I can't lose you."

Lunara smiled. "And you won't. I promise." She hugged Varila.

"Who else is going to teach Tedris the wonders of books and reading?"

Varila gave a broken laugh. "I'll kill you if you die."

When Varila looked up at Salvarias, her message was clear. If Lunara got hurt, Varila would send him to his old home in the catacombs under Warton. He tilted his head in acknowledgement.

It is about time you realized how much you need her, Vegos said. *She is vital to your success, boy. She will be escape from the darkness closing in. Listen to her. Accept what she can gift you.*

I will, my friend.

"Well, now that's settled, let's talk about travel," Okulu said.

Wilhelm's eyes darkened.

Okulu continued undeterred. "Enemies escaped last night. No doubt they're fleeing to their friends to tell them what's happening. We need to beat them to the cities, take over everything, and force them toward Bren and Humar's army. If we take our time, each city will increase in difficulty, and we'll lose more men."

"Okulu is right," Salvarias said. "With Lunara's help, spells take half the amount of energy."

"What spell is this?" Brice asked.

"In a blink, I can travel as far as I can see," Salvarias explained. "I could travel to our next city and open a portal in the amount of time it takes my brother to eat breakfast."

Wilhelm crossed his arms over his chest, ignoring the laughter, his eyes locked on to Salvarias's. "You swear you won't overdo it?"

"With Lunara, I can take you with us as well, Brother. The three of us could find a place for camp and set up the portal. And you yourself can ensure I do not overly exert myself."

Wilhelm's eyebrows shot up. "She helps that much?"

"Yes."

"You can't argue with that," Okulu said. "With the time we're saving, we could even stand to give Salvarias a day to rest before each siege. We can take over Windlous in a month instead of two."

"Can we get word to Humar?" Wilhelm asked Kisra.

She nodded. "We're at the ocean. I'll send the message through the sea, and my father will have it within a day."

"I hate to say it," Brice said, resting a hand on Wilhelm's shoulder. "But it's the best plan."

Wilhelm shook his head, but he gave Salvarias an infectious crooked grin. "I've always said you're the most amazing mage to ever live."

Salvarias grinned back.

"First, we're going to see my parents," Varila said. "Kisra, go create a portal."

Lunara bit her lip. "You think it wise?"

"Not for you," Varila said. "But Father won't be mad at me."

KISRA HAD the portal set up in no time, and Salvarias, his brother, the sisters, Okulu, and Brice walked through, Lunara's hand gripping his painfully tight.

Warm air hit Salvarias first, and the afternoon sunlight flicked off into the middle of the night. Stars hung high, the moon peering down at them. Gunder's former estate had transformed since they had left over a month ago. The portal opened up into the old gardens, now a staging area for transporting troops and supply wagons adjacent to the barracks.

Wilhelm nodded in approval. "Looks good."

"Shh," Varila hushed. "If anyone sees us, you'll be stuck here signing paperwork for days."

The group snuck through the estate grounds and found the secret entrance in the wall butting up against the Bellerum estate. Squeezing past thick vines, Salvarias dumped into the servants' garden of the Bellerum home. Empty and smelling of Jasmine, Salvarias mused it was nearly as nice as the formal garden. The servants' rooms had balconies as well, but no one stood on any, and the windows were dark.

Varila led the way, soundless, the rest following as silently except for Okulu's metal armor clanking every now and again. They slipped in through the kitchen and all of them snapped to a halt.

Lord Bellerum stood by a fire, dressed in a robe, face contorted in barely controlled anger. Lady Talura stood at her husband's side, robe pulled tight about her.

Sira and Saval darted from the shadows and ran up to Salvarias and Lunara. Sira rubbed Lunara's stomach, purring deeply. Saval's greeting was so enthusiastic Salvarias was pushed back against Wilhelm, his brother's immovable frame all that kept Salvarias upright.

It took time to calm the griffins, but when they did, Lady Talura said, "Well hello, dears." She looked them up and down. "You all look alive. See there," she said to Lord Bellerum. "Alive and well."

Lord Bellerum merely glared at Lunara and Varila.

"Boys," Lady Talura continued. Her gaze rested on Salvarias, so bright and warm. "Hello, sweetness." Gliding across the room, she stopped in front of Lunara and whispered, "Say you love him and all will be forgiven."

Lunara nodded and walked a few steps forward, never unclamping her hand from Salvarias's. "I know you're upset, Father, but I had to. I want to help."

Still nothing. At this point, even Salvarias shifted under the man's stare.

"I ..." Lunara forced out a smile. "I love you."

Lord Bellerum's glare faltered, tears fled into his eyes, and he gave a soft cry before he swept Lunara up in his arms. "I was so worried," he said. "So worried."

"I'm sorry," Lunara said, finally releasing Salvarias's hand. "It was important I go."

"You're safe here."

"It's my choice," she said. "Not yours."

Lord Bellerum looked to Varila. She nodded subtly, and any objection he might have made died. "I understand," he said finally. "I should have trusted your judgement."

"I brought her for you to see," Varila said. "She's fine, and she's going back with us."

"Of course," Lord Bellerum said. "But your mother and I are going with you."

"What about the city?" Sir Brice asked.

"And Tedris?" Varila asked.

"I've got old man Gryn here. He'll take care of it, and Tedris is visiting Zehnia and the prince and princess. I'll make sure she knows to keep him there."

Whoever Gryn was, Sir Brice seemed pleased by the lord's explanation.

Lady Talura paused in front of Wilhelm. "You look especially well, son."

"I banged some sense into him," Varila supplied.

Okulu choked out a laugh, and Wilhelm flushed red.

"Well, welcome back," Lady Talura said, unruffled. "I'll get us packed, Edium." Turning a smile to Salvarias, she said, "Come along, Son. I need some help."

Oddly, he found himself walking beside her without looking for an excuse to leave.

Smiling up at him, she said, "I've missed you."

"And I you," he said, yet again surprised by the truth of his words.

The smile blossomed up to her eyes, brimming with love and pride. He yearned for it as much as he recoiled from it.

He pondered what it would have been like if she had been his mother. He wondered if she would have hugged him when he had seen the man hanged in the gallows in Falar when he was a small child. Would she have looked upon him with disgust, or would she have held him tight and told him he was good, that the smile was just a mistake, that he was not a monster? When he confessed his evil, would she have beaten him with a skillet, strapped him to a chair and bled him with leeches, cut open his head? Or would she have encased him in enough love that the evil could not survive it?

He almost laughed aloud at his pathetic desires. There was not enough love in the world to drive the evil from him. No mother could ever gift a monstrosity such as him her love. Mother's knew good and evil. Salvarias's mother had known. Lady Talura was toying with him, waiting until he wanted her love enough to lower his guard, then she would laugh at him, hurt him, and cut him.

Lowering his head, he shifted from her reach. He would not allow it to happen again. No one would cut him anymore.

20

SUMMER 1022 A.R

Salvarias stared absently at the mound of bodies, Saval sitting stately at his side, the setting sun bathing the sky in plum. Hyde had fallen easily that morning, and the task of piling up the bodies of their enemy was near an end. The stench should have discouraged his lingering, but he found himself lost in a trance of exhaustion and relief that held his feet and eyes captive.

Over the past three weeks, their determined army had taken over eleven of the thirteen largest cities and towns. Tomorrow they would head for Lynta, and after that, they would meet Humar's army in Bren. Victory was so very close. Salvarias swore he could reach out and almost touch it, taste the sweetness of it, smell its end, and it scared him.

Instincts left him feeling cold, an odd hopelessness creeping by his side, whispering defeat in his ear. There was no reason for it, no sign victory over Lynta would not come as swiftly as the last eleven cities they had seized. Yet, he could not shake the feeling. Perhaps it was merely exhaustion. Spells upon spells were all he had done for weeks. Any other time he was sleeping. His life had taken on a repetition he found tiresome. Certainly it allowed him and Kisra to perfect their timing and spells, but Salvarias's mind was not made for redundancy. He pondered if his bleak outlook was merely his mind trying to sputter back to life.

Once the knights had lit the bodies aflame, the men dwindled out of sight, each off to sleep after a long day of cleaning up Hyde and returning it to its few surviving citizens. He should return with them. He should sleep. But he was as tired of sleep as he was tired. At least tonight he would sleep in a real bed. One of the inn owners had insisted on housing as many knights as his establishment would permit. The rest of the knights were welcomed into people's homes.

Okulu sauntered up to the now flaming pile of corpses and extended his hands, rubbing them together as if cold. "When I need to think, I always look for a pile of burning bodies. Really gets the mind moving." He glanced over his shoulder and grinned at Salvarias. "Smells like a pig on a stick."

"I lack your same fondness."

"I've got him, Qwyn," Okulu said. "Go get some rest."

Sir Qwyn saluted and headed back toward the inn, his shoulders slouching and feet dragging.

"The army needs rest," Salvarias noted.

"I think Wilhelm plans on allowing us a day or two in Lynta. He's eager to be as close to Bren as possible. Why are you out here?"

Salvarias shrugged and pulled his gaze from the bodies. So much death. "I have a bad feeling."

Okulu frowned. "Your instincts are usually spot on. Any idea why?"

"I have not a single clue, my friend." A change in the breeze sent a line of smoke in Salvarias's eyes. He blinked back the tears and fought the urge to gag at the odor. "I cannot say if our problems will arise in Lynta or Bren, or perhaps some later battle I have yet to learn of."

Okulu waved away the smoke. "No sense in pondering it. What will be will be." He took a swig from his flask. "You look tired."

"I am."

Okulu nodded, his gaze roving over the deserted streets. "I bet you're bored out of your mind. No time to come up with new spells or read."

"And I bet your soberness has nearly made you insane."

Okulu grinned. "That noticeable?"

"Perhaps not to everyone. Your flask has not yet gone empty this week. It is merely my observation."

"A lot of lives depend on us … on me. Despite my charming and carefree disposition, I do take that seriously."

"I never doubted you did, my friend."

"Must be nice having Lunara with you."

"It is. I am sorry you have been separated from Cessia and the twins for so long."

Okulu took a swig. "It's been rough, but we'll meet up with Cessia in Bren. And I doubt the kids miss me. Zehnia has all sorts of things to keep them occupied."

Salvarias smiled. "From what I observed of them, Humar will have assigned guards to keep them out of trouble."

Okulu laughed. "I don't understand it. They find it as easily as you. Speaking of children …"

Salvarias ran his hand along Saval's feathered head, realizing the griffin had suffered another growth spurt. When sitting, his head came up to Salvarias's waist. "I do desire children. However, I am not sure it is wise. The forces living inside Lunara and myself should not be approached lightly. Nor do I have any confidence I would be a good father."

"Ah, children are resilient little beasts. And I've seen you with Tedris and my kids. They all love you." Okulu glanced at the darkening sky. "Let's head back."

Salvarias fell in line with the merc.

"I've been wondering something," Okulu said. "Have you noticed how no child you've ever met has shied away from your eyes?"

Frowning, Salvarias shook his head.

"I've always thought children to be free of evil. They meet the world with wide, open eyes. They see things …" Okulu pursed his lips. "It's like they see inside people, past the layers of facade we put up. Briana once told me I always look sad. Remarkable she noticed what I harbor in regards to my sister. I'll never be free of it, and no matter how much I smile, she saw it. Makes me wonder what they see when they look at you."

Salvarias shrugged off the comment. He did not want to think on it. To do so would make him confront something he absolutely refused to face.

At the inn, Salvarias ate a quick dinner with Lunara and her family and then retired to his room, leaving Saval with Lunara. He needed to study the same spells once again.

Vegos's voice rang in Salvarias's mind, though the bear had remained downstairs with Wilhelm. *You put too much pressure on yourself, boy. Take the night off.*

I must be prepared. Good night, Vegos.

You're as stubborn as that brother of yours. The bear muttered a curse before falling silent.

Sighing in resignation, he plopped down in a chair, ignited his magic, and opened his spell book. With each word, his mind wandered here and there, and only his magic's call pulled him back to study.

After one such lapse, his magic suggested, *Perhaps we can rest and study tomorrow. Honestly, we are not getting anywhere. Your mind was not made for the mundane of routine. You must challenge and awaken it.*

Salvarias leaned back in his chair and rubbed his eyes. *I am sorry, my friend.*

His magic snorted out a laugh. *I could use the rest. I fear I am exhausted beyond what I have shared with you. I promise, tomorrow morning we can study and be ready in time.*

Then rest and let us continue tomorrow.

With that, he let his magic fall away and shivered instantly as its warmth left him. He rummaged around in his pack and came up with a book Lord Bellerum had given him in the buried city of Quind. They had presumed the writings to be that of a mad man, but the longer Salvarias had studied the book, the more he believed there to be a barely coherent story hidden within: two or three words strung together to make sense amongst ten words that could not possibly be linked. It would take him hours of puzzling through the text. He smiled at the book and reverently placed it on the table.

Laying out his quill, ink, and fresh parchment, he began jotting down passages he found. Hours passed by uncared about, his mind reveling in a new task, awakening from a long slumber, and it made him feel alive.

At some point Lady Talura brought tea, Lunara visited and left him be once she saw him occupied, and Wilhelm had wished him good evening, Varila hanging drunkenly on his brother's arm.

After Salvarias had gone through the entire book, he set it aside and picked up the parchment. Settling in his chair, Salvarias sipped his cold tea and read.

I FOLLOWED THEM, I did. The mighty Firth Brothers, the sons Nevlar created for his lover's war. The forest was dark, oh so dark, and it screamed. It screamed and screamed. The trees pleaded me to end it. To chop, chop, chop them down. They didn't want to see it anymore. I told them to hide me; I lied and told them I would kill them when I saw what I needed. Foolish little things believed me.

I knew what no one else did: Zerana couldn't be dead. No, no, no. No. Not her. No. Not her. Not Veedran's love. He wouldn't kill her. You can't. You can't kill what you love.

I'd prove it to Nevlar. I'd find a way. Everyone knows his fury and what he created in the depths of darkness, what eats souls for eternity: Oblivion, it is; the root of horror and never-ending suffering. I didn't want to go there. I didn't want my love to go there. I'd show him we're not all evil. Not all of us listened to the Dark One.

I heard them, I did. The roar of gods. The ground trembled with it, the trees pissed themselves of their leaves. Anger of the gods bled into the soil, tainting the nectar of life. Lights flashed through the forest. Blood red and ink black.

Then the brothers were in a clearing with the gods. Nevlar a ball of

blackness and anger, darkening toward the center; Veedran a red cloud of
hate and evil, dripping blood from its center.

I wanted to cry as I hid, and I did. Blood. My eyes rained blood. The
power of the gods are not meant for men. No, no, no. We are weak. Weak
little things. Easily tempted, easily killed, easily forgotten. And the gods had
forgotten us. They had forgotten the fragile world in which they battled
upon. The forest changed and wept, corrupted itself with power, a mixture
of hate and anger, despair and loss.

"You will not kill me," Veedran hissed. "You don't have the strength."

"No, I do not, my dearest therro."

The ground shook and surged up black rocks; skipping stones like I
played with in my youth, in times when things were bright and happy, and
when smiles were true and death had not come to my parents.

One stone rose above the others and flew into the center of Veedran. Oh
gods, the scream. My ears bled, and we screamed together with the dark
god. Screamed until our throats bled.

I saw them, the Firth brothers, huddled together, covering their ears,
screaming with us. Screaming and screaming.

Then Veedran's cloud started to take shape, twisting and imploding.
Organs and bones formed, and veins began to encase the blood dripping
from the dark god.

Two tendrils of black smoke snaked out from Nevlar and each grabbed a
Firth brother. The men screamed and writhed against the god's touch, and
their hands smoked and sizzled. I screamed too, screamed and screamed but
the trees hid me, muffled me, and no one came for me.

The rock shot from Veedran's newly constructed heart and flew into
Travard's burning hand as the black smoke entered his skin, sinking in and
in and into his arm. His howls were deafening.

Wilhelm tried to help, but the other tendril penetrated him too, sending
him in a fit of convulsions.

"You are my Guardian," Nevlar said to Travard. "You will keep it safe
and secret. You will not listen to its calls. You will be strong in this." To
Wilhelm, he said, "And you are the Protector. You will give your brother
strength when he has none. Your life is bound to him. Forever will your
bloodlines be enslaved to my cause; forever will you and your children be

vessels to your duty. I offer this salvation to my children. You are their only hope. Keep it hidden from him. Keep yourselves hidden. Now run! Flee! Flee!"

The black fog left them, and the brothers clung to one another and ran far, far away.

Skin grew over Veedran's exposed insides, wrapping him in human form. All that was left was a man—beautiful if not for his eyes, the eyes of darkness and hate.

And then it happened. I knew it happened. The trees knew it happened. And we all shook in fear. Nevlar's curse took hold of all the gods still on Arden. The trees heard their screams, all enslaved into the weakness of a human form, stranded here, on a world so fragile.

"What have you done to me!" Veedran cried, looking at his hands in horror.

"I have taken from you what you value most," Nevlar said. "I have taken your disease and all the power the stone could hold and have given it to my children."

"Curse you!" Veedran screamed. "Curse you from your home, curse you from your children."

Nevlar laughed—dark and sad, dark and angry, dark and hopeless. "These are not my children. I care not for them. I hate them. I will leave you here and smite this world. I hate this place! And I hate you!"

And with that, Nevlar left.

Veedran spoke strange words that held in them a power of their own. Worms crawled up from the earth, already grotesque from the power mutating them into the unholy. They'd grown cat-sized, boils and blisters bursting on their mucusy green flesh. Teeth chomped on their own mouths, caking yellow blood around their gaping maws.

"You, my little pets, will hunt for me. Hunt and hunt until you find what was taken from me. Hunt and send my servants to kill!"

The worms' mouths opened in silent assurance, and then they wiggled their way to the depths of the world.

Veedran raised his face skyward, spread his arms, and shouted, "Father! Creator of all! I have been betrayed!"

"No, my son." A lean and beautiful man appeared, oh so beautiful. I wanted to look away. I did, I did, but I could not. He owned me: my mind, my soul, and my heart. He looked around with an air of indifference. "My first-born sons, and look at what you've done with your power."

"He took her from me," Veedran spat. "She was mine!"

"She was her own." He ran a hand through His sleek black hair. "She made her choice. Nevlar made his. And you've made yours."

"Will you do nothing, Father?" Veedran pleaded, falling to his knees. "At least take back what he has stolen from me."

The man laughed, coarse and hallow. "You two have amused me since the first day I created you both. And this ..." His vibrant purple eyes flared with sick hunger. "This will be the ultimate game. I will curse Arden so no gods can enter or leave it, including your beloved therro. Just imagine his anger when he learns Zerana lives and he is unable to help her. Imagine it!"

Veedran smiled and licked his lips. "Make him suffer as I have, Father."

"Yes," the man continued. "Nevlar will live in agony and never be allowed to set foot upon his world unless he wins. I will set the game's rules for you both to follow. Do not lie down and take what Nevlar has done, what he is about to do. And for your life and Zerana's, do not allow me to become bored. If you do, I'll set in motion events to end you both."

"Take this weak form from me!" Veedran demanded. "I can do nothing trapped in this."

The man laughed. "With all the creatures that can contain a god's power, he chose the weakest, but I dare say one of the more beautiful, for Nevlar has always had a love for beauty. I would have made you into an abarimon, or a nian, or even a naga, though simply a dragon would surely strike fear into the small creatures living here. But no, your dearest brother chose a human." The man laughed again as he turned to leave. "I will not change your form, Veedran. You must learn to grow outside that confine." He paused, glancing at Veedran over a shoulder. "Oh, and Son, do you remember when you defied me, when you went to save your brother—your therro—and I punished you?"

Veedran nodded.

"Nevlar was crafty," the man continued. "He has stolen the seed I gave you. He put it in that rock."

Veedran bolted to his feet, spit flying from his lips as he cursed.

"Yes," the man purred. "I'd forgotten. I made you love what I gave you, didn't I? Like a man consumed by the Thirst." The man laughed. "Oh my dear, dear Nevlar. He has tried to save you so many times, and this is yet another attempt. He took my seed so you would have a chance to see light, but he does not realize the darkness has infected you, does he?" The man looked sympathetic as if watching a crippled dog trying to walk. "I will help you, my son. The Guardian was poisoned with a portion of your power so the seed does not kill him. It will think him a servant of yours. Nevlar is such a smart child." The man smiled affectionately. "Here is what I will do for you. The seed will lay dormant within the stone unless someone learns what lives within it. When they do, the stone will link them to you and you will find it without fail." The man gleamed a smile. "Nevlar has made his Guardian ignorant, but in time someone will uncover what has been documented this day. After all, knowledge is power."

The man looked at me. Right at me! And He smiled. Smiled! I ran, gods how I ran. But I heard Him. Through my screams not to, through my feet pounding on the forest floor, I heard Him.

"You can run all your days, child of Arden," the man called after me. "But you will learn what it is, you will write it down, and you will die a mindless idiot." The voice rose, tinted with humor, with some sadistic satisfaction. "What lives on Arden, what is in the stone, is the seed of all Evil. The seed of darkness. The seed of murder. The seed of hate. And once one poor soul seeks answers to the stone's beginning, the seed will awaken and find its master. But that is not the worst of it. For the length of the stone's life, it will grow more powerful by feeding on its Guardian, taking away his light one nibble at a time. Infecting him as it did Veedran."

SALVARIAS SHOT up from his seat, stumbling as he tossed the parchment into the fire. Grappling with his robes, he found the rope holding the stone around his neck. One harsh tug freed it, and he threw it across the room.

"Brother!" Salvarias cried, backing away quickly, tripping over furniture.

It was too late. The stone knew.

21

SUMMER 1022 A.R

Wilhelm jolted awake to his brother's haunting screams. Throwing aside his blankets, he stumbled out of bed, not bothering with a shirt or shoes. In the hall, other doors were opening, and Lunara and her parents were barreling up the stairs. Wilhelm sprinted to the next room and flung open the door. What he saw turned his blood to ice.

Salvarias was speared in midair by what must have been twenty tentacles—like the arms of an octopus—jutting out from the corner of the room. They were made of the same red fog that had attacked his brother before, but this time it dripped blood onto the old stone floor. They impaled Salvarias, taking turns plunging in and out of his limp body. His screams had stopped, and blood soaked his robes to the old burgundy color he used to wear.

The tentacles froze, then slowly shifted until they were pointing at Wilhelm. They had no eyes, but their presence was undeniable and the weight of their stare unmistakable.

"The Protector," they hissed in unison. "You are too late. He is ours. Ours and not yours."

Wilhelm gritted his teeth and lunged. The tentacles did nothing to stop him as he batted at them, but they flinched and hissed from his touch.

"Get off him," he roared, frantically swiping at them.

They dodged and plunged their way in and out of his brother. Salvarias hitched each time, and a low mewl sounded in his throat.

"Gods, help me," Wilhelm pleaded, but nothing came.

Cursing them all to Oblivion, Wilhelm wrapped his arms around his brother's shoulders, clinging to Salvarias's back, and then lifted his legs to circle his brother's. His weight made no difference.

The tentacles screeched in hatred filled anger. At first, he thought he had succeeded, that he was immune to their efforts, but then sharp pain shot through his back and warm blood spread across his stomach as the tentacle burst up and into Salvarias.

Wilhelm didn't realize he'd screamed until he tasted blood from his raw throat. He'd been stabbed before, but this was fire and ice, and the touch of the fog erupted a feeling of *wrong* in him; as if his very soul had been fondled by something sinister, by the truly evil.

Out of the corner of his eye, he caught Edium leaping off a chair the man must've positioned nearby. He crawled on top of Salvarias, and it only took a breath for Edium to scream.

Lunara took a step forward, but Vegos stood in front of her, shaking his head.

It cannot learn of her, the bear said.

Wilhelm barely registered one of the tentacles burrowing its way into his brother's right hand. Flesh sizzled, and the stench of it reminded Wilhelm of the night the shadowfires had swept through Falar, burning and killing.

Help him! Vegos commanded. *Remember, he has shared his soul with you. You can fight for it as much as he. Use your powers, boy, before it consumes him wholly!*

Edium screamed again. Then it all stopped. Wilhelm fell hard to the floor. Edium rolled off Salvarias and his brother rolled off Wilhelm.

"Salv," Wilhelm gasped, resting a hand on his brother's shoulder.

Salvarias stood slowly, and Wilhelm used the surrounding furniture to pull himself up. Edium was curled on the floor, blood spreading across his white tunic.

Salvarias cracked his head side-to-side and turned around. What stood before them was not Salvarias, not the brother Wilhelm had grown up with and loved. Salvarias's cold black eyes scanned the group before boring into Wilhelm.

"You should have left me for dead, dearest brother. All those times, you should have left me dead. I told you there was evil inside me. I warned you it would win. And here it is."

Help him! Vegos roared.

Whenever Wilhelm used his mark to enter Salvarias's mind, he knew it hurt his brother, knew it took days for Salvarias to recover, but gods if there ever was a time when he needed to do it, it was now.

"All our lives you've trusted me," Wilhelm said. "Trust me again." He thrust out his right hand, palm up.

Salvarias regarded it, smirked, and raised his gaze to Wilhelm's. "Always trying to save me. Always sacrificing yourself for me. My perfect big brother. The one everyone loves."

"We love you," Talura said from behind. "Gods, we love you so much, Son."

Salvarias flinched.

"Take his hand, dear," Talura said in a motherly order.

Salvarias reached out, hesitant, his fingers slowly uncurling. "It is too late for me."

"Oh my dear sweetness," Talura said softly, coming to Wilhelm's side. "It'll never be too late. Now do as I say, Son."

Salvarias's gaze flicked over to her. "You are not my mother."

"I would be if you'd let me."

His brother's jaw clenched, and his hand started to withdraw.

"For me, Salv," Wilhelm said. "For me."

As if removing a mask, Salvarias's stern expression melted, and he reached out to Wilhelm, tears glistening in his eyes. "Brother, hel—" He jerked as if shoved back, and his expression hardened.

Wilhelm didn't wait to see what happened next. He grabbed his brother's hand and forced their marks together. Then everything disappeared.

Wilhelm stood in a blank space, lit but by what he couldn't determine. Turning around, he came face to face with a ball of condensed red fog.

"How did you come to be here?" it asked.

"He's mine," Wilhelm said. "He always will be."

He felt its quizzical look better than if it had eyes. He also felt its sense of amusement. "He is not. Let me show you."

In a blink, Salvarias stood, head cocked slightly to one side, eyes dead of emotion.

"He thinks you belong to him," the creature said. "What do you think?"

The corner of Salvarias's lip curled up in a cruel smile. "I think I have fought too long. I think I am tired. I think he should have left me for dead when I was born."

"Tsk tsk," the creature said. "Somehow you would have been brought to life. Creation grew bored with His son's game, and He would have found a way. He gifted you the ability to make a choice. The Soul, the one that decides it all: light or darkness, life or death, happiness or sorrow, freedom or enslavement." The fog snuggled up against Salvarias. His brother shivered. "Tell me, my poor pet. How does that make you feel?"

"I ..." Salvarias's brow furrowed.

"Come now," the creature said. "All your years, hated by those who saw. Hated because He made you this way. He made you look like Veedran on purpose, you know? He did it so every time Nevlar looked upon you, his joy would be tainted by the memory of his brother, of the one who betrayed him. And let's not forget your mother. Such a sweet woman until she was impregnated with you. Every time she looked at you, she had to remember that night, that violation. Now tell me, my sweet sweet pet, how do you feel?"

Salvarias's eyes darkened. "Angry."

"Ahhh." If the creature had a face, it was smiling. "Anger is the root, my pet. But hate ... don't you hate her?"

Salvarias flinched. "I could never hate her. I loved her. She was my mother. I have to love her."

The creature tsked Salvarias again. "Why do you have to?"

Salvarias cringed from the creature. "Because if I do not, I will be evil. I must love her." Tears welled in Salvarias's eyes. "I do not want to be evil."

The creature pulsed with anger. "Come now, my pet. You killed Thia. Do you remember the sweet, innocent girl you murdered? Evil has owned you since your first breath."

"No, Salv," Wilhelm said. "Look at me." His brother raised his stricken face. "You're not evil. It's trying to make you evil. You have to lock it away, Salv. Lock it away with the Hunters. Put it in a dungeon."

Tears fell down Salvarias's cheeks. "Do you not see, Brother? I am too tired. I have fought for too long. My mind ..." Paranoia infected his voice. "I am going mad, Brother."

"Not as long as I'm here," Wilhelm said. "You can do this, Salv. Think of Lunara. She needs you."

"No," the creature purred. "She is better off without you, without your evil infecting her. You've seen it: the innocence leaving her, her light dimming. It's your fault, pet."

Ever since Salvarias's resurrection, he had confided in Wilhelm, told him things he'd never shared before. He'd educated Wilhelm on how he battled the evil. It was all in the mind. No swords, no physical prowess, which was opposite of how Wilhelm fought. But for this, Wilhelm would do his damnedest. For Salvarias, Wilhelm would die trying.

Ignoring the creature hissing temptation into Salvarias's ear, Wilhelm built an image of a prison in his mind: a bubble of seamless impenetrable steel. A small door, just big enough for the creature to fit, would be all that could open. Just a small door with a simple lock controlled by Wilhelm and his brother. No keys could be hung in such a dangerous place, so he made the key a word. But what word? What would be trusted between just the two of them? Then he had it.

Grimacing, Wilhelm constructed the image in his mind into something solid before him.

"What are you doing?" the creature hissed.

Ignoring it, Wilhelm kept his focus. Searing pain lanced across his side. Gritting his teeth, he pushed it away. Dull pain dug into his back, building and building until it drove him to his knees. It felt like a hand clawed its way inside him and clutched at his organs, squeezing his lungs closed.

A familiar cry at his side made his heart leap, but he refused to look away, refused to give in to the need to check on his brother. No matter how hard he tried, he couldn't tune out his brother's choked cries of utter agony.

Then the steel prison started growing faster, and he knew his brother was helping. With the evil split between them, they each had mind to give to a fight, and they were doing their damnedest.

Blood filled Wilhelm's mouth. He spat it out and rasped, "Good job, little brother. Just a bit more."

Salvarias's next scream sent gooseflesh over Wilhelm's body. Cursing, he felt the evil slide from him to his brother.

"Hang on, Salv." Hot tears streamed down his face as he listened to his brother wail.

The prison formed as he imagined it. All he had to do was build the door and lock. Darkness began to bleed into his vision.

"No," he wept, feeling himself starting to fall into nothingness, grasping for something solid. "Please, help me. Someone help me."

Dull warmth encased Wilhelm, and for the first time since entering Salvarias's mind, he felt grounded. Brilliant sapphire light glowed around him.

"You must hurry," a voice said. "He's dying. My wizard is dying again."

The light propped him up, tingling his skin in such an irritating way he had to fight the compulsion to scratch at it. Three eternities seemed to pass before the door formed, lock in place, ready for its prisoner.

Wilhelm pooled the last of his strength and looked around. Salvarias hung in the air, gaping holes ripped through his body, blood running out of him in a river.

Wilhelm gave a short cry and bolted to his feet.

"Remember," the magic said. "This is a battle of the minds. His soul has been ravaged, not his body. My wizard will heal with time if you stop this."

Wilhelm caught sight of the ball of red birthing from Salvarias's heart, visible beneath shredded skin and muscle. It wasn't watching Wilhelm. It was savoring Salvarias's torment.

"He's mine!" Wilhelm roared, and leapt.

Clutching the ball in his hands, he wrestled to keep hold of it. Salvarias landed hard on the ground but lurched up and helped control it. The two of them took the few agonizing steps together, each sweating, and each groaning in torment over their wounds. With one roar of determination, they shoved it into the prison. The door snapped shut and both shouted in unison, "Bear!"

The lock clicked and they collapsed.

WILHELM HUDDLED IN THE CHAIR, shivering under the three blankets Varila had piled on him. Apparently he'd slept for an entire day. It was night again, dark and silent except for the hum and occasional pop and crackle of the fire. The warm summer air and the dancing flames did nothing to heat the cold embedded inside him. Varila insisted his skin was warm, but it couldn't have been. All the hot baths and cups of tea had done nothing.

"You're doing it again," Varila said.

He clenched his jaw to keep his teeth from chattering.

"No better?" she asked.

Wilhelm nodded, and his voice shook when he said, "Surprisingly, I feel warmer than when I first woke. Do we have any extra blankets?"

The ten piled on top of Salvarias trembled as if plagued by the Retribution itself, despite Sira and Saval curled up around his brother, purring softly and nuzzling him.

"I'll see if I can find anymore."

She left quietly. Alone, the fire seemed unusually loud. Lunara had left to bathe for the first time since whatever they had lived through had happened. She'd refused to leave Salvarias's side until Wilhelm woke to take watch.

Vegos also stood vigilant, though he could provide no aid to either brother. The bear had turned melancholy, growling at nothing.

"I am cold," Salvarias said from under the covers.

Wilhelm, keeping his blankets wrapped around him, crossed the room and sat on the edge of the bed. Salvarias's eyes were struggling to stay open, and he twitched and spasmed with shivers.

"There's a fire going," Wilhelm said. "Varila is looking for more blankets.

"Varila?"

"My wife," Wilhelm prompted. "Lunara's sister."

Salvarias was silent a moment before he nodded. "I remember." He struggled against the pile and the griffins and eventually managed to sit upright, tucking himself in the corner of the room. Sira and Saval curled around one another at his feet. His tired gaze rested on Wilhelm. "Forgive me. I did not know what the book was."

"I know, Salv." Wilhelm scooted back to sit beside his brother. "The parchment had burned except for the last paragraph, the one that said what the stone is."

"I am a fool. It seems everything I do ends up turning on us."

Wilhelm let out a soft chuckle. "If that were true, we would have been dead a long time ago."

"In case you have forgotten, death has visited each of us more than once." Salvarias threaded his hands through is hair and rested his forehead on his propped-up knees. "I am so cold."

"Me too. I haven't figured out why yet."

It was not your bodies that suffered, Vegos explained. *The wounds you saw and felt were not there when you woke. Edium is healing as well. Evil does not feed on flesh. It feeds on our light.*

"There was blood on us. I saw it, felt it."

A powerful delusion of the mind, Vegos said. *An attack on the soul can be so traumatic the human mind must find ways to explain it. You saw what you thought you should see. You saw on Edium what you assumed should have been there. It is your mind's way of trying to alleviate the potency of the attack and the violation your soul suffered. Your wounds run deeper than physical. With time, you will warm.*

Wilhelm pursed his lips and passed his brother the puzzle box. "Something didn't make sense. When the ... thing was talking, it said Salv was made in the image of Veedran with the purpose of hurting Nevlar."

Salvarias rested his head on Wilhelm's arm, his fingers spinning the box into odd shapes. "I am confused by that statement as well."

Wilhelm slumped against the wall as a thought manifested itself; so quickly in fact, he wasn't sure it came solely from him. "Adok."

Salvarias tensed. "What about him?"

"Adok was Nevlar."

"That makes no sense, Brother. If Nevlar were here, he would have helped us find Zerana. He would have told me who he was."

"No, remember what Vuddruk said? He said we were pawns in a game. He said there were rules, and Adok was adamant you never learn of him. I think he helped us, Salv." Wilhelm sat up straight, his mind turning with all that fell into place. "The shadowfires are his. They made you. They gave me power in the barbarians' arena. Don't you see? Nevlar is your father!"

Salvarias shook his head. "It cannot be. I have Veedran's power—"

"Nevlar made the Guardians and Protectors." Wilhelm planted his palm on his forehead. "I can't believe it, Salv. Think about it! I'm a descendent of Wilhelm Firth, a man created by Nevlar. You're Nevlar's son. We might not be brothers in the traditional sense, but in the eyes of gods, we are. Our connection is stronger than any other Guardian and Protector because we're both Nevlar's sons. Adok, you always said he lectured you. He was always telling you to be careful. That's because it was Nevlar guiding his son. Nevlar's servants healed me in the arena so I could save us. They gave me my power, not my father. They did it so we could survive."

Salvarias frowned, looking at Wilhelm like he'd gone mad. "Veedran confirmed I was his son."

"No, you said it first. What better way for him to tear you down than to agree to it?"

Salvarias shook his head. "It cannot be. He would have told me. Adok would have told me."

Enough, Wilhelm, Vegos said. *Between you and me, you must give him time. Remember, Terror owns him, and because it always hunts him, he has buried himself in a cave of lies that help him cope with what he endures. He has concocted imaginings that break my heart to see, but it has kept him alive. In time, with the right influences, the right situations, his lies will show themselves to him. But he is not lying when he says he is going mad. The power within him will eventually devour his mortal mind. He was made ... special. But even with most of his godhood locked away, his vessel cannot contain the minute amount of power seeping through. He is so very fragile, Wilhelm. He must uncover truths in his own time. We can only encourage these thoughts, point out what he should be seeing for himself, and let his mind digest it slowly.*

"It's all right, Salv," Wilhelm said, reining in his own enthusiasm. "Just think on it for me. Piece together what I have, and I think you'll see what I mean."

Very good, boy.

Settling himself back comfortably, Wilhelm said, "How's our prison holding up?"

Salvarias seemed grateful for the change in topic, and his body relaxed as best it could while still shivering. "Yet one more thing for me to focus on. The Hunters, the evil, and now this. I do not know how much longer I can endure it, Brother. The pain is near unbearable."

"You mastered the evil with time," Wilhelm said confidently. "Soon this will be no different."

Salvarias held out his right hand, palm up. Burned into the center was a red circle. "It has marked me." His voice trembled. "Veedran will come for me."

Wilhelm inhaled a deep breath and let it out slowly. "They've tried to tear us apart, take you from me. They'll try again and again, but as long as you remember that all I want is for you to be safe and happy, they will never succeed. You understand me, Salv? No matter what Veedran whispers to you, no matter what that stone says, no matter what the world itself might proclaim, and no matter what your heart feels or your brain thinks, you have to remember that fact. You understand me, little brother?"

Salvarias looked up at him and gave a tired smile. "I do."

"Then they'll never win, and Veedran can't take what is not his."

22

Salvarias sat astride Mithal, huddled in his cloak and covered by a blanket, barely paying heed to the army behind him pounding along on their way to Lynta. Wilhelm had been insistent Salvarias not strain himself unnecessarily, and with Lynta a mere day and half from Hynd, his brother had demanded they march. Travel had been uneventful, and by midafternoon they would be close enough they would need to look for a safe place to camp.

The army, however, was not what consumed Salvarias's thoughts. If he allowed himself to believe Nevlar was his father, and if it turned out Wilhelm was wrong, it would crush the life from Salvarias. Better to think he was the son of Veedran. It was safer for his heart not to hope and face disappointment. Better to expect the worse; nothing could hurt more than what he had already prepared himself for.

Furthermore, Salvarias doubted his brother understood the implications. If indeed Nevlar's servants created Salvarias, it would have been this Creator that had seen to Salvarias's birth. Nevlar was banned from Arden. Which meant the Creator had used the shadow-fires to infect Salvarias's mother with His seed. And if Nevlar was banned, how could he possibly be Adok? None of it made sense, but he knew of one who could provide answers.

Mithal switched directions and weaved his way to Mafarias. Without looking, Salvarias knew Wilhelm followed.

"Hello, grandson," Mafarias greeted when they arrived.

"I have questions," Salvarias said, fighting the burgeoning fear of being near the god.

"I'll answer what I can," Mafarias said.

"You are stuck here."

Mafarias frowned. "Yes. After Nevlar struck our world, no gods could leave, and no new gods could visit."

"So there is no chance another god could ... inhabit a being from this world?"

Mafarias rubbed his cheek. "That's a more complicated question than you're thinking, boy. No, a god cannot inhabit a being fully. A god could, if powerful enough, speak and see through a creature. It's a different sort of link, and only a higher god could do it. I couldn't, nor could say ... Crutar."

"How many higher gods are there?" Salvarias asked.

"Oh ... I'd say it's near fifty."

"And lower gods?"

"Hundreds."

"Am I Nevlar's son?"

Mafarias's eyes opened wide. "Well now, you're asking me a very specific question."

"More rules?" Wilhelm rumbled. "More games."

Mafarias shrugged. "Everything is a game, my dear boy. Love. Hate. Life. Death. It's all just pieces moving around. Winning and losing."

"Answer the damn question," Wilhelm growled.

"I will not." Mafarias looked at Salvarias. "Unshackle me, boy. Let me help. Let me show you I can be trusted. I want to help you kill Veedran and save your grandmother. Once we reclaim Lynta, I'll tell you what you want to know. I swear it."

"Absolutely not!" Wilhelm snapped. "I don't—"

"Do it, Brother," Salvarias said, narrowing his eyes at Mafarias.

"You can't be serious, Salv! After what he did to you?"

The god cannot be trusted, Vegos echoed.

"We need his help," Salvarias said simply. "I am tired, Brother. Weak. We need another mage."

Wilhelm's jaw clenched, but he made no further arguments. Salvarias glanced at Vegos, but the bear looked away stubbornly. It was unfair to place the burden solely on Salvarias and Kisra when there was a god here that could help. It seemed Vegos knew the truth of it, or else the bear surely would have argued. Perhaps Kisra sleeping in Sir Brice's saddle had something to do with it as well.

Turning in his saddle so he fully faced Mafarias, Salvarias tossed back his hood and glared at the god. "Understand this, Grandfather: I know how to kill a god. Betray us, hurt us, and I will cut out your heart, set it aflame, and behead you without giving it a second thought. You are not my family. I do not care for you or your guilt. I do this for answers and nothing more."

Mafarias winced. "You never used to be so cruel, boy."

"That merely shows how little you know me."

Salvarias urged Mithal on, and they trotted away, Lilly plodding along at their side. Wilhelm's curses had yet to stop.

THE CITY of Lynta was as Salvarias remembered: bright and cheery in an otherwise dreary landscape. The homes were colorfully painted, the lake warmed by the summer sun, and the trees in which Salvarias hid among smelled alive. The only differences were the octrils patrolling the streets, a giant ogre guarding the gate, and the swarm of magically inclined, human-sized leathery birds circling above the castle of Okulu's home.

"This isn't good," Okulu said from behind.

There was a chorus of murmured agreements from the group at Salvarias's back.

"What do you think?" Idolar asked Wilhelm. "Three thousand?"

"Five," Wilhelm said flatly. "There'll be additional forces in the barracks, homes, and the castle."

"Five thousand against our mere ninety?" Edium said. "I hate to say it, Son, but we don't stand a chance."

"I agree," Mafarias said.

"I didn't ask for your opinion," Edium growled. "You—"

"Enough," Wilhelm said absently. Salvarias's brother had become a mediator between the two men, constantly breaking up their fights.

"Can you eliminate the magical creatures, Mafarias?" Salvarias asked.

"How many do you figure there are?"

Salvarias counted. "Fifty-three."

"Perhaps." Mafarias rubbed his cheek, squinting up at the sky dulling with the setting sun. "Yes, I suppose I could. I'll be worthless afterward."

"No different than usual," Edium muttered.

"It is time for you to accept my proposal, Brother," Salvarias said.

"No. I won't have you go in there with only ten men."

"I hate to say it," Edium said to Wilhelm, "but your brother is right. Have faith in him."

"I have faith in him," Wilhelm said defensively. "I don't have faith in the ten Vipers accompanying him."

"Replace two with me and Varila," Edium suggested. "You trust me, don't you?"

Wilhelm glanced at his wife, then Edium. Grunting, he looked back at the city. "I'm going too. Idolar, you'll lead the charge. Brice will be second in command."

"And me?" Lunara asked.

"Whatever pleases you, my lady," Salvarias said. "Stay with the squires or come along."

"I'm coming with you," she said before he finished. Sadly, she understood the depths of his exhaustion better than any, even Vegos. It had manifested itself in her own slouch and dark-rimmed eyes.

"Questions?" Wilhelm asked. When no one said anything, he nodded. "Then tonight we get Okulu's home back."

Okulu made a sour face. "I'm not all that fond of it. I'd be fine if you wanted to move on."

Salvarias arched an eyebrow. "Are you sober?"

"I was." Okulu drained his flask.

WILHELM SQUEEZED, huffing and puffing his way through the opening Salvarias had created in Lynta's wall. He was tiring of trying to fit through these openings; tired enough he entertained the thought of eating less. Of course with each meal he had forgotten his struggles and devoured his ration along with any left over from his command staff. Hunting parties had kept their supplies stocked nicely, and the group had yet to feel the hardships Wilhelm was sure afflicted most armies.

"Gods, you need to eat less," Okulu complained.

"Shut up," Varila snapped. "I like him that way."

Okulu bowed. "Of course, my lovely golden—"

Varila held up a hand. "Finish that sentence and I'll cut out your tongue."

Wilhelm finally managed to wiggle free his shoulder and dumped on to the narrow alley. Breathing hard, he glanced around to be sure they were all there. Qwyn stood at Salvarias's side, hand on the hilt of his sword, gaze scanning for any commotion. Okulu was on Salv's other side, sipping his flask and leaning against the wall as if they weren't in the belly of the enemy. Lunara was sidled up to Salvarias, her hand clasped in his. Edium and Varila took point, and the other five Vipers lined up behind them.

"All right, little brother, close it up," Wilhelm instructed.

Salvarias whispered words, and his shaking hand trembled out a rune. The stones slid back into place. Salvarias pulled his cloak about him, shivering. For the most part, Wilhelm had recovered. Cold still clung around his heart, making him want to reach for a cloak, but the warm night air reminded his skin how much he hated summer.

Winking at his brother as he passed, Wilhelm took his spot at the head of the group and led onward into the heart of Lynta.

Unlike other cities the Knighthood had taken back, Lynta had life. The enemy's numbers granted them the luxury of regular patrols, and they were more alert than they had been in other cities. Guttural conversations drifted up into the night air, offering Wilhelm the alleys and streets to avoid. Overhead, the magical creatures' wings beat in discord, the cacophony thumping through the city. Wilhelm glanced up often, but the leathery beasts paid them no mind. They appeared to be lookouts for encroaching armies. Luckily, Wilhelm had taken his knights by way of the forest to Lynta's north. The canopy provided cover, and he no longer regretted the extra time they'd needed to navigate the woods.

A door on Wilhelm's right banged open, and a drunken octril staggered into the alley. It blinked at them in surprise, and as its mouth opened in alarm, Qwyn pounced. Covering the creature's mouth with one hand, he shoved it backward and brought up his sword. So close together, the blade gouged upward along the octril's torso before finally cutting into its throat. Blood bubbled out of the slit, and the creature's feet scraped against the cobblestones. It seemed to take forever for the creature to still. Qwyn dragged the body to a pile of overturned crates and another knight helped cover the evidence. Then they were off again.

On and on they climbed until coming to the second to last street. From the shadows, Wilhelm surveyed the estate. It was too quiet. This was where the prisoners were being held, and unlike other cities, there was only a meek patrol of five octrils. They looked nervous.

"I do not like this," Salvarias whispered. He held up his new mark. "They must know we are here, Brother. This is a trap."

Wilhelm scrutinized the dark windows, the lack of any noise other than the shuffling feet of the octrils on guard, and the words of his brother. Of course it very well could be a trap. It very well could not.

"Humar's reports are months out of date," Qwyn said.

"They've been out of date since we landed," Okulu pointed out. "So far, they've been accurate." He tilted his head toward the estate.

"The prisoners were said to be in there. Besides, if it is a trap, what then? Do we turn back? Tuck tail and run?"

"We carry onward and address the estate after we start the siege," Qwyn said. "It isn't worth the risk."

"If we do that, then we don't know what will come out of there and corner us," Okulu said. "I don't see we really have an option."

"I can take Salvarias out of here," Edium said. "We don't need to risk the boy. I'll bring Kisra back."

"I will not endanger her life over my own," Salvarias said, as Wilhelm knew his brother would. "My spells are suited for tight quarters, which is what we face inside."

They bickered more, all with opinions, all valid, all their ideas racing through Wilhelm's mind. He missed Humar desperately in that moment of indecision. What would the king do? Humar was so certain in his choices, moving forward without hesitancy.

A good leader is riddled with doubts, my dear boy, Vegos said. Even though the bear had remained with the army, his voice rang strong in Wilhelm's mind. Absently he wondered how far they could be separated and still communicate. *However,* Vegos continued, *he or she will hold them close and secret. Others cannot see them. I guarantee Humar would be just as unsure, but once decided, no one would know how much the decision cost him. You must decide. And you must be strong.*

Wilhelm inhaled a soothing breath and let it out slowly. Okulu was right. Leaving an unknown at their back was worse than walking into a situation prepared for the disaster. "We go in," Wilhelm said. He didn't need to look back to feel his brother's approving smile.

23

Every muscle in Salvarias wanted to turn and run. His fingers glided over the new mark the stone had left on his right hand. The red circle nearly took up his palm, taunting him with what lived within, what even now was nibbling at his tiny, precious soul. Veedran knew they were here. Salvarias was almost certain of it, but he did not say so. The reason was his mother, walking at his side, her glare burning his heart. How much of his own mind could he really trust anymore?

As Wilhelm set off through the shadows in the estate's courtyard, Salvarias followed. He had wiggled his hand free of Lunara's, needing it available for his magic. He would have taken her hand in his right, but he refused to let the mark touch her. Even last night when they had rolled in their sheets, he kept the mark from her skin. He pondered if it would heal as his left hand had should he decide to flay it away. Perhaps after the battle he would try.

Wilhelm stopped them behind an overturned charred carriage. A blackened hand hung out one of the windows, burned to the bone.

"Anyone see more?" Wilhelm asked.

No's were murmured amongst the group.

"All right, little brother," Wilhelm whispered. "Take them out."

Salvarias easily generated his five small ice shards, peeked over the carriage, and whispered, *"Rulose."*

The shards whizzed through the air, each ending in a wet thud in an octril's neck. The bodies collapsed upon one another with a soft clang of armor.

Wilhelm kept them hidden a long moment, waiting for others to respond to the disturbance. No creature came to check, and Salvarias's worry grew.

Cursing softly, Wilhelm crept from cover, all following soundlessly. At the door, Salvarias's brother pressed an ear to the wood and waited. Nothing happened.

Wilhelm, uttering out another colorful curse, unsheathed his broadsword, the knights following suit. Slowly he inched open the door. Blackness was all that lurked beyond.

"Once inside, we'll need light, Salv."

Salvarias nodded to his brother, and then they filed inside. The door thumped closed and any minor light from the moon blinked out. The estate was quiet.

"Definitely a trap," Qwyn whispered.

Grunts of agreement rippled amongst the group.

"Lumous," Salvarias murmured, lighting his dim sparrow.

The entrance cut through the width of the rectangular home, ending at double glass doors opening to what Salvarias assumed would be the gardens. Long, dark hallways flanked the middle of the entry, leading to gods only knew what. Centered in the room was a woman chained to a chair. Brown hair frayed from a braid, and the tatters of a once fine gown hung on her voluptuous frame. Her blue eyes widened in alarm, and she shouted muffled words through a gag. What surprised him most was the amount of powerful magic flowing inside her.

"Haleen," Wilhelm breathed. He rushed to the woman, Salvarias and the others a step behind. Kneeling beside her, he fumbled with the ties while Qwyn pulled the gag from her mouth.

"Run!" she screamed. "It's a trap, Wilhelm. Run!"

It was too late. Chaos erupted.

Creatures spilled from rooms and hallways, a flood racing toward them. If he used too much magic, he would be useless for the main battle, yet if he did nothing, they would all be dead.

"Salv!"

Wetness seeping into his leg made him look down. A brilliant orange tentacle was wrapped around his ankle. If he did not know any better, he would assume it was an octopus. Frowning in confusion, his gaze tracked it to a hallway. Octrils poured around it, and as far as Salvarias saw it had no end. Before he could call out to his brother, the tentacle yanked him off his feet and hauled him through the mass of enemies.

Desperate, he grabbed at the carpet runner, then at the edges of a door as it mercilessly spirited him into another room. When he twisted his body so he could see, he gave a yelp of surprise.

The tentacle disappeared down a hole in the estate's floor, hidden beneath a bookcase now moved aside. Salvarias grabbed for the edge as his body slid into darkness, but his two-fingered hand could not hold his weight, and he fell.

Landing hard, air rushed out of his lungs, and he lay gulping and moaning. Helplessly he watched the stream of light above disappear as an octril repositioned the bookcase. Once he choked in a few musty-laden breaths, he whispered, *"Lumous."* His sparrow greeted him, illuminating the dark stone surrounding him and the dank hallway branching out to either side. The tentacle had released him at some point, which was the single positive thought Salvarias could summon.

Looking above, he followed along the ceiling in both directions, then closed his eyes and whispered his spell. The ceiling let off a glow of soft light, hopefully above on the upper floors as well so as to help his brother.

Resisting the urge to connect to Wilhelm, Salvarias shoved himself to his feet and staggered to the wall, calling his staff to him. His brother would need all his wits to survive the horde above. And Salvarias needed to escape quickly or else his friends were doomed, unless Haleen had the magical stamina to keep up with his brother.

Salvarias! Lunara cried.

I am alive. My brother?

We're cornered in a room, but holding them off.

I will try to find a way to you.

The tunnel leading up to the hole was too long and slippery to use for escape. Nevertheless, Salvarias tried several times before giving up, his fingertips raw from scraping against the stone for purchase. He had a spell that could project him upward, but the bookcase blocked his exit. Of course blowing it up was an option, but he dare not try it for fear some of his friends might be in the room. Furthermore, there was always a risk using that much magic in a confined space. It could cave in the walls and kill him.

Slouching to keep his head from hitting the ceiling, Salvarias followed the trail of mucusy liquid the tentacle left behind and muttered out some of Durak's favorite curses. The light along the tunnel ceiling followed him, marking his path not only for himself, but perhaps his brother if he made his way down.

The trail ended at a spewed open hole running down into infinite darkness. Rocks were strewn about the edges, clearly exploded from underneath. No doubt the creature had been instructed to attack this specific estate. The hole surely led deep underground and probably ended up in the lake. They had walked right into an artfully laid trap.

Following the tunnel to the lake would do no good. The creature had finished its mission. It had pulled Salvarias into the belly of the estate. But to what end? And how had it singled him out amidst such a large group?

They want you alone, Vegos said. *They have separated you from your Protector. They have divided your strengths. You must find a way back to Wilhelm, boy. Do not linger. Your power is a beacon, and those who seek you will find you soon. Run!*

Salvarias did not hesitate or question Vegos. He hobbled down the hall as fast as his bad leg would let him. Ignoring the passing halls, he kept straight, certain it would lead to stairs or some other means of escape.

Passing one such room, he heard a soft cry and Tedris call, "Uncle Salvarias!"

Do not! Vegos commanded. *It is a trap. Find your brother and come back for the boy.*

Uncertainty never tempted Salvarias. He would turn himself over to the darkness before he would let harm come to Tedris.

No!

Salvarias took a few steps back and peered into the room. Tedris was huddled on the floor, hands chained to the wall, tunic stained and rumpled. Tears fled down his cheeks, but when he saw Salvarias, his amber eyes lit with hope.

"Help me!" he pleaded. "Uncle, help me!"

The instant Salvarias stepped through the door, blinding pain flared on the side of his head, sending him sprawling to the ground.

"Leave him alone!" Tedris cried.

Salvarias blinked his vision clear and looked up into the red eyes of Eludar. Blood flowed like a river over its human-shaped form, its armor moving as if liquid itself. One gloved hand hovered above Tedris's head.

"Hello, Salvarias," the creature said. "And I thought you would have been smart enough to leave your nephew with me until you found Wilhelm. Yet here you are. Alone and unprotected."

Hot blood ran into Salvarias's eye, blurring the other chained-up figure in the room. Slate-blue robes hung off his hunched frame, and his white beard was stained and matted.

Vuddruk raised his head and gave a weary smile. "Hello, brother of mine. In trouble again, I see."

"You cannot win," Eludar said. "I am immune to magic, and you have no brother to run me through." It raised an ungloved hand toward Tedris's cheek. "You know my blood is poison. One touch and a child this size will be dead in a few breaths. I give you a chance to save him. Come with me."

Salvarias wiped the sleeve of his robe across his temple and eye, ridding it of blood and clearing his vision. Slowly he got to his feet. "How did you find him? Did you kill the queen?"

"Of course not. We have servants, boy. More than you could ever know. She whisked the boy away in the dead of night and met us here. We have been waiting your arrival." Eludar spread his arm wide. "Do you like our trap?"

"You have played your game well," Salvarias conceded. "But even if I go with you, my brother will hunt you down and kill you. It is time you realize it is your side that will fail. I give you one last chance to surrender."

Wilhelm's anger roared to life as Salvarias conveyed the conversation. Vision dimming with it, Salvarias smiled. "My brother will kill you."

Eludar returned the smile. "I assume you've kept connected to him? It matters not. If you do not come now, he will be too late."

"I will never go with you."

"So be it, boy."

Just as Eludar lowered his hand to Tedris, Salvarias flicked out his rune and funneled the energy. The creature's hand rested a hair's width above Tedris.

"You may be immune to my magic, but the boy is not," Salvarias said. "I cannot hurt you directly, but now you will not hurt either of them to manipulate me. Run and you may live."

Eludar turned burning eyes on Salvarias and roared out in anger. It blurred in movement too fast for Salvarias to track, and when it stopped directly in front of him, cold spread across his stomach, followed by sticky warmth. He looked down at the blade protruding out of him.

"No!" rang aloud and in Salvarias's mind, the voices of Tedris, Vegos, Lunara, and Wilhelm muddled together.

"Do not think we require you to live, boy," Eludar hissed in Salvarias's ear. "We prefer it, certainly, but there are other ways to victory."

Eludar yanked the sword clear, and Salvarias coughed on his own blood, his hands clamping on his stomach to staunch the flow of blood as his legs gave out from under him and he sank to his knees.

∾

WILHELM CURSED as he drew his second sword. Confusion, joy, and fear warred within his heart as he watched Haleen shoot off a bunch of fire shards that impaled her targeted octrils. They'd made it to the room where Salvarias had been taken, but Qwyn, five other knights, and himself were barely holding the entrance. Soon they would be overrun.

Varila and Okulu grunted and groaned as they shoved against the bookcase.

Reaching over Qwyn's head, Wilhelm rammed his sword down, skewering two octrils. Hot blood splattered up his arm when he jerked his blade free.

A wave of dizziness staggered him back, and the room blurred in and out of focus. One breath clear, the next he stood looking at his son and Vuddruk chained in a room with Eludar standing near. Muffled voices sounded in his mind, as if they spoke from behind a thick door.

Tripping and staggering, he lurched over to Varila.

"What is it?" she said tersely.

Wilhelm didn't have the mind to respond. The room bleeding in out of focus clamped his throat closed in attempt to keep his stomach under control. His brother's mind whirled within his own, giving him an instant headache, but he pushed it aside and tried to strengthen their connection.

One more shove and the bookcase slid away to reveal a tunnel. Sheathing his swords, Wilhelm dropped down without hesitation, landing hard and awkward. Using the wall for support, he sprinted toward his brother, heart pounding as Eludar's hand neared Tedris's head.

Vaguely he was aware of a terrible thunder ricocheting down the tunnel, the plume of dust engulfing him, and the vibration that shook the ground.

The image of Tedris blurred, and the rush of movement freed Wilhelm's stomach. Leaning over, he vomited as he stared into the glowing eyes of Eludar. Then he saw the blade sticking from Salvarias's stomach and the vision shattered.

What felt like clawed hands raked across his mind, stealing his connection to Salvarias. The sudden jolt knocked him back physically, and the tearing in his head leached a cry from him, followed by a roar of anger and pain at remembering the blade stuck in his brother.

When his vision cleared and the room stopped spinning, Wilhelm stood paralyzed by fear. Not again. All that blood. So much blood.

Run! Vegos's voice rang around in his breaking mind.

Blinking aside tears, Wilhelm ran down the hall, eventually passing a hole littered by loose rocks, twisting his ankle in the process of stumbling over them. He rounded into the room with a war cry, drawing his sword and swinging it at Eludar's surprised face.

The creature danced back, clumsily raising its sword to parry aside Wilhelm's strike. Glancing down, he saw Salvarias on his knees, blood flowing over his fingers, speckled on his lips.

"Forgive me," he gurgled, and collapsed to the ground.

Warmth exploded within Wilhelm, driving him backward, punching the air from his lungs, and constricting his muscles with such intensity he cried out. Then it stopped. Red blanketed over his vision, his body surging with strength, but it did not stop his heart from ripping in two.

Pouring his pain into a shout, he charged Eludar. The creature whipped up his sword in another parry, but Wilhelm's strength drove Eludar's blade aside, sparking it against the stone. They were face to face, and Wilhelm smelled its fear. He breathed it in and grinned. Dropping his sword, he clamped his hands around the creature's neck and whirled it to the other wall, slamming it hard enough to cause it to drop its sword. His hands smoked and sizzled, and nausea set deep in his stomach. He fought the urge to vomit and hauled the creature up and then down to the ground with all the force he could muster. Blood splattered across the stone.

Vuddruk shuffled by, shielding Tedris and yelling for the others.

Salvarias was dragging himself to the other side of the room. Seeing his brother's blood again only fueled Wilhelm's anger. He would lose his brother. Salvarias would die, and Wilhelm would be alone again. Dead again.

Fury leached from his throat in another shout, and he pummeled Eludar. Blood gushed all around, covering him. He didn't care; pure rage controlled him. He beat and beat at the blob in front of him, swallowing the creature's blood as he shouted out his hatred, as he cursed every god he had ever heard of.

Brother.

The word tore through Wilhelm's mind like a tornado, clearing his rage and leaving behind horrible pain. He raised his tear-blurred gaze to his brother. Salvarias's head lay in Lunara's lap. His breath hitched and wheezed past the blood leaking down the corner of his mouth. His body jerked in spasms, but his gaze was steady.

Vuddruk stuck his head in the room and whistled. "By the gods."

Wilhelm looked down at Eludar. There was nothing left but a pool of blood and red acid eating away at Wilhelm's hands and knuckles. Bile rose in Wilhelm's throat, his stomach cramping and churning. His muscles seized up.

Salvarias held out his left hand, mark up, shaking and wet with blood. Wilhelm couldn't move, couldn't tear his gaze from the blood pouring out of Salvarias.

Vuddruk dodged around the splatter of Eludar and knelt beside Salvarias. "I feel what you are, boy. I told you we were brothers." Vuddruk drew Salvarias's dagger and rammed it into his own heart. Lunara cried out, and Salvarias's eyes widened. "Gods cannot be killed." Vuddruk pulled the knife free and tore open his robes enough so they could see the hole. "We can heal ourselves, Brother." He shut his eyes tight and grunted, face twisting in pain, sweat beading up on his brow. The skin melted closed, and Vuddruk slumped. "It's not easy," Vuddruk continued. "It's hard the first time you do it. It'll hurt like Oblivion, but you'll live."

Salvarias's brow creased, his body tensing, and a fresh stream of blood surged up from his mouth. Wilhelm vomited, clutching his stomach.

"Your brother will die without your help," Vuddruk said. "But you can't help him until you help yourself. Come on, boy. Concentrate on the wound. Force your power to heal it."

Salvarias closed his eyes. A breath passed before a shimmer appeared around Salvarias, like a heat wave distorting the air. Then his blackfire burst alive.

Vuddruk yelped in surprise and fell back. Lunara shivered, but did not move.

Sweat burst over Salvarias, his eyes clamped tight, and he screamed between clenched teeth. Curling up, he hugged his wound and screamed again.

Darkness bled into Wilhelm's vision. His body gave out from under him, and a terrible cold sank into his bones. Breathing was too much trouble. The darkness pulled him into its depths, wrapping around him like a blanket of ice.

No sooner had he succumbed to it than a building warmth sparked in his heart. It spread outward, heating cold muscles, calling his soul home. It was hard to leave that darkness, as cold as it was. It had a hold of him, like the many other times he had died. He wanted to stay there, free of pain and fear, and free of his failures and burden of what he had to accomplish. But the warmth insisted, bringing his body to life, settling in his soul, and feeding him love and strength. It imbued a feeling of wrong toward the darkness, as if it were a horrible beast feasting on him. The warmth was what he wanted, what he needed, and what he lived for. Inhaling deeply of it, it filled him completely, making him lightheaded with such peace and strength he puzzled over how he could have ever given up so easily.

It hauled him up and up toward light, embedding in him such euphoric comfort that he thirsted for more. He drank deeply of it, pulling it inside him. It blotted out his sorrow and bludgeoned his doubt until it consumed him in utter happiness. He never wanted to leave it, never wanted to be parted from it.

Like a candle flickering out, it all vanished. A dank mustiness pervaded what was once clean. An uncomfortable heat washed over him, and a stone room blinked into existence. He was soaking wet, and Salvarias was sitting next to him looking exhausted but alive.

Salvarias smiled sleepily and wiped the blood dripping from his nose. "Welcome back, Brother."

Wilhelm pulled his brother into his arms and held him too tightly, but he couldn't help it. When finally he had assured his heart his brother was alive and it was not a dream, he sat back and patted his brother's shoulder, grinning wildly. "So you can heal yourself now?"

Salvarias grinned back. "Apparently I can. Should save us quite a bit of trouble."

Wilhelm laughed and ruffled his brother's hair, grunting when a strong punch landed in his ribs. "Ouch." He shook out his soaking hair and checked himself over. No blood was on him.

"Papa!" Tedris flew into Wilhelm's arms. Tedris raised his gaze to Salvarias. "I knew you were both special. I felt it when we first met. Am I special like Papa?"

Salvarias leaned his head back and closed his eyes. "Yes, you are, little bear."

Tedris grinned. "Does that mean I can fight with you?"

Salvarias chuckled along with Wilhelm. "Not yet, but soon."

"Will you save me if I die?" Tedris asked.

"Yes," Salvarias said without hesitation.

"Is it because of this?" Tedris asked, holding out his palm to show the same mark as Wilhelm's.

Salvarias opened his eyes and regarded the child. "Partly, but more so it is because you are my nephew, and I ..." His voice trailed off and his brow furrowed.

Yes, you have perceived your actions correctly, Vegos said. *Like you did with your brother, you have claimed Tedris's soul as your own.*

How have I done such a thing?

Vegos chuckled. *Because you are a god, my dear boy. And like Zerana owns her clerics, you own Wilhelm and Tedris. Even Lunara to a certain degree.*

Salvarias shifted and looked around at their friends. Wilhelm hadn't noticed they'd arrived. Varila grinned at him, and he smiled back.

"Luckily I used to play in these tunnels when I was little," Okulu said. He looked left to right, shrugged, and pointed the opposite way they had come. "I think we can get out this way."

"Just like the caves outside Sundil," Varila muttered. "If I remember, you got us lost."

Okulu frowned. "Did I? I don't recall."

"You were drunk, bastard," Varila snapped. "Tedris, stay close to your aunt. I get the feeling we won't escape out of here without some troubles."

Wilhelm looked Vuddruk over. The old man looked tired. Studying his brother, Salvarias didn't look much better. Healing Wilhelm had taken its usual toll, not to mention whatever Salvarias had done to heal himself.

"I will be fine," Salvarias said. "We must hurry. Dame Kisra and Sir Idolar will be worried about our delay."

Wilhelm hopped to his feet, legs shaking from the remnants of Salvarias's power coursing through him. He pulled Lunara to her feet and passed her Tedris before helping his brother up.

"Edium," he said, "you lead the way with Okulu. Varila, stay close to Lunara and Tedris."

Once they were lined up, they started onward. The tunnel was uncomfortably low, dank, and stinking of rot. He hadn't noticed it on his way to his brother, but now his back ached from how far he had to slouch, and he wanted nothing more than to breathe fresh air. Salvarias's breathing, though steady, sounded wheezy. Glancing behind, he smiled at Haleen. She hadn't changed much since last he had shared her carriage. A few extra wrinkles around her eyes and maybe soft lines around her mouth, but her figure was every bit as voluptuous as he remembered, and her eyes ever more inviting. She smiled at him, wincing and raising a hand to her bruised cheek.

"You look well," she said, taking a few quick steps to join his side. "I've missed you."

"I would have come for you if I'd known you were taken," he said. "Brenil told me you'd died from plague."

She nodded. "A wise decision. You couldn't have saved me then, Wilhelm."

"Why did they keep you ... I mean, you're barren. I don't understand."

Her bright blue eyes darkened, and she wrapped her arms around herself. "A few grew fond of me and decided to keep me as their play toy."

Wilhelm clenched his fist. "I'm sorry."

She shrugged. "It kept me alive."

"I never knew you were a mage."

"Not something I ever wanted known. Money can buy peace for my kind. I remember you praising your brother's skill, but I am still amazed."

Salvarias bowed his head. "Thank you, my lady. You are quite accomplished yourself."

"My dearly departed husband paid for private tutoring from Himiks. The man was easily bought."

"Master Himiks was not nearly versed enough to teach you all you know," Salvarias said. "Did you have another instructor?"

She cast him a sultry smile. "Are you married, Master Salvarias? You've quite the handsome face, and I'm curious how you might compare to your brother."

"I am, and you avoided my question."

"I see you settled down," she said to Wilhelm. "Your wife is beautiful."

"She's an amazing woman."

"And a child? I'm sorry I missed so much of your life. I'd hoped we'd be life-long friends."

Wilhelm smiled at her, remembering those times in her carriage, their soft conversations and the deep thoughts he'd entrusted to her. "We are," he said. "You were always my closest friend."

Okulu stopped and motioned to a ladder leading upward. "This will put us in the garden. From there we can get back to the streets and up to the castle."

"What about the creatures inside the estate?" Edium asked.

Okulu took a swig from his flask. "I think they'll be digging out of the collapse Haleen caused for some time yet. But when we give the signal to Idolar, we can hope they'll join ranks at the front gate instead of continuing their pursuit of us. If not, we're in for a long fight."

Climbing the ladder in the narrow tunnel was a bit of a challenge, but Wilhelm managed his way up and into a shed. Dusty hay covered the floor, and gardening tools hung from the walls. Once they all squeezed in, Okulu closed the hatch, covered it with hay, and led the way out.

Luckily for them, the garden itself was overgrown from lack of care. Massive bushes, limp trees, and weeds as tall as Okulu lined their path to a small side gate.

Wilhelm kept his eyes and ears alert, but heard and saw nothing. They eventually ended up in an alley, empty and quiet. The estate was a street away from the main castle; their final destination. All huddled together and watched. It didn't take long for the first patrol to pass. Once it did, they waited again until the next patrol. With their frequency, sneaking through as a group wouldn't be an option. One or two at a time, however, had promise.

"Edium, Qwyn," Wilhelm whispered. Once the two were at his side, he motioned to the open gate leading into the castle grounds. "You two go in, clear any standing watch inside, and then give the signal. We'll follow two at a time."

When the next patrol passed, Edium and Qwyn darted across the street and slipped through the gate. Wilhelm exhaled a sigh of relief when no cries or alarms were raised. After the next patrol passed, Edium stepped from cover and motioned them.

Wilhelm sent two knights. They made it through with plenty of time, but he realized Salvarias wouldn't, not with his bum leg.

Between the next patrols, he sent Varila, Tedris, and Lunara, followed by two of the other knights and Haleen. Looking over his shoulder, only Okulu and one other knight were with them.

"After Salv and I make it," he told Okulu. Wilhelm draped an arm around Salvarias's shoulders. "Don't worry about your staff," he said to his brother.

When the patrol went out of sight, Wilhelm darted ahead. Salvarias hobbled along, but the pace Wilhelm set made his brother's leg give out a few times. Wilhelm didn't bother with letting his brother help. He just carried him across the street.

Past the gate, Wilhelm rounded the corner and tucked them into the shadows. Salvarias gasped in silent lungfuls of air, sinking against the wall. With one more inhale, he pointed at a stake near the entrance. A head was mounted upon it, swollen and infested with flies. Rust colored blood stained the ground at the base.

"Okulu's father," Salvarias rasped. He pointed to the other side where a second head was mounted, long hair matted with blood. "His mother."

"Oh gods," Wilhelm breathed.

When the steady footfalls of the other patrol passed, Wilhelm peered around the corner and tried to motion them back, but Okulu and the knight were already headed for them. In the middle of the street, Okulu stumbled to a stop. His eyes grew wide.

"Okulu," Wilhelm hissed. "Okulu!"

The man just stood there, staring at his dead parents. Then for the second time, chaos erupted.

24

Salvarias's heart lurched into his throat as octrils surged out of the estates surrounding the gate, including the one they had just escaped. Behind him, a thunderous roar erupted from the shadows of the castle. The ground shook once, twice, and then a troll stepped from the darkness, spreading its arms wide, spiked club held in its gnarled hands.

"It's another trap!" Qwyn shouted.

Okulu stood alone in the street, tears glistening in his eyes. In that moment, Salvarias witnessed the look of a man who'd lost the last of his family, and to see such a tragedy unfold within his dearest friend tore Salvarias's heart. Anger simmered at the creatures surrounding his friend, at the darkness plaguing Arden, at all the death Salvarias's home had endured.

Clenching his fists, Salvarias stepped from behind the wall and strode into the street, ignoring Wilhelm's alarmed cry.

"Kill them," Salvarias commanded.

Whether it was him or his magic, he did not know, but twenty octrils burst apart, entrails and blood splattering homes and their allies.

Salvarias thrust his hand to the left, palm held up toward the horde approaching from that side. He wanted them dead, and they were. Turning to the right, he glared at the creatures standing there, gaping at him with fear-stricken faces. Then they were gone. Left on the street was nothing but chunks of flesh, globs of organs, and a stream of blood.

As his anger receded, Salvarias stared at the carnage. "What have we done?" he whispered.

It was not ... me, my wizard, his magic said.

"I did this?" he asked, appalled.

When you are angry, you're susceptible to blackfire's power. Your anger calls to it, and it will do your bidding.

A heavy arm wrapped around Salvarias and hauled him back behind the castle gate.

His mother sneered and hissed, "Monster."

Through the streets, the sound of pounding feet thundered up to them. Behind, the troll roared again.

Varila slapped Okulu and shook his shoulders. "Snap out of it! You want to do something? Kill the bastards that did this!"

Okulu blinked at her and then nodded slowly.

After the two had darted inside, Wilhelm and Edium closed the gates, but they were merely decorative iron. They would not hold off the enemy.

"Now, Vegos!" Wilhelm shouted.

A roar rang through Salvarias's mind and sounded far off in the forest. The thunder of drums started a breath later.

Wilhelm grabbed Qwyn's arm. "Get my brother somewhere high up where he can see. He has to cast the spell or else we're dead. If he gets hurt, I'll castrate you and then banish you from the Knighthood. Take the rest of the men." Turning to Edium, Wilhelm said, "You promised to keep him safe. Do it." To Varila, he said, "You're with me."

Okulu led the way wide to the right, steering Salvarias and his group far from the troll.

The troll looked no different than the one Wilhelm had slain in the barbarians' arena. The thing stood near thirty feet, covered in ashy-brown leathery skin. Gnarled callouses stood up on its knees and elbows. The thing roared again, spraying Wilhelm in spittle reeking of old graves.

"I get it!" Varila yelled. "You got the last one."

"I think it'll take both of us."

She looked it up and down. "Fine, you bastard. But I get left, you get right." She flashed him a quick grin. "If I win, you have to do that thing with your tongue."

Wilhelm laughed. "I'll do it if I lose!"

"Oh, and by the way, I'm pregnant." She winked and darted off after the creature.

He stood rigid, joy burgeoning in his heart. He'd always thought they would only be blessed with one child. It seemed implied by his father's stories and his brother's suspicions. He'd accepted it, as had Varila, though both had wanted another child.

His wife's war cry shook him from his bewilderment, and he sprinted after her.

The troll cast them an amused look before it swung its club. Wilhelm dove. A whistle of air pressed him to the ground, ripping petals from nearby flowers. The beast wasn't slow, quite the opposite. Before its one arm stopped swinging its club, it reached out for Varila with its other. But gods, his wife was faster. She dove under the grab and summersaulted up, never losing her momentum. She was underneath the creature before it could react. Gripping her sword in both hands, she hacked into the creature's heel. It roared in pain and hopped up and down. Varila dodged the thudding footfalls.

Wilhelm finally made it to the other side and mirrored his wife's strike. The troll wailed as it slammed its fists on the ground, pounding around to find them. They kept in its blind spot, looking for an opening.

A sound like a thousand hissing snakes filled the air. It chilled Wilhelm's bones. Varila looked equally alarmed.

Then the troll teetered back and plopped down on its ass. It was smiling at them.

Wilhelm looked to the castle and the origin of the noise. Up a few floors, Salvarias stood on a balcony protruding from the castle's side. His hand was moving in a rune. Lunara clung to him, her head angled backward. The men on the balcony were shouting in alarm and pointing up. Wilhelm craned his head further, and his breath caught in his throat. The flying creatures were spiraling downward, gazes locked on his little brother. Their maws opened and liquid fire poured out.

"Salv!" Wilhelm cried.

Mafarias had betrayed them. Again. Just as Wilhelm thought the bastard would.

Salvarias's head jerked up. Anger and betrayal churned in Wilhelm's heart, spun around in his head.

"Come on, Salv," Wilhelm muttered. "Get mad."

His brother raised a hand, readying a spell, but the creatures, all of them, gurgled and gagged on their fire. Bright orange blood rained down. Squinting, it took Wilhelm a few blinks to see the thousands of ice shards tearing into their flesh.

"Mafarias," Varila said.

Their grandfather might have kept his word, but it was too late. A flood of fire raced for his brother. Salvarias flicked out his hand and a flat white ceiling appeared over the balcony. Lava cascaded over it, deluging the ground below, splattering far enough a few drops sizzled close to Wilhelm, and dumping shredded creatures into the court-yard. Salvarias flicked his hand again, and that beautiful spell of destructive wind raced over the rooftops of the city. Wilhelm didn't need to see to know it would curve down at the last moment and chop half the army off at the waist. Another quarter would be dying from being flung into one another. That would leave only a thousand or so.

He looked up at the troll and smiled. "That's my little brother. And he just killed half your army."

The troll's eyes lit with rage, but before it could rise, Varila leapt on its stomach and raked her sword upward. Entrails and organs spilt out, liquids in putrid shades of yellow and brown pooled on the ground, reeking so badly it made Varila retch. She was covered in it.

Wilhelm looked back up at the balcony. Salvarias was leaning on Lunara and the railing, his hand drawing another rune. A ball of fire appeared, small and insignificant, but as Salvarias sent it sailing through the air, it grew, spreading wide enough to take out a few blocks as it disappeared from view behind the rooftops. A breath later screams erupted from near the gate and a plume of black smoke exploded in the air. It only took a light breeze to bring the stench of burning flesh up to the castle.

Salvarias sagged completely, but his head turned to Wilhelm.

Wilhelm grinned and whispered, "Nicely done, little brother." Turning to Varila, he swept her in his arms and kissed her, despite the stench and slime. When he pulled his lips from hers, he said, "I love you."

"I know. Now, if you don't mind, we've got a big problem."

Wilhelm followed her gaze to the horde of creatures flooding into the courtyard. Glancing up at the balcony, he saw his brother holding his sliced hand aloft, bright red blood visible even in the dim light. Salvarias's soft voice said, "Unlock your inner beast, Brother."

Power surged through him; wonderfully warm power that imbued itself in his muscles, expanding his skin to try to contain his growing girth. Inhaling an exhilarating breath, he drew his second sword and grinned at the creatures rushing him.

LUNARA WINCED at the heat emitting from the ball of fire floating in front of Salvarias. More of his weight pressed down on her shoulders as he sent it forward, and she stood straighter, trying to offer additional support, purposely ignoring the blood running in a steady stream from his nose and pushing aside her own deep exhaustion. She shielded herself further from their connection in an effort to keep awake.

Intense heat simmered the balcony, and along the blackened railing, where the creatures' liquid fire had passed before cascading down to the courtyard below, still smoked. Bodies littered the grasses; heaps of unrecognizable flesh. She didn't want to look, but her gaze sought the battle at the gate.

Salvarias's wind spell had left a path of destruction in its wake. The higher chimneys were toppled, and at the gate, creatures were piled upon one another in what she assumed was a mess of gore. Any spared from being cut in half had been flung against the stonewall. To her amazement, the wall itself had shook dangerously with his spell, causing their own army to give pause. Few creatures recovered.

"You don't need to do anymore," Qwyn said. "Please, Lord Knight, reserve your strength."

But Salvarias whispered under his breath, and the fireball sailed forward, expanding into an oval disc, barreling toward the poor, dazed enemy. It hit with an explosive cloud of flames, erupting screams of alarm and sending bodies flailing about, igniting more of their comrades. A cheer rose up from the knights as they cut their way into the city. Amongst them, Lunara made out Vegos tearing through the creatures, shredding any who got in his path. Victory would be hard earned, but they would prevail.

"Unlock your inner beast, Brother," Salvarias whispered.

She looked over to see blood running down his hand. Below, Wilhelm's booming laugh erupted over the chaos. Inside her own body, her bones sagged, and she wanted nothing more than to fall asleep. He wasn't going to leave this balcony upright.

"Let us go help," Salvarias said.

When he turned, his eyes rolled back and he collapsed. She tried to ease his fall, but both landed heavily. Blood trickled out of his mouth, nose, and ears.

"Uncle!" Tedris cried.

"He's fine," Lunara assured him. "Just tired."

"By Zerana's love, that boy is stubborn," her father muttered. "Is there a safe place inside we can take him, Okulu?"

The merc stood despondent, staring over the destruction, eyes glossy with unshed tears.

"Dammit," Edium muttered.

A gust of wind blew Lunara's hair in her face. Quickly she brushed it aside and raised her gaze skyward. Sira and Saval spiraled down and landed lightly on the balcony. Sira pressed her head against Lunara's belly and squawked softly. Saval let out a low keening whine as he nudged Salvarias. Her husband didn't move.

"Do you think they can carry his weight?" Edium asked.

"It's worth a try," Qwyn muttered.

Lunara and Tedris wedged themselves under Salvarias's side and shifted him enough that Sira managed her head beneath him, lifting him higher so Saval could wiggle under him. It took effort from the four of them, but they eventually had him draped over both griffins' backs.

"Let's get down to Wilhelm and Varila," Edium said.

She leaned over the railing to see the mayhem below. Wilhelm and her sister were drenched in blood, swords spinning wildly. Despite their talents, they were losing ground. Tedris's hand clasped hers, and he looked up at her with wide eyes.

"Papa and Mama will be all right, won't they?"

"Of course," she said, sweeping him up in her arms and balancing him on her hip. "Your Mama can beat those creatures with one hand tied behind her back."

Tedris grinned at her. Such a trusting child.

Her father led the way at a brisk but cautious pace. They hadn't had time to check the rooms along the way when they had first entered the castle to ensure no enemies lurked within. Anything could be awaiting them.

At the second floor, Edium gave up caution and ran. They heard swords clanging, and fear for Wilhelm and Varila sent them running, even the griffins though they had a harder go of it.

By the time they made it to the lower level, Wilhelm and Varila had been driven inside. More creatures were pouring in, their numbers increasing. Hundreds must have been hiding in the estates.

Haleen rushed to Wilhelm's side and began spouting off spells. Her father drew his sword and sprinted to their aid, calling over his shoulder to Vuddruk, "Keep my grandson, daughter, and the boy safe."

"Come along, dearie," Vuddruk said, taking her arm and ushering her down a hall.

"But I can help," Tedris said. "I can lift a sword."

"Certainly you can, boy," Vuddruk said. "But adults are paranoid over children. They'd be so worried about you—without reason, of course—that they wouldn't be fighting to their best abilities."

Tedris sighed heavily, head craning to watch the fight fading from view. "One day I'll be as good as Papa. Did you see him? Two swords, Aunt Lunara. Two! And did you see Mama cut open that troll?" He swiped his hand down. "One stroke, just like that!"

"Hush now," Lunara whispered. "We need to be quiet."

Sira and Saval followed awkwardly, their bodies nearly taking up the entire hallway. Despite their efforts, several times Salvarias's head knocked against the walls.

They ended up in some sort of foyer. Mirrors hung all around, rich carpets muffled their footfalls, and a horrible stench clogged the air.

"Gods, what is that?" Lunara said, covering her nose with her arm.

Vuddruk grimaced. "That's the smell of unbathed bodies."

Studying the room, their gazes fell on a door barred with beams of wood. Now both were silent and far from the fighting, she heard the sound of coughing and soft sobs.

"The prisoners," she said in unison with Vuddruk.

"Dear gods," Vuddruk said. "Help me, child."

She shooed the griffins and Tedris off to the side and joined the old mage at the doors. They both pulled and punched at the beams, but she wasn't strong enough and he was too weak from his days being held captive. Saval gently shimmied his way from under Salvarias. The griffin rose on his haunches and grabbed the beam with his front talons. Muscles bunched along his arms as he heaved and pulled. Much to her surprise, he let out a deafening roar, a noise she never knew he could make, and the beam gave way, sending the straining griffin stumbling backward.

Vuddruk threw open the doors. Beyond was what she guessed to be a grand ballroom; ornamental murals covered the walls and ceiling, and the polished marble floor was now stained with human waste.

People flooded out, knocking her and Vuddruk down as they fled for freedom. Saval let out an indignant squawk as people shoved him aside, but he managed his way to Lunara and Vuddruk and helped shield them as they scrambled to the side of the room where Sira huddled protectively with Salvarias and Tedris.

"Well then," Vuddruk said, grinning widely while watching the thousands of people rushing by. "I guess we found the help your father and sister needed. Who said the old and un-murderous type couldn't save everyone."

Relief let loose laughter from them both.

25

Wilhelm raised the sheet over Sir Vin's face. They had lost too many this battle, and the weight of it hung heavy on his shoulders, despite Vegos's best efforts. The bear nuzzled him gently, a comforting rumble vibrating Wilhelm's chest.

"Take heart, Lord Knight," Paull said. "He died peacefully and without pain."

Wilhelm nodded and attempted an assuring smile.

Outside the inn where the wounded and dying were housed, a palpable cloud of death hung over the city. Breathing shallow did not save the stench from invading his mouth, coating his tongue like spoiled milk. Vuddruk stood waiting, his beard gleaming white and wearing a borrowed set of robes from Salvarias that pooled at his feet. He smiled kindly, though his eyes bore heavy exhaustion and a deep sadness.

"You!" Vegos roared. "You left me in that cave to die!"

Vuddruk raised his hands in surrender. "You must believe me when I say I did only as Nevlar demanded. He said he would one day send someone to free you. To gods a thousand years is nothing, though I'm sure for you it was an eternity."

Vegos snorted, looking at the mage with disgust. "You live only because my Travard trusted you, and time and again you saved him. And Wilhelm has told me you have saved his life and that of his brother's."

"Can you do anything for the injured?" Wilhelm asked. "Like you did for Salvarias outside Zeeas."

Vuddruk shook his head. "I merely shocked his heart to start beating again. His injuries would've healed with time, unlike those inside who will not make it until morning. Gods cannot heal those whom Death has already claimed as his own."

"Salv healed Edium," Wilhelm snapped. "Zerana's healed Lunara. Salv's brought me back from death."

Vuddruk patted Wilhelm's shoulder. "I know it's confusing, boy. Salvarias did not heal Edium, Nevlar did. And I assure you he pays handsomely for doing so. And as for you and Lunara, those who healed you own your souls. I own no souls, and therefore none are mine to save."

"More rules," Wilhelm growled.

"Alas, that is true. I do not approve of them myself, but I must abide by them."

Grunting in annoyance, Wilhelm headed back to the castle, Vuddruk half running to keep up with Wilhelm's long strides, Vegos ambling along beside them.

"Why did they leave you here?" Wilhelm asked.

Vuddruk gave a sardonic laugh. "They had not anticipated their victory in kidnapping your son. I was a contingency. They assumed Salvarias would have done what they asked in order to save me. I dare say they were right. I saw it in his eyes. Why he would sacrifice himself for me is a mystery. Certainly I have given him little reason."

"You keep saving his life. It's all the reason Salv would need."

"A generous man."

"You don't know the half of it."

I would trust him, Vegos advised. *In all the years I have known him, he has been loyal to Nevlar, if not cryptic at times. He likes to be mysterious with his knowledge. I suspect that is why he has been so vague in answering your questions. He is also very careful at walking the thin line bordering terribly close to disobeying the rules. He is clever, but infuriating at times.*

Wilhelm grunted an agreement.

Vuddruk grabbed Wilhelm's arm and leaned close. "You have traitors among you, boy. I don't know whom, but Devoar knew too much. It had to have come from someone in your ranks."

"My grandfather, no doubt," Wilhelm muttered. The answer was immediate, and even as Wilhelm gave voice to what he had feared ever since they had brought the bastard along, it hurt for it to be a truth. He'd always loved his grandfather.

"I cannot say for certain. Mafarias and I are merely acquaintances. He's always been recluse and never cared for the war, never picked sides, and his love for women occupies much of his time. Even after the curse, he kept far from me and any ties to either side of the war. I say this because I find it hard to believe he would ever devote himself to light or darkness."

"They took our grandmother."

Vuddruk looked puzzled a moment and nodded grimly. "He must love her very much to betray you. Still, I would not be so sure it is only he. Someone took Tedris from Warton. Someone besides your grandfather, and he or she had to have been a mage."

"When we get to Bren, I can ask Zehnia." Wilhelm glanced at the old man. "I haven't had a chance to thank you for helping my brother. With him able to heal himself, you've definitely given us a chance. I wish we would have known about it sooner."

"Ah, you mean his death?" Vuddruk shrugged. "I doubt all those years ago he would have possessed the power. It's grown exponentially since his resurrection. He is opening himself up, and every time he uses it, it will strengthen. When he is well, I will caution him against it. If he unleashes too much, his mortal mind will cave under the strain."

"He fears he is going mad."

"With good reason. Likely he is. All I know is your brother was made special. Any other god trapped in this mortal form releasing as much power as he would have been dead long ago. He is an anomaly amongst gods, rest assured. I do not offer this to ease your worry. Quite the contrary. No one can guess his breaking point but himself, and I doubt he would spare his mind if it meant saving Arden."

Wilhelm grunted an agreement as he stepped inside the castle, pleased to see the bodies had been carried away and the blood cleaned.

"Well," Vuddruk said. "If you don't mind, I'd like to get some rest. The past two years have been arduous, to say the least."

The mage tilted his head before climbing heavily up the stairs leading to the upper rooms. He passed Brice bounding down two at a time and Kisra trailing the young knight.

"Wilhelm," Brice greeted, a smile taking up half his face. "I can't believe we pulled this one off."

They clasped hands, and despite his grief, Wilhelm found Brice's enthusiasm infectious. "That we did."

As they ambled along, Brice reported on the number wounded, how many citizens had been saved, how many were sick, the army's provisions, what they could take from the city, and several more facts Wilhelm could not muster the energy to care about.

At long last, the brief was complete and Wilhelm found himself in the dining hall, platters of food covering the table. Apparently, the castle's staff had been taken alive and was now repaying their rescue by offering their services. Wilhelm picked up a plate and piled on as much meat as it would hold.

"I need you to find my grandfather," Wilhelm said to Brice as he plopped down. "Bring him to me when you do but be cautious. I don't know if I can trust him. How's my brother?"

"Qwyn reported that he's up and bathing right now. Despite the amount of magic he used, Qwyn said he looks remarkably alert."

Kisra nodded. Her smile conveyed pride in their victory, but dark rings hanging under her eyes betrayed its cost. She'd grown thin over their campaign, and Brice hardly left her side. Even now she leaned on him, and Wilhelm couldn't help notice their hands entwined. He'd not realized they'd grown so close.

"He's recovering faster these days," Kisra said. She ran a trembling hand across her brow, brushing aside a few locks of hair.

"Can we create a portal to Zehnia?" Wilhelm asked. "I'm sure she's worried about Tedris."

"I cannot," she said. "I have no soil from Warton. The only link we have is from the Knighthood headquarters. I could go back, if you like, and travel to Warton from there and deliver the news."

Wilhelm shoveled down another mouthful of roasted pig and nodded. "I think it's the least we can do. I'd like you to stay in Warton and figure out who's betrayed us. Someone kidnapped Tedris from right under the Queen. I'd think she'd know them. Vuddruk suspects a mage."

"Likely," she agreed. "They would've required access to a portal to be here before we were."

"Take your time and rest a day there," Wilhelm said. "A nice bed would do you good. Take Brice with you."

Brice blushed but grinned. "I'll keep her safe."

"Bring me the traitor," Wilhelm said. "Alive if you can, but I won't shed tears if you bring me just the head."

"Vegos!" Tedris cried. The boy barreled into the room and collided with the bear's leg, hugging it tightly.

Vegos shook his leg. *Don't be so needy, boy.*

Wilhelm grinned at them when his son grabbed hold of a chunk of fur and climbed up Vegos, despite the bear's snapping jaw and threatening growl.

You're pulling, Vegos complained.

"Don't be such a baby," Tedris chided. Once mounted, he hugged Vegos's neck. "You stink."

So do you, the bear said indignantly.

"We'll be sure to return by noon tomorrow," Brice said. "If we can't find the traitor ourselves, I'm sure Marcus could help."

Wilhelm tore his attention from his son and nodded an agreement. Marcus was Humar's most trusted friend in Warton. He'd finish whatever Brice and Kisra could not. "We'll leave early, but you two can catch up. And before you go, post a guard on Vuddruk. At this point, I can't trust him completely."

"I understand," Brice said, his smile falling. "I must say, having Vuddruk and that lady both here is odd to say the least."

Wilhelm frowned. "They were bait."

"Bait?" Kisra snorted a fake laugh. "There was no need for bait. They knew we'd go to the estate for prisoners. Why they had the woman there is a mystery to me. Tedris and Vuddruk I understand. After all, they wanted Salvarias. But this Haleen?" Kisra shook her head. "I don't understand it. Then again, I don't have a mind for this plotting and deceit."

"She makes a good point," Brice said softly.

Wilhelm hunched closer to his plate of food. "No, I've known Haleen for years. More likely they were going to use her to get me to do what they wanted."

Kisra narrowed her eyes. "Why not use Tedris?"

Wilhelm wolfed down a few more bites, turning the question over in his mind.

"We best be going," Brice said.

"I'll meet you outside," Kisra said. "I want to check on Okulu. I'm worried about him."

The two left Wilhelm in thought. Odd, yes, but they didn't know Haleen as he did. She was a survivor. Perhaps she'd hinted for them to use her, knowing Wilhelm would rescue her from years of imprisonment. Of course she would be suspected. No one understood her as Wilhelm did. No one understood his relationship with her, how close they were, how much he had valued her, how her friendship and comfort had kept him going in his youth as he watched his brother deteriorate.

The musky scent of long-ago memories filled his nostrils, and he looked up to see Haleen settling in a chair next to him. Her bright blue eyes were as inviting as he remembered, and when she spoke, it was in that same breathy voice.

"I can't tell you how good it is to see your face."

He smiled at her. "And yours. Thank you for your help."

She shrugged and popped a grape in her mouth. "It was the least I could do. Though you hardly needed it. Your wife is an amazing fighter and a beautiful creature. And your son has taken the best of you both."

Wilhelm looked over his shoulder to see Vegos lying on the cool floor, Tedris curled up in the crook of his arm, both snoring. "I've been blessed."

"Indeed. I never expected you to achieve anything less in life. You were destined for greatness."

"How did you survive?"

"A creature fancied me, and I was given to it." She looked down at her hands. "I bid my time with it, pleasing it enough to keep me alive. I never gave up hope of escape. It wasn't easy; quite horrible, if I'm to be honest. I'm sure I'll never be free of nightmares." She inhaled a deep breath and cast Wilhelm a small smile, bringing attention to the new wrinkles around her mouth that had not been there when last he had kissed it. "But that is the past. I'm free and intend to help in any way I can."

Wilhelm rested a hand on hers. "I'm so sorry, Haleen."

"Don't. None of it was your fault. You're here now, and saving the world at that. You've done more than any. I only hope to pick-up our friendship." She smiled slyly. "It is a shame you're married. I would have liked your company to drown away the horrible memories."

Wilhelm laughed. "You give me too much credit. But I am here should you ever want to talk."

She cast him a bright smile and then kissed his hand. "Gods I've missed that laugh."

They fell into easy conversation as if they had never been separated.

SALVARIAS STEPPED into Okulu's room, closed the door, and made his way to the fire. His friend sat in a cushioned chair, elbows propped on his knees as he leaned forward, a half empty bottle of brandaline loosely held in one hand, his other holding his head.

It had taken the army the entire day to clear the town, set up patrols, and find rooms inside the castle. Okulu had retired only an hour ago, yet two empty bottles of brandaline rested on a nearby table.

Salvarias sat in a chair and set a tea mixture in front of Okulu.

"Something to make me sleep?" Okulu asked, voice dead, breath reeking of alcohol.

"I think it best."

"They never blamed me," Okulu said. "Not once. I wanted them to. Gods how I wanted them to." He leaned back in his chair and took a long swig from the bottle. He had not bathed, and the stink of battle hung heavy in the room because of it. His eyes were as red as rubies. "I told them they were horrible parents. I told them they should punish me for letting my sister go alone, that they should be angry with me, something, for godssake. But they didn't listen. I hated them for that. I really hated them." Tears welled in his eyes. "And I told them as much. I did it right before I left."

Salvarias pried the bottle from Okulu's hand and pushed the tea closer. "Drink, my friend."

"Every time I close my eyes, I see their heads. I don't want nightmares," Okulu said thickly.

"You will have none."

Okulu picked up the cup in a shaking hand. "Promise?"

"I promise."

Okulu drained it, hauled himself up, and tripped and swayed to his bed. He collapsed on to the mattress and buried his face in a pillow.

Salvarias covered his friend with a blanket and sat on the edge of the bed. He waited until Okulu's shoulders stopped shaking and his breath deepened in the steady rhythm of sleep before rising and searching for bottles. Salvarias found four hidden and another empty one. Taking them all, he left the room. Kisra was waiting outside.

"How is he?"

"Sleeping," Salvarias said, handing her the bottles. "I would dispose of these." Looking her over, he frowned at her pale face and dark rimmed eyes. "You should sleep as well, my lady. He will not wake until late tomorrow."

"I'm heading to Warton for a day, and trust me, I'll be utilizing the queen's softest bed."

"You did well. Sir Brice told me of your spells. You were integral in our victory."

Kisra snorted. "Cessia would be better. It's hard for me when the numbers dwindle. I feel like a wild boar in a glass shop."

"Your power is vital in wars. Trust in yourself will hone the precision of your spells."

She nodded, offering a tired smile. "I'll see you tomorrow."

Bowing, he bid her farewell, went two rooms down, and slowly opened the door. Lunara had already fallen asleep with the two griffins curled about her.

As tired as he was, his mind was not yet calmed enough for sleep. Shutting the door, he navigated the hallways leading to the dining hall where his brother had surely set up camp. Halfway there, Lady Talura intercepted him.

"Hello, sweetness," she said.

He hated how much he liked her endearment. Bowing, he said, "My lady. You should be resting."

Lady Talura shrugged. "I'm not tired." Picking at her nails, she frowned at them. "I can't get the blood out from under them."

She had spent the day helping the healers with the wounded. When Salvarias had seen her, it had been a shock to see her covered in blood. He had nearly passed out from fear it was hers. The memory did not sit well with him.

"Would you take a walk with me? Edium is already asleep, but I can't ..." She smoothed her dress and blinked a few times.

Of course a cleric of Zerana would be linked closely to life. Such gentle people should not witness the tragedy of war. He had concocted a sleeping remedy for Lunara so his wife would not relive the horrors in her dreams. "I can mix you—"

"Not yet. I need time, but before I sleep, I'll take whatever you think best."

"As you wish, my lady," he said, bowing. "But I should meet with my brother."

"He's still eating, believe it or not. By the time we're done, you'll have your brother all to yourself." Lady Talura laughed softly. "You'll have hours, as a matter of fact. Varila can't get the troll's smell out of her hair. She'll bathe for days until it washes out. Now come along, sweetness."

She led the way down a few halls and then out to the warm summer night. The garden had been trampled, but the scent of flowers helped battle the smell of burnt bodies. Salvarias fought a shudder at remembering the creatures screaming as he set them aflame.

"You did well today," Lady Talura said. "You nearly took out the entire army on your own."

"I could not have done it without Lunara's help."

She frowned up at him. "Lower your hood, dear."

He pushed it down without hesitation.

"The stars are lovely," Lady Talura said. "So full of hope, don't you think? Beacons of light."

Salvarias regarded them for a moment. "Stars die just as hope dies. Darkness has an insatiable appetite."

"Yet we are winning our campaign."

Salvarias conceded her point. "Though it is bloody. We have lost twenty knights."

"And without you and your brother, Arden would be consumed in darkness."

Salvarias rubbed the red mark on his right palm. "This city was a trap. The dark god knew where we were headed."

"Yet we prevailed, my dear. You must see the positive even as you acknowledge the negative. Holding one over the other leads to hopelessness or carelessness. Balance in all things."

Lady Talura stopped at a bench and sat down, patting the spot beside her. Salvarias sat as far from her as he could.

After a moment of silence, she said, "I want you to tell me what she did. Everything."

Salvarias tensed. "I do not wish to discuss such things."

"All the more reason to tell me. The heart cannot bear such burdens alone. You haven't confided in your brother or in your wife."

"They know—"

"They know she hurt you. They don't know what she did or said."

"And why would you think I would confide in you when I have not done so with my own brother or wife?"

She smiled up at him, looking as though she was explaining the complications of the heart to a child. "You would not lay your burdens on them. You would not want to add to your brother's guilt or make Lunara relive what you endured."

"And you think I am so cruel as to make you suffer?"

She laughed light and airy. "Surely not, sweetness. You're denying me, aren't you?" She smoothed her dress. "You're misguided, of course."

"How so?"

"It's quite simple. Mothers can bear the weight of the world as easily as you cast your light spell."

Salvarias glanced at his sparrow of light. He did not remember casting it. "My mother could not."

"Oh, well, there's a simple explanation." She shifted to face him. "Remember what Mafarias said: she was a demigod, and her mind was not made to withstand such power. I, on the other hand, am blessed by Zerana. My mind is quite capable of shouldering such suffering."

Narrowing his eyes at her, he mulled over what she had said. His mother's eyes had always gleamed oddly when she had hurt him. Perhaps those were the times when her madness was upon her. "And you think speaking of what happened will drive away the horror of it? You think it would help."

"Absolutely."

He startled at her confidence. Thinking it over, he shook his head. "I do not believe you."

Grinning mischievously, she said, "But aren't you curious if I'm right? What harm could come of it? Do you think it would drive me to hate you? You care not for my love, so what would it matter? And as I said, Zerana strengthens me. The burden will reside with her, not me. Now, tell me what happened."

He sat in silence for several long moments, churning over her statement, wondering if it were true. He had not realized he spoke until half way through his sentence. "It started the day I was born." Gods, was he really going to tell her? He thought to stop, but the first words had been spoken, and the rest gushed out in an avalanche of pain and remembrance.

He recalled his mother's hateful stare when Mafarias had placed him in his mother's arms the day he was born. She had shoved him back and declared him a monstrosity, a demon child. Despite being new to the world, he understood her hate. She looked at him that way for all the years she lived with him.

The joy of Tobin coming into his life was immediately snuffed out by the horror he endured when the guard would take Wilhelm away. The books, the skillets, the boards—anything she could find to beat him with. When that did not help, she used leeches to drain his 'evil' blood. She yelled at him, told him how horrible he was, how miserable he made her life, how eventually he would taint his brother with evil. Then the worst came: the cold sting of metal as it sliced down his head, the sound of his blood dripping into a washbasin, the taste of her own blood running hot down his throat, the burning of his tears, and the forlorn song of the sparrow.

He wept as he did then. He wept as only a broken child could. A part of him wanted to stop, to save himself from reliving such nightmares, but the storm had been unleashed, and he barreled on.

Through teeth clenched in self-hatred, he recalled to her the times late in the night when he was taken from Wilhelm's side. Shame did not stop his confession of the people he had killed in that horrid house by the docks. He recalled the weight of the knife in his hand, the warm, slick blood staining his small fingers, the overwhelming scent of cloves and fish guts, and the cries of those he murdered. He wept out how much he hated himself afterward, but blurted his admission of the joy he felt as he cut into them.

He choked on the memory of the night his mother had died: what he saw and heard, the smell of it. He balled himself up, tight and tucked away, at voicing Tobin's betrayal. His father's abandonment, just when Salvarias had accepted the man. Alone. He felt so alone.

He rambled on about his time in Zeeas. The knives and cold, the humiliation and the sick need for Sansis's comforts as the man cut him up.

Try as he might, he could not curl up tighter, could not hide from it nor forget it. It lived on him as a fresh wound, always opening, always bleeding. He heard the low broken keening coming from his own throat when he had finished spilling his torment. Rocking himself, he hugged his knees tight to him, burying his face in them, holding the back of his head, and feeling the bump of the scar beneath his fingers. He hated it. He wanted to scalp himself, cut away the memory. He wanted to flay away the marks Sansis and his mother had left on his soul. A new wave of tears choked out as he wept, "I do not want to feel anymore."

He was not sure how long he sat there crying. It all fled out of him, draining him the longer he let it go, the longer he did not care if he was weak, and the longer the tears owned him.

When at long last they subsided, he felt heavy with exhaustion and lightened of an unknown burden he had carried. Lady Talura hummed a song, and the melody instantly brought him safety and love. He wanted it, needed it, and he clung to her voice for some time before he hesitantly raised his head. He was curled up against a tree, though he had no memory of leaving the bench. His arms ached with how tightly he had held himself. The sleeves of his robes were wet with his tears.

Lady Talura was knelt in front of him. Though she had dried her face, her eyes were red and glossy with unshed tears.

"I'm proud of you," she whispered. "It takes courage to face your pain. Burying it away will never do, sweetness. I'm here, and I'll always listen to you."

Salvarias gave her his one secret, one he kept buried in shame. "I hate her." His throat tightened, and it took effort to keep going. "I love her, I do. But ... But gods help me, I hate her." The instant the words came, he did not think he could disgust himself further. Voicing it only solidified his evil, but he wanted her to know how dark his heart truly was.

Lady Talura gave a soft laugh, seeming filled with relief. "I hate her, too."

The words struck Salvarias dumb. She could not. She was a mother. She sensed good and evil. She should know Ashra was the good one, he the evil. All those around him, who swore they saw good in him, did not feel the evil inside as he felt it. It called to him even now, urging him to strike her dead and to kill all around him, to save himself from more pain. A horrible part of himself *wanted* to do it. Shaking his head, he said, "You cannot. You are a mother. You know good from evil."

She stared at him as if he spoke a different language, then her eyes lit with some understanding. "Oh my dear sweetness. Mothers have no such knowledge. We're just people, dear. No different from you, your brother, Edium."

"She knew."

"She only knew of the shadowfires. She let fear own her. She let it whisper in her ear and drive her mad. She let fear turn her against her own child."

Salvarias had built his world on this principle. It was his way of understanding why his mother had done what she had done.

"Is Varila evil?" Lady Talura asked.

Salvarias shook his head.

"Yet her mother beat her. Tell me, if mothers know good and evil, why would she have hurt Varila?"

Never had he thought of it that way. He had warped everything around him to fit into his explanation.

"Your mother was sick," Lady Talura said gently. "She had an illness of the mind, sweetness. Nothing more."

Could it be? But where would that leave him? Was he the

monstrosity his mother had always said he was, or had a god created him with a god's soul and power, with a god's eyes? Was it possible he was good? Then he remembered the knife. The blood on his hands.

"I killed them," he said. "She was right about me. I killed them."

Lady Talura smoothed her dress, eyes downcast, lips pursed. When she spoke, her tone was filled with skepticism. "So you say."

"I remember everything that has happened in my life. *Everything.* There is no doubt. I held the knife."

Shrugging, she gave him a wane smile. "I don't believe you're capable of it."

"The evil ... it lives within me. I *am* capable of killing. I have done it."

"Not the way you're describing. You've killed those who've killed others. You've never taken the life of an innocent."

"I want to," Salvarias said. "There is a part of me that wants to kill you right now."

She gazed at him for a long moment before nodding. "I see the truth in what you say. I do. But you're a good person at heart, Salvarias. I don't believe you'd ever kill an innocent." Frowning, she said, "It was heavy in your hand, was it not? That's how you described the knife. Heavy and awkward. You were a small child: small hands, small arms. You think you were strong enough to get a knife through skin and muscle? Through bone?"

The knife had been heavy. He recalled the image of it teetering in his hand, the hilt bigger than he could grip with both hands. But when he killed them, he had held the knife securely. His hands had taken up the hilt. Straining his mind, he tried to pry out details of the killings. Now he did, they seemed ... hazy.

"If you had done it," Lady Talura continued, "then the knife could not have been as large as you say. For you to have done it, you'd have stabbed them in places that could kill, but would not be as brutal as you're remembering. Something's wrong, dear. I don't know what, but your memory is flawed. You're not a killer."

He distinctly remembered the sickening smell of blood, the screams, and the wet knife in his hands afterward. But always hazy was the act itself. The eyes of his victims were behind gauze, the splatter of blood blurry, and the knife had no real feel to it—no weight, no coldness from the metal hilt. What it meant, he had not a clue. No question he had been in the home. No doubt the people had been murdered. But what it all meant ... He could not connect the facts.

"Can a mind be forced to believe it did something? Is magic capable of such a thing?" Talura asked. "Can memories from one be given to another? Perhaps someone did kill those people, and perhaps you were given the memory of it."

The possibilities for magic were endless, as he was discovering. The number of spells seemed infinite. Of course it was possible, but he did not know how to do it.

"Shh," Lady Talura said, grabbing his attention. "You've been through enough tonight. Let it lie until morning." She smiled sweetly. "By the time we leave this garden, you'll know the joy one can receive if they merely share their sorrows. You're not alone, Son."

For the first time, he wholly believed her. Her smile grew as if she knew his thoughts, and its happiness infected him. She saw good in him. A mother. She cared for him even after all he confessed. She saw simply him: all his flaws were bared to her, and she did not deny them as his brother did, or overlook them as Lunara did. Lady Talura *saw* them, accepted them, and despite it all, the care in her eyes never lessened.

Bending to keep his attention, she said, "I love you. With all my heart."

He had a sudden urge to call her mother, to open to her what he knew dwelled in his heart. Ashra was dead. She could not touch him anymore and fill his mind with self-hatred. He could have a new mother: one that would love him unconditionally and stay with him when he was frightened; one that noticed all the things he needed and made plates of food out of love. He could have what he always longed for. A mother. And all he needed was to accept it, to voice it.

Inhaling a deep breath, he built up the courage and opened his mouth.

"Hello!" Wilhelm boomed.

Salvarias jumped, his heart knocking in his chest, breath sucking in to choke him. Lady Talura startled as well, but immediately burst into laughter.

"You nearly scared us half to death," she said. "Come join us. We were just going for a walk."

Wilhelm plucked Salvarias up from the ground, wrapped a heavy arm around his shoulders, and ruffled his hair. Salvarias elbowed his brother's ribs.

"Ouch," Wilhelm muttered, rubbing his side. "You should be resting."

"I am fine," Salvarias said, smiling as he let his weight fall into his brother's hold. He glided forward, not needing to move his feet.

"We're going to leave early in the morning for Bren," Wilhelm said. "I don't think Varila will be emerging from the tub until then. I told her we could send her ahead. The stench of her hair might scare away the other army."

"I'm surprised you're still alive," Lady Talura said.

"There's some furniture that didn't make it," Wilhelm said, winking.

"Edium was asking after your grandfather," Lady Talura said. "He hasn't seen him since the fighting stopped."

Wilhelm frowned. "I've asked to have him hunted down."

"I am sure he has taken a room," Salvarias said to assure his brother's churning worry. "The spell he cast surely made him tired."

"Even so, we have questions for him," Wilhelm said, his voice hesitating enough for Salvarias to know there was more to it.

Salvarias tilted his head to Lady Talura. "If I remember correctly, you fancy owls?"

Her eyes lit. "I do! Is there one about?"

Calling the bird in his mind, Salvarias asked if it would join them. It swooped down in a lazy spiral and settled itself on a branch of a nearby tree. It blinked its large eyes at Lady Talura.

Pressing a hand to her heart, she gasped. "It's beautiful!"

"You may approach it," Salvarias encouraged.

Tentatively, she walked up to it. When it cocked its head, she let out a small laugh and stroked its feathers. "How truly remarkable."

Wilhelm released Salvarias and, crooked grin spread, ambled up to the owl.

The bird's eyes flicked left, and it startled from the branches, taking flight. A chill inched its way up Salvarias's spine. Glancing over his shoulder, his heart skipped when he saw his mother gliding toward him. Closing his eyes, he silently repeated it was not real. When he opened them, she stood in front of him.

He stumbled back a step and looked at his brother. Wilhelm's eyes were wide, mouth hanging open. He was looking directly at their mother.

"It can't be," Lady Talura breathed. "You're dead."

Ashra brushed back a lock of auburn hair and smiled. "I've come for my sons."

Horror as he had not experienced since he was child roared to life in his veins. Frozen, he could only listen to her chant her spell and let the soil fall between her fingers. A portal opened.

"I'm sorry," she said. "Truly. But this must be done."

Salvarias staggered backward, collided with a tree, and sank to the ground, unable to tear his gaze from his mother. She walked to Wilhelm and placed an owl feather in his hand. He looked at it puzzled, then his eyes rolled back, and he crumpled to the ground.

Lady Talura lunged forward, dagger gripped in her hand. Ashra leaned back, letting the blade slide past, and stuck an owl feather in Lady Talura's hair. The woman shook her head, hissed out a curse, and toppled to the ground.

Ashra turned to Salvarias.

"You are not real," he pleaded. "You cannot be real."

"It's time to go, Son."

Tears burned in his eyes. Shaking his head, he pressed himself to the tree. "Help me," he wept to his brother. Wilhelm did not move. "Help me!"

Pale blue light flickered in his vision, and then darkness claimed him.

~

UNUPTURE BROODED ALONE in a tent nestled in the middle of Veedran's army, wincing when he shifted in his chair. The last beating Devoar had given him when he'd tried to escape hadn't completely healed. His ribs still ached with each breath.

For months he had tried to pass messages to Salvarias, and each one had been intercepted. His only option had been escape. He had needed to warn Salvarias they were coming and that their grandfather was going to commit the ultimate betrayal. But the time for warnings had passed, and once again, Unupture's foolishness would lead to Salvarias's suffering.

Through the tent flap, Unupture caught sight of the stars and glorious moon lighting Devoar speaking just outside the tent. Soon, if not already, Salvarias would be taken.

"After we get the stone," Devoar was saying, "you'll leave here and go to Zerana. There you can build your powers free of harm."

A silhouetted figure nodded. "And once the Guardian obtains our victory here, you will kill Wilhelm and send Salvarias to me. With my power fully returned, I will claim Salvarias's soul and end this fight."

"You are certain Salvarias will not resist? He has proven strong."

"You will have broken him by the time you hand him over to me. Remember, we know his secrets. And with the Soul broken and alone, the boy will cave. Victory will be mine."

"Wilhelm will not let you take Salvarias again," Unupture called to them. "He's too strong for you, and Veedran is vulnerable as long as the Protector lives. And Salvarias will never let him die. No amount of planning or hiding Veedran away will save him. Wilhelm and Salvarias will kill him."

Devoar stepped inside, and Unupture's stomach dropped when Veedran followed. Devoar's armor flowed with its movements, the slithering souls beneath wailing in near silent torment. "Some of what you say is true," Devoar conceded. "But we have made plans. Infallible plans."

Unupture laughed, but it held no warmth. "Time and again you have underestimated the brothers and their companions."

Devoar knelt in front of Unupture. "You don't understand, betrayer. We have spent three years preparing for this scenario. It was always a possibility Wilhelm would rescue Salvarias before we could turn him. For three years we've prepared."

"They have gods that will help them," Unupture said, desperate for it to be a truth. "They are not alone."

"You mean Vuddruk? Yes, I admit he has been a hindrance, but Mafarias cannot save his love unless he takes care of his brother of magic. Vuddruk will not live out the night."

The tent flap opened and a mess of octrils entered lugging Wilhelm's limp body. They dumped him on the ground at Devoar's feet. A woman entered behind them, lean and beautiful, eyes bright with intelligence. Sweat-soaked locks of auburn hair clung to her face. Flung over her shoulder was Salvarias. Gently, she lowered him to a bed of blankets. Pale blue light flickered around Salvarias and then disappeared.

Turning to Devoar, the woman said, "I've done what you've asked of me, now let her go."

"All in good time," Devoar said.

"That wasn't the deal," the woman snapped.

In her anger, she looked just as she had in Salvarias's memories, yet what stood before him was not their mother.

Devoar circled Ashra. "Flawless, absolutely flawless. You must have had free reign of Lynta. No man would stop a woman of such beauty. Tell me, is this how you tricked the Guardian when you would steal him in the night?"

"Yes," she said shortly.

"Her own son—a god!—could not tell you two apart. How truly remarkable."

"Let her go," she demanded again. "I have kept to our agreement. Release her."

Veedran knelt beside Salvarias. "Indeed you have. Bring in his lover, Devoar. We must not keep Mafarias waiting."

"It is not wise to cave so easily," Devoar said. "We can still use Jepine as leverage against him."

Veedran held out a hand, and Devoar placed a dagger in it. Slowly, Veedran cut down the front of Salvarias's robes and parted the slate-blue fabric. Unupture looked away from the young man's mutilated body.

"You see," Veedran said, smile growing, eyes gleaming, "I have what I want. There is no more need for clever ploys."

"You can see it?" Devoar asked.

"Yes," Veedran said.

Devoar motioned to one of the octrils. "Bring Jepine."

Veedran reached out tentatively, hand shaking. "I have waited so long. Over a thousand years."

"Be careful not to touch the boy," Devoar warned. "I do not trust sleep to keep him from stealing your power." It pointed at the red circle burned into Salvarias's right hand. "Will it remain?"

Veedran nodded. "The boy has been marked by my power. Nothing can undo it. I will forever be linked to him."

Veedran touched the air just above Salvarias's chest. Though Unupture saw nothing, the god clearly found something. Lifting and then wrapping his fingers around whatever he had, Veedran yanked it free. He fiddled with it a breath before it became visible. It was a rock, black, oval, and flat. Along its surface, a red line began to glow, subtle at first, more a trick of the eye. Then it grew and grew, lighting up Veedran's black eyes, casting long shadows in the tent.

Mafarias took a step back and Unupture cringed in his chair.

Then the light burst alive, bleeding out Unupture's eyesight, touching upon his skin. It left behind a feeling of wrong, of hopelessness, of true despair. When Unupture blinked back his vision, only dust was left in Veedran's hand. The god's eyes were closed, his breathing light and even.

After a long silence, Devoar asked, "How do you feel, Master?"

"Alive," Veedran breathed. "I finally feel alive."

An octril walked in and dumped a naked body on the ground. It was bloated from rot, face covered in burst boils, skin blue and black from death. Withered locks of auburn hair covered its head, and the once form of a woman was barely noticeable.

Mafarias sucked in a breath, and when Unupture looked up, it was not the young woman who stood before him. It was a God of Magic. Mafarias's eyes were raining tears.

"You've betrayed your grandchildren for nothing," Veedran said softly. "She has been dead for some time."

Mafarias's eyes lit with unbridled rage, and he roared out as he charged Veedran. Just before his hands closed around Veedran's throat, he stopped and struggled against some invisible hold.

Veedran sidled up to Mafarias and spoke in a rich seductive tone Unupture had never heard the god use, but it made him shiver with adoration.

"You see now," Veedran breathed. "You see you cannot win. They cannot win. Arden will be mine. I will break my brother's son and use the Guardian's power to annihilate this world. Father will be pleased. He will end this curse, and I will leave this world in ruin. And you, my dear pet, made it possible. You gave me the advantage time and again. I've squandered them in the past, but not this time. This time I will use it, and you will help me."

"Never!" Mafarias spat pass tears. "Never!"

Veedran rested a hand over Mafarias's heart and smiled. "You will have no choice. You will serve me. You will do as I say."

"Master, no!" Devoar roared.

A thin tendril of red burrowed its way inside Mafarias's chest. The man screamed such a harrowing scream it chilled Unupture to the bone. Spittle bubbled up on Mafarias's lips, his body went rigid, and his eyes darted and rolled wildly.

"You cannot control a god!" Devoar shouted.

"I can do anything," Veedran hissed.

"He will be mad! You've ruined him!"

"I do not need him sane to do what must be done," Veedran snapped. To Mafarias, he gently said, "Change into her for me."

The air shimmered around Mafarias like a mirage. When it subsided, Ashra stood before Veedran.

"Very good," Veedran said and released him. Mafarias toppled to the ground, eyes too wide, and drool fell from his open mouth. "You will obey Devoar. Do you understand?"

Mafarias gurgled some reply and crawled to the corner of the tent. He rocked, blubbering quietly.

Devoar shook its head. "You risk much of our mission."

"I have my power back," Veedran snapped. "Nothing is more powerful than me!"

"As long as the Guardian and Protector live, you are in danger. You must leave and nurture your power. Only you will be able to kill the Guardian, but not until he has been weakened."

Veedran clenched his hands into fists. "I can kill him now."

"I would not risk it," Devoar said. "Remember, Salvarias killed Lakvra. He is strong in his own right, and every time you touch him, he takes a part of your power. You must be at full strength, and he must be broken."

"You forget," Unupture said smugly. "He killed Crutar as well. You have no hope of winning against him."

Devoar laughed. "You think Crutar is dead? Do you think any would know how to kill a god? I assure you, Crutar is alive and with our other army. People made up that story about the heart and beheading with the purpose of giving Arden hope. Only a god can kill another god. Why do you think Salvarias did not die?"

Unupture shook his head, unable to grasp what Devoar meant. "Salvarias did die."

"Not really," Devoar said, seemingly amused by Unupture's puzzlement. "A god's body might lay dormant if he is ignorant enough to heal himself or be healed by another."

Unupture's mind tumbled with revelations. "You mean if Salvarias had known he was a god, he could have healed himself?"

Devoar shook its head. "I cannot believe Arden to be so ignorant of gods and their history. Do they not know of the Creator?"

Veedran looked at Unupture as if he were vermin and said, "Nevlar and Zerana wanted them pure, innocent, and free of the complications gods bring. They told them nothing." Veedran gave Salvarias's peaceful face one glare, then marched out of the tent.

Devoar motioned a group of octrils over to Wilhelm and Salvarias. "Take them and do what was discussed."

"What are you going to do to them?" Unupture demanded.

Devoar turned sympathetic eyes to Unupture. "It is not your fault you fell in love with the Guardian. Gods have sway over mortals, and any looking deep enough into Salvarias will be mesmerized by him." Shaking its head, it made its way from the tent, softly saying, "Such weak creatures, these mortals. It is not even a real fight."

VARILA HELD TEDRIS CLOSE, smoothing his hair, happy to see his silent tears had lessened. Vegos paced the dining hall, growling low. Varila herself wanted to succumb to a tantrum of sheer anger, but held her worry close to her heart, murmuring comforts to her son when she trusted her voice.

"You're sure it was Ashra?" Edium asked her mother again.

"Certain," Talura confirmed. "I'd seen a drawing of her in Jyfil's home. There's no mistaking a woman that beautiful."

Her mother pressed fingertips to her temples and groaned. The sleeping spell had apparently given her a dreadful headache, and the tea Lunara had mixed had yet to help.

Lunara blinked to keep the tears that had threatened all during their conversation at bay. "Salvarias knew they would come for him. The stone marked him. It was only a matter of time."

"The guards were not looking for Ashra," Idolar said apologetically. "She would have been able to travel through the city unmolested."

"You remember nothing else?" Edium asked Talura.

Her mother closed her eyes and said, "I remember I tried to stab her. Then I felt a tug in my hair, from the owl feather, I assume, then darkness too deep to be restful. It was if I were awake, screaming all night before the spell finally ended." Her features tightened, and she whispered, "He was utterly petrified. His eyes …" She shook her head gently. "I … Blue … I remember seeing something blue, but I can't recall."

"Salvarias's magic?" Varila asked. "Dark sapphire?"

"No … No, not dark. Pale, like a sun-drenched sky."

Edium stopped pacing. "You're sure?"

"What is it?" Varila asked.

"Mafarias," Edium growled. "When he touches the boy, he uses some sort of blue light. It's the only way he can do so without hurting Salvarias."

"I saw Ashra," Talura said stubbornly. "I've never heard of a spell …" Her eyes widened. "Oh gods. Mafarias was the one who took him in the night."

"What?" Edium said.

Her mother dropped her face in her hands. "It was Mafarias. He betrayed his own grandchildren. He tormented Salvarias in his youth. It was not solely his mother who abused him."

Her father paled, jaw rippling. "We have to go get them. Qwyn, bring me Vuddruk."

Haleen pressed a cold cloth to the back of Talura's neck. "If indeed it was Mafarias, you could not have done any more. I sensed his magic. He's quite powerful."

Lunara's battle finally ended in a broken sob, and she sank to a chair. The griffins gave pitiful cries as they nuzzled her, wrapping their tails around her. Haleen was quick to offer comfort, hugging Lunara's shoulders, standing awkwardly among the griffins. "There, there, dear," she said gently. "Salvarias is extremely powerful. More so than Mafarias."

No one said anything in response. They'd seen what happened when Salvarias thought he saw his mother. With her now solidly in front of him, no doubt he'd cave to his paranoia and revert to his childhood; no doubt he would do nothing to his mother.

They sat brooding until Qwyn came back into the room. The knight looked death white. "He's dead. Burned alive."

Vegos stopped his pacing and raised his gaze to group. After taking a steady breath, Tedris said, "Vegos said only a god could kill Vuddruk. He thinks it was Mafarias."

Dark silence settled over the room, blanketing it in the realization of how deep the mage's betrayal had gone.

"There's no time to waste," Okulu said darkly. "He won't last long, not in his state, not with all the magic he's used over our campaign. It's up to us now."

"I can stay with your son," Haleen offered Varila. "My magic is about all we have to keep him safe."

"I want to come, Mama," Tedris said, eyes set with determination.

Varila couldn't imagine leaving him behind. Wilhelm might have trusted the woman, but Varila didn't. "He'll come with us, and so will you."

"Of course," Haleen said quickly. "Anything I can do."

Varila noticed Lunara's eyes narrow at the woman. Haleen was hiding something.

WILHELM CLIMBED his way from darkness. First to greet him was a musty smell tainted by the metallic stench of old blood. Second was the cold. Summer had been hot in Windlous, and he had a sudden fear he'd been unconscious or dead for months. Perhaps he'd been killed and Salvarias had just brought him back. He remembered seeing his mother, but of course that had to have been a dream. She was dead.

Squinting past the haze of his vision, he saw a wall of tightly packed gray stone and a window that looked into another room. He puzzled over the pointlessness of such construction until he made out a figure beyond the glass. The person's hands were shackled to chains hanging down from the ceiling, barely long enough so the person's toes scraped the ground. Wilhelm blinked in comprehension at seeing the mutilated, naked body of his brother hanging limply, blood running from underneath the wrist manacles holding his weight.

Wilhelm went to stand but straps cut into his wrists, and his lurch almost toppled the chair. His feet were tied as well.

"I want you to fully understand your situation," a voice said from behind. "You hear the storm, do you not?"

Wilhelm did, the steady drumming of a heavy rain and the whistle of wind. It wasn't a normal storm bringing the crispness of fresh rains. It was heavy with decay, unnaturally cold.

"Your brother woke up once to see his predicament. I fear his mother scared him senseless." Devoar came into view.

"You hurt him and I'll—"

"Rest assured, Wilhelm, I have every intention of hurting your brother. I want you to fully understand my plans. I want you to think on what I tell you. Think of your brother and what is best for him, not you." Devoar leaned against the wall, staring out the window. "First, know I have given him brandaline. He is incapable of casting spells. He is helpless. After our talk and if you do not agree to my terms, I'll authorize a special servant to break his body. That will be the easiest for him, but I daresay the hardest for you. But look at him. You must know physical suffering is something our dear Salvarias has become all too accustomed. I merely do so to weaken him. When he is barely alive, I will drug him. A simple concoction and one Sansis used on the boy before, a hallucinogen that warps reality. Our young Guardian tends to revert to childhood. He will think he is a helpless child. That is when we will send in Ashra. She will reenact Salvarias's childhood, all his beatings. He will weaken mentally to the torment, just as he always did when he was a boy. The death will come. He will be on the verge of caving to us. That is when I will send you to talk to him. And you will talk to him, of your own free will or not. You will tell your brother you do not love him. You will tell him you are scared of him, of what he's done. You will tell him he is alone. You know your brother well. He will go mad and the evil will consume him. I offer you a chance to spare him this pain. I offer you the chance to give him to me. Tell him, with all your love, to do as we say. Command it of him, for his own good. Let him die quickly, pain-lessly. Let him die knowing you love him. Give him to me."

Wilhelm blinked aside building tears. "I will never give him to you. He's mine."

"You understand I am not bluffing. I will do everything I say. But at any point, all you have to do is agree, and I will end it. Am I not merciful?"

"Go to Oblivion."

Devoar sighed as it turned to face Wilhelm. "It's important to me you understand what is going to happen."

A door opened in the other room and a creature entered. Wilhelm had never seen the likes of it, but it was clearly demented. The yellow eyes alone shone with madness, eagerness even. It was humanoid, naked, and clearly male, covered in smooth red skin. Two horns protruded from its head, and a fork tongue darted out, impossibly long, and flicked over Salvarias's skin. The feet were hooved, the hands human, but instead of nails it had talons. A floor length tail swept the ground, twitching in excitement. Gripped in its fist was a whip, barbed with metal spikes, short and utterly wicked looking.

"You understand," Devoar whispered in his ear.

Wilhelm hadn't noticed the creature had moved behind him. The demon beyond had held his attention.

"Give him to me," Devoar breathed.

"Salv!" Wilhelm shouted.

"Did I not mention this room is enchanted?" Devoar asked innocently. "No sound will escape these walls, but rest assured you will hear his screams. And he cannot see you either. To him, it's just a wall. Come now, Wilhelm. Spare your brother this torment. He deserves peace. All you must do is give him to me. Release your claim on him."

Wilhelm clenched his jaw. "Never."

"So be it."

The demon uncoiled the whip, snapping it against the wall. The spikes chipped the stone. Turning to Salvarias, the demon leaned back, looked at the window, grinned, and then struck Salvarias.

Bright blood sprung up instantly, and a line of skin parted. Salvarias's sharp intake was followed by a soft sob of shock and pain.

The demon cracked the whip again across Salvarias's back. His brother arched, gasping in confusion and pain.

Fury erupted in Wilhelm, building a tidal wave of absolute rage as his vision tinted the same color as Salvarias's blood. Wilhelm yanked on his bonds, shouting for Salvarias, cursing Devoar and the demon. Hot tears of anguish and hate rolled down his cheeks as the whip struck again and again.

26

Time was meaningless; a never-ending night of horror. No amount of struggling had loosened Wilhelm's ties. No amount of begging had made it stop. Devoar's only words were "Give him to me" and with Wilhelm's every denial, the demon increased the torment it inflicted on Salvarias.

Surely Salvarias was near death. His brother's sobs and screams had stopped hours ago. He hung limply now, head bowed, bloodied black hair falling to cover his face. New welts and gnarls of burnt flesh overlapped the old.

"Why," Wilhelm wept. "Why him?"

Devoar gave a wane smile. "It is a game, dear Wilhelm. A game of the gods. For Veedran to be victorious over his brother, he must obtain the Soul. Once he has it, he will leave. Simple as that. You must see now. You must see that Veedran will never leave your brother alone. He will hunt him for eternity and torment him as a means to turn him. End it. Save your brother."

Wilhelm closed his eyes. He saw his wife's face, his son's. His hand warmed under the memory of resting it on Varila's stomach, trying to connect with his new child. He remembered the times Salvarias huddled in a corner, crying and scared. He remembered his brother's mutilated body.

"Free him," Devoar whispered in Wilhelm's ear. "Free him."

Hopelessness broke Wilhelm to sobs. Either way he was sending his brother to his doom. Then he remembered the fierceness in his brother's eyes when he'd said they would fight, that they would kill Veedran. Salvarias would rather suffer a million tortures than to give in.

Hoarsely, Wilhelm whispered, "My brother is mine and mine alone. You can't have him."

"Fool," Devoar hissed.

But the demon stopped. Wilhelm blinked back tears of utter joy as the creature unshackled his brother, dumping him to the cold floor. It took too long for Wilhelm to see Salvarias's hitching intake of air.

The demon went to a dark corner and came back to Salvarias holding a cup. It forced Salvarias to drink, though his brother hardly fought. After it was done, it left the room.

"I am not weak to admit your brother has a powerful mind," Devoar said. "He can fight the effects of certain poisons and oils, whereas any other person could not. However, in the right environment with the right words, he tends to succumb. Rest assured I have studied your brother, his mind, in detail. I know exactly when to push him."

Wilhelm looked up at the creature, trying to hide hope from his eyes. "You know you can't make him do certain things. That's why you need me."

Devoar frowned, and shifted its feet. "The boy's mind is complicated, I admit. Yes, there are things we fear cannot be said to him. There are things we cannot yet request of him. But as I said, I have been planning a long time, and I know how far to go and how far I must break him before he will succumb. We will take our time, Protector. There is no chance of failure. I ask again, give him to me and I will end his torture."

Wilhelm didn't bother to respond. They both knew his answer.

Some time passed before the door opened again and their mother stepped inside. She knelt beside Salvarias, brushed back his hair, and whispered, "Son."

Salvarias's eyes fought to open past all the blood crusted around them. He blinked at her once, then his eyes widened in absolute terror. Scrambling backward, paying no heed to his injuries, Salvarias crammed himself into a corner of the room. His gaze darted around and he whispered, "Brother?"

When nothing happened, Wilhelm watched helplessly as sanity drained from Salvarias's eyes.

SALVARIAS PRESSED himself further into the corner, burying his face against the cold stone. He told himself over and over that the leeches were not real. He begged his mind to surface from this nightmare, but every time he raised his eyes, the dark room encased him and his mother's wild eyes glared at him. She had gone mad, he was certain of it. Drool fell from her lips, her normally silky mane of hair frazzled, and her ranting made no sense.

Bowing his head, he looked at his hands. One blink they were small, the next blink large and one nearly fingerless. Reality grew hazier, his surroundings clearer, and his body weaker. All he could cling to was his brother. Wilhelm would come for him. Wilhelm always did.

He had not realized he had feinted until groping hands woke him. Struggling instantly, he looked wildly around. He was still in a home, wind howled outside, and the clattering rain and booming thunder still reverberated in the room.

The hands hauled him backward. Glancing over his shoulder he saw the chair. He saw the straps. He saw the knife. A cry of utter terror ripped from his throat. Writhing desperately, his mother's hold never loosened. Helpless and weak, just as he had always been. His body had no strength against hers, and the room spun in lazy circles, tipping this way and that. Sounds drowned in and out. Always so weak and small.

She threw him into the chair with little effort. Sharp pains shot all over, a dizzying wave that made him want to retch. The straps cut into his wrists, small and fragile.

Hoarsely he begged her to stop, pleaded her to love him, and wept his apologies. As usual, it did no good.

"Accept it!" his mother commanded shrilly. "Accept the evil and this will end!"

Salvarias stared at the dark ceiling as a strap went around his forehead, pinning his head back. He felt the evil trying to surface, beating against his wall and roaring in fury. It was so much stronger than he remembered, so much stronger.

Cold metal slid into his scalp, and his eyes widened in pain. As the blade sliced down, he screamed and screamed, his voice rising over the new lullaby his mother started singing.

The evil pummeled his wall, and he cried out when it cracked.

27

W ilhelm had no more tears to give. For days he'd watched as his mother cut open his brother's head, dump leeches on him, and beat him with whatever was lying around. For days he'd watched Salvarias sink further and further into insanity and had listened to Salvarias plead for him to come. For days Wilhelm had stewed in his own filth, accepting the offered bread and water to maintain his strength, and at every opportunity he had tried to escape. He was nearly as beaten as his brother. Consciousness was blessedly rare, and when capable, he fought, but those times were as scarce as consciousness. When he could, he tried to connect to his brother, begged him to hear him, but Salvarias's mind was too far gone.

What he knew now as he stared at Salvarias was that his brother would not be able to fight the evil much longer. The storm had gotten colder, and dead insects and vermin were crammed in corners. The house shook with each roll of thunder, and outside hail constantly pummeled the home.

Time was running out, and he was forced to concede no one was coming for them ... or couldn't.

A cold gust of air whistled behind as the door opened and

someone stepped into the room. Weakly, Wilhelm rolled his head around to see a mage holding out a vile of purple liquid to Devoar.

"King Frisliasi's package, as you requested," the mage said.

"Send word to our ships to attack Meitholias," Devoar said. "Leave no Winsire alive." Devoar turned a curling smile on Wilhelm. "Your brother's time is up. I give you one last chance, Wilhelm."

"Go to Oblivion."

Neithelas's betrayal shouldn't have shocked Wilhelm, but for some reason it stung. The list of people he could trust seemed doomed to evaporate before his eyes.

Devoar went into the other room and passed the vile to Ashra. She sprinkled half of it on her and then knelt beside Salvarias. Behind Wilhelm, the patter of feet drummed as a rush of octrils entered. They untied him and hauled him outside. Despite knowing what to expect, the sight still chilled his bones. Lightning was all that lit the absolute darkness surrounding the cottage. Flanking him were high hills swaddling a valley where the cottage nestled. Trees had once soared high but now were nothing but broken wood, rotting. The sky itself had succumbed to defeat. No moon or sun shone through the thick clouds. Decaying animals and bugs sloshed against Wilhelm's legs as he staggered through calf-high standing water, his feet sinking into too cold mud.

Wilhelm's legs kept giving out on him, forcing the octrils to support his weight. Days of sitting had stiffened him, but he played up his weakness, buying time and giving the enemy a false sense of security.

They walked a good ways before stopping at the edge of the valley. Below, lights twinkled from hundreds of lanterns, spreading near a mile. Beyond that, the city of Bren stood. It had yet to be taken, though by Veedran's numbers they could have.

An octril gagged him and drew a hood over his face. He hung his head, listening and waiting. Thunder shook the ground beneath him, and lightning flashed bright spots across the black fabric blocking his view. Then he heard his mother's voice.

"You will do as I say, Salvarias," she said.

"Please, mother!" Salvarias wept. "Please do not make me."

Devoar whispered in Wilhelm's ear, "The Winsires have a wonderful oil that forces a person to do whatever is asked of them."

The hood was yanked off, and Wilhelm blinked against the sudden bright flash of lightning. A good twenty feet in front of him, Salvarias was kneeling, naked and shivering, beside their mother.

"Salv!" Wilhelm yelled, but the gag muffled his voice.

"Ashra will force him to kill Humar's army," Devoar whispered. "If you give him to me, I will let Humar and his men leave to fight another day. Deny me and your brother will kill them all. Tell me, dear Wilhelm, could your brother live with himself if he were to do such a thing?"

Of course the answer was no. Nor could Salvarias live if he gave himself to Veedran. But Devoar didn't know how deep Lunara had connected to Salvarias. His brother's eyes lit every time she walked into the room, and his voice filled with love every time he spoke to her. With Lunara's help, Wilhelm could save Salvarias.

"He's mine," Wilhelm growled through the cloth.

Devoar sighed. "So be it."

With a flick of its hand, Ashra nodded. Her glance at Wilhelm made him shiver. His mother had always been strong and willful, but now her eyes lacked sanity.

Pointing at Bren, Ashra shrieked, "Kill them!"

"Please do not make me!" Salvarias wept.

"You will do as I say!" she yelled. "I will show you what you are capable of, monstrosity! Do it!"

Salvarias grabbed his head and cried out.

"Fight it, Salv," Wilhelm called to no avail. His brother couldn't hear him past the gag and the increasing rolls of thunder.

Salvarias doubled over and let out an agonizing cry. From his mouth poured red fog. It ate over the ground, speeding its way between the legs of octrils surrounding his brother. It bled down the hillside, startling creatures from its path. To those who didn't move, it knocked them to the ground and dissolved through flesh and bone, leaving pools of red blood swirling in the standing rain.

Wilhelm watched helplessly as it butted against the trench Humar's army had dug that was supposed to save them. Salvarias's power paid it no mind. It built up like a tidal wave, rising and rising. Though they were far away, Wilhelm swore he heard the shouts of alarm erupting from Bren, a crescendo of helpless cries. Then the wave toppled and crashed down on the army camped outside Bren's walls. This time, Wilhelm was certain he heard the screams.

The flood of red butted against the wall, swelling high, but it did not penetrate it. Then Wilhelm remembered his brother's spell; the protection spell the mages would have cast along the wall.

Salvarias crumbled to the ground, convulsing, blood running from his mouth and nose. Whatever power he had been feeding the wave ebbed, and with it the tidal wave receded, thinning until there was no sign it ever existed or that near a thousand men had just died.

"How many more times do you think he can do that and survive?" Devoar asked. "This will kill him. I beg you, end his misery. He will pass painlessly into Nevlar's waiting arms. He will be free of this world and the body that holds him hostage. Give him to me, and I will spare those you care for. All Veedran wants is victory. Once Arden kneels before him, he will leave here. You will live to start anew. Your brother will be free. It can be this very night if you just give him to me."

Wilhelm closed his eyes against it all. His determination wavered. Perhaps it would be better. Salvarias would be with Nevlar. The darkness in Arden would be gone. One horrible night for a lifetime of peace. But if Salvarias gave himself to Veedran, his brother's soul would be lost, and that price was too steep. Devoar was merely feeding Wilhelm lies. False hopes. Deceit.

Opening his eyes, he glared up at Devoar and shook his head.

A gust of wind nearly toppled Wilhelm. The freezing rain came down with new ferocity. Thunder shook the ground, knocking a few creatures over. Lightning fingered down from the sky, striking not only the army but also the city of Bren.

Salvarias was kneeling, hands threaded in his hair, his body shaking violently. Ashra was whispering in his ear, and Wilhelm didn't need to hear to know what she said.

"Yes," Devoar hissed. "It worked!"

Wilhelm looked down in horror at the crimson rain staining his skin, leaking between his lips and tainting his tongue with metallic blood.

"Kill Wilhelm!" Devoar ordered.

All the strength Wilhelm had saved exploded in every muscle. Springing up, he used his weight to knock aside the octril on his left. One quick spin freed him from the other octril and then he was running for his brother. A few tried to block his path, but he bulled through them. Cries of alarm rose from behind, which gained the attention of the group ahead. Swords struggled to come out of sheaths, eyes widened, and a few managed to strengthen their stance before he barreled into them. None could stop his weight at a full run. A few stings erupted on his arms and across his back, but he ignored them.

His eyes were focused on his little brother looking up at him with all the hope of the world. By the time he dropped to his knees, he had his hands unbound and the gag removed. Time was of the essence.

Sliding on his knees, Wilhelm collided with Salvarias, wrapped his arms around his brother, and draped his body over Salvarias's.

"You have to fight, Salv!" Wilhelm ordered. "You were drugged. You didn't kill them, Veedran did. He just used you to do it."

"Help me!" Salvarias sobbed, curling up in Wilhelm's arms. "Please help me! She hurt me! She hurt me!"

Sharp pain shot up Wilhelm's back, and the world flashed white. Cursing, he fumbled for his brother's hand, found it, and pressed their marks together. "Fight!" he roared.

"Don't kill him!" Devoar shouted. "We need him again!"

Then Wilhelm understood his fatal mistake. Ashra had only used half the oil. They would use the other half on him to force him to turn over Salvarias once they broke his brother down again. Devoar said Wilhelm would agree eventually, whether of his own accord or not.

Calmly and without any order in his voice, Wilhelm said, "You're not a child anymore, Salv. Mother can't hurt you unless you let her. You have magic. Powerful magic. I want you to fight her, Salv." Hands grabbed him, trying to pull him from his brother. Pain shot all over as things clubbed his body, but he kept calm and let none of it reach his brother. "All I want is for you to be happy. You believe me?"

"Yes," Salvarias wept. "I do not understand, Brother!"

"I need you to remember where you are, who you are, and what you're capable of. I need you, little brother."

He untangled himself from his brother, struggling against Salvarias trying to claw his way back into Wilhelm's arms. Rounding on the nearest creature, Wilhelm grabbed its sword and plunged it into his own chest. The last thing he heard was Salvarias's tortured scream.

SALVARIAS TORE his numbing gaze from his brother's lifeless eyes and looked around. Surrounding them were creatures—hundreds, thousands. He remembered nothing but his brother. Nothing of how he got here or why the creatures surrounded him. But none of the answers would have mattered. His brother was dead, and the world so utterly empty.

"Monster!" a woman shrieked. He should know her. He should, but did not. "Look what you did!"

"Kill him!" a creature belted.

For some strange reason, Salvarias did not want to die. He raised his hands and wished the creatures to pause. And they did. He was cold and wanted sun, so the clouds left and the moon lurched sideways and the sun appeared.

Plopping down, he stared at the dead insects floating atop the water. He wanted it dry, so the soil soaked up the water. A part of him knew his listlessness should be alarming. The numbness spreading through his heart was wrong. But to deal with Wilhelm's death was too harrowing. Better to tuck away his heart, his vulnerability, and his pain.

Life is cruel, is it not, my little pet?

Salvarias frowned at the voice. It was as familiar as it was strange. So many questions, and he was too tired to figure them out. Glancing down, he noticed he was naked, cold, and shivering despite the hot sun. Cuts and bruises covered him, and his body suddenly felt too heavy, the world moving too slowly, sounds too deep. Wilhelm's dead eyes stared at him, begging him for something. Sharp pain shot through Salvarias's heart, but he bottled it away, locking it in a dark corner.

You have killed him, the voice said. *You killed hundreds of innocents. Remember the city. Remember the men you murdered.*

Salvarias did not remember, but if it were true, he did not care. He was so very tired.

You killed them, the voice said exasperated. *How can you live with what you have done?*

He glanced at all the creatures frozen mid action: most lunging toward him, swords half drawn, clubs half raised, spit from their roaring mouths suspended in air. Salvarias curled up next to Wilhelm and rested his head on his brother's chest. There was no deep intake of air, no steady lifebeat, and no bright smile. His brother was cold and dead, just as Salvarias felt inside. Closing his eyes, he slept.

28

SUMMER 1022 A.R

Neithelas stood on his balcony, watching the far away orange glow and listening to the screams of his friends as they burned. Hearing such torment had hardened his heart, and his eyes had no more tears to give. He had betrayed the trees and his people, had gotten in bed with darkness, and now all would pay for his treachery.

Behind him, Jenthia gave orders of evacuation, Pathelone resting on her hip. She was a good queen, a good woman, and she did not deserve his anger or bitterness. It was all so clear now. He never should have married. His heart forever belonged to Lunara.

"The creatures are upon us," General Brayd said. "We must flee. We are outnumbered three to one."

"Go," Jenthia urged. "Do not wait for us. Get as many to safety as you can."

"My king?" Brayd asked.

Neithelas waved an annoyed hand, never turning to face the general. "Be gone."

Hesitation, but eventually the man's boots thumped their retreat.

"Husband," Jenthia said gently. "We must leave."

"You must," Neithelas said. "I will go my own way. Catch up to Brayd, and he will guard you with his life."

"I will not leave without you, my lord. You cannot stay here and burn!"

Neithelas finally tore his stare from the fires and regarded his wife. Such beautiful eyes and face, yet he found no love for her, no desire. "I do not love you, Jenthia. I never have. I have no desire to rule, and now I have nothing left to rule over."

"Think of your children," she said. "I have never asked or needed your love, but your children do."

Neithelas ran a finger down his son's cheek. "But I do not love him, nor do I love the child growing in your womb. I wanted *her* children, not yours. I do not love my son, and I do not want him."

Jenthia's eyes darkened. "I hope you rot for all eternity in your selfish cruelty."

She whirled away, a flash of such beauty, and then she was gone. Neithelas turned back to his friends and blinked aside wetness in his eyes. Finally, he had found more tears.

THE TREK to the army should not have taken long, but with the rains, entire valleys had been flooded and new rivers had formed. Lunara held tight to Tedris as he dozed in the saddle, cuddled up against her under blankets that never seemed to do any good.

Though not connected to Salvarias in an attempt to shield her own body from his torment, his fear and sorrow nevertheless weighed on her heart. But more shocking was the sadness of her son. She mused he was as connected to Salvarias as she, despite her husband's ignorance to Lumus's existence—at least she hoped her son would be named Lumus. She'd listened every time Salvarias had cast his light spell, but her pronunciation always seemed off. He'd once told her no soul besides those blessed with magic could speak the words properly.

He will be fine, she told her son. *Your father has been to Oblivion and back, and each time he has returned stronger. He will not leave us.*

Yet the farther they walked, the thicker her doubts became. Her husband was tired, beat down, and losing hope. He might not have said as much, but each city they had taken had come with a price of exhaustion for him and Kisra. Dumping such burdens on two people had made her livid, but no one had listened, and her husband and Kisra continued to abuse their gifts, pushing themselves to save others.

Upon cresting a hill, lightning flashed across the dark sky, revealing the sprawling army of the enemy. No fires could be lit in the downpour, and Lunara and her friends would have blindly wandered right on top of the creatures had the storm not warned them.

"Damn it all to Oblivion," her sister cursed. "How are we supposed to get past all that?"

Vegos growled, stirring Tedris from sleep. The boy wiped at his eyes as he said, "Vegos said he can't connect with Father." The boy stiffened. "He said he must be hurt and has no mind to listen."

"It'll be all right," Lunara whispered, casting Vegos a glare. The bear was smart enough to look abashed.

"Sleeping," Tedris said, his voice lighter. "He said he must be sleeping. But he does know Father and Uncle Salvarias are in that army."

"Thoughts?" Edium asked.

"Get drunk and charge in?" Okulu suggested.

Varila rolled her eyes. "How about something that doesn't involve death. Or spirits."

Okulu grunted. "Picky woman."

"Disguises?" Haleen said. "Perhaps we could spy on what makes up their ranks, then we can get armor or servants' garb."

"A sound idea," Talura said, her voice somewhat cold.

Lunara didn't care for Haleen. She'd sensed deceit in the woman, though for what Lunara could not tell. It appeared her mother had sensed the same.

Varila nodded. "I'll go with Father and see what we can see."

Just as she nudged her horse forward, the clouds suddenly disappeared. Bright sunlight shot down, blinding them, making them all cover their eyes.

Tedris clenched Lunara's arm, and in a voice thick with a building sob, he said, "We must hurry! Papa! Papa!"

"What did the bear say?" Edium demanded.

"Nothing," Tedris cried. "Can't you feel it?"

Lunara's eyes grew wide as she noticed the unnatural stillness of the army, and the absolute sorrow piercing through Salvarias. Lumus churned in her stomach, and she swore she could hear his sobs.

"Papa!" Tedris screamed.

The child's grief spurred them all forward at a run.

SALVARIAS WOKE TO A SOOTHING MELODY—A woman's voice though not his mother's. A warm blanket was draped over him, smelling strongly of jasmine.

All his body ached, and he was certain there was no blood left in it. He wanted to sleep, endlessly and blissfully, but the song persisted, switching from a hum to soft words.

"Salvarias," a light voice said.

Annoyed at the interruption, he opened his eyes. Whatever irritation he felt vanished when he saw her blue eyes and a smile to quell the most horrendous of storms. She was light in the darkness. Purity amidst evil.

Beside her knelt an older woman with the same blue eyes, white flowers wilting in her hair. She was the one that had been humming. "Sweetness," she said.

The one word nearly cracked the wall around his pain.

"I know you're scared," the woman continued. "But we're not here to hurt you. We want to help."

Behind her were three men: one older, one young half-Winsire, and another Erthla around Salvarias's age. Tearing his gaze from them, he regarded the young woman. He knew and trusted her.

Turning to the other woman, he felt the same. But this woman offered him something he had begged for since he was born. She loved him as he had always wanted his own mother to love him.

That weak, vulnerable side pushed harder to surface. Surveying the creatures, he realized he must have been asleep for some time. All their eyes were bloodshot. Ashra stood, eyes glaring with nothing but hatred. Slowly he found the fresh cut on the back of his head. Tears began to well. He willed them away, but they came regardless.

Turning to the woman, he said, "She hurt me."

"I know, sweetness. But I won't let her hurt you ever again. You're safe now."

All his pain swept over him, all his suffering, his fear, and his anger. "She hurt me!" he cried, cradling his head.

"Which is why we need to leave," the woman said. "These creatures will hurt you again. She will hurt you. We need to get your brother out of here."

"She hurt me!" Salvarias roared as his anger overcame him. Bolting to his feet, he released his hold on his mother. "I hate you!" he cried.

"Demon!" his mother rasped. "Demon born of darkness!"

Wonderfully warm blackfire erupted over Salvarias as he took the last step forward and grabbed his mother's throat. "I will show you darkness," he hissed.

He set her aflame with no care for her screams, with no mercy for her writhing. He watched with satisfaction so intense, it made him lightheaded. Then everything faded until he stood before a massive gate surrounded by roiling black fog. Beside him knelt a man, weeping.

A voice purred out of the fog, "Hello, Son. You must remember."

Salvarias stepped back from the gray tendril snaking toward him, but one from behind wrapped around his ankle, circling its way up until it cocooned him. Wilhelm's voice echoed within the fog.

Remember where you are, who you are, and what you're capable of.

His brother's last words had been spoken with confidence, with calm, trust, and without fear.

"Remember," the fog whispered.

And he did. He remembered everything.

When the fog retreated, he glared down at his grandfather.

"I didn't have a choice," Mafarias wept. "He took your grand-mother. I didn't have a choice."

Salvarias touched the doors and they swung open. He made no sentence, no rebuttal, and no sentiment. He merely shoved his grand-father into Oblivion, blinked, and found himself holding a charred corpse.

He dropped it, wanting nothing more than to wipe off the flesh stuck to his palm. Mustering every ounce of his courage and calm, he turned to Edium. "Please carry my brother."

Gathering the blanket about himself, he walked onward, head lowered to avoid Lunara's gaze. To avoid Talura's that surely would not be filled with love. Not anymore. Not after what he had done to Humar's army. To what he thought had been his own mother. His own mother ... He had burned her alive with all the hate he had harbored for his entire life. And with the action, he was forced to face the truth: he had never loved her. Never. What kind of evil being did not love its own mother?

They marched to the gates of Bren that swung open upon their arrival. Salvarias walked through, ignoring the soldiers lined up and the hateful mutters. He ignored Humar when the king asked ques-tions, anger barely suppressed in his voice.

Salvarias plodded through the hostile city until he reached Okulu's uncle's inn. The old man welcomed them and showed them to a room where the men deposited Wilhelm's body.

"I need to be alone," Salvarias said.

Everyone left, silent. He could hear Tedris crying in the room next door.

Salvarias sat down by his brother's side. The one person who loved him and would not care what he had done. Wilhelm would save him from himself, from the evil barreling toward him, and from the self-loathing that now darkened the sky.

Wilhelm would save him. His brother always did. And Salvarias hated him for it.

~

WILHELM TOSSED ASIDE the book and settled back in his chair next to his brother's bed. Salvarias had yet to wake from the last healing he had done for Wilhelm. He had hoped his brother would not remember killing half of Humar's army, but by the sickening green clouds churning outside the window, his brother had remembered everything. How the world had stayed alive, Wilhelm would never know.

The enemy seemed too shocked to take action after whatever spell Salvarias had cast had worn off. Surely they were planning something horrendous, something sneaky. Edium had received word the knights were waiting. No one seemed to have a plan anymore.

Salvarias stirred, a low groan escaping when his shoulders moved. He'd probably cracked open a scab on his back. White dressings covered his entire torso, and Lunara had restitched the cut on the back of his head.

"Salv," Wilhelm said softly.

His brother's large black eyes opened slowly. There was no love in them, no fear, no hate, and no anger. Nothing. He'd seen it before, and he knew when his brother feared losing to the evil, he would tuck himself away, give the evil room but never surrender himself. Somewhere inside Salvarias's soul, he was waiting for Wilhelm to save him.

"Leave me," Salvarias murmured. "I have no desire to hear your encouragement or excuses for what I have done."

Wilhelm rose from his chair and sat on the edge of the bed. "I won't say a word." Holding out his hand, palm up, he smiled. "Give me your hand, Salv."

His brother smirked. "You always think I am lost. This is me, Brother. This is me tired, done with it all. I care not for Arden's fate. I care not for Veedran or Nevlar. Any of them."

"If that's true, no harm will come from taking my hand."

"Always the savior," Salvarias sneered. "Always swooping in to rescue me from myself. The big brother. The perfect man everyone loves."

"I'll take it forcibly if I have to."

"You never listen to me. I am tired. I do not want to fight anymore." Tears welled in his eyes. "I am so very tired. Leave me in peace. I beg you, do not make me fight anymore."

"I know you're tired, Salv. I know you want peace. But you'll never have it unless Veedran is dead."

"And you think I could kill him? He's a god, Brother. A god!"

"So are you."

Salvarias flinched. "I do not want to be one."

"I know."

Wilhelm snatched up Salvarias's wrist and pressed their marks together before his brother could even think to pull away. Salvarias gave a soft cry and yanked his hand, but Wilhelm held firm.

"I'm here, Salv. You have to fight it." He wrapped his arms around his brother. "I need you. Lunara needs you. You can't be done."

A soft sob left his brother, then Wilhelm's strength drained out of him. By the time Salvarias stopped, Wilhelm shook with fatigue, but he managed to hold tight to his brother and whisper, "I'm proud of you."

Salvarias's sobs deepened, and he curled up against Wilhelm, pressing an ear to Wilhelm's heart. "Forgive me," Salvarias wept. "Please forgive me."

"There's nothing to forgive, little brother. You didn't do anything wrong."

29

SUMMER 1022 A.R

Salvarias woke to fingers running through his hair and the fresh scent of spring. No images of death fleeted across his vision, and his mind was calm. Her thin nightdress did not dull the warmth of her body snuggled up to his, her head resting on his chest, a leg entwined with his. Sira and Saval were curled up together at the foot of the bed, purring softly.

Outside the open window, stars and a half moon shone bright, and a breeze wafted about, warm with summer, fluttering a candle and disturbing the embers of a dying fire.

"How do you feel?" Lunara whispered.

In honesty, his entire body hurt, and his pounding head made him nauseous. "I am fine, my lady."

"Liar." Resting her head on her propped-up hand, she smiled. "You look better."

Her eyes were so full of life, of love, even after what he had done. Of course she would still love him. He could murder the world and she would stand by his side while he did it.

Threading a hand through her hair, he pulled her lips to his and kissed her. It was selfish on his part when he rolled on top of her, deepening his kiss. All he wanted was to drown his sorrow, forget his pain, and hide away. Her body gifted him escape.

He took his time savoring her taste, the feel of her smooth skin beneath his hands, and her moans in his ear. He felt and thought of nothing but her.

Too soon it ended and the world came barreling back to him, his body aching from his exertion, spinning the room and threatening his vision.

"Let me make you some tea," Lunara said.

She rose from the bed, wrapped herself in a thin robe, and crossed the room to the fireplace. A kettle was hanging, and she used a thick towel to grab the handle. He watched her, half awake, half ready to succumb to unconsciousness, as she mixed herbs, the light of the candle and moon playing with the colors of her hair.

Once mixed, she poured a cup and joined him on the bed. It took effort from both of them to get him sitting upright. The tea was an earthy root mixture laced with a few herbs to ease whatever swelling was happening on his back. He drank it eagerly and accepted her offer for a second and third cup. Finally by the fourth, his pain subsided. He considered healing himself, but the pain last time had been unbearable. Unless it was a mortal wound, he saw no need to endure such suffering. His body would heal on its own.

"You have not slept," he said, noticing dark rings under her eyes.

"I wanted to be sure I was awake when you were."

Hauling himself up, he leaned on his staff as he walked around the room, working out stiff muscles. By the time he returned to bed, Lunara was sleeping. The griffins had moved up around her, cuddled up on either side, deep in dreams.

He covered her with a blanket, washed, and dressed himself, pulling his hood low. With the late hour, he hoped no one would be about, and he could sneak into the city and find out how the battle faired.

Slipping silently from his room, he walked down the hallway, descended the stairs, and found himself in the main dining room at the Seatide Inn. It was late enough no guests were up, but Harriot was cleaning a table. She glanced at him and beamed a smile.

"Salvarias! Kuly will be so happy you're up. He's been worried sick, you know. Are you hungry, dear? I have some roasted vegetables left from dinner."

Salvarias remembered Herald's heavy hand with seasoning and, despite his hunger, shook his head. "You are too kind, my lady. I am—"

"Don't you worry yourself one bit, deary. I cooked these myself. I promise you won't be disappointed. Come now. Have a seat. I have some wonderful apple juice I just made this morning."

He bowed. "As my lady wishes."

She beamed him a smile. "Such a sweet boy! I'll be right back, dear." Bustling around tables, she disappeared into the kitchen.

Salvarias slowly lowered himself to a chair, wincing against the tightness of his back. No sooner had he settled in than Okulu came sauntering in from the kitchen. He had a mug smelling of apples and cinnamon, and another that was unmistakably brandaline. The scent made Salvarias want to vomit. Brandaline only brought painful memories.

The merc plopped down in a chair and pushed the apple cider to Salvarias. "Humar wasn't too happy with you."

Salvarias took a tentative sip of the juice and found it delightful. "With good reason."

"Wilhelm told us Neithelas gave them the drug they used on you. You didn't have a choice. When Humar found out, he was quite forgiving."

"I should have fought off the effects," Salvarias said. "I almost did. Had I been healthy, I believe I could have."

"Ha! Of course you could. Gods have amazing powers."

And there it was: a god, and not just of magic. Salvarias could no longer run from the fact. He grimaced at Okulu. "I fear I have little control over my power."

"I can sympathize."

Salvarias arched an eyebrow. "Can you?"

Okulu flashed him a grin. "My charm pours out of me. I've tried to control it, but it's just so damn ... powerful. Women fall prey to it, worship it."

Rolling his eyes, Salvarias could not stop his smile. "What a horrible burden."

Okulu squinted at Salvarias. "You look like you went to Oblivion and back again."

"I have."

The merc chuckled. "What now?"

"I wanted to see how the city faired."

"Veedran's army is setting up siege engines. I suspect they'll start with the catapults tomorrow night. Wall won't last but for a few barrages. Wilhelm sent word to his knights that once it starts, they're to attack. We'll start at the same time."

"Suicide."

Okulu shrugged. "At least we'll go down fighting. That is unless you have some trick up your sleeve. I saw you freeze that entire army."

"I did not do so consciously. As I said, I have little control over my power."

"Then we'll do it the old fashioned way. Swords and blood, my friend. Swords and blood."

They spent time talking of nothing important. As usual with Okulu, Salvarias felt no pressure to be strong, to be smart, to be powerful, or to be optimistic. They ate and drank, laughed and talked of the mundane. They joked until the dark sky lightened with the first signs of morning and Lady Talura entered the dining room.

She looked both of them over with an arched eyebrow. "You know it's morning?"

Okulu downed the rest of his brandaline. "It's nighttime somewhere in Arden." Standing up, he swayed a bit. "I guess I better go find that wife of mine."

Lady Talura nodded. "Her and Varila have become quite close.

The two of them were up late, deep in their wine. I'm sure she's sleeping."

"We'll see about that." Okulu staggered to the stairs and lurched his way up.

When alone with Lady Talura, she motioned to the door. "Shall we go for a stroll?"

Salvarias nodded and used his aspen branch to rise. She led the way outside, winding slowly through the streets. Women, children, and the elderly were being ushered to the back of the city, far away from the wall and the enemy at the gates. Children wailed when their fathers left, women shed silent tears, and boys too young took up a sword.

Lady Talura ended up at the wall and climbed a set of stairs to the top. The sights before him made Salvarias feel small. The enemy sprawled across the hills, massive wood engines being constructed at unnatural speeds.

"The battle will begin tomorrow night," Lady Talura said. "Or so Humar thinks. I don't suppose I could persuade you to leave the city?"

Salvarias glanced at her out of the corner of his eye. Tears glistened unshed, her chin high, fresh white flowers decorating her braid. She looked older today. Wrinkles struck out from the corner of her eyes framed by dark circles.

Of course she would want him to leave, to draw the army away from her family, to send the abomination far from her daughter. Even if he did flee, the army would decimate Bren. Looking back over the hills, he hid his pain and said, "Leaving would accomplish nothing. They would still attack. These people would still die."

"I ... I just ..." A few tears fled down her cheeks. "I couldn't bear it if something happened to you."

Salvarias flinched. Shock bled into his voice when he said, "I killed half of Humar's army." He motioned to the dead grass, the fallen trees, and the mounds of dead animals piled outside the city. "I did that."

"And I've told you before: I know what lurks within you. I know what you've done, Son. I know, believe me. But none of it has changed my heart. Do you think love so fragile? That one wrong deed can shred it?"

"One?" Salvarias said exasperated. "Hundreds! And you forget Tobin. His love shattered after one deed."

"My dear son, if Tobin had lived, I guarantee he would have forgiven you. I swear he would have held you close and told you it was going to be all right. He had no chance to think on it, to realize love cannot be extinguished so easily. As for me, those 'hundreds' of acts are only in your own mind. And honestly, I don't have one example. You were drugged and tortured. You've done nothing wrong, sweetness." She held up a hand to stop his rebuttal. "Nothing you say will change my mind. I love you. I always will."

Salvarias blinked aside tears and stared at the stones beneath his feet. What he desired so desperately in Lynta, what he almost had accepted, was still there for the taking. He could have everything he had ever wanted: his brother's happiness and a wife, father, and mother who loved him unconditionally. Everything he had ever dreamed of.

"I hope I've proven myself to you," she said. "Proven I know a thing or two about life and can offer you wisdom. Even to a man of your intelligence. I hope you've realized you can trust me. Though you may not accept my love, at least trust I would never do anything to hurt you. Can you do that for me, sweetness? Can you trust I have your best interests at heart?"

He wanted to say no, cast her aside, and stay in his shell of safety. But it was not the truth, and he found he could not form the lie. Reluctantly and with a note of bitterness, he nodded.

"You didn't kill those people when you were young. It was Mafarias, manipulating you into thinking you did. Remember the knife, how heavy it was? Remember how hazy the actual act was? Remember the blue light? The light Mafarias uses whenever he touches you? It wasn't you, sweetness. Do you believe me?"

With what Mafarias had done, it was not a stretch to think he could be so cruel. After all, he had impersonated their mother and stolen the brothers away to be tortured and killed. Despite his actions being done out of love for their grandmother, Mafarias had been untrustworthy, desperate. A traitor to his own grandchildren. Yes, yes Salvarias believed her. But did it matter? He had killed others. Blood was on his hands.

"Do you believe me?" she asked again.

He nodded.

"When you confronted your parents' murderer, your brother killed half the men there. Do you think him evil?"

"No," Salvarias said.

"Yet you are evil for killing the leader of that group. The man who set your mother aflame and who tormented countless mages. If you think you are evil, then surely your brother is as well."

"My brother could not be evil if he tried," Salvarias said shortly. "To even propose ..."

"You see my point. If you are so willing to condemn yourself, you must condemn Wilhelm as well. He has killed as many as you have."

"The little girl in Xeroth. Humar's men. Those were innocents."

"If anyone is to blame for their deaths, it is Veedran and Nevlar. Nevlar bore a son and never taught him how to be a god, how to control the power within. Veedran manipulated you repeatedly, drugged and tortured you. But ..." Talura tilted her head at him, studying him. "From this point on, son, every action you do is your own. You are a god, whether you want to be or not. You might have been ignorant to it before, but you can no longer deny it. That means, if you continue to shun your powers, to flee from your destiny, then every death by your hands is yours to bear. However, if you embrace your godhood, if you accept whom you truly are deep inside, then victory is already yours. If you try your best with the knowledge you have, then nothing can be faulted to you. Cowards wear failures as stones on their backs. They fall into caves and skulk around the ground. Heroes wear failures as a crown of thorns, bared for all to see, proud they tried. It is time for you to decide, sweetness. Do you want to be a hero or a coward?"

Who was he deep down inside? A killer or a prisoner? Afraid or brave?

Uncertain. That was what he was. Who he was. "I do not know what is right or wrong," he confessed. "There are powers inside me I do not understand. Deep down, I am uncertain."

"Indecision is a coward's best friend, my dear, and a hero's constant companion. You are a good person. You want to make the right choices. Find something inside yourself and trust it. You have to trust *something*, sweetness."

There was one he could trust, one that could help him, could protect him from things Wilhelm's sword could not touch. Inhaling a calming breath, he ignited his magic.

My wizard, it greeted. *Are you truly ready to embrace the power within?*

I am frightened of them.

As you should be. They are not to be trifled with, my dearest friend. But believe me when I say I will always give my life to protect you. We venture into the unknown, but I am with you every step of the way.

Salvarias gripped his aspen branch tighter, pulling it close and taking comfort in its warmth. He had lit his sparrow, though he did not remember doing so. It glided above his shoulder, gifting him calm and serenity as always; light in the darkness, a happy song sung to him in his most harrowing moments. The sparrow had always been there for him, and though it had no power, he drew strength from it now as he had done as a child.

I am ready, he told his magic.

We must proceed with caution. The power was not made for a human mind. We cannot unleash its full potential. All we can do is acknowledge it, accept it, and see if it will work with us without overpowering you. Black-fire is who you are. The other power ... that is an infection, a disease in your mind. It is not our friend, and it will kill you if given the chance. I will call blackfire forth, and when it speaks to you, it is time for you to listen and respond. Are you ready?

Salvarias glanced at Talura for strength. She bestowed it upon him in a smile; one that gave him love, pride, comfort, and safety—everything he had ever longed for. *I am ready.*

He cried out when the power roared to life in the depths of his soul, as it pounded awake his once sleeping heart, as it imbued strength into every muscle. Initially all he felt was the usual hate and anger that came with blackfire, but that could not be who he was deep inside. Instead of fleeing from it as he had done in the past, he faced it. All that hate and anger lived because it had no choice, just as Lakvra had no choice in her need for lust. She had been angry, hurting, and scared. She had no choice in who she was. At the root of Salvarias's power was the insatiable need for vengeance. He wanted it, needed it, and loved it. But that could not be all he was. Certainly there was more to his soul.

There is, my dearest friend. Look closer. See what you have denied yourself for all your life. See what I see.

And so he did. The power was not separate from him as he had assumed, not like his magic was. It was merely a second half of himself, another Salvarias living within, brimming with traits that he had buried beneath layers of fear and self-hate. Existing there were qualities he had considered himself unworthy of: confidence; self-love; the recognition of his power; the exhilaration of his godhood; the seed of his goodness; the power of his smile, joy, and love. It affected everything around him, and so far, he had only fed it his self-loathing, his hopelessness, his fears, anger, and his sad memories.

Deep inside, Salvarias saw the good. Deep inside, hidden from the world, was a confident and angry man who had been denied for far too long. Closing his eyes, he balanced his doubts and thoughts of unworthiness with his other half. For the first time, he forgave himself for those he had killed with blackfire. For the first time, he admitted he was as good as he was evil, that he enjoyed killing those who killed the innocent. For the first time, he snatched up the love and acceptance Talura offered him and held it close to his heart.

He was neither a servant to the light nor a servant to darkness. He was the in between, a balance of the two, his own man who owned his own soul. He chose his own side, and with his decision, joy as he had never experienced bloomed. Laughter built until he had no choice but to release it, let it shake through his chest, let it unburden himself.

For the first time, he felt *alive*.

A LOUD BOOM echoed over the valley, reverberating through the wall beneath Talura's feet. A gust of wind burst out from Salvarias, nearly knocking her over. Above, blinding sunlight split the clouds. The standing water was gone; one breath there, the other not. The dead animals had disappeared as well. Below, directly beside a dead tree, a sapling surged up from the ground, rising near a foot before it shivered out a wealth of branches reaching for the sun. The ground beneath Veedran's army blossomed thick grass, greener than she had ever seen in her entire life. The sun above bathed the hillsides in crisp yellow, and a flood of green grasses devoured the once dismal gray hills. Air filled Talura's lungs, making her realize how dull every breath of her life had been.

The world she had lived in her entire life had been dead. She had just never been shown what true life felt like. Now it surrounded her, and she looked at her son with wide eyes. He was watching her, his laughter finally quieted, his gray irises churning in rhythmic swirls. He was a different man. In one action, he had changed. She saw it in his eyes.

He inhaled a deep breath and said, "I love you ... Mother."

All the love Talura had ever felt from Zerana did not compare to what his words embedded in her soul. "I love you too, sweetness." Looking around, she whispered, "I don't understand."

Salvarias regarded the area with an uneasy gaze, but not alarmed. "I am the son of Nevlar. I am a god." He held out his hand and dull flames of black ignited along his skin. It did not burn his robes or seem to cause him any discomfort. If anything, he looked at it somewhat awed and a tad dubious. "I have feared this power," he continued. "But there is another within me that is now the root of my fear. This power ..." He rested a burning fingertip on the ground and lightly ran it along the stone wall. A sprout burst between the mortar and branched out rapidly, creeping down and along the wall, birthing simple leaves and white flowers, filling the air with the sweet scent of jasmine.

A drop of blood fell from Salvarias's nose, but he wiped it away nonchalantly. "I do not want to be afraid of who I am anymore."

"Nor should you," Talura said. "I'm so proud of you."

Salvarias closed his hand in a tight fist and the blackfire disappeared. "It is you who gave me what I needed most. You never gave up, Mother."

Looking up at him, his face relaxed as she'd never seen it before. He bore the expression of a man who had come to terms with his destiny. Smiling, she whispered, "Gods help any who stand in your path, Son."

Troops along the wall had backed up from them, swords half raised, eyes wide and frightened. If Salvarias noticed, he gave no indication. Surveying the enemy, he said, "If I were angry, I could kill this entire army. I do not want to be angry anymore, and honestly, I lack the apathy to murder all those creatures. Surely some are innocent. I want to believe that, to hold that hope close. Am I a fool, Mother?"

"Hope is never foolish, my dear. But denial is. Those creatures will kill us if something isn't done."

Salvarias frowned. "I do not want to destroy anymore. I want to create." He picked up two small rocks and covered them in his hands. "Death is inevitable, and I have dealt my share. But life ... Life is a blessing, and I have yet to explore it." He opened his hands, and where once there had been two stones, now were two baby owls, pure white, who turned their heads and looked up at Talura with large golden eyes. Defensively he said, "There is more inside me than destruction. There is more inside me than darkness."

"I never doubted it, sweetness," she said, trying to keep her voice even and comforting, fighting the awe and sheer dumbfounded shock that threatened to mute her. She needed to be here for him, to give him words of encouragement, and to help him with what he had just become. For no doubt existed, beside her stood a god. And he was a child: uncertain, emotional, volatile, emitting waves of wonder and curiosity, seeking answers and his place in a new world. What stood beside her was no longer a timid young man who feared his power. She'd awakened a god. "I've always said you're a good man with a good heart, Salvarias. I've never been more certain than I am now. I know you don't want to fight. You opened yourself up to something, something you want to explore, and trust me when I say I support you. But you won't be able to explore life if Veedran wins. He will command this army to kill everyone living in Bren, including yourself and your family."

"You do not understand, Mother. Even if I wanted to destroy the army, I could not. I am ... trapped in this ..." He held out his hands, turning them over, studying them as if seeing them for the first time. "I am trapped in this form. My power is not a quarter of what it should be, and it is governed by my emotions. Right now, I am utterly happy." He let out a soft laugh, eyes betraying his youth, the simple truth a mystery to him. "Always before I was happy because something happened: my brother's marriage, my marriage, a joke my brother told. But now ... Now I am happy for no reason, Mother. None at all." He looked up at the sky and smiled. "For no reason. Do you have any idea how wonderful it feels?"

She couldn't help but smile. His was infectious, glowing with so much joy it seeped inside her own heart. "I do, sweetness. I've lived nearly every day feeling it."

"How can the world be so dark if feelings like this exist?"

"Because like you once were, some are addicted to sadness. It is a disease, and the cure is often never given or never accepted. Trust me when I say no one wants to live in sadness. It sneaks up and snags hold before you realize it. Then you are trapped, and escape seems impossible."

"How could I ever go back? How could I ever allow myself to feel that again?"

"Oh sweetness, life seldom plays nice." She scooped up the owls, marveling over how beautiful they were. Looking up at her son, she said, "Sadness will visit you again. I have no doubt of it. But you must be strong. You mustn't let it win as it did before. Promise me you will rise above it. Promise me you will always look up at the sun and see hope."

Salvarias smiled at her. "I promise, Mother."

30

Lunara jumped up from her seat in Herald's dining hall when Salvarias strode in, his laughter carrying through the room along with her mother's. Wilhelm also stood, his eyes widening. Lunara had felt the change in Salvarias, felt his joy so intently that she had withdrawn from his mind. She didn't need their connection to feel it now, and apparently neither did Wilhelm. His mouth hung open, twitching to try to smile past his shock.

When Salvarias's gaze fell to his brother, the air itself seemed to hum with utter joy. He hobbled across the room and flung his arms around Wilhelm's neck.

"It is wonderful, Brother! Utterly wonderful! I feel alive!" He laughed again.

Wilhelm blinked a few times and then lifted Salvarias in a bear hug, his own laugh booming out with his brother's. "What happened?"

Salvarias wiggled free and held out his hands. They ignited in blackfire. "It is who I am. I am a god, and I cannot deny it. But this power is not an infection. This power is simply me, Brother. Me. And I am not evil."

"I know, Salv. I've always known."

It wasn't long before others joined them. Edium, Okulu, and Cessia were first, Varila, Qwyn, and Idolar next. Humar came at one point, but Lunara's father was quick to quiet the king from discussing the army threatening Bren. Edium seemed to understand today was special, that today Salvarias should be gifted a day of joy, a day of no pressures to solve Arden's problems, a day to revel in his new power and happiness.

Hours of staying connected to his happiness, wonder, and curiosity over his new power drained her energy and made her tire early in the night. He took notice, and begged the others his leave and escorted her to their room.

"You didn't have to go," Lunara said, plopping down on the bed and rubbing her tight stomach. The bulge she had so artfully hid was growing. Soon, she'd not be able to hide her pregnancy, especially from a healer as gifted as Salvarias. If he had not had the weight of Arden on his shoulders, no doubt he would have already seen the signs. Yawning, she said, "You should have stayed with the others."

He knelt in front of her and began unlacing her boots. "I want to be here." He glanced up at her and smiled. "Do you wish to be alone?"

"No, of course not."

He gently tugged off her boots. "I will try to lessen our connection. I can see it is taking a toll on you."

"No," she blurted. Too long had she begged him to lower his walls. She never wanted them raised again. "I can handle it."

He winced when he stood, his hand going to his bruised ribs. "As my lady wishes."

"It's a wonder," she mused absently. "You can heal mortal wounds, yet cannot grow back your fingers or ear."

He frowned at her. "Grow back?"

"Certainly you've tried after you found out you could heal yourself?"

"I have not. I have never thought to attempt it." He let out a soft laugh. "It seems so logical, does it not?"

Smiling, she nodded.

Bowing his head, he closed his eyes. A few short moments passed before his blackfire came to life. The heat of it bathed her in warmth, and the sight made her want to fall to her knees before him, offer her adoration. It was so much more powerful.

He gave a heavy exhale, part disbelief and awe, but mainly brimming with pain. The bruise on his cheek faded in a blink, and her mouth dropped open as the three missing fingers on his right hand grew from nothing. He flexed his hand and laughed. When he raised his gaze to hers, it was filled with astonished relief. He ran his hand along the back of his head and, this time, tears welled.

"It is gone," he breathed. "All of it."

Her own eyes widening, she reached out and brushed back his hair. A new ear had replaced the gnarled flesh of his missing ear. Rising, she pulled him up with her, untied the rope around his waist, and lifted his robes over his head.

His body was perfect: no scars, old burns, or fresh wounds. Reaching out a tentative hand, she ran it along his smooth chest.

"I can't believe it," she said.

Then he kissed her. His blackfire caressed over her, tingling along her skin, humming its way through her entire body. The feel of it, of being touched by something so powerful made her heart pound in her chest. Warmth settled itself in her stomach.

Salvarias pulled back quickly, his eyes widening as they lowered to her belly. He knew.

"I wanted to tell you," she said feebly. "I was worried it would burden you more."

His gaze darted back and forth between her eyes and stomach. He took a step back. Joy and fear waged war inside him.

"I promised you before it would be all right," she said. "Nothing has changed."

"How can you be sure?" he said hoarsely.

"Because we will love our child. And that is all that will matter."

Slowly he sank to his knees in front of her and pressed his forehead to her belly. His shoulders shook, and he half laughed, half cried. "It is a boy, and he has magic." He raised his gaze to hers, cheeks wet with joyful tears. "I am going to be a father." He swept her up in a hug, spinning her around. "You have made me the happiest man alive, Lunara."

Laughing, she hugged his neck. "You deserve nothing less, love."

SALVARIAS CARESSED the book Tobin had given him all those years ago. He did not need to open the cover and read the inscription; the words were forever burned across his soul. Yet the burn did not hurt anymore. It was just a scar, old and crusted over. He had a new family, one he was certain would never cast him aside. Hugging the book, he looked into the flames of the fire flickering in the hearth and thought about freedom. For so long he had tortured himself with the past, his sins and evil, but now he wanted to look into the future, to be free of his old burdens. He wanted so badly to be free.

Giving the book one last caress, he tossed it in the fire and watched the flames devour it. No weight lifted off his shoulders as he had hoped, but he did feel the taut rope of guilt loosen.

Inhaling deeply, he turned his back on the fire, gathered up his staff, and silently left the room, leaving his wife asleep with the two griffins. He should be tired, but his happiness was relentless. For too long he had walked through life half asleep. The night was still early and laughter from the dining hall trickled up the stairwell. Wilhelm's laughter boomed above the rest, and with a smile Salvarias made his way downstairs.

"Salv!" Wilhelm roared. Three empty ale pitchers were in front of him and Okulu. "Come join us!"

The room had quieted some, and he felt gazes follow him to his brother, but he paid it no heed. He found he no longer cared about the stares he received, and the only reason he raised his hood was out of general politeness.

The mood was melancholy except for Salvarias's friends. It was too easy to forget the army camping outside the walls when he was so happy. Accepting his powers certainly accounted for most of his joy, but having a body free of scars was a first.

It was odd not to rely on his staff as he headed to his brother. He carried it, but more for the comfort and coolness it provided than any real need for its aid. Ever since he had accepted his power, the unnatural cold in his bones had vanished. Now he experienced the true heat of summer for the first time. He had half a mind to change the season, but it was a petty wish and not worth the effort.

"How's that wife of yours?" Okulu asked as Salvarias settled into a stool at the bar between the two men. "She's been looking tired lately."

Salvarias grinned up at his brother. "She is pregnant. I am going to be a father."

Wilhelm blinked in surprise, then his crooked grin spread and his laughter seemed to shake Salvarias's stool. He found himself whisked into a rib-crushing hug, one he eagerly returned. Okulu ordered a new pitcher of ale along with tea for Salvarias.

"About time," Okulu said after Wilhelm had lowered Salvarias back to his stool. "Now my little runts can have a friend."

The three of them talked late into the night until the dining hall finally emptied and Herald heaved sighs with every sip Okulu took of his ale. Taking the hint, the merc bade them farewell and headed to his room.

Wilhelm rose, wrapped an arm around Salvarias's neck, and led him to the stairs. "I'm really proud of you, Salv."

"Thank you, Brother. Never could I have imagined being this happy, and I owe it all to you. You believed in me and loved me when no one else did. You kept me alive, kept me from succumbing to the darkness inside. If not for you, I would have been lost after my first breath."

"I only did what was right, Salv. I only saw what was truly there."

Smiling, Salvarias elbowed his brother's ribs.

"Ouch!" Wilhelm said, and ruffled Salvarias's hair.

The door to the inn burst open and Kisra marched in, Brice behind her. Both looked pale.

"It's Haleen!" Kisra said. "Zehnia said she had a cousin come visit, the only newcomer she'd allowed around the children. Haleen Avral, daughter to Wunhur's brother."

"It can't be," Wilhelm argued. "I knew Haleen when I was young. It can't be."

Salvarias winced at the hurt in Wilhelm's voice. How naive to think Veedran would not have sent spies after his brother as well. And what better than a pretty woman, one who had not looked at Wilhelm as a boy as so many had.

"Zehnia said Haleen had moved to Dalnar for a while," Kisra insisted. "The times line up. I swear it's her. She left the same day Tedris disappeared."

Wilhelm! Vegos roared. *Salvarias!*

Salvarias bolted up the stairs, hearing his brother rushing behind him. It felt awkward to climb so quickly, his leg not once giving out. His heart, however, stuttered painfully. At the top, Salvarias flung open his door. His wife was gone. Wilhelm had already darted past and opened the door to his own room.

Salvarias rushed to his brother's side and peered inside. In the far back, he made out a distortion in the air, shimmering in the moonlight seeping through the window. Haleen stood in a corner, eyes wide, and tears falling freely.

"He came with no warning," Haleen wept.

Varila was not in the room; no doubt locked up with Cessia as she often was. Talura had probably been watching Tedris.

"Lumous," Salvarias snapped.

His sparrow lit up Veedran and a portal Haleen surely had created. The dark god's arm was snaked around Talura's neck, and he held a dagger to her ribs, angled perfectly for the heart. Her eyes were calm, but her chest rose in shaky breaths.

"They took Tedris and Lunara," she said.

"Yes," Veedran hissed. "You thought you could win, boy? You

thought choosing a side would end this? You might have saved Arden, pet, but you have doomed those you love. I will never stop until you lie dead at my feet, boy. The time for games is over. Come find me and let us finish this."

Talura looked at Salvarias with complete calm, and smiled. "Remember your promise to me, Son. Everything will be all right, sweetness. *You* will be all right."

"I beg to differ," Veedran said past a grin and rammed the dagger into Salvarias's mother.

"NO!" Salvarias cried, lunging forward.

Veedran dropped Talura, stepped through the portal, and vanished. Salvarias sank to his knees beside his mother, but it was too late. Veedran's strike had been true. Vaguely he heard Haleen hiss words, and the portal flickered shut.

Gathering his mother in his arms, he wept, "You cannot leave me. You cannot!" Warm blood soaked the sleeve of his robes. "You cannot!" he screamed.

Happiness stolen from him, pried from his desperate grasp. It could not be. Gritting his teeth, he shouted out his defiance. It *would* not be. Sweet black flames erupted, warmth spreading through him.

"You cannot," a voice said calmly.

Salvarias raised his head and regarded Balance. She stood resolutely, her eyes stern, her mouth set with the same determination flowing in Salvarias's veins.

"Life cannot be restored once taken," she continued. "No matter how much you desire it. If you try, Father will strike you down. It is the way of it, dear brother."

"I am not your brother," he snarled.

"The Creator is your mother, Salvarias. Nevlar is your father. Ashra was merely a vessel. You are my brother, just as Veedran is, just as was Vuddruk. And all of the Creator's children must follow His rules."

Salvarias sprang up, grabbed hold of Balance's neck, and shoved her against the wall, lifting her so her feet dangled and she was eye level. "Tell the Creator that He can go to Oblivion. I will not abide by His rules, and I certainly will not let my mother die."

"It is impossible to bring an unclaimed soul back from death," she warned. "Think back on it, dear brother. No one has brought back the dead."

"Nevlar brought back Edium."

"Edium had not yet passed. Nevlar merely healed him, against Father's wishes. He pays dearly for what he did."

"Zerana brought back Lunara both times I died."

"Zerana owns Lunara just as you own Wilhelm."

Salvarias glanced over his shoulder. Why then was Zerana not healing his mother?

"Zerana is too weak," Balance said. "She cannot give her power to both mother and daughter." A flicker of sadness passed through her eyes. "You are powerful, Brother, more so than Nevlar, Zerana, and even Veedran. But even you could not defeat the Creator. Many of us have risen up against Him and have failed. How do you think Veedran came to be the way he is? He tried to save Nevlar, and as punishment the Creator turned him mad and made Nevlar watch. It is why Nevlar could never kill his brother. Veedran sacrificed himself for his brother." Tears skimmed down her cheeks. "He is Creation, Brother. He is the Beginning and the End. Life and Death. You have no choice."

"One day I will. You tell Him I will come for Him. One day I will kill Him. This is a promise I make to Him."

"As you wish, Brother."

Salvarias dropped her. Before he even took a step back, she was gone. Inhaling a deep breath, he turned around. Wilhelm stood over Talura, his chest rising in even breaths, but his eyes were deadened with horrible sadness ... and anger. Without warning, he whirled on Haleen. Salvarias had not seen his brother's dagger until a red stain spread along Haleen's side.

The woman gasped, wide eyes locked on Wilhelm.

"Will you deny it?" he whispered low.

Tears welled in her eyes. "No," she rasped.

"I trusted you," Wilhelm said. "I always trusted you." He twisted the knife and yanked it free. Haleen crumpled to the ground, the light of life fleeing from her eyes. Salvarias cared not. If Wilhelm had not done it, he would have.

Varila rushed into the room. Upon seeing Talura, she gave a heartrending cry and flung herself over her mother's corpse.

The pain of loss nearly stole Salvarias's legs from under him. Of course he could hide again, tuck himself away and try to stave off the waves of pain tearing through his heart. But he did not want to be that person anymore. He could not go back to being half dead, to letting sadness own him as he once had. He had lived, and death was no longer an option. More importantly was the promise he had made to his mother, to the woman who had loved him as he had always wanted to be loved. Just a day. One day was all he had of that love. He could have had it for months had he only risen above his fear. Now it was gone, and it left a deep dark void, one he filled with anger, but not his old uncontrolled anger. This was deadly calm. It granted him clarity and purpose.

Turning slowly, he left the room. It did not take long to reach the outer wall. The siege engines were nearly complete. The soldiers lining the wall looked on hopelessly, whispering doom to one another. Boys and girls too young held swords, women crowded with the men, and a few feeble retired warriors tried to lift their own blades. Defeat was in the air.

Salvarias looked out over the army and prepared himself for what he must do. He had told Talura he lacked the apathy to murder, but if he were to be honest with himself, he *wanted* to lack it. Now faced with what had to be done, the act was too easily swallowed. His heart even raced a bit in eagerness.

Remembering his mother's words, he raised his head and looked up at the dark sky. Hope sometimes came in blood. Hope was not always light.

He realized life, though wondrous and infinite, did nothing to satiate his thirst, what roared pleasure through his veins when using his power. Now with his anger alive, it was what drove him. Fight. He was built for war, built to annihilate, just as Lakvra was built for lust, Zerana built to adore life, and Veedran built to hate. And who was he to deny his destiny? After all, there could be no life without death, no death without life. There were times when violence was the only means for peace. It was a contradiction indeed. For gods such as Zerana, killing was something they could simply not do. She loved life too much to destroy it, even one as horrible as Veedran; that was why she had armies do her bidding. But to Salvarias, he understood the necessity. He did not agree or want it to be so, but he understood it.

This army would die. Veedran would die. And Salvarias would be the one to kill them. This was who he was deep inside.

Violence.

The reluctant killer.

UNUPTURE WATCHED from his perch on the highest hill as a single figure cloaked in black stepped through the city gate below: a tiny spec facing an ocean of evil. He would have been ignorant to the man's identity if not for the sparrow of light floating over Salvarias's shoulder. Moonbeams lit the unsavory army crowding the hills, all watching the young man. The scene was epic, and Unupture doubted he would ever forget the details. A lone man against thousands.

"My name is Salvarias Laybryth." His voice was soft and lulling as always, but as clear as if he stood by Unupture's side. "Some of you serve your master with unbending loyalty, and those who do will die this day. For those who think they have no choice, for those that follow out of fear, I give you one chance at freedom. Whisper loyalty to King Humar and I will spare you. Those who stay silent will burn with the rest who have betrayed Arden. Do not attempt to lie. I will know."

If any around him declared such devotion, he did not hear them.

Devoar had fled when life touched the hills, when joy imbued itself in the very air and soil of Arden. Veedran had lost, and no doubt his anger would be great. No doubt Salvarias and any who followed him would pay.

Unupture closed his eyes to the wave of blackfire racing toward him and whispered, "I give my loyalty to you, Salvarias."

31

Wilhelm watched Salvarias packing spell components, sipping his fifth cup of tea. He had refused to rest after he killed the army. The amount of power he used was tenfold what he normally unleashed, yet he was upright and awake. It should have calmed Wilhelm, but instead dread settled itself in his gut. Glancing around to make sure his wife was not with them, he said, "I'll leave Tedris, Salv. I'll leave him there. I'll let him die, but I ... I can't lose you. Not again."

Salvarias paused in his packing and raised his gaze to Wilhelm. "I will not. Veedran has killed Talura and taken Tedris and Lunara because he knows I will follow him. He has set a trap, and I willingly walk into it. If I do not, I could not live with myself."

"He has the stone, Salv. He has his power back. You can't use all yours or else it'll make you mad. He can use his, and he will. If you even touch him, it'll kill you. You understand that, don't you?"

"I do."

"Then how are we supposed to defeat him?"

"You, my dearest brother. Do you not remember the times you have met him? He is afraid of you. You can hurt him."

"He'll kill me before I can lay a hand on him."

334

"My magic cannot hurt him, but it can protect you until you reach him. I need him subdued so I have time to focus my power. I need to feel safe, that he cannot hurt me. Only you can gift me that. Once you have him, I will use my power to kill him."

"That sounds a little too simple."

"Simple is not something we have tried before. Perhaps it is time."

"How do we find him?"

"My connection to Lunara. I know where to go."

"I can't lose you, Salv. I won't survive it again."

Salvarias's expression melted into sympathy, and he moved to stand directly in front of Wilhelm. "When will you realize, Brother? When will you see it? My life will not be long in this world. Perhaps I will die today, perhaps tomorrow, perhaps in five years. Regardless, it will be sooner rather than later. It is a fact we cannot escape. You must understand, you saved me every day. Every day. All I have I owe to you. When I die, it will be more important than ever that you live. You must be there for Lunara and my son. All I love I entrust to you."

Wilhelm shook his head, eyes burning with a wave of tears.

"Promise me," Salvarias said. "Promise you will care for them. Promise me you will live—truly *live*—once I am gone. Raise my son as you did me. You must do this, Brother. You must do this for me."

"You can't ask that of me, Salv. You can't ask me to sit by while you die."

"Nor am I. We will fight, Brother. Together, until my last breath I will fight. But one day we will lose. You must see it."

Wilhelm couldn't bring himself to look at his brother. "Now's not the time to talk about it, Salv. We—"

"This is the perfect time, Brother." A light hand rested on his arm. "I never want to be parted from your side, but I have had to face the truth. It is your turn. Promise me."

He is right, Vegos said gently. *But remember what I said before. Always, always, your brother will return to you. It might take time, but Salvarias owns you, and he will not leave you forever.*

Wilhelm nodded and choked out his agreement.

∼

VARILA STOOD IN HER ROOM, glaring at her brother-in-law. "You can't be serious."

"I cannot save Lunara and your son if I must be worried about you, sister," Salvarias said. "I can heal my brother, bring him back from death. I cannot do the same for you." The mage glanced at Humar. "Nor you, my friend. I must go alone with my brother."

"Salv's right," Wilhelm said, taking a step back when Varila turned her gaze to him. "I want you to come, Varila. I do. But we have to be smart about this. Veedran can kill you with a snap of his fingers. Me too, but Salv can fix that."

Varila looked to her father, but Edium merely gazed at the jasmine flower in his hand and her mother's ring. Pain shot through Varila, and she quickly looked away. Her mother would have told her to listen to Salvarias. She would have said Salvarias would know what to do. She would have promised her everything would be all right.

"I swear on my life I will bring back your son and sister," Salvarias said.

"It's suicide," Humar snapped. "Create a portal once you get there. Let me bring my army."

Salvarias sighed and sank into a chair. He looked near exhaustion. "Veedran has his powers back, my friend. He will kill your men as easily as I did. My brother and I are the only ones that can defeat him and have a chance of returning. When I have Tedris and Lunara, I will send them back to you through a portal." He raised his gaze to her. "You must trust me, sister."

Varila swallowed hard and turned to look out the window. Charred corpses littered the hills, most still smoking. So much death around her and so much pain in her heart. She'd lose them; she knew it. Blinking aside her stupid tears, she nodded. "I trust you, little brother. You bring back my husband, and that means you have to come back too."

"That I cannot promise, but I will try my damnedest."

"I need time alone with my husband."

Humar gently tugged Edium up and led him from the room, Salvarias following. When they were gone, silence stretched between them.

Eventually Wilhelm broke it. "I'll bring him back."

Varila nodded and turned to face him. "I know you will. And I know you'll leave him there if it means saving Salvarias."

Wilhelm's gaze dropped, shame reddening his cheeks. She hated him as much as she loved him for it.

She strode over to him and cupped his face in her hands. "Either way, I'll love you. Either way, I'll be here for you. Forever. I love you."

Fresh tears welled in Wilhelm's eyes as he kissed her.

32

Wilhelm didn't like his brother's spell. Certainly he supported Salvarias's accomplishment, but men weren't made to fly. Just thinking about it made his stomach churn, and standing atop Bren's wall did nothing to alleviate his suffering. The ground seemed miles away, and the breeze far too warm. Running a hand along his sweaty forehead, he tried to ignore his brother's eyes lit with amusement.

"I wish you'd take me with you," Humar said for the hundredth time. "You two shouldn't go alone. There could be an army awaiting you."

"And if there is, you'd just die with us," Wilhelm muttered.

"It's suicide," Okulu snapped, then took a long pull from his flask.

"It is the right decision," Salvarias said, voice calm.

If Wilhelm hadn't known his brother so well, he wouldn't have picked up on the subtleties of Salvarias's nerves: his hand pressed to his robes to keep it dry while the other gripped his aspen branch needlessly tight, or the slight shift in his stance. They were doing exactly as Veedran wanted, and the alternative was to flee and abandon everyone. While he would have done it to keep Salv safe, his brother wouldn't have been able to live with himself.

338

"Let's get this over with," Wilhelm said.

Salvarias bowed to Humar. "Take care, my friend."

"You as well."

Wilhelm shook Humar's hand and then Okulu's.

"Try not to die," the merc said.

"It's my main priority."

Salvarias locked arms with Wilhelm. "Are you ready, Brother?"

Taking in a deep breath, Wilhelm nodded and snapped his eyes shut.

It was as it was the last time his brother had performed the spell. A huge weight settled itself on Wilhelm's shoulders, like a mountain trying to sit on him while at the same time his feet pushed up. How he wasn't smashed in two by the opposing forces he'd never know. One whispered word from his brother launched them forward. If Wilhelm had been thrown from a catapult head-on into granite, it would have been less painful. Wind seared his face and drove air from his lungs. The pressure gave him an instant headache and made his bones ache. In a breath it stopped, and then he was floating, weightless. This time he managed not to flail around like a beheaded chicken. He kept his body rigid, locked tight against Salvarias's. His stomach flipped from the change, from the sensation of nothing grounding him. And then they were falling. Wilhelm swallowed his rising gorge and peeked between narrowed eyes.

Blue ocean as far as he could see raced up toward him. He bit back a scream and snapped his eyes closed.

They stopped in midair, and for the briefest of moments, he heard sea gulls and the wind playing with the ocean. Then the force built once more, pushing him up and crushing him down. The sensation made him lightheaded, made him want to pass out so his head didn't feel like it would burst. Salvarias's whispered word flung them forward.

Wilhelm wasn't sure how long it went on. He focused his mind on calm, trying to ease his sickness from infecting his brother. He thought of his swords, heavy and comforting against him. He imagined driving them through Veedran, hearing the bastard scream, and seeing him writhing in agony. He imagined Salvarias, cloaked in flames, killing the dark god, freeing the brothers from this game, from this life of torment. He imagined returning home where they would rule the Knighthood and usher in an era of peace.

"Brother," Salvarias said.

Wilhelm came to himself and felt blessed ground beneath his feet. He also felt his brother's trembling arm unlock from his. Forcing open his eyes caked in dried wind-blown tears, he surveyed the white, cracked ground stretching as far as he could see. Wind ripped about him and angry clouds roiled overhead. Lightning thrashed the sky, marrying with thunder loud enough to shake the ground.

Cracking his head side to side to rid the lasting effects of the spell, he glanced sideways at his brother. A white cloth was pressed to Salvarias's nose, and a spreading red stain told Wilhelm all he needed to know. As he suspected it would, the spells and amount of power his brother had used were taking a toll. He would have prayed to a god if he could have thought of any to trust.

"Where to now?" Wilhelm asked.

Salvarias flicked a shaking hand straight. Wrapping an arm around his brother's shoulders, Wilhelm led the way, holding his brother up so he needn't bother walking. As he hoped, Salvarias began to doze, his weight sagging.

The longer Wilhelm walked, the more thankful he became for the clouds and wind. Hot as it was, it would have been otherwise unbearable. The dark sky kept tricking his mind into thinking it should be cold, however the warm wind was a reminder of the desolation he wandered. Dried grasses crunched beneath his feet, and the occasional husk of a tree with its spidery, broken limbs spoke of life that had long ago fled. He didn't like this place. Not one bit. How could this go anyway other than horrible?

Salvarias jerked violently and exhaled a sharp cry. His hand clamped over his chest, and Wilhelm's heart thumped in his ears when blood ran between his brother's fingers.

"What happened?" Wilhelm demanded, gaze darting from one empty place to the other.

"Lunara," Salvarias rasped. He winced, jaw rippling, and then the blood eased. "The goddess is healing her, and I was too connected. I am relieved to know I was right. Zerana will never let Lunara die unless it is what the goddess desires."

"Healing ..." Wilhelm surveyed the desert, squinting against the wind. "There." Far off he barely made out a tree and what looked like a cocoon dangling from its branches. Of course if he allowed himself a bit of logic, it made more sense for it to be a body. But he couldn't let his mind go there.

Salvarias shielded his eyes. "Lunara is not there. Brother ..."

Wilhelm shook his head and started forward. If his son were dead, Salv would bring him back. Wilhelm had an irrational idea to knock his brother overhead and somehow build a raft out of the dead trees and sail far away. Gripping the hilt of his sword, he fought to draw it, yet all he could see was Tedris running from him, squealing in delight as Wilhelm swooped him up and tossed him high in the air. Glancing to the side, he watched his brother striding forward; no limp, no missing fingers. He stood tall, confident, and alive. All his brother's years were full of fear. Salv deserved a chance at happiness.

"Just so you know, my dearest brother, I have a protection spell around me." Salvarias glanced up at him, smiling slightly. "While I cannot tell you how much your gesture means to me, you have no choice in the matter. I will bring your son back to you."

They walked on in silence, Wilhelm dreading every step, dreading what he would see, what would happen.

When finally they came to the tree, nothing Wilhelm could have done would have prepared him for what he saw and for what had been done to his son.

Tedris hung, crucified to the tree. Neck down, he'd been skinned, and by the slackened horror of his expression, he'd been alive when it happened. The ground had soaked up the blood, but the body still glistened.

Wilhelm couldn't move. He just stood at the base of the tree, staring up at his son, imagining the terror his little boy suffered.

"Brother!" Salvarias said sharply.

Wilhelm jerked and tore his gaze free.

"Help me," Salvarias said, holding Tedris's sagging body. "We must get him down."

Wilhelm lurched over and cut the ropes holding Tedris. The boy fell hard in his arms. Tears broke free, and he cradled his son close and sank to the ground.

Salvarias knelt in front of Wilhelm and met his gaze. "He will remember. There is nothing to be done. You understand?"

Wilhelm nodded.

Salvarias gently took Tedris's right hand in his left and closed his eyes. Skin grew back over his son, pink and untouched by the sun. A soft cry built in Tedris's throat, and when he opened his eyes, it wailed out in a harrowing scream.

"It's all right, Son," Wilhelm murmured, holding tight and rocking. "I'm here. You're all right."

Tedris screamed and screamed, clawing at Wilhelm, flailing about hysterical.

Salvarias rested a hand on his forehead and whispered, "Peace."

Tedris's screams turned to sobs, and he opened his eyes. "Papa!"

"I'm here," Wilhelm assured, holding him tightly. "Everything's going to be all right." Burying his face in his son's wavy hair, he shut his eyes and whispered words of comfort.

Salvarias threw some dirt on the ground, chanted, and drew his rune. A shimmer appeared.

Holding out his arms, he said, "Give me Tedris and go through to make sure it is safe."

Wilhelm reluctantly handed over his hysterical son and went through. Varila stood waiting, chewing on her nail. Humar and Okulu were there too.

"Well?" she demanded.

"They skinned him alive," he said hoarsely. "He remembered it, Varila."

Tears built in her eyes but she blinked them away, nodded, and then stepped through the portal. He followed her.

To his surprise, his brother was humming, rocking Tedris to the melody that poured out smoothly. It made Wilhelm's eyes heavy, and he realized Salvarias was subduing Tedris, easing his stark terror with drowsy comfort.

Salvarias walked up and passed Tedris to Varila. Their son looked at them with heavy eyes and smiled. "Hello, Mother. I've missed you."

She held him close, half laughing and half crying. "I've missed you too. How ... Are..."

"Uncle Salvarias helped," Tedris murmured, eyes closing. "He made the pain go away. I really don't remember it."

"Take him from here," Salvarias said, motioning to a portal. "I will leave this open. Once Lunara is through, with or without my brother or me, Kisra must close it. If my brother and I survive, I will open another."

Varila nodded, gave Wilhelm a quick kiss, and disappeared.

"Let's get going," Wilhelm said.

They made it a few steps before Salvarias collapsed to his knees, doubled over, fists balled in his hair. His breath came in short, sharp intakes. Blood ran from his nose and a thin stream fell from between his lips.

Wilhelm dropped by his brother's side. "You used too much, didn't you?"

Salvarias nodded, choking on a thick river of blood. He snatched hold of Wilhelm's hand, and strength drained from Wilhelm's legs. It didn't last long, thankfully. When Salvarias released him, his brother spat out a glob of blood and pressed a cloth to his nose. He shook badly.

"Use more," Wilhelm encouraged. "I can handle it."

Salvarias shook his head. "You will need your strength, Brother. I will be fine."

Wrapping an arm around Salvarias and muttering out a curse, Wilhelm hauled himself and his brother up. They kept walking, worry knotting Wilhelm's gut with every step.

LUNARA COUGHED ON BLOOD, gasping past the pain lancing through her heart. It only lasted a breath before Zerana's power flooded the wound, erasing any lingering pain. Her son's lifebeat remained strong throughout, but Lunara had the distinct impression of the baby absorbing Zerana's power, of pulling it from the goddess with each touch. Her only physical proof was warmth in her womb with every healing, and the blissful sense of peace flooding from her son. If her suspicions were true, Zerana showed no signs. The goddess's tearful eyes merely stared at Veedran, full of sympathy.

"You have to love me," Veedran wept. "Love me and I will leave your daughter in peace. I beg you, love me!"

His voice held such desperation that it tugged at Lunara's heart. So much pain trapped in one soul.

"I love you, but not in the way you seek," Zerana said gently. "I cannot force my heart to feel what it does not. You are sick, Brother. Let Nevlar help you. Let me. Give up this need for blood. If you do not, I fear your fate."

Veedran's cold eyes darkened. "You think the boy will kill me?"

Zerana said nothing.

Veedran's face reddened, fury flooding his voice. "I will kill him. I will kill everything he loves." The god turned to Lunara. "He thought to hide you from me? Thought to keep a child of Zerana safe in his arms? Safe from my wrath? He thought he could have you? Light? Love? He was a fool! A fool!"

Lunara braced herself for the knife as it plunged toward her breast. Horrible heat burst alive in her belly, hazing the scene before her, erupting an agonizing cry from her throat. She felt the kick of her son, felt anger in him, and then it suddenly vanished. It passed so quickly she doubted it happened. Blinking in surprise and confusion, she stared at Veedran's knife sticking from his shoulder. He gaped at it, looking as puzzled as Lunara.

A sudden sense of exhaustion throbbed within her child. Fear lurched her heart to her throat. *Son?*

Warmth blossomed from her womb and love swelled in her heart.

No more, she scolded gently. *Your father will save me. Do not drain yourself again, my sweet.*

"You touch him and Salvarias will not be merciful," Zerana warned. "Leave the child be."

Lunara had not noticed Veedran's wide gaze locked on her belly. A slow smile spread across his face, and he looked into Lunara's eyes. "Your husband is coming, child of the light. Let us welcome him."

It wasn't long before the mirage in front of Wilhelm gave way to a dark hole in the ground. Salvarias urged them on faster, his fears manifesting in Wilhelm. The sky overhead boiled with clouds, lightning fingered down, and thunder boomed often. Still, the clouds held their fury.

They reached the edge in time to see Veedran standing beside Lunara. Her dress was covered in blood. The air itself crackled, and the hair on Wilhelm's arms stood up. He looked over to see black flames erupting over Salvarias, his eyes dark with murderous intent.

"We do this together," Wilhelm barked, gaining his brother's attention.

Lunara was suspended in air, limp, cheeks wet with tears, but eyes bright with defiance. Beside her stood a woman with pure white hair, same ice blue eyes as Lunara and same slight build. Her eyes widened when she looked up at Salvarias.

"Help me!" she cried.

Veedran yanked the dagger from Lunara, smiling wickedly. "Salvarias! My sweet nephew, how fairs Bren?"

"It is free," Salvarias said, his voice eerily calm. "I have killed your army, Veedran. And I will kill you."

The wound in Lunara's chest flashed white, and the blood ceased.

"Do not touch him!" Zerana cried to Salvarias. "Physical contact with him will kill you!"

"Your wife is with child, nephew," Veedran said conversationally. "Poor soul will live in agony. I sensed it. A child of light and darkness.

You think you suffered, child of the shadows? Ha!" He ran a hand down Zerana's cheek. "My lover is weak, you see. She has kept her daughter alive as long as possible, but her powers have been spent. Sadly, it is the way of such vessels. But it gives me the opportunity to do something for you, my dearest nephew. I will free your child of his burden. I will not let him live with such torment."

"No!" Salvarias cried.

It was too late. Veedran rammed the dagger in Lunara's stomach. Then the world began to shake.

FURY ROARED in Salvarias's veins, deafened him to the thunder shouting overhead. The ground beneath his feet shook with his rage, and the clouds answered his anger with flashes of lightning and booming thunder. Wilhelm's arms grabbing hold of Salvarias was all that saved Veedran. He could only watch as blood spread across his wife's stomach. He could only struggle weakly in his brother's arms as fresh grief shredded apart his heart, as his knees gave out as he listened to a wail reverberating in his mind: the cry of his unborn child.

"You have to pace yourself, Salv," Wilhelm said. "You can't kill him now. We have to save Lunara and Zerana first." He shook Salvarias. "You have to calm down."

His brother was right. His son and wife could not be avenged if he flung all his building fury at Veedran. Not yet.

Gritting his teeth to keep in the rage, he flicked his hand and sent Veedran flying out of the pit, sailing through the air and out of sight. Taming his need for blood and relaxing in his brother's hold, he looked down into the darkness. It would not permit him to enter, nor did Zerana have enough strength to save herself. Only darkness and light were allowed in, and Salvarias had chosen shades of gray, living in neither light nor dark. He had but one choice. One that chilled him to the bone.

Turning to his brother, he said, "The creatures within that pit will only accept a child of light or a servant to darkness."

"No, Salv. You can't do it."

"I have no choice, Brother. You can save me as you did last time. Lock it away once I am free. If I seem as if I will not help them, you must command me. Force me to do it."

Wilhelm looked into the pit, then back to Salvarias and nodded. "I won't let it get you, Salv."

He knew his brother would not. Wilhelm always saved him. Wilhelm was always there for him.

Closing his eyes, he found the steel prison his brother had built. He could hold off the worst of it, he could hide a portion of himself until Wilhelm came for him. For Lunara, he could do this.

"No!" Lunara cried, cradling her stomach. "You can't, Salvarias!"

He whispered "bear", and the world went dark.

33

Lunara cried out when Salvarias leapt down into the pit. His eyes were dead of love, pools of black hate.

"What has he done?" Zerana breathed.

Blinking aside tears, Lunara pressed both hands over the wound in her stomach. Her son still lived, but he was fading.

Salvarias looked around, as if confused as to why he was here.

"Salvarias," Lunara whispered, reaching out to her husband. "You have to help us."

He cocked his head at her, eyebrows stitching together. "Why?" he asked.

"Because if you don't, Zerana and I will die," Lunara said.

He looked at the goddess. "Why should I care? She never helped me. She never stopped my mother. She never answered my prayers."

"I couldn't," Zerana wept.

"I care not for you," Salvarias said. "I care for nothing."

"Salv!" Wilhelm barked from above.

Salvarias flinched and looked up. A sneer slid across his face, and his voice dripped with hate when he said, "My dearest brother. Have you come to save me?"

"Not yet. Help Zerana. Now."

Lunara knew that fluctuation in his voice. That command.

Salvarias's jaw rippled, but he turned to Zerana, grabbed her hand, and whispered under his breath. A ball of blackfire formed and plunged into her palm. The goddess cried out, collapsing and convulsing. Lunara shielded her eyes when blinding white light filled the pit. The creatures within screamed, and so did Salvarias.

A wave of dizziness spun around Lunara, knocking her to her hands and knees. When finally it passed, she blinked spots from her vision and stared down at the dry ground beneath her. Zerana was lying near, blood pouring from her mouth and nose. Salvarias was staggering up, blood matting his robes.

"Salv," Wilhelm rushed to his brother, reaching out.

Salvarias gave a shout of utter anguish and tackled Wilhelm, clamping his hands around his brother's throat. "She would be alive if not for me!" Salvarias cried. "She did not deserve to die!"

Wilhelm's face turned red, and he gasped for air that never came.

"She did not deserve the curse placed upon her when she called me her son!" Salvarias screamed. "I should have died! You should have let me die! Then she would be alive! Lunara would be safe! And my son would not be doomed!"

Veins popped out on Wilhelm's forehead.

"You should have left me dead!" Salvarias cried.

Lunara struggled to rise, holding her stomach tightly, begging her son to hold on. Zerana coughed up blood, lurched to her feet, and practically collapsed on Salvarias.

"Don't do this!" the goddess cried.

Salvarias rounded on her, red fog drifting out of his eyes, mingling with blackfire. "You never helped me," he spat. "I prayed to you when she cut me. I prayed and you never helped me." He wrapped a hand around Zerana's throat and lifted her eye level. "No one took me from that place! I was alone!"

Zerana clawed at his hands, gulping for air. Wilhelm had rolled on his side, gagging on his breath, face red.

"Salvarias, no!" Lunara screamed.

It was no use. His anger was out of control. Blackfire and red fog encased Zerana. The goddess flailed wildly, choking near silent screams. The stench of charred flesh filled the air.

Lunara staggered to her feet, collapsed, and tried to rise again. It was too late, though. The world darkened without Zerana's light. All the love Lunara had lived in for her entire life faded, leaving behind an empty hole. Coldness. Her son's grief was ten times that of hers, aching in her belly, tearing at her heart. Not even out of the womb and he drank from sorrow. For the first time, she doubted her son would live a happy life.

Salvarias tossed aside the charred corpse and pounced on Wilhelm, who'd just gotten to his feet. They both went down, and once again, Salvarias locked his hands around his brother's neck. Instead of trying to walk, Lunara dragged herself across the ground, digging her fingers in between the cracks of dried mud.

Wilhelm's fight had stopped by the time she reached her husband. Using the last of her strength, she grabbed his arm and cried, "Salvarias!"

He whirled around, fist raised, but stopped when he met her gaze. The hate in his eyes melted and instant tears fled down his cheeks.

"Help me!" he choked.

No sooner did the words trail off then his eyes darkened, and hate came flooding back. It was all the break Wilhelm needed. He grabbed his brother's hand and shoved their marks together. Salvarias clutched his hair with his free hand and shouted in pain. Wilhelm breathed through clenched teeth, eyes shut tight and raining tears.

"Not this time," Salvarias growled, his voice not his own. It was raspy, dark, and hateful. "You cannot have him! He is ours!"

Lightning fingered down from the sky, blowing up dust and rock. The clouds unleashed a fury of rain, stinging Lunara's skin. Shielding her eyes, she looked through the downpour and saw Veedran off in the distance marching toward them.

"Hurry, Wilhelm!" she cried.

"You can't have him!" the evil shouted through Salvarias's lips. "He's mine!"

Salvarias cried out again. They wouldn't make it in time. Veedran was too close. Then Lunara saw it, a lumbering mass barreling toward them. Vegos. And, above him, two griffins.

Salvarias sucked in a sharp breath and coughed up a pool of blood. Wilhelm lay nearly motionless now, face twisted in concentration and pain.

"Help us!" Lunara shouted at Vegos.

The bear roared out, a deafening sound that shook through Lunara. She snapped her eyes shut and clamped her hands over her ears. When finally the ground ceased vibrating, she pried open her eyes. Wilhelm wearily sat up, his face gaunt and shadowed like he'd been sick for months. With shaking arms, he pulled Salvarias to him. Her husband wept hysterically, clinging to Wilhelm.

"It's all right," Wilhelm whispered, rocking Salvarias. "I've got you now. You're safe."

SALVARIAS CLAWED AT WILHELM, horror closing in all around him. He had murdered her, murdered light and good. The act had scarred his soul, left a gash on it that would never heal, that could never be forgiven.

He had killed light.

"It's all right," Wilhelm said. "It was my fault, Salv. You didn't do anything wrong."

Fear owned Salvarias, locked his limbs tight against his body, and he curled up to make himself as small as possible, tiny enough to lose himself in the safety encompassing him. He required it. Pressing an ear to his brother's chest, he drowned himself in the comforting beat and whooshing breaths.

"I'd never let it take you from me," Wilhelm said gently. "Never. I promise you're all right. You believe me?"

He would never be all right. Not after what he had done. Some acts were against the nature of worlds. Zerana's death had darkened entire universes. He felt the loss as if they were all his home, as if they were all his own loved ones. Screams wailed from all the worlds she had touched and all the souls she had loved. He felt their emptiness and the emptiness in his wife's own heart.

Regardless of how much his deed had dried up his own soul, he had to finish what he had started. Choking in a deep breath, he let Wilhelm's rumbling voice beat down the last of his fears. Gathering his courage, he left his brother's arms and crawled to his wife sitting beside them. Blood poured over her hands.

"I'm sorry," Lunara choked. "Our son ..."

"Shh," he comforted, pulling her into his arms and kissing her hair. "Everything will be all right."

"Salvarias, there's something I haven't told you," Lunara said.

"We will talk later."

His power flowed easily from him, bled into her, and mended her wounds. His son's life was ebbing though, growing fainter and fainter. Closing his eyes tight, he sent his power to strengthen his son, to give back life that had been taken. "Please," he begged. "You cannot leave us. Fight, Son."

He released more of his power, willing his son not to die. His power dimmed, and he was about to pull more when he realized his son was taking it—using it, strengthening his life. In that sacred exchange, Salvarias touched upon his son's soul, upon his powers, upon light and darkness.

Tears rained freely, and he had to bite back a sob. It was as he had feared. His child would have Salvarias's thirst for blood. His child would kill without prejudice, and he would enjoy any death, whether that of a good soul or not. But life was sacred, even those who did not deserve it, and his son would feel the loss deeper than even Zerana. The power she had used to heal Lunara would see to it. Death and life would war forever inside him. He would laugh when he killed and weep afterward. He would be haunted by his actions and would suffer when the smallest of creatures died.

"Forgive me," he wept. His son was healed, stronger now he had taken some of Salvarias's power. He would live a life of torment.

"No," Lunara said, cupping his face. "We will love him and help him. He will not be alone with it as you were."

She had known what they had done.

"His life will have more joy than suffering," Lunara said. "I swear it, Salvarias. I swear it."

She was so certain. Her eyes held not a single doubt, nor her heart.

"Salv!" Wilhelm said, voice tight with alarm.

Vegos was tearing into Veedran, spraying the god's blood over the muddy ground, but with each slash and bite, Veedran's own power cut into Vegos. Blood matted nearly every inch of the bear, and the rain pouring off him was red.

Salvarias pulled Lunara to her feet and motioned toward the griffins. "You must go."

"I can help," Lunara said, voice small. She knew she could not.

"I love you." He kissed her softly. "Now go."

She hesitated a moment before resting a hand over her belly. No doubt she would have stayed if not with child. She mustered up a smile that did not reach her eyes, then Sira lowered herself enough for Lunara to jump on her back. Saval nuzzled Salvarias before taking off after them. Lunara's grief swelled in his own heart.

A tortured roar turned Salvarias's attention back to Veedran. Red fog leaked from the god's body, and he held Vegos overhead.

"I will kill everything you love!" Veedran shouted.

Vegos exploded, chunks of muscle and fur splattering the ground, drenching the god in blood.

"No!" Wilhelm roared, and bolted for the god.

Salvarias hastily cast his protection spell, throwing an enormous amount of power into it. It leached from his bones, and a sudden wave of absolute exhaustion robbed his vision.

When he blinked it clear, he was on his knees, blood running freely from his nose, rising in the back of his throat.

Veedran's first wave of attack was nothing but fog, yet Salvarias had no doubts it would have driven his brother mad. It bounced off the protection spell, the force of it rattling Salvarias.

Wilhelm charged, feet kicking up mud. Veedran's eyes widened. He had expected Salvarias to attack. The surprise was exactly what

Salvarias had bet on. The dark god stumbled back, barking out another curse. The fog turned into hundreds of stakes.

Salvarias strengthened the spell around his brother, choking on the blood flooding his mouth. His insides felt on fire, and lances of pain shot all over inside him.

We cannot continue this, his magic warned. *I am nearly out of your control. I will tear you apart.*

Salvarias ignored it.

Wilhelm roared out and leapt, driving his swords down. Veedran screeched and tried to turn, but the swords impaled him. Wilhelm wasted no time in wrapping his arms around Veedran.

"Now!" Wilhelm roared.

Salvarias called forth his blackfire, but paused. To kill a god—his uncle, a being without control over his actions—was wrong, despite Veedran's victims screaming at him to do it. They wanted their vengeance, and he doubted he could resist. Still, he hesitated.

"Salv!"

Without help and after using his power to kill Zerana, what he needed to do would drive him mad. With certainty. Salvarias had chosen a side, a decision that vanquished the spell blocking Nevlar from this world, yet the god had not come. Raising his face to the sky, Salvarias said, "Help me, Father. I beg you. I did not mean to kill her. I swear it."

Nothing came to save him; nothing lifted the horror of what had to be done. Yet he could not blame Nevlar. Salvarias had killed his father's lover and now had every intention of killing his brother. Why would he help?

Salvarias looked back to his brother struggling to keep hold of Veedran. He could not spare his own mind and still save those he loved. He had always known he would go mad. He had just hoped it would have been later in life, perhaps blessing him with time to watch his son grow up, to spend time in peace with his new wife, to see his brother flourish in the Knighthood. But life had never been so kind to Salvarias. Why would it start now? And did he not deserve such a fate? Did the victims of Veedran's murderous whim deserve an eternity of reliving their deaths, all that horror, and all that pain? Did a god that killed a goddess of light merit anything less?

Closing his eyes to Lunara's erupting pleas, he sent forth his blackfire. He would never forget his wife's hysterical sobs or Veedran's scream. He would never forget the utter sorrow ebbing from Nevlar, infecting the air itself and bursting black rain from the clouds. Never would he forget the tear in his own heart even as roaring elation erupted from the sighing relief of Veedran's victims.

34

AUTUMN 1022 A.R

E dium gently cut away the jasmine crawling over his wife's tombstone so her name was visible. Months had passed, and the pain in his heart had not subsided in the least. If not for his children, life would not have been worth the energy. But they needed him, so he gently kissed his wife's tombstone and left the garden, feet suddenly too heavy.

His estate was quiet this late. He welcomed the change. Humar had taken it upon himself to give up rule over Arden. No one man could undertake such a feat without the help of a god, and apparently they had all left. Or at least none showed themselves. With Humar focusing his efforts on Loutsil, he had offered Edium rule over Dalnar, insisting he would be the fairest King, but Edium could not find room in his heart nor would his mind be up for the task. He'd suggested Idolar, and Humar had reluctantly agreed. The old knight had a family; two sons raised morally, both with kind hearts. They would be good princes. They would help their father lead Dalnar into an era of peace and prosperity. Of that, Edium had no doubts, which thankfully left his heart free of guilt. Even Varila agreed with his decisions. Never had he been prouder of her. With all the sadness surrounding them, she kept a bright face and light air. Inside she must have been miserable, but she kept her family together.

As he did every night, Edium climbed the stairs to his son's room. He paused at the door, took a deep breath, squared his shoulders, and stepped inside. Salvarias lay limply on his bed, eyes distant and unaware, his mouth slack. It was a relief to see him docile. Half the time he was a raving mess, shouting at anyone around, attempting to kill everyone but Wilhelm or Lunara. When with them, his body finally gave out and he stayed in the state he was in now. Needless to say, Wilhelm and Lunara spent as much time with him as possible.

They'd barely kept Salvarias alive by force-feeding him. Gods, how he screamed when they did, as if they were shoving daggers down his throat. Alas, the boy's fear had finally come to pass. He'd gone mad.

Wilhelm was by the boy's side, marks pressed together in yet another vain effort to break Salvarias's insanity. Neither Lunara nor Wilhelm had any success.

Edium waited patiently, absently stroking Saval's neck when it snuggled against him. The griffin was the size of a horse. He doubted it would get much bigger. The dramatic growth spurts had finally dwindled. It had filled out nicely, broad chested, head high, feathers preened to perfection and inky black. The beast was regal and utterly beautiful to look upon. Edium always felt a sense of awe when it stood near him. Sira was probably with Lunara. The beast never left his daughter's side and only permitted Paull to examine her bulging stomach.

At long last, Wilhelm dropped his brother's hand and sank heavily into a nearby chair. His whole body shook.

"Hello," Edium said softly. "Anything?"

Wilhelm leaned back and closed his eyes. "No, nothing."

"You need rest."

Wilhelm didn't respond. The boy was a walking husk. Stretched between being a husband, a father, ruler over the Knighthood—

which was currently locked in a campaign to take back the Winsires' home from the army that had invaded it months ago—and caretaker for an insane god had drained him of weight and energy. He sagged upon himself, dark rings under his sunken eyes. Certainly he did not give into hopelessness, but the body was simply not made to endure such stresses. No arguments had changed the boy's grueling pace. All he ever said was he had made a promise, and he'd see it through.

Edium sat in a chair beside him. "I'm proud of you."

Wilhelm said nothing. He'd fallen asleep.

Edium gazed at his son. Salvarias's body hitched as it did often, a line of drool fell from his open mouth, and a single tear leaked from the corner of his unseeing eye.

How could life be so cruel? Victory only to suffer defeat. A life fleeing from terror, only to lose to it when happiness had finally been obtained. How could a god be so helpless?

All Edium's life he had thought he understood the world, its wickedness and its kindness. But now ... now it was a monster towering before him, and he had no defense against it.

WHEN FINALLY SALVARIAS battled through darkness and the beasts holding him, he found himself standing among wheat colored hills, the sky painted a familiar sickening hue of pink. No blood stained the ground anymore. No dead roamed the hillsides. He had freed them when he killed Veedran.

He walked in relief and with no purpose for what felt like hours before he saw the man. He stood as tall as Salvarias, hair the color of blood. His features were delicate, high cheekbones, thin eyebrows, lips pulled back in a grimace. He looked up when Salvarias approached, and his eyes were the color of dying grass.

"Hello, Son," the man said.

Salvarias recognized the voice from the hours of lectures he used to receive. Swallowing the tightness in his throat, he bowed. "Father."

Nevlar looked over the hills. "You have given them peace. All those Veedran killed."

"I did not want to kill him or her. I swear it, Father."

Nevlar shrugged. "What we want and what must be done seldom align. My brother was infected, but I loved him. Regardless of whether he deserved it, I hate you. I've tried to overcome it, to tell myself you did what was necessary to keep you and your family safe. However, I have not convinced my heart. I offer no apology for it. It is what it is. As for Zerana ... that is another matter entirely. I will never call you my son. You are dead to me. Dead to me."

Salvarias tried to hide the hurt from his voice. "I understand completely, Father."

"I know you do. Despite my loathing of you, I will never harm you. You must know that. Your world is safe from me. I have no desire to ever go there again. I wanted ..." He looked over at Salvarias. "I just wanted to say goodbye."

Salvarias blinked aside his tears and looked at the horizon.

"You've been asleep for a long time." Nevlar turned to go, but paused. "Zerana loved you. She blamed me for your torment. She could not fathom how I could be so cruel as to agree to my Father's terms. So for her, I will give you something. You will remember everything when you wake. For once in your life, you will wake free of Terror's grip. But you will remember." Nevlar shook his head. "You will remember."

Salvarias blinked at the darkness. It took his eyes a moment to adjust to the dim moonlight seeping through a part in the drapes. He inhaled deeply the scent of a spring meadow. Lunara was sleeping in a chair situated beside his bed. Her stomach bulged, whereas when he had last seen her, he had not noticed.

Heartache pierced through him, so deep he did not think he could survive it. Loss, emptier than he had felt with his mother's death. The loss of a goddess of light. He curled up upon himself, tears pouring out, body racked with silent sobs. His soul was damaged, permanently scarred by his taking of good. Yet just as horribly painful was the loss of Veedran. Higher gods touched so much in so many worlds, and now those who worshipped Zerana felt the loss, and those sick souls that had idolized Veedran were now filled with hate. All of that grief and anger was directed at Salvarias, as if every living being in every world knew he had been the one to kill them.

An image of his mother appeared in his mind, and her words rang all around him: *"Promise me you will always look up at the sun and see hope."*

For her, he would rise from this bed and live. For her, he would always live.

Inhaling a deep breath, he slowly sat up, waiting until the dizziness passed before he swung his legs over the ledge. Every muscle was stiff, and his bones creaked and cracked in annoyance. He must have been bedridden for months.

Finally managing to get to his feet, he took a few turns around the furniture, recognizing his rooms in Serinity with ease. Once he felt better, he walked over to the chair, leaned down, and kissed his wife.

Her eyes fluttered open, and she looked at him as if he were not real. After glancing at the bed, it seemed she understood, and she flew into his arms.

"We've been so worried," she wept. "Months, Salvarias. It's been months!"

He held her tightly, reveling in her smell, comfort, and the familiarity of her. Easily he felt the strong lifebeat of his son, and it brought him a guilty happiness.

Eventually Lunara released him, snatched his hand, and led him to the door. "Wilhelm's been worried sick. He's hardly slept." She burst through the door, dragging him behind her. "Wilhelm!"

His brother emerged from his room along the opposite hall, pulling on a tunic over his gaunt frame. He paused with it half on, his eyes growing wide.

"Salv?"

Salvarias grinned. "Brother."

Wilhelm's tears were instant, and he closed the distance in a few leaping strides. Salvarias found himself whisked up in a bear hug, air squeezed out of his lungs.

"You did it," Wilhelm boomed. "My little brother is the most powerful god alive!"

Salvarias could not contain his own laugh. They had done it. And more the miracle, they had survived it.

35

Salvarias ran down the halls of his home, leaving the messenger carrying the news of his wife's labor behind. Finally the time had come when he would get to hold his son and to see his wife's joy. To be a father. Excitement quickened his steps, and he reveled in the ease in which he ran. He had yet to grow tired of his health.

He rounded a corner and stumbled to a stop. Standing before him was a slender man with sleek black hair and vibrant purple eyes.

"It is time for you to return home, Son," the man said, smiling, teeth straight and too white. "And I think the timing is perfect."

His hand jutted out and went *inside* Salvarias, straight to his soul. The shell around his power cracked.

"Did you honestly think a long life was your destiny?" the man said. "Did you honestly think happiness would be yours for eternity? Hope is nothing but lies the heart tells. And you have much to answer for, Son."

The shell around his power exploded and blackfire surged up through Salvarias. He looked down at his hands. Blood seeped from his pores and dripped to the ground. Salvarias saw nothing else but red. It ran from every orifice, from every pore. His insides liquefied. Bones cracked under the strain of the burgeoning power.

"Salv!" Wilhelm roared.

Salvarias blinked, and his vision barely cleared enough for him to see his brother. Choking on blood, Salvarias rasped, "You promised me, Brother. You promised."

I cannot stop this, his magic said. *I cannot mend it. I cannot save you.*

It will be all right. Salvarias knew what was coming, and he knew his magic would forever be a part of him. Even so, he tried to heal himself, tried to encase the power again, but it had been freed. *He* had been freed. It was a bittersweet feeling: finally feeling whole, uncaged, free of his life prison, but at such a great cost. Never again would he be able to walk in human form unless the Creator allowed him.

"Ah," the man whispered. "Do you think me so merciful, Son? Do you think I would honestly allow you to stay here? To witness your son's birth? To watch him grow up? Foolish boy."

"No!" Salvarias choked.

The world went black, and the last thing he heard was his brother calling his name.

LUNARA SCREAMED. Sweat fell down her face as she squeezed Varila's hand. She knew what was happening, despite not being at Salvarias's side. She felt his power growing, eating away his human form, freeing him into the beautiful being she had always sensed beneath the layers of flesh. She'd never lived in a false world where Salvarias would remain in human form. However, she had fed herself hope that he would remain here, by her side, watching their son grow.

Tears fled from her eyes when she felt him pulled from the world. She heard him calling for her, heard his anger and despair, but his voice faded the further he was taken from her.

The pain in her heart overrode the pain of her labor. She lay sobbing, barely following Paull's orders to push. All she wanted was to be by Salvarias's side, in his arms, his soft voice telling her everything would be all right.

11111111

Clasping her sister's hand tighter, she said, "You have to raise him, Varila. You have to be a mother to my son. Love him as I would. You cannot disappear from his life or sink into darkness. Promise me, sister."

"What are you talking about?" Varila said, her voice breaking with coming tears. "What's going on?"

"Promise me!"

"No," Varila said, her forehead pressing against Lunara's, her sister's hot tears falling on Lunara's face. "You can't leave me. You can't."

"I have no choice."

She heard her son's cry before the room went black. A chill crept toward her and a voice hissed in her ear, "You suffer because of him. Your child will suffer because of him. Deny him your love and I will let you live with your son. If you refuse, your child will grow up alone."

Lunara cried openly, and in her mind she responded, *I will always love him. Always.*

"So be it."

Cold settled into Lunara, and try as she might to cling to warmth and light, darkness won.

SALVARIAS WOKE IN NOTHINGNESS. No color. No light. No darkness. He went to look at his hands, but he had none. No limbs. He was not standing nor lying. Before him stood the Creator.

"It takes some getting used to. Especially being born into a form. You are a god, Salvarias, and are not tethered to anything unless I deem it so."

Salvarias looked over at a cage. His father was in it.

"Seems you have doomed us both, boy," Nevlar said. "I curse the day I ever asked for you."

Salvarias tore his gaze from his father and focused all his attention on the Creator.

"Your life is mine to do with as I please," the Creator said. "Indeed, you are my greatest creation. So complicated, so intricate in your conflicting layers. You see, they asked for you, and so I gave them what they wanted. You, Vengeance; vengeance for your father, for your uncle, and Vengeance for the world. But you are an infant in your godhood. You cannot even sit up on your own. One day, one day far, far away, you will grow strong enough to kill me as your heart so strongly desires. I've seen my doom in your eyes. Of course I could kill you now, spare myself. But in all honesty, I grow tired of this existence and look forward to the day when one could actually challenge me. To feel fear again. To just ... *feel*. Oh, and ours would be a duel written in the histories of all the worlds. When my death comes to me, I will give you a battle to scar you for your eternal life. Until then, you will suffer for what you've done."

The man waved his hand, and Lunara appeared by his side. Her body was transparent, a wisp of a form merely for Salvarias's sake. Souls had no form.

"You see," the creature purred. "I have taken her from Arden, from your son. Your father and your dear wife will be my prisoners until such a time as you come to lay me to waste. I'd kill your brother as well, but with how entwined you two are, I doubt death would keep you separated, and then it would be out of my control. But rest assured, he hurts enough to appease me."

Salvarias's anger exploded, and he sent it all to the figure before him. The Creator brushed it aside as if batting away a fly, his eyes darkening in utter fury. Even so, Salvarias saw the spark of fear.

The man leveled a finger at Salvarias and screamed, "I curse you, Salvarias Laybryth, God of Vengeance! I curse you to live your existence on Arden. Oh, do not think me merciful, boy, for when I send you there, it will be in the form of a monster! You will not remember who you are. Those you care about will not think for an instant that you could be their long-lost brother, son, or father. No, you will live in ignorance of one another. But the heart is the heart, the soul the soul, and some things cannot be stopped. You will grow to love them as they will you, despite your form. And when your heart is full, they will die of old age, but you will live on in solitude. You will watch everyone you love wilt away, and because you are a god, you will not age. You will live alone and grief ridden by all your losses. Those who hunt the killer of Light and Evil will find you and bring war to your home and your child, and your child's children. Arden will be cursed just as you. This is your future, boy. This is the future of a son that betrays me!"

The Creator struck out, and Salvarias fell. He fell and fell for an eternity, darkness his closest friend. He wept until he could not remember why.

36

AUTUMN 1022 A.R

Wilhelm stood at the altar, holding the crown of Dalnar in his trembling hands. He hated speeches, but as Lord Knight, Humar had insisted Wilhelm be the one to crown the new kings. He had just returned from Windlous not but a week ago, gifting rule to Humar's sister, Falisa. Today he was crowning Idolar. All good choices, to be sure, and ones the Knighthood supported.

He glanced over at Varila. She stood in her armor, their daughter Alurana on her hip, Tedris—now five winters old—at her side. Beside him, Salvarias's son stood; Lumus, though that wasn't quite the right pronunciation for Salvarias's light spell. Lunara had spent days trying to figure it out while Salvarias had slept after his fight with Veedran. Even with Kisra's help, no one besides mages could pronounce it correctly, so they had gone with the closest, and upon his waking, Salvarias had agreed to it, his eyes lit with amusement at the time. At only two winters old, Lumus was the spitting image of his father if Salvarias had been a healthy child, save for a white streak of hair positioned the same as his mother. His voice even sounded the same. Wilhelm could not say Lumus was a happy child, nor could he say sorrow stalked him as it had done Salvarias. The child was always insisting he was fine, patting Wilhelm's hand as if he were the child and not Lumus. Tedris, however, had become thick as thieves with the boy. The two were inseparable, and sometimes Tedris would leave Lumus's room with tears in his eyes. Like Lumus, he would put on a smile and say he was fine.

Humar cleared his throat.

Wilhelm blinked away tears he hadn't realized were building. He placed the crown on Idolar's head and babbled out some nonsense. The gathered crowd cheered, flowers flew in the air, and music started.

Wilhelm mingled for a while but soon escaped to a quiet spot to watch the ocean. It wasn't long before Lumus found him. He swept the child in his arms and both gazed over the waves rolling in.

"You seem sad," Lumus said.

"I miss your father." He dug in his shirt pocket and handed over the puzzle box. Just like his father, Lumus was infatuated with it, and it moved with the same grace Salvarias had conjured.

"I miss him too. I miss hearing him count."

Wilhelm smiled. It hadn't taken long to discover the boy had been aware of everything since first Salvarias's seed had taken. They didn't know what Lumus was, if he was a full god or merely a demigod. Wilhelm guessed it was something altogether new.

"I miss mother humming," Lumus said.

"Your mother did hum beautifully."

Lumus held up the puzzle box proudly. "Can you guess what it is, Uncle?"

Wilhelm frowned at it. "A sparrow." Though it looked nothing like a sparrow to him. It was a game he played with the boy. Over the years of Salvarias constantly manipulating the device, and of all the times Wilhelm had asked what it was his brother had made, he had been able to find patterns. Lumus was intent on stumping Wilhelm.

Lumus smiled sadly. "Father loved sparrows. Their songs."

"And do you hear their songs?" Wilhelm asked, gently prying for information. Lumus was not an open child. He kept secrets. Wilhelm was certain the boy was powerful, blessed with many gifts, but

Lumus coveted his abilities like they were the most treasured of secrets.

"Of course I hear them," Lumus said. "I am not deaf, Uncle."

"I know. But do you *hear* them?"

Lumus's smile faded, his gaze never leaving the puzzle box. "I hear much, Uncle. I hear you cry at night."

Okulu sauntered up. "We've spotted something." The merc pointed up at the sky. "See it?"

Annoyed at the interruption, Wilhelm shielded his eyes from the sun and looked up. There was a black dot, growing bigger, dropping from the sky.

"Bird?"

"I don't think so."

Varila joined them and grunted at it. "Been watching it. It's certainly big, whatever it is. And it's dropping fast."

"It could be anything," Okulu muttered. "With the curse gone, I've lost track of how many new creatures have sprung up across Arden."

Wilhelm shrugged. In their short conversation, the object had grown closer, and Wilhelm now saw that it was falling with force, as if thrown.

"Get everyone inside to the lower levels," Wilhelm commanded.

He gave Lumus a squeeze, but before he could pass the child off, Lumus clasped his arms around Wilhelm's neck and whispered in his ear, "Have faith, Uncle. Father will not leave us alone forever." When the child pulled away, he glanced at the object. "Nothing is what it seems, but some secrets must be kept until the time is right for them to be spoken."

Varila's shouted orders pulled him from confusion, and before he could think clearly, Kisra whisked the boy up in her arms and began herding the children to safety.

Wilhelm inhaled a deep breath and turned his gaze back to the creature. It was balled up, massive wings wrapped around itself, plummeting fast enough they saw the air speeding around it. It shot overhead, leaving behind a screech of passing wind, and it bored right into the mountains east of Serinity. The crash thundered all the way to them; the plum of dust seen from their distance.

"Get me Saval," Wilhelm ordered. "Okulu, send Cessia on Sira with soil for a portal. Tell Brice to get us a full battalion. That creature was bigger than three houses."

It didn't take the griffins long at all to cross the distance to the mountains. Wilhelm often wondered if his brother had intentionally made them fast flyers.

When they landed, he told the griffins to guard Cessia while she set up a portal.

"Stay out of sight," Wilhelm told the mage. "I want a look."

Wilhelm clambered over the rubble created when the creature had punched inside the mountain. He crept silently into the tunnel, amazed at the sheer size of it. It opened up in a cavern, wrecked by the creature's plunge, dust hazing the air, and small rocks still tumbled from the ceiling. Soon the light dimmed to where he could barely see in front of him. Using the wall, he snuck farther in, planting each foot softly, testing for loose rocks. Soon, not even the light from outside could penetrate the darkness.

Wilhelm was about to turn back for a torch, but the dimmest of light glowed from beyond. Taking another step, he realized with a rush of terror that it came from the creature's eye. It was bigger than his head, dark sapphire blue with a slitted pupil. It regarded him without fear or malice.

"What do you want?" Wilhelm demanded. Ever since Salvarias's death, foreign creatures had been popping up demanding the head of the one who killed Zerana or sometimes even Veedran. When Wilhelm told them his brother was no longer on Arden, they said he lied, that they could sense him close. Wilhelm guessed it was Lumus, and his protective nature over the boy had led to many deaths of those stupid enough not to turn away. Needless to say, caution and suspicion had bred quickly across Arden.

The eye blinked slowly, and the creature groaned in pain as it shifted. "I want nothing. I ..." Its head butted against the ceiling. It keened out a low whine. "If you wish to kill me, I suggest you do it now. I am hurt."

"I don't kill unless it's deserved. Do you deserve it?"

It gave a dry laugh. "I do not, but I doubt you believe me."

Wilhelm shrugged. "Depends on what you want."

"As I said, I do not want anything."

"Where are you from?"

"I … I do not remember. I do not remember my name."

Wilhelm frowned at the uncertainty and slight fear in its voice. "It'll be all right. What are you?"

"A dragon," it said without hesitation.

"Dragon? Never heard of it. There are certainly none of your kind here."

The dragon shifted again, rumbling out a groan and bringing down a shower of pebbles and a fresh wave of dust.

"Why don't we leave this cave before it crashes in around us?" Wilhelm suggested, waving the air clear. "Be warned. I have over a hundred men out there with weapons."

The creature nodded. "I have no desire to fight."

Wilhelm grunted and led the way out. When light fell on the creature, he sucked in a breath. Inky black scales covered its massive body, and webbed wings curved around it, their points sticking well past its mass. A tale flicked back and forth, its diamond-shaped end flinging around rocks the size of a large dog. The blue eyes regarded him thoughtfully, intelligent and powerful. He should've been scared half out of his wits, but he found himself suddenly protective of it. It was in pain, and the eyes were sad, widened slightly with fear.

Wilhelm reached out and ran his hand along the creature's scales. They were smooth and warm to the touch, and the creature shivered under his hand. A tingle shot up his arm, and he quickly pulled away. The blue eye was regarding him curiously. Flexing his hand, he reached out again. No tingle this time, just comforting warmth. "I lost my brother two years ago," Wilhelm confessed, though why he didn't know.

"I am sorry for your loss."

"So you don't remember your name. What's the first thing you remember?"

It shook its head, dim light glistening off its smooth scales. He was suddenly struck by how beautiful the creature was, how majestically regal. Once again, he reached out and ran a hand along the scales. Certainly they were hard, but their texture felt like silk against his calloused hand.

"I remember nothing but falling. And then pain." The creature shrugged its wings. "I only know what I am."

The creature's fear embedded itself in Wilhelm's own chest. He rubbed a hand along its shoulder and said, "It'll be all right. For now, I guess we'll call you dragon."

"As you wish, human."

Wilhelm chuckled. "That's fair. How about ... Sparrow."

"You cannot keep trying to name me after a species, *therro*."

"Actually, my brother loved sparrows. It was meant as a compliment."

"And why would you compliment a creature you just met?"

Wilhelm frowned up at it. "Honestly, I don't know."

It grinned, showing a row of sharp white teeth. "You are a complicated man. What is your name?"

"Wilhelm."

"Wilhelm ... I do not like it. I will call you *therro*."

"What does that mean?"

"I do not remember. It just ... it fits you."

Wilhelm laughed. "And you call me complicated."

It lowered its head to be level, the bottom scraping slightly across the ground. "Can I stay with you? I fear I find myself without a home, and for some reason, I desperately want one."

Wilhelm couldn't stop another bout of laughter. "You'll scare the sanity out of the citizens."

"Oh ... I see."

"But I've never been one to care about such things." Wilhelm winked at it. "Tell you what, you join the Knighthood and fight at my side, and I'll build you the most wonderful home I can."

The creature blinked at him, but a slow smile spread. "Are all knights as small as you? You must need protection."

"I can handle myself just fine."

The creature clicked a talon at Wilhelm's chest, and he went sailing across the ground. Sparrow shrunk back.

"Forgive me, *therro*. I did not know you were so fragile."

Wilhelm rolled up, dusted himself off, and grinned. "I guess we could use a little protection."

Sparrow bowed its head. "Then I am yours, my dearest *therro*."

Wilhelm sidled up closer to the beast as they emerged into the sun. The dragon uncurled itself, rising to its full height and glory, towering over the hundred men grabbing for swords.

"No one will hurt him," Wilhelm barked.

He startled over his sudden possessiveness. The creature had cowered back from the men, trying to huddle its mass behind Wilhelm. He stood straight, challenging anyone to say anything, while at the same time he breathed hard against an urgent hope. Could it be his brother?

The thought washed away as quickly as it came. No. His brother was lost to him. Yet, even with this dark reality, the usual sadness did not overtake him. The dragon nuzzled him, and Wilhelm smiled at it.

Softly he said, "He's mine."

AUTHOR NOTE

Thank you for taking time to read my story. I hope you found it enjoyable. For those of you that have followed the series, you might notice I have left several minor story lines open. I have done so intentionally. I'm not sure if I'll ever visit Arden again, but I wanted to leave myself the opportunity.

If you have questions, comments, or would just like to talk, you can reach me through my website (booksbylkevans.com), or send me an email at booksbylkevans@gmail.com.

www.ingramcontent.com/pod-product-compliance
Lightning Source LLC
Chambersburg PA
CBHW051318250626
47155CB00007B/2376